POISONWELL

This is a work of fiction. Names, characters, organizations, places, events, and incidents are either products of the author's imagination or are used fictitiously.

Published by 47North, Seattle

www.apub.com

Amazon, the Amazon logo, and 47North are trademarks of Amazon.com, Inc., or its affiliates.

ISBN-13: 9781477827871

ISBN-10: 1477827870

Cover design by becker&mayer! Book Producers

Illustrated by Magali Villeneuve

Library of Congress Control Number: 2014953467

Printed in the United States of America.

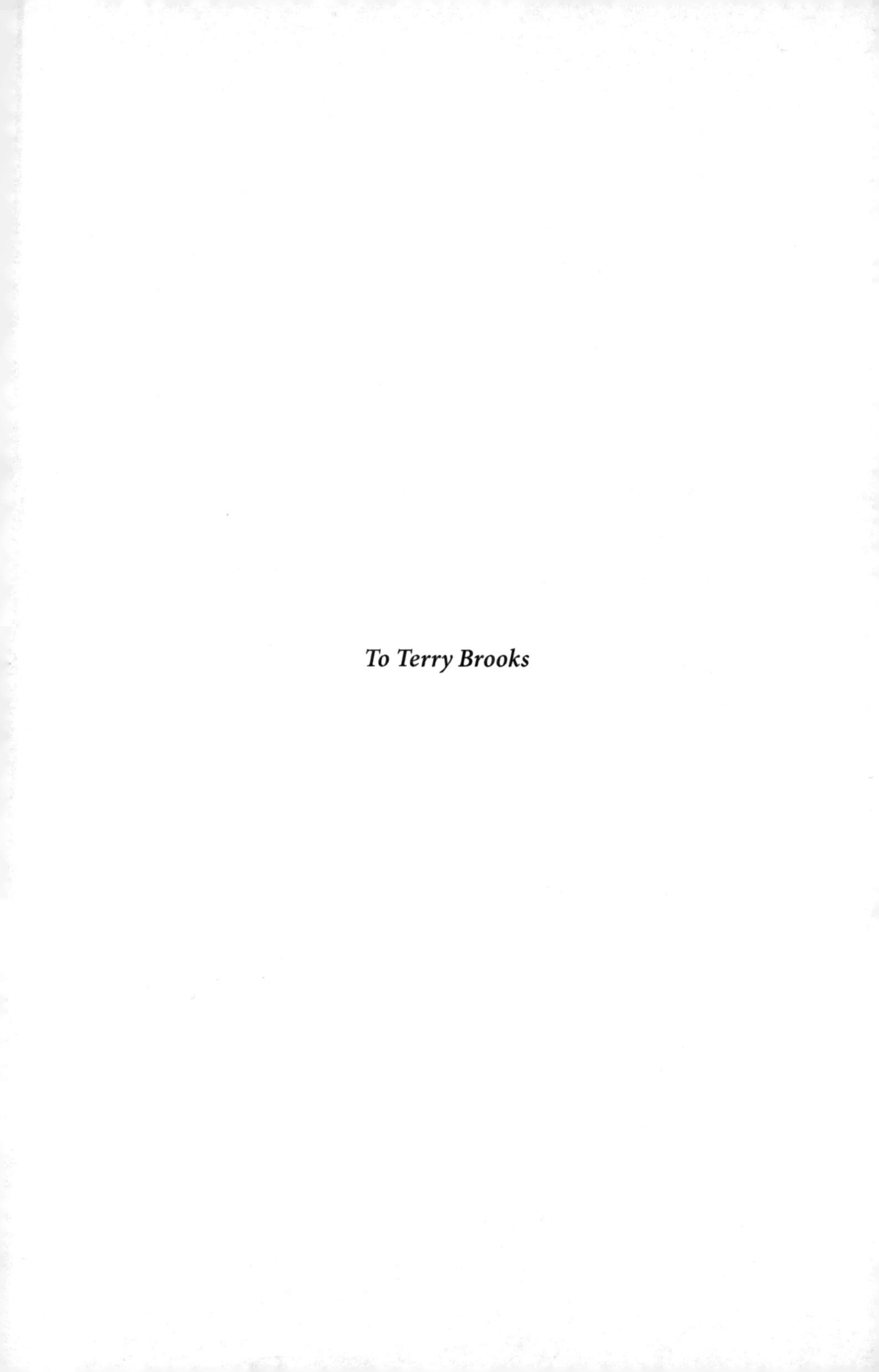

To Terry Brooks

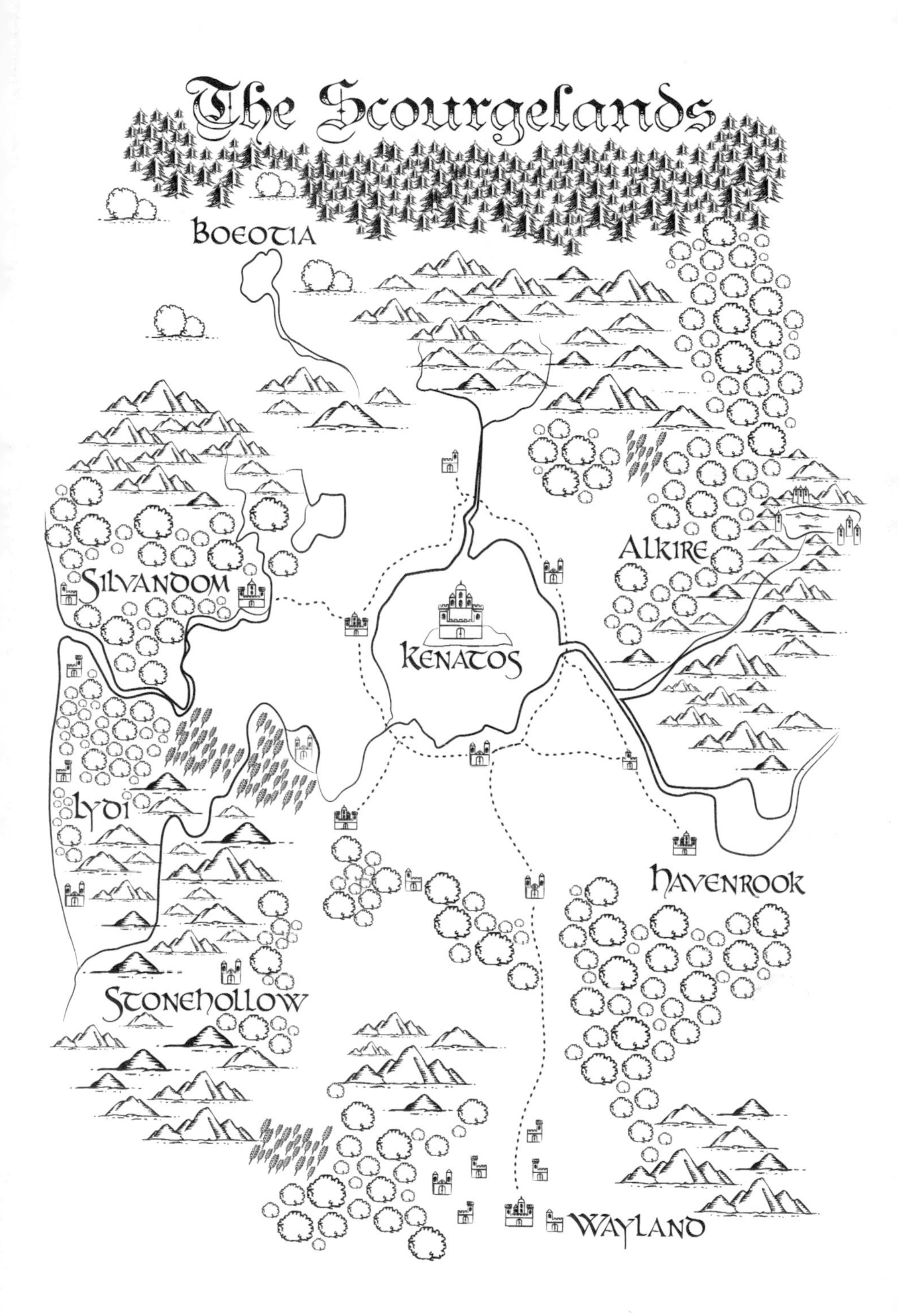
The Scourgelands
Boeotia
Silvandom
Alkire
Kenatos
Lydi
Havenrook
Stonehollow
Wayland

I

The snapping sound of a branch was Tyrus's only warning. He managed to sidestep as the creature hurtled past him, but its claws raked his arm as it passed, opening slits with its razor-tipped points and unleashing searing pain. The beast landed, coiled like a spring, and launched back at him again, its fangs snapping toward his throat. Tyrus managed to catch its thick ruff of fur and then channeled the fireblood into it. The blue flames made it shriek with pain before snuffing it out in a plume of ash. Pain shot through Tyrus's arm down to his wrist, but he did not have time to dwell on it. Three more of the creatures were coming at him.

Tyrus's mind was frozen in time, all things slowing to the syrupy texture of dreams, his senses as sharp as the claws of the beasts. The sound of battle raged all around him as the survivors fought against the onslaught that came like an avalanche. He could hear the whistle of blades, the spray of blood from fur, barks and whines, and the almost-giddy chuckle of men driven past the point of exhaustion.

He tried to dodge the next creature as it swiped at him savagely, misjudging the blow and feeling it score his leg. Another turned into ash from the fireblood and Tyrus knew his hold on sanity was starting to slip. With all his heart he wanted to unleash it fully, to blast the relentless demons into whatever oblivion awaited them. Control—he had to control his anger and desperation.

One of the catlike creatures landed on his back, knocking him off balance. Tyrus nearly fell from its weight, but managed—if barely—to keep upright. His knees knotted with pain as the weight drove on him. The cowl of his cloak was wrenched aside by sharp teeth as the creature prepared to sink its bite into his neck. Tyrus swiveled, blasting the third Weir full in the chest with the fireblood just as it launched at him. The flames guttered out as the creature slammed into him, knocking him backward. The interruption may have saved his life, for he landed on the creature still clinging to his back and it let out a hiss of pain and surprise. Glowing yellow eyes shining with madness loomed over Tyrus and he summoned the Vaettir words again.

Too late.

A swipe of the claw raked Tyrus's face, slashing his lip and chin as he tried to jerk away from the blow. Pain and blood drowned him, and again he nearly lost his self-control. He throttled the beast by the throat and sent flames streaking down its body until it vanished.

With a jerk of his shoulder, Tyrus twisted away from the creature pinned beneath him, its limbs thrashing to free itself as well as to attack him. Tyrus pressed his weight against it, slamming its head into the crackling nest of desiccated leaves. He pounded on the creature's head again and again, his fist glowing blue with the fireblood. A terrible fury rose inside of Tyrus's soul. He felt his own teeth bared with hatred and wondered whether he would start biting the demon next.

The creature lay limp and still as Tyrus managed to stagger to his feet. Howls filled the air, coming from far away. Mopping his bleeding face on the back of his hand, Tyrus turned to see who was left, who had survived. The baying sound signaled retreat. They had experienced it before.

The catlike creatures loped into the woods, vanishing like quicksilver, their hide glittering with dusty frost that made them turn invisible when they were not attacking. Fear began to replace the fury. The demon-spirits were cunning and deadly. The Druidecht Merinda had called them Weir. It was from some lore she had been taught.

One by one the creatures slipped away, leaving the remnants of Kenatos to bleed.

Tyrus tried to still his breathing and subdue his mounting panic. Why had the creatures run off? He could discern no pattern in their attack or retreat. They seemed to have no reason. Perhaps a more cunning intelligence controlled them?

He looked down at his hand and saw the smear of blood. His mouth and chin throbbed with pain, as did his leg and arm. He clutched the wound on his arm to try to stanch the bleeding and started to hobble, seeing who had survived.

There was Merinda, face ashen, her untamed red hair clotted with leaves. Her fingers still burned blue as she rocked back and forth, not sure if the reprieve would last. Her eyes were lucid. That was good. She was hunched forward protectively, elbows in. Sweat mixed with the mud on her cheek.

Standing just behind her was the Bhikhu. Tyrus was so grateful that Aboujaoude was there. The Vaettir-born Bhikhu were all dead. Nothing had prepared them for the ferocity of the attacks, and their instinct to preserve life had defeated their chances of survival. Aboujaoude was Aeduan, trained in the Bhikhu Temple in Kenatos. Street fighting was natural to him. Survival was an instinct he did not lack. He had shed his Bhikhu sensibilities after the first attack of the Weir. So far, their threatening time in the Scourgelands had revealed he was an efficient killer. As Tyrus panted, staring at the man, he realized the Arch-Rike would make Aboujaoude a Kishion when they returned.

If they returned.

The doubt's whisper was so soft, he almost didn't hear it. It made his knees quaver and nearly start clacking together. *If* was a terrible word. It was the hinges of a door leading to thoughts that, once contemplated, the mind could never abolish. He was never one prone to other men's fears. In his heart, he had believed he could defeat the Scourgelands. Losing half of the party already had begun to fill his mind with the seeds of doubt.

Their Romani Finder was the first to die.

The three Vaettir Bhikhu from Silvandom. Dead.

The brutish Cruithne warrior named Glebbon was still alive, still as deadly as ever. He was a menace with sword or pike, shrugging off the Weir as if they were merely feral street cats. Tyrus was grateful he was still alive.

Then there was Declan Brin, the Preachán. He avoided combat when he could and was helpful to analyze the situation afterward, pointing out symmetries to the attack. Where was Declan? Tyrus looked around, not seeing him.

"Declan?" he called.

"Over here, Tyrus!"

That was Mathon's voice, and it was hard-edged and frantic. Alarm swept inside of Tyrus. He turned and found Mathon kneeling over Declan's body, fingers working deftly to try to save the Preachán's life. Declan moaned and gurgled, his head thrashing one way and then the next. Mathon was a Rike and one of the best healers in the city. He was young looking, nearly the same age as Tyrus. He had short, dark hair, a slightly bulbous nose, and an expression that was perpetually sad, except that at the moment it was frantic with desperation.

"I'm working as fast as I can," Mathon gibbered, "but he's losing blood quickly." He jerked loose his belt and then fastened it like a strap to the Preachán's arm, twisting the leather viciously to try to stanch the bleeding. Declan groaned with pain, digging his fingers into the clutter of leaves.

"I'm losing him!" Mathon said, panting. He leaned close and listened to Declan's breath. He cinched the strap tighter, causing another groan of pain from the injured man. Mathon was full of scrapes and scratches himself, his black cassock soaked with blood and sweat. His own wounds were untended.

"Tyrus?" Declan said with a quavering moan.

Tyrus dropped to his knees next to the man. "I'm here."

Declan shuddered fitfully, his eyes opening wide but with a blank look, as if he couldn't see. "There's something you should know. The trees . . . I've been noticing that when . . . I'm seeing that . . . what I can't say is that I don't recall . . . or remember . . ."

"Declan, I don't understand you," Tyrus said, grinding his teeth. "What have you seen in the trees?"

"The trees," Declan breathed. His head lolled and he looked at Tyrus, though his expression was still blank. "I can't remember . . . the trees."

"What trees?" Tyrus said, placing a calming hand on Declan's shoulder.

Mathon pressed his mouth against his own forearm, shuddering with emotions as he watched his friend dying. Blood seeped from the arm, draining away the Preachán's life.

"Declan," Tyrus implored.

Mathon clenched his teeth and began working again, jamming a stick into the knot of belt and twisting it around, tightening the knot more. Declan let out a scream of pain and began thrashing.

"Hold him down," Mathon ordered Tyrus.

Tyrus did, surprised at the wiry man's sudden strength. It took more effort than he expected to pin him still, knowing the suffering he was causing to his friend.

Merinda wandered up. "Can I help?"

Mathon shook his head. "Not unless you can summon a Shain spirit."

"There are no helpful spirits in this forsaken place," Merinda said with despair. "We are at the mercy of the Scourgelands."

"What mercy," Mathon mumbled, torquing the stick more. The bleeding began to subside. He gazed at Tyrus deeply. "Nothing could have prepared us for this place. What little lore we got from Possidius was absolutely useless."

"I'll remember to tell him that," Tyrus said darkly. "This is not a place for scholars."

"This is not a place for the living," Mathon said, scanning the trees surrounding them. "This place repels life."

Howling started again. Tyrus looked up, experiencing the shiver all the way down to his toes.

"They are coming again," Merinda said with dread. "We must go."

Mathon hung his head. "I may have saved him . . . but for what? We won't last another wave from those beasts. My healing orbs are all spent, Tyrus. They were spent the first day we arrived. I only have my hands and skein threads to make stitches. We were not prepared for this!"

Tyrus lifted himself from Declan's body, realizing the man had probably fainted from the pain. His breath was so shallow it wouldn't have rustled paper.

"If we stay here, we all die," Aboujaoude said.

Tyrus stared down at Declan's shrunken face. His eyelids quivered and then he blinked awake.

"Declan?" Tyrus said.

The Preachán let out a grunting breath. His teeth were clamped together. "Tyrus," he hissed.

"What is it, my friend?" Tyrus leaned closer.

"Must . . . leave me. I cannot flee. I am . . . not going to survive this. You all go on."

Merinda's face flushed with sorrow.

Mathon shook his head angrily no.

"Logical . . . conclusion," Declan said. "One dies. Five live. For now. Maybe none of us will live through this. Improve . . . the odds. Must . . . survive and warn. Must leave a record. The trees, Tyrus. The trees aren't dead."

"What does that even mean?" Mathon said, wiping tears from his eyes. "For pity's sake, you've never made sense to me, Declan!"

"Tyrus," Aboujaoude warned. Glebbon gathered around as well, his face smeared with blood.

Staring down into the fading eyes of his friend, Tyrus knew that what Declan had said was true. But it did not make the truth any easier to accept.

"I did what I could," Mathon said, wiping his face. "This is impossible. How could we have known what we would face? Birds that turn you into stone if you look at them? They nest in these woods. The Weir. Or those scorpion beetles. Oogh, how I hate those. The poisons in this place. Everything is poison here. No food to eat. No clean water."

"We still have provisions," Tyrus said. "We can make it two more days. We are getting closer. The attacks come more swiftly because we are nearing the center."

The Cruithne Glebbon chuckled darkly, his voice echoing like a deep kettle. "We've poked a stick into a living hive. We are nowhere near the honeycomb. These are just the outer defenses. They are swarming us, Tyrus. The next wave comes."

"A bee swarm," Mathon said, nodding. "Good analogy. I'm feeling the stings. What do we do, Tyrus?"

Tyrus saw that they were all looking at him. Every one of them had trusted their lives into his hands. The Arch-Rike had warned him that it was folly. Possidius the Archivist of Kenatos had said they would likely all perish. The lack of information about a threat did not lessen its reality. Only scraps of knowledge existed about the Scourgelands. Those scraps had been carefully and methodically collected by the Archivist over a period of years, if not decades. Small little scraps. Little hints. Danger and threats masked in a fog of history that was too impenetrable, a fog dating further back than the founding of Kenatos itself.

The city of Kenatos had been founded to survive the Plague so that each race and each culture might endure despite the ravaging diseases that afflicted the world. Yes, Tyrus had gleaned everything he could from those scraps and tales that Possidius collected.

But Tyrus never shared his own knowledge with others. He hoarded his secrets like a miser hoards coins. He did not tell Possidius that he knew something the older man did not, that he had learned it while living in Silvandom as a young man when the Plague had struck previously and the gates of Kenatos had locked Tyrus out.

There was another source, a book that had never been copied into the Archives of Kenatos. It was a book he had found in the vast library of the royal house of Silvandom. On an obscure page, written in the Vaettir tongue, was a single word, scrawled onto the margin. It was an ancient word. It was a word that bore no direct translation. Tyrus had fussed over that word for a long time before finally giving it a name in his own Aeduan language.

Poisonwell.

It was a defense, a barrier—a locked gate deep in a cave that barred the only way into Mirrowen that mortals could travel. A shaft that connected both worlds. The umbilical cord of the worlds. How to summarize those meanings in a single word? Tyrus had stared at the page for days, thinking thoughts so deep that he desired neither food nor drink. He was just a young man, of course. And he had stumbled upon a great secret that seemed to shout in his ear. Poisonwell was the lost gate to Mirrowen, a land beyond the grasp of death. There was a way to get there, to be free from death after all. Poisonwell was not just the cause of the Plague. It was also the cure.

And no one knew where that word was inscribed except for Tyrus. If only he had shared that knowledge with someone else—like Possidius.

He looked up at the others, who were each staring at him with looks of hopelessness and despair. They could see nakedly that he had no answers for them. He had no plan that would guarantee their survival. He had led them into death itself.

His heart began to shrivel.

He stared down at Declan, who seemed surprisingly lucid for a man bleeding to death.

"What do you advise?" Tyrus whispered to his friend Mathon, a friend he had known since their shared days in an orphanage.

Mathon swallowed hard. His face was full of sadness and despair. "We thought you knew, Tyrus. We believed in you."

It was the first crack in the eggshell. The rest of it crumpled around him.

He had failed. The despair of that knowledge hurt worse than the claw marks ravaging his face.

"Our best chance is to flee these woods," he heard himself saying hoarsely, as the sadness nearly unmanned him. "If we separate and go our own ways, our enemy will hunt us separately and some of us may survive." He licked his bleeding lip. "I'm not certain any of us will make it out of here alive."

Looking down, he watched Declan Brin shut his eyes, and an expression of peace crossed the Preachán's face. He would lie there, still, and wait to die.

It was the hardest decision Tyrus had ever made in his life. He was twenty-five years old.

"Over the years, I have periodically, though seldom, received requests to understand the lore of the Scourgelands. There is very little in the records about that forbidden place. I ascribe the lack of history to the fact that it is so lawless and dangerous that few who venture there have ever survived. Some menace lurks in those woods, a cunning menace that even the Boeotians fear. The only man I know personally who has survived a journey there is Tyrus Paracelsus. And even he rarely speaks of it without shuddering."

- Possidius Adeodat, Archivist of Kenatos

II

The fire snapped and spat out a cluster of glowing sparks into the night air. Even the wind was timid. Phae glanced surreptitiously at the faces surrounding the camp, all eyes fixed on her father. She could see her own feelings mirrored in most of their expressions—horror mingled with dread. Only two seemed impervious to the emotional tale, namely Kiranrao and Baylen.

On the other side of Tyrus sat Annon, a Druidecht. He was Aeduan and only slightly older than Phae, but his eyes were haunted and his clothes showed the scorch marks and stains of his rough journeys. The talisman and a torc around his neck gleamed in the firelight and he absent-mindedly stroked the fur of a spirit cat, Nizeera, nestling beside him. By Annon, she saw his twin sister, Hettie. Both were the children of Merinda, the only other person who had barely survived the Scourgelands journey with Tyrus, but who had lost her mind overusing the fireblood's magic. Hettie wore leather hunter garb and smoothed her hair over her ear as she watched. She had been abducted by a Romani as an infant, though she had eventually renounced her Romani heritage and begun Bhikhu training under the man seated next to her.

Paedrin had the dark skin and slanted eyes of the Vaettir and he was an outspoken Bhikhu. His hair was shorn short and he wore stained gray robes that were spotted with blood. His eyes were always expressive as he had listened to the tale, eager to learn more. There were several other Vaettir in the party as well. Prince Aransetis wore the black tunic of the Rikes and his cousin, Khiara, wore paler colors, clad in the formal robes of her order—the Shaliah, the healers of Silvandom. The last Vaettir was the Romani lord Kiranrao, who had listened to the tale with a curl of derision on his lip. He dressed like shadows and his very presence reminded Phae of smoke. Baylen was slightly apart from the others, a hulking Cruithne warrior from Kenatos who had multiple blades strapped to his back and wore armor and battle gear. He showed little emotion on his face or in his eyes, and had listened to the tale with only small coughing chuckles to mark his surprise.

Seated next to Phae, his knee just touching hers, was Shion, her protector. He had the look of an Aeduan and he had once served their enemy, the Arch-Rike. His face was raked with scars from some previous vicious battle. His gaze was intent as Tyrus spoke. Phae believed that Shion was connected to the Scourgelands somehow.

Tyrus's voice resumed, breaking the stillness as the sparks winked out. "That was the moment when I broke," he murmured softly. "That was the moment when I failed. I rarely share this experience and still feel the shame of it. I left one of my best friends to die. But it is important—crucial, even—that you understand the horrors we will all face inside the Scourgelands. That was eighteen years ago. Only Merinda and I survived, and only because she sacrificed herself and unleashed the fireblood's full force to save my life."

He took the small, charred stick he had been using to stir the fire and prodded it once more, shifting the weight of a glowing log. "There was something we had in that previous journey that we lack among us now. Any thoughts as to what that might be?" He raised an eyebrow curiously.

"A Preachán?" Kiranrao said with a smirk, earning an aghast look from Hettie. Phae observed how the Romani girl was always watching him, covertly, but still Phae noticed the subtle deference. Paedrin's frown was a sullen curl at the remark.

Tyrus ignored it.

Prince Aransetis leaned forward. "You replaced a Rike gifted at dispensing healing magic with a Shaliah, whose power is innate."

Tyrus nodded, but Phae could tell it was not the answer her father sought. "No. What we lack is a single word. Trust." He gazed at each one of them. "They were each tested and loyal, or so I thought. Looking back now, I think my friend Mathon was sent by the Arch-Rike to poison my thoughts. I've learned since then that our enemy is quite adept at such arts. It is probably his key power of influence—the ability to sow doubt. It was right at that moment, with Declan Brin dying before my eyes, that Mathon's words affected me so much. I failed because I chose, at that moment, to surrender to my doubts. We disbanded, each going our own way. I was hunted and chased and later stumbled upon Merinda, which is when I learned she was pregnant." He shook his head, frowning with determination. "I have since learned that trust is essential to an endeavor such as this. If we cannot trust one another, then we will fail. I've shared with you this story to show you my trust. It was trust that won Phae's protector from the Arch-Rike's service. Trust is a powerful motivator."

Tyrus set down the stick, setting the smoking end amidst the coals. "Trust is where it begins. I would like each of you to describe why you are here. Before you decide whether to accompany me on this suicidal quest, you must know what you can about each other and then make your choice to stick with us or leave." His gaze shifted to the Cruithne. "Baylen. Why are you here?"

Phae rubbed her chin with the back of her hand as she stared at the giant Cruithne. He was easily three times the size of anyone else there, his skin shadowy in the night. Streaks of gray swept through his hair along his temples, but the rest was a lustrous brown. He had big jowls and an expression of sardonic amusement. "You chose me first because you trust me the least?" he asked, and then waved it off as a joke. He sighed and then stared at the fire, his meaty fingers tugging absently at the prairie grass. "I observe people. It's what I was paid to do at the Paracelsus Towers in Kenatos. I observed those coming in and going out. I judged the threat that each individual presented in their countenance. I wasn't only hired for my ability to see people, though. I'm pretty good in a fight. Maybe not as tough as Glebbon, but I learned something of street fighting from a fellow named Aboujaoude who rescued me from a scrape I couldn't win. I suppose I have always felt indebted to that Bhikhu. I've spent most of my life fighting one thing or another."

He tossed a clump of prairie grass into the fire pit. The pieces flamed brightly for a few moments. "I suspected that you were planning another trip to the Scourgelands, Tyrus. You never said it in your words, but I could see the intent in your eyes. Part of me wanted you to ask me to join you. When you vanished in a cloud of dust and rubble, I thought my chance to join you might have passed. Seems now like I was just in time."

Tyrus nodded slowly, giving the big man an appraising look. "Are you in league with the Arch-Rike of Kenatos?"

The Cruithne's expression went flat. His eyes glittered. "No."

Tyrus nodded again. "I don't have one of those rings the Rikes wear, Baylen. I've learned that it isn't wise to trust a man by his words alone. I was just asking." Then turning his look to Prince Aransetis, the Vaettir lord, he nodded deferentially. Aransetis wore the black cassock of a Rike, which gave him an incongruous appearance amidst them, especially in light of her father's last question. Though Tyrus said nothing, the Prince understood his meaning.

"My name is Aransetis," he said in a distinctly formal tone. Phae had first met him in the barn at the Winemiller orphanage in Stonehollow where he had tracked her down. He had warned her that her life was in danger and had tried to persuade Master Winemiller to let her accompany him to safety. The natural distrust of those from Stonehollow had thwarted his effort, and she had managed to sneak away that night. She shook her head with the memories that followed, glancing at Shion, who stared fixedly at the Prince.

"I am from one of the noble houses of Silvandom and my family has been allies of Tyrus for many years. We sent three Bhikhu with Tyrus the last time, one of them being my brother. I was a young man myself at the time and believed in the quest to rid the world of plague. I was not allowed to go and grieved when I learned what happened. I decided at that moment that I would train to kill that I might be useful if a second attempt was made."

His eyes shone with intensity, his frown a sign of dark strength. "I trained to protect Tyrus's daughter." His gaze met hers and she felt a shiver run through her. "To give my life so that she might reach the center of that hideous maze. I gladly step aside, relinquishing that role to someone better suited than I. Many of you have asked me why I wear these black robes. The answer is simple. To better understand the cunning mind of our enemy, the Arch-Rike. Like Tyrus, I suspected Lukias was a traitor among us. I did not recognize that he *was* the Arch-Rike himself. Because of that betrayal, I suspect each one of you of deception. I will be watching you closely. Expect that."

Kiranrao snorted. "This speech is supposed to help us trust one another? Even black hens lay white eggs."

Aransetis frowned at the comment, but Tyrus held up his hand. "Have a care, Kiranrao. We just watched the Thirteen of Canton Vaud get murdered by the Arch-Rike and we took the blame for it. Trust is improved when we understand one another's motives. Prince Aransetis is explaining his rather candidly."

"And so are you?" Kiranrao challenged.

"You heard my speech to the Thirteen," Tyrus replied heatedly. "My motives have ever been the same. The Arch-Rike ascribes it to a lust for glory and fame. As you no doubt have realized, we will get very little of that if we succeed. Khiara—what about you?"

The Vaettir girl did not raise her eyes but continued to stare down at her hands. "A Shaliah is a healer. My purpose is to keep you all alive. Had I been there, Declan would have survived and you might have made a different decision." She sighed, her voice trailing off very softly. "I go where my cousin goes."

Phae saw the unmistakable flush in the girl's cheeks and her heart throbbed with pity. Khiara was in love with her cousin, Prince Aransetis. It was painful to look at, for it reminded her of her own feelings for Trasen. As a Dryad-born, she had erased all of Trasen's memories of their time together because the Arch-Rike was using him to hunt her. Khiara's feelings were simple and uncomplicated.

But Phae could see that Prince Aransetis did not reciprocate them. His jaw clenched at her mumbled words, his stern expression becoming even more so.

"Thank you, Khiara," Tyrus said. "We are grateful you are with us. Without you, we cannot succeed." He said a few words in the

Vaettir tongue, which Phae could not understand. Khiara sat as still as a stone, saying nothing in return.

"Annon."

The young Druidecht was only a little older than Phae, but he seemed to have aged in the hours since the destruction inside Canton Vaud. He had connected with a Dryad in the woods of Silvandom and her tree had been destroyed by the Arch-Rike shortly after the death of his masters—the Thirteen. He absently stroked the fur of a spirit creature nestled in the grass next to him, a big cat named Nizeera.

"My mother was Merinda Druidecht," Annon said in a hoarse voice. He gazed around the fire at each of them. "For years I believed that Tyrus was my uncle. I thought he abandoned me in Wayland to be taught by a mentor because he was ashamed of me. I've learned that he was only trying to protect me, that Kenatos is a prison, and he was a prisoner." He snorted with disdain. "I am here because the Arch-Rike must be stopped. I seek his downfall. He knows about the Plague and its source. There is a shrine . . . a sanctuary of some kind in the mountains north of the island city. He has stonecutters from Stonehollow working on the outer façade. As we learned from Tyrus this evening, there are Calcatrix in the Scourgelands—these are serpent-like birds that have poisonous claws and can turn you to stone if you look at them. Khiara and I faced them in the Arch-Rike's secret temple, which he calls Basilides. The doorway inside Basilides leads into the Scourgelands. It may even lead into the heart of it."

Tyrus held up his hand and made a gesture and Annon quieted. The young man sighed deeply, the expression on his face pained. "The Arch-Rike has struck me quite personally. He destroyed the Druidecht hierarchy. And he took someone from me as well." His voice hushed as he mastered his emotions. Phae noticed a slight blue glow appear in his hands. "I will do whatever I must to defeat this man."

The firelight was beginning to dim, but Tyrus did not feed it with another log. He turned his face to the Romani girl, Hettie. She was looking at Annon with softness and compassion.

"Why am I here?" she said with her particular accent. She reached over and took Annon's hand, giving it a gentle squeeze. "This is my brother, if you did not already know. We are the twins of Merinda Druidecht. I was raised by the Romani." Her voice did not betray any emotions, but Phae noticed that she had chosen her words with care. "Though now I no longer wear a hoop in my ear. I seek my freedom. I seek a change in the order of things. I am a Bhikhu in training." She glanced over at Paedrin, giving him a slightly mocking smile, one that shared many memories.

All eyes went to him next, another Vaettir who squatted low on his haunches, his sandaled feet flat against the ground. He looked over at Tyrus and then shrugged. "I do not know why I am here. I think I took the wrong road back in the woods and ended up with all of you by mistake."

Phae smiled, appreciating the Bhikhu's sense of humor. She saw the effect on all of them, the lightened mood, except for Kiranrao, who looked disdainful.

"We're all so serious. I thought it might be best to try levity. I am here to keep all of you from dying. I will do my best." He looked at Tyrus shrewdly. "I understand your warning about the dangers we face. I am not afraid to kill. I would prefer not to, but if the odds are against us, then I will do what must be done. When this is finished, I intend to return to the Shatalin Temple in the mountains along the coast. I have a promise to fulfill there. It seems the Arch-Rike keeps some of his servants training there." His eyes went straight to Shion. "It is time they were sent away."

He glanced around the fire ring and then fixed Kiranrao with an evil look. "I do not trust Kiranrao. I don't care how many nights we spend around the fire holding hands and singing songs. I don't think that I can ever trust him. Prince Aransetis, maybe we can take turns keeping a watch?"

"Paedrin," Tyrus warned.

"I'm just getting started," Paedrin said. "We would be better off without him."

Tyrus fidgeted angrily, but the Romani was quick to interject. "Let the lad speak his mind," Kiranrao quipped with an exaggerated yawn. "He's more to be pitied than laughed at."

"A goose is still a goose, even if you call it a duck. I made that proverb up myself. I rather like the sound of it compared to all of yours."

Kiranrao's eyes narrowed—that was the only indication of his displeasure.

"Paedrin," Tyrus said, "be silent. If you can." The Bhikhu bowed his head to Tyrus, but his look was unrepentant. "Kiranrao? Of us all, you bear a grudge against the Arch-Rike. His machinations are destroying Havenrook as we speak."

The Romani snorted. "That is well known, so I won't give any flowery speeches. I am here for one simple reason—revenge. Since I escaped the hangman's noose in Kenatos, the Arch-Rike has repeatedly earned my scorn. His armies attack my people and cripple my city as we sit here mumbling in the shadows. When this is through, I will see him dead. As for a strategy, Tyrus, I see you are overlooking the simplest one. We could end this by tomorrow night."

Tyrus clenched his teeth. "Kiranrao . . ."

"It will only take but a moment to explain." The lanky Vaettir was as mercurial as a cat. His hand never strayed far from a dagger belted to his waist. The look of the dagger made a pit inside Phae's stomach. "Just give me the Tay al-Ard now. I will venture into the

Scourgelands alone. None of the beings skulking in there will be a match for me. When I find the Dryad tree in the center of the woods, I will come back to you and we can all enter together. You can all have a little . . . a little picnic while I am gone." He smirked at Tyrus.

There was a moment of silence. The Tay al-Ard was a device invented by Tyrus of incredible Spirit magic that could transport whoever was holding it to any location he or she had previously been. It was a power Kiranrao hungered for almost as much as his blade.

"It won't protect you from losing your memories," Paedrin challenged.

Tyrus leaned forward. "We will see if your plan is wise after we've survived our first encounter in the Scourgelands. You may be surprised by the power of our enemies. But even so, they will fear facing you, Kiranrao. The weapon you carry is anathema to them. We will not succeed without you among us."

Kiranrao seemed mollified by this and said nothing in reply.

Tyrus turned to Shion and gestured.

Phae sat next to Shion, feeling the coolness of the night air settling into her bones now that the fire was nearly burned out. Up close, she could see the faint scars on his cheek, scars that seemed to be a matching set to the ones on Tyrus's face. Shion was the Arch-Rike's most ruthless servant, the Quiet Kishion, a man without a name and without a past. Somehow the mystery surrounding him was shrouded in the lore of the Scourgelands. His scars, his lack of memory, his invulnerability. She had watched him plunge his hand into a swarming beehive without a single sting and then plummet from the roofline of a house and walk away as if it were nothing. The Arch-Rike had sent him to capture her. He had succeeded, but somehow her father had persuaded him to join the quest. She was afraid of him, but she was also afraid of not being near him. His very presence was a source of comfort, a man beyond the reach of death.

"Call me Shion," he said, his voice rich, as if he had studied in the theater. "If Tyrus's motives are not what he claims them to be, then I will be the first to abandon him. I am Phae's protector. That is all you need know about me."

"How did Tyrus persuade you to forsake your master?" Kiranrao probed. "If there is anyone here to be distrusted, it's you, for you were his servant."

Shion looked at him, a little wrinkle of annoyance on his brow, and said nothing in reply, holding true to his nickname. Phae had been the recipient of his sullen silence in the past. She concealed a smirk.

"Daughter?" Tyrus said patiently, eyes focused on her face. She stared back at him, feeling that complex mixture of emotions. They were still such strangers. She wanted to know him better, but the more she learned about him, the more fearful she was of the cost of knowing him. His enemy was the most powerful man in all the kingdoms. His quest took them into the most dangerous land. How should she feel about a man who willingly took his daughter into such a place?

Phae saw that they were all looking at her, waiting for her to speak. With a blink of her eyes, she could steal their memories away. She could make them all forget the quest they had joined. It caused a wild thrill inside her heart. She could make them forget all about her and then she could walk back to Stonehollow and rejoin her lost family.

It was a sad wish.

But she could not do that. Not after each of them had suffered so much. Not after all the world had suffered.

"My name is Phae Winemiller," she said simply, crossing her arms over her knees. "And I am here to end the Plague."

"Havenrook has fallen and the Romani have dispersed. An army of the Cruithne reached the trading city before the King of Wayland could penetrate the woods. I am astonished at how swiftly the collapse occurred. Despite the great wealth of the Preachán and their Romani allies, they apparently took no thought for their own city's defenses. I am certain they will resent the presence of the mountainfolk amongst them. But what choice do they really have but to endure it?"

- Possidius Adeodat, Archivist of Kenatos

III

Phae was not certain what sort of reaction she would get from her words. She did not enjoy being the subject of so much attention and began to fidget. "I am Dryad-born," she continued in a low voice, grateful for the darkness that shadowed her face. "I'm of the age where I can bond with a tree and gain access to its memories. My father hopes . . . that doing so will help us understand the Plague's origin."

Kiranrao leaned forward. "You *hope*?"

"I'm convinced," Tyrus replied, gesturing for Phae to say nothing more. "The place we seek is deep inside the Scourgelands. A place called Poisonwell. It's a cave."

"I know that name," Annon announced in the dark.

Tyrus turned to him, his expression changing to alarm. "I have never spoken it to you before."

Annon sat up straight and picked at the whiskers on his chin. "It was in the tunnels of Basilides. There was a Rike who kept asking me what I was seeking there. He wanted to know what you had sent us to claim . . . a treasure from the sarcophagi hidden there.

He was certain we were seeking an artifact, not the doorway itself. He said that word—Poisonwell—that was the source of the Plague."

"What else did he say, Annon?"

The Druidecht began to rock back and forth, his face twisting with frustration. He wiped his face with his hands. "I don't remember it well. He warned of the dangers in the Scourgelands. My memories are so faded. I used to be able to remember every word. Now I can hardly recall a thing. Erasmus said something as well. He figured out something about the Arch-Rike."

"Try to remember."

"I am trying, Tyrus." Annon rose quickly and began to pace around the circle, his brow furrowing deeply. "Khiara? Do you recall what he said?"

The Shaliah's eyes were closed and she seemed to be asleep. "He spoke about the lost blood. The forgotten blood. A persecuted race."

"Go on," Tyrus murmured, his eyes twinkling with excitement. The others were leaning forward as well, waiting.

"Yes!" Annon said, stopping. He pumped his fists in concentration. "He spoke about the fireblood. No one knows the name of our race. We look Aeduan, but there was once a name for our kind. It is lost now. But there were crypts, you see. Around in a circle, filled with treasures."

"Treasure?" Kiranrao murmured inquisitively.

Khiara nodded in the darkness, the moonlight starting to reveal her face. Her eyes were wide open. "There were crypts for each of the kingdoms—"

"Yes, but the names on the crypts were of the *living*." Annon stopped, his face brightening. "The one with Kenatos had the name Band-Imas on it. The current Arch-Rike, not one of those from the past. Erasmus said the Arch-Rike was masquerading. Wasn't that the word he used?"

"Yes," Khiara answered. "A disguise. The crypt marked Wayland had the current king's name. Again . . . the living."

Tyrus was deathly still.

Annon shook his head in frustration. "He'd realized a truth, Tyrus. You know how Erasmus was always making predictions. He perceived something about the Arch-Rike. There was a pattern there amidst the stone boxes that he understood. Before he could explain it to us, he died. There were serpents everywhere. Several bit him before attacking us."

"There are serpents in the Scourgelands as well," Tyrus said. He steepled his fingers, drawing deeply into himself. "Is that all you can remember?"

Annon began pacing again. "I'm trying . . . but we nearly died too. I had not even thought of it until now, when you said the word *Poisonwell*. It triggered the memory."

"And where is this hidden temple the Arch-Rike is so secretive about?" Kiranrao asked.

"You've lost your treasure and so you are seeking a new one now?" Paedrin mocked.

"You test my patience, boy. I could go there and seek new information. I can get past its defenders."

Tyrus shook his head and waved his hand. "It is probably the place the Arch-Rike expected us to flee to from Canton Vaud. Undoubtedly there is an overwhelming force awaiting us there. Your magic is strong, Kiranrao . . . I do not doubt that. Because Annon was there, we can go to the tunnels whenever we wish. I chose Boeotia because it is the one place the Arch-Rike cannot hunt for us unmolested. He is expecting us to enter the Scourgelands right away out of desperation. Our advantage lies in being unpredictable."

"The Uddhava," Paedrin said.

Tyrus nodded. He rose to his full height and Phae felt insignificant in his shadow. "Poisonwell is our destination. It is a strange nexus between our world and Mirrowen. The entire forest of the Scourgelands exists to thwart us. My plan is simple. We will pass the Arch-Rike's defenses by being unpredictable. We will skirt the borders of the Scourgelands north, testing its boundaries, bringing its defenders after us. Then, with the Tay al-Ard, we will come back to the different points we have been to, causing some fires and attacking its defenders, and then come away again. The Tay al-Ard is critical because it can bring us to a place where we have been before. It will allow us to flee quickly when the beasts threaten to overpower us. By moving constantly, we will penetrate the woods at various points. The defenders will not know where we will strike next. If we focus carefully and don't gaze at the trees, we'll avoid the eyes of the Dryads, which will try to trick us into looking harder. That is the secret Declan began to deduce before we abandoned him. Any tree with mistletoe must be avoided at all costs."

Baylen spoke up. "You won't kill a bear if you keep poking its hide with needles. You will only make it angrier. We want to kill this one."

Tyrus shook his head. "No, Baylen, we cannot kill this one. You do not understand or appreciate the number of defenders in the forest. We must distract them. Make them hunt us. And we must stay out of their reach. If the King of Wayland marched his entire army into the Scourgelands, they would be decimated. There is no weapon we could use, not even the blade Iddawc, for there is no single enemy to slay. A smaller force will stand better odds of slipping through. When we're attacked on all sides, we will gather around me and disappear. This is the part where you will all have to trust me. I will be the judge of when it is time to flee.

The creatures who oppose us are driven by an intelligence. They do not always fight to the death. Sometimes they flee and then come again soon after. I have faced these threats before and survived." His look was hardened with the experience. "I will decide when to flee. When I give the command—Hasten!—you need to come to me immediately. Grab my arm or grab each other and I will use the Tay al-Ard to bring us to another place. When I say the word, I will count in my mind for five seconds. Like this . . . one—two—three—four—five. You must be with me by the end or you will be left behind."

Phae felt coldness go down her spine. She looked up at her father in shock.

Kiranrao snorted.

"You do not appreciate the savagery of our enemies. You do not comprehend how lethal they can be." He sighed. "I do not expect that all of us will survive. That would be foolish in the extreme. We must have faith in each other and you must trust me fully to know when the right time is to pull away. Our foes are powerful. The Scourgelands have been a land of death for too long. In the city of Kenatos, there is a game the Paracelsus play called Bad-kejon. It moves very quickly and often turns unpredictably. Once we enter that place, we are playing Bad-kejon with a ruthless enemy who seeks our death. I won't have time to explain my motives or my thinking to you. I won't have time to persuade you why I'm trusting my instincts in a given situation." His voice grew ragged and he took a leather flask from his belt and gulped down some water. "Those who survive this ordeal will do so if you obey and observe to perform every word of command from me . . . with exactness."

There was stillness in the night after he spoke. Phae felt herself starting to shiver. Shion nudged closer to her, giving her a look of concern. She shook her head, biting her lip. Her father's words conjured images of blood and death in her mind. How many of those joined around a smoldering fire would survive to the end? She did not know them, but she cared about the welfare of each of them. She believed some might die. The thought that most of them would was a price too horrific to consider.

"Taking into account that the last group you brought there met such a terrible fate," Kiranrao said disdainfully, rising to his feet with the grace of a cat, "I supposed we cannot expect any better."

Prince Aransetis rose as well. "If you are not up to the challenge, you are permitted to withdraw."

Kiranrao looked over the Prince skeptically. "I do not fear you. I fear no one. There is nothing those haunted woods can send at me that I cannot handle. Know that."

"Proudly spoken," Paedrin quipped. "My master always accused me of arrogance."

Kiranrao's face contorted with anger. "Why do you waste our time, Tyrus?" he seethed. "If you do not trust giving me the Tay al-Ard, then let us go together. Just the two of us. I will get you to the center of that maze and then you can bring your daughter there in an instant. All this talk and worry is madness. None of these fools need die. I will bring you there myself. I swear it."

Phae felt a shiver of fear go through her at the Romani's words. She stared at her father with worry. *Don't trust him. He only wants the Tay al-Ard. If you go with him, he'll kill you.*

"We cannot succeed without you, Kiranrao," Tyrus said softly. "I've known that from the beginning. You are impatient because of what is happening in Havenrook. Ending the Plague will do more to aid your people than anything else you do. We all go together. We will succeed if every person does his part. Including you."

Kiranrao scowled and muttered something under his breath. He looked at Tyrus fiercely. "Are we going to wait around the coals all night? It will be dawn soon. What then?"

"We leave now. Hettie, conceal the traces of our camp. We go deep into Boeotia."

There were no roads in the wastes of Boeotia. Annon had wandered through many valleys surrounding the kingdoms, but he had never entered such an inhospitable land before. There was no prairie grass, only dirt and rocks and stunted shrubs. The trees were gangly and full of thorns, with wispy leaves and pollen that drifted when the wind shook the branches. There were occasional pockets of denser vegetation clustering around tiny rivulets of water. Annon rubbed the sweat from his neck, craning his head to gaze up at the burning sun.

There were spirit creatures, however, in abundance.

As he walked, Annon reached out to the life populating the prickly shrubs and weed-choked hills. Most were in the form of brown-skinned lizards that concealed themselves and studied him from the shade, or grasshoppers that hopped and flew. He sensed spirits in the millions of tiny red ants that came from clods of cracked dirt. They greeted him warily but deferentially, recognizing him for who he was. They gave him conflicting sentiments.

Welcome, Druidecht. Beware this land. They will hunt you.

Beware, Druidecht. You will not be harmed.

Your friends will all be killed.

One of Nizeera's ears twitched as she padded near him, sniffing the air and testing it for the scent of Boeotians. His heart was heavy as stones, and he walked with a feeling of ever-mounting dread. He glanced back at the others, watching the order that Tyrus had assembled for their march through the region. Tyrus was in the center with the Kishion and Phae. Aransetis covered one flank and Paedrin the other. Baylen walked with Khiara ahead of Tyrus. Kiranrao and Hettie came up the rear, with Hettie doing her best to cover their trail and watch for signs of pursuit. Tyrus had sent Annon and Nizeera to go out in front and survey the land and find the trail. Should trouble find them, all sides would pull in toward Tyrus and await his instructions.

You are grieving.

Annon glanced down at Nizeera, seeing her saucer-like eyes boring into his. *I am.*

I fear that you will be reckless because of it. Do not seek your own death, Druidecht.

He sighed deeply, feeling a strange mixture of guilt and denial at her intruding thoughts. Tyrus's speech had not filled him with dread. If anything it brought a promise of respite from the terrible pain inside his damaged heart. He dreaded the thought of never seeing Neodesha the Dryad again. Was she in Mirrowen at that moment? Was she dead? Was there a way he could be reunited with her? Would death separate them forever? He did not know. Not knowing made the pain all the worse.

The more they walked, the less the gravelly ground and shrubs bothered him. It was dusty, to be sure, and the air was dry and made his throat parched, but he found a strange beauty in the land, especially the shape of the rugged mountains deep to the north. There were no signs of dwellings, but he understood that the Boeotians lived in movable tents. They were wanderers and did not plant or harvest crops. They lived off the land and raided the kingdoms to the south when they needed more. Theirs was a guttural language and he recalled, having faced Boeotians twice in his wanderings, that they were not to be reasoned with. Their warriors were quick to attack and assume danger. Annon did not expect that he would be able to cross their kingdom without stumbling across their clans.

Nizeera, do you smell anything on the wind? Any trace at all?

She growled softly. *Nothing but our own scent. The wind comes from all sides. I will smell something if it approaches us.*

Annon wondered how far they had penetrated into the Boeotian lands. The day was long and hot and his legs throbbed from the pace of the walk. He glanced back repeatedly to make sure he was not outdistancing the others. He saw several talking amongst themselves as they traveled, but he felt no desire for companionship. Perhaps Tyrus knew his heart couldn't bear it, that it was one of the reasons he had been chosen to lead the way.

A bird fluttered in the gray-blue sky, soaring overhead. He heard its thoughts come down to him as it passed. *Your band is being followed, Druidecht. Others are summoned to join the pursuit. They will come at night when you cannot see them in the distance. Be warned, Druidecht. They will come at night.*

Annon felt his heart constrict and stopped, holding up his hand as a warning. He did not know how many were in pursuit, but he got the sense from the bird-spirit that it was a sizable host. He looked ahead, seeing nothing but unending plains with sharp brown rocks and tumbleweeds. Pausing, he stopped and inhaled the air, tasting the dirt on his tongue. He could hear the crunch of boots as the rest of Tyrus's band approached him.

It was hardly past noon and the Boeotians had found them already.

"As iron is eaten away by rust, so the envious are consumed by their own passion. I heard it said once, and this by a wealthy man in Kenatos, that what he needed most was to love and to be loved. Happily he wrapped those painful bonds around himself, and, sure enough, he would be lashed with the red-hot pokers of jealousy, by suspicions and by fear, by bursts of anger and quarrels. Some fools cannot discern the difference between love and jealousy."

- Possidius Adeodat, Archivist of Kenatos

IV

Studying emotions at a drab and colorless monastery, with all its cracks in the cobbles and moldering stone walls, had not truly prepared Paedrin for the rest of his life. He had been taught by Master Shivu that emotions could be controlled, directed, and would ultimately provide a calm assurance and peace that would persevere until the stubble of black hair on the dome of his head had frosted over. Always Master Shivu had a quirk of a smile on his face as he waggled his fingers at his young pupils, warning them not to be caught in the snares of the heart. Men murdered for love. Fools bargained with Preachán for tastes of it.

But there was something about seeing Hettie walking side by side with Kiranrao that made Paedrin forget all of Shivu's cautions.

The young Bhikhu sighed deeply, wrestling against his surging feelings. How could he describe it? The tranquility Master Shivu promised was still there, woven link by link like the chain he had fastened to his wrist and now used as a weapon—a series of conscious choices that had purified his body and his mind and allowed him to perform feats of great discipline and grace. Tranquility was as subtle and sweet as a juicy grape. But at the same time, he experienced the red-hot burning on his tongue brought by a mouthful of fiery peppers—hate, jealousy, revenge, contempt. These were powerful emotions, and their presence nearly drowned out the calmer ones completely. He realized that it was difficult to be patient and wise when his mouth was blistering with unspoken insults.

What galled Paedrin even more was that Tyrus would not address his concerns or explain his reasons for allowing Kiranrao to join the expedition. It was like bringing along a snake and trusting it not to bite you. Tyrus would offer no reason. He only said it would become very clear once they entered the Scourgelands.

The walk through an area like Boeotia normally would have required his concentration, but with such vast open plains and rolling, scrub-packed hills, there was little that could advance on them unawares. No fearsome Boeotian warrior could possibly be squatting behind such stunted weeds or barren brush. Paedrin wanted to fight. He wanted to challenge Kiranrao right at that moment. He recognized his own tempestuousness, but recognition didn't help him cope.

Why did he care so much that Hettie seemed accepting of Kiranrao's company? Was he, a Bhikhu, attempting to *own* her in his way? She was a Romani girl, stolen at birth by a midwife and raised to be sold every ten years starting at age eight. Paedrin had snapped off her earring in Kenatos, and she had become a disciple of the Bhikhu ways. But he also knew that she was a cunning liar. Conflicting memories of her bashed around inside him. He had grown to trust her at last, through all they had suffered together to reach the Shatalin monastery and claim the Sword of Winds. A shiver went through him at the memory of huddling close to her at a cliff face. She had nearly plummeted to her death that night and he had saved her. In return, she had saved him from the Kishion training yard.

Yet Kiranrao was her old master. He who pays the piper calls the tune. Was Kiranrao calling the tune or was Tyrus? Was Hettie showing deference to Kiranrao so as not to provoke him? Would Paedrin fare better if he stopped provoking him too?

The man is insufferable, he thought blackly. How would Shivu have handled him? Black thoughts scudded across his mind. It did not matter for Master Shivu was dead, killed by Romani poison.

Annon stopped and the lack of motion caught Paedrin's attention instantly. He shoved aside his teeming feelings with great effort and began searching the area for signs of a threat. The big cat was nestled by Annon's leg, its tail lashing like a snake. Annon turned and began to hurry to Tyrus. Paedrin, not wanting to miss any of their conversation, reached the Paracelsus first.

"What is it?" Tyrus asked Annon.

"The spirits tell me we are hunted," Annon answered in a low voice. Some of the others gathered around as well. "They will stay out of sight until after nightfall, but I fear we may be surrounded. Our progress is being tracked."

"From behind?"

Annon nodded. "For now. Word is spreading about us. They may seek to box us in. Should we change direction?"

Tyrus shook his head. "No, I don't want them to realize we know of their plans. We can escape easily enough with the Tay al-Ard. Escaping is not my concern. I intend to face them."

"You do?" Annon asked, his face betraying his surprise.

"I have trained for years to fight Boeotians," Paedrin said, edging closer. "They are the principle enemies of Kenatos and have sought to destroy us since the founding."

"Yes, yes, I know," Tyrus said impatiently. "They are a proud race. Honor motivates them, but not the form of it you might be thinking."

"Honor?" Phae asked, brushing a long strand of hair over her ear. "What do you mean?"

Tyrus glanced at her and did not answer her question. "It is important that we learn how to fight as a group. It is crucial that we understand each other's abilities. We will not molest the Boeotians if they leave us alone. But if their hunting party attacks us, they will be surprised." Tyrus cocked his head a moment, pausing as the others approached. "They have a strange ritual among them. Their leaders are always the fiercest warriors and they constantly challenge each other for supremacy. When they come, Paedrin will challenge their leader."

A glow of excitement welled in Paedrin's heart. That was exactly what he needed. "I would be honored."

The glow turned sour when he saw Tyrus's smirk. "I'm confident in your abilities, Paedrin, but I mean to tell them that you are our lowliest fighter. It will send a message through their ranks and to their chieftains that we are not to be trifled with. They will test us before committing all of their force. We will pass their test."

It did not help Paedrin's feelings that Hettie was smiling at Tyrus's comment. She gave the Bhikhu a look, her expression revealing her unspoken words. *Lowliest fighter?*

"Very well, Tyrus," Paedrin replied with as much dignity as he could muster in such a moment. "But I have a ploy that I need to warn you all about. The Sword of Winds contains a potent magic. It cannot be drawn from its sheath without triggering the effect. This is what happens. The stone set in the pommel glows, and anyone who sees it will become blinded and suffer terrible pain. These effects do wear off after many hours, and the pain is not without benefit. In some way, the magic strips away the need to use your eyes at all. When it happened to me at the Shatalin temple, I was able to see just as well with my eyes shut. My other senses were amplified and I still feel those effects even now. If the leader succumbs to the magic, it will be a quick victory, for the magic is quite painful."

"Let me see it," Tyrus said, holding out his hand. Paedrin swiveled the scabbard around from his sash and quickly untied it. He offered it to Tyrus, who examined the pommel and the stone embedded there.

Annon drew closer. "There is a spirit trapped in the stone. I cannot hear it, but I can sense it."

"I thought that as well," Paedrin said, nodding.

Tyrus bent close, looking at the design. "This blade was not forged by the Paracelsus. There are no binding runes. The ancient stone set in the pommel was part of the original design." He adjusted his grip on the scabbard but did not attempt to draw the blade. The hilt was narrower than the types of guards made by the blacksmiths in Kenatos. The polish had long rubbed off and part of the hilt had tarnished.

"What is it then?" Kiranrao asked curiously.

"This is a Mirrowen blade," Tyrus answered with a curt nod, handing it back to Paedrin. "It was a gift by the spirits to a Vaettir lord many centuries ago. It's been handed down during the generations and was brought across the sea when the ships came, escaping the fate of the Vaettir homeland. The stone is a protection against the unworthy handling the powers of the blade. As you no doubt learned, it empowers someone to fly and will help in your natural abilities. This is important, Paedrin, because some of the creatures we'll face, like the Calcatrix, attack from the air and if you look at them, you will turn to stone. This weapon was designed to help destroy such creatures."

"I cannot draw the blade from the sheath," Paedrin said. "I can only use it in the scabbard until the master of the blade draws it. I've tried." He looked at Hettie, for she was the one who had explained the properties to him.

Tyrus turned and faced her.

"It's true," Hettie said. "I learned in the temple that only one man can draw the blade. It's fused solid otherwise. It must be given freely or taken from the one defeated in battle."

"Cruw Reon," Tyrus answered. "The traitor of Shatalin."

"The man standing right next to you may be the one who can draw it," Hettie finished, holding her hand toward Shion, the Quiet Kishion.

Paedrin stared at him, saw the look of amused surprise flicker momentarily on his scarred face.

"Is my name Cruw Reon, Tyrus?" he asked in a soft voice.

"That cannot be," Tyrus answered. "I learned of Cruw Reon from Master Shivu and he lived a generation ago. You cannot be him. But if the blade passes from master to master through defeat, you may have the right to unsheathe it. Draw the blade and we shall see."

"Or not," Kiranrao suggested. "Especially if we all go blind."

Tyrus handed the scabbard to the Kishion, who studied its length as if it were some unnatural, disgusting thing. Phae watched him intently, her eyes drawn.

"Unless you all have a deep fondness for ravaging pain," Paedrin said dryly, "I would recommend shutting your eyes before he draws it."

They did, except for the Quiet Kishion and Paedrin himself. The Kishion stared at the weapon, some dark emotion crossing his face. Frustration? Worry? The man was always so silent. Had he discovered a way to tame his emotions? Perhaps he could teach Paedrin how.

The two of them looked at each other a moment, the Kishion inquisitive.

"It hurt worse than any pain I have ever experienced," Paedrin offered calmly. "Even when you broke my arm. But the pain brought insights. It also brought new abilities I did not have before. Truly pain is a teacher. Perhaps the origin of that saying was Shatalin."

"Perhaps," the Kishion answered. Gripping the pommel firmly, he stared at the scabbard, studying the markings on it. Most averted their faces, not wanting to be stung by the blade's painful magic. Phae clutched her father's arm, her eyes squeezed tightly shut.

Gripping the scabbard tightly, the Kishion slid the blade free of its sheath in a fluid motion. It loosened without difficulty. The orb fastened to the hilt began to glow, making Paedrin wince in anticipation, but not painfully bright as it had before. He saw looks of fear on the faces of several of the women and Annon.

Paedrin squinted and then relaxed. "You truly are the master of the blade. It did not blind as it did before." The others looked up nervously, seeing the stone in the hilt glowing softly.

"I have no memory of this blade or that name," he announced coolly. "That part of me is lost until we find Poisonwell. The blade is yours, Paedrin. I give it to you freely."

Despite being a constant reminder that there was one man in the world that Paedrin could not defeat, he was starting to like the Kishion fellow.

The attackers came at midnight with smoking torches.

Tyrus's small band was expecting them.

The Boeotians had elected to swarm them from all sides, offering no way to escape a ring of death except through clashing weapons. Paedrin exulted in the anticipation of a duel with the leader and had practiced his forms well past sundown. He had his chain whip in one hand and the Sword of Winds in the other. Tyrus had positioned the companions around a campfire in a square formation. Paedrin stood in the middle of the square so that he would be the center of all eyes.

The tromping sound of charging men erupted from all around them, making the earth tremble with the force of feet. Spears clashed with buckler shields like thunder cracks. Whoops and shrill cries came at them from all sides.

Excitement thudded inside Paedrin's heart, matching the quickening pulse. He was ready for this. He felt as if he were a bow flexed near to bursting. He was ready to launch an arrow.

"Not yet," he heard Tyrus murmur, allowing the Boeotians to surge closer. Paedrin's lip tasted like salt.

A streamer of blue fire arced into the air, rising high before exploding into a single pulse of white-hot flames. Crackles of energy sizzled in the sky, illuminating the area and revealing the rush of attackers closing in. A deafening boom followed the light flash and its echoes reverberated across every rock and boulder nearby. The Boeotians halted suddenly, shielding their eyes from the glare and the noise, their charge interrupted.

"Now," Tyrus said.

Paedrin swallowed and then took in a breath of air to begin to rise, becoming the focal point for all eyes as they recovered from the flash. Tendrils of smoke and magic seethed in the air, fading slowly. He raised the Sword of Winds as if stabbing the sky with it and felt his rise accelerate.

"Is there a man brave enough to face me?" he shouted defiantly. "I am Paedrin Bhikhu of Kenatos. You are sorry worms to be blinded so easily. Does a little light make you squirm? Who among you dares to face me? Where is your leader? I will kick him into the dirt and spit on him."

There was a roar of anger and rage at the insults. Using the sword's magic, Paedrin swooped toward those coming from the northern side. "Well?" he shouted. "Who leads these quivering pups? Name yourself! I am Paedrin Bhikhu and I challenge you!"

A single spear came at him from the darkness. He saw the huge man who threw it and jerked his shoulders so that the shaft sailed past him.

Paedrin let out his breath and came crashing down to the ground, his face livid with rage. "Am I a sparrow to be pecked at? Are you the leader of these cowards?"

The man was enormous with graying temples and a long, knotted beard. There was a torc around his neck and the veins standing out on his skin gave him a purplish cast.

"I am Cunsilion Uchitel," the giant-like man said gruffly. "I defy you, Bhikhu!"

Paedrin had the Sword of Winds in his right hand, the chain rope in his left. He bowed, leaning forward, dropping into a low stance. "I am honored to be the one to shame you in front of your dogs. I serve Tyrus Paracelsus of Kenatos and am his lowliest servant. When I am finished with you, I will gladly defeat any else who dares to face my skill."

The man lumbered forward, large as a bear. His hidebound boots thudded in the packed earth, with little tendrils of things tied into his braided mustache and beard. Tattoos covered his left arm up to his shoulder and up past his neck, full of designs that offered the appearance of the bark of a tree. His eyes were full of fury and passion. Little flecks of spittle sprayed from his lips as he huffed.

Paedrin felt his muscles soothe and relax. This was what he longed for.

The brute of a man hefted another short spear and Paedrin readied for it. A huge axe was also strapped to his back.

"I do not prick so easily," Paedrin taunted.

"We shall see," Cunsilion Uchitel replied in a guttural tone. "Atu vast! Atu vast!"

Then planting his lead foot as if he were about to split the world in half, the giant-man hurled the spear directly at Tyrus.

Annon recognized the Boeotian words. He did not recall what they meant, but he knew they were the precursor of a vicious attack. He had heard those words spoken at Reeder's death and he had used them himself when a pack of Boeotians had hunted them along the trek to Basilides. He watched the man loose the spear and saw it sail toward Tyrus before anyone could react. Anyone, except for the Cruithne Baylen. He stepped forward and shattered the spear with one of his broadswords. The fragments exploded and the Boeotians whooped and screamed and charged from all sides.

Pyricanthas. Sericanthas. Thas.

The ancient Vaettir words sounded in his mind as Nizeera screamed in warning. He had already summoned the words previously but he wanted to make sure he kept control of them as Tyrus had warned. He saw the flames proceed from Hettie and Phae and Tyrus before loosing them himself. The sheet of flames expanded from their core, as if a large boulder had suddenly been heaved into a pond, sending out ripples in all directions at once. Annon felt his blood start to sing with the pleasure of the magic and knew it would be dangerous to play with the fire for very long. The scrub and brush exploded into yellow, setting the land alight with flames. Annon saw Paedrin rush the Boeotian leader, whipping the chain over his head as he charged. Hearing Nizeera growl, he saw a rush of Boeotians heading right for him.

Turning, he focused the fireblood on the approaching men and watched them become consumed into plumes of ash.

"How many?" Baylen asked.

"At least a hundred," Khiara said from above.

"Hold the flames," Tyrus ordered. "Now we can see, and the smoke will add confusion. Bring the fight to them. Now!"

"Was only waiting for you to say it," Baylen said with a chuffing laugh. The bulky Cruithne rushed toward the advancing foes.

Prince Aransetis put his hand on Annon's shoulder, looking him in the eye with deep seriousness. "I will keep them away from you." Then he shot like a lance into the midst of the Boeotians. Annon watched him, no weapons in hand, attacking the larger men with crisp, curt movements, standing like a dam against a flood. Each stroke was painful and Annon could hear the sound of snapping bones. An axe coming down at Aransetis's skull was caught, ripped loose from the attacker's grasp and tossed aside, followed up with a sharp kick to the kneecap and an elbow into his nose. Annon watched in amazement as the Vaettir prince struck with brutal efficiency, tossing men nearly twice his weight as if they were nothing. His black Rike cassock clung to him, snapping like a flag on a pole as he whipped from one victim to the next.

Nizeera growled at Annon's feet, staying next to him in case others broke through.

None did.

Paedrin's chain struck Cunsilion Uchitel's cheekbone, hard enough to slit open the skin and spray blood, but the giant-man was tireless and determined. Again he swung the axe down hard to split Paedrin in half vertically and again the agile Bhikhu sidestepped the blow and delivered three of his own in return for the one doled out.

Paedrin whipped the chain around once more, but the Boeotian leader ducked and double-stepped forward, seeking to crush the young warrior with his hands. The Sword carried Paedrin directly over the rushing man and the Bhikhu landed behind him, pivoting the blade under his own armpit and stabbing backward. He felt the blade strike flesh and muscle and withdrew it and swung around again. The giant barely managed to avoid the killing stroke by diving forward. He seized a fistful of dirt and thrust it in Paedrin's face. The tactic was an ancient one. It normally worked.

As Paedrin closed his eyes to deal with the abrasive pain of the dirt, his other set of eyes seemed to open and he could see just as clearly with his other senses. He lashed the chain whip down and the Boeotian rolled to one side. He lashed it again, forcing the man to roll the other way. The Boeotian struggled to get to his feet and Paedrin caught him around the neck with the chain, wrapping it in quick circles, and then jerked hard, unbalancing him. With the leash in his left hand, he raised the Sword of Winds to finish him off. His heart hammered in his chest. This would be a deathblow, his first deliberate kill. He sensed the Boeotian kneeling in front of him, chin out defiantly, his breath coming in winded gasps. Could Paedrin do this? Could he end a man's life on purpose?

"Hasten!"

The command was issued by Tyrus. Had he seen the indecision on Paedrin's face? Was something else amiss in the battle? From what he had seen, Tyrus's small band was making short work of their foes. Was the summons to return to him and use the Tay al-Ard a result of something Paedrin had done—or failed to do?

One.

He could not waste time thinking about it. He left the chain around the leader's neck and summoned the power of the Sword to bring him to Tyrus's side.

Two.

Paedrin could not see, but he sensed the others were gathering swiftly. His eyes hurt from the dirt, but he ignored the pain. Reaching out, he clasped onto an arm. He recognized the bracer and the shape. It was Hettie. He squeezed her forearm, wanting so much to be away from the nightmares facing them. Where would Tyrus take them? Into the Scourgelands?

Three.

"Quickly!" someone called. From the commotion, Paedrin was almost sure it was Phae.

Four.

The magic of the Tay al-Ard gripped and flung them far away.

Five.

"There is something in humility which strangely exalts the heart."

- Possidius Adeodat, Archivist of Kenatos

V

The battle with the Boeotians horrified Phae. She felt no physical threat or personal danger, but the abilities of those surrounding her had left her with a deep sense of her own helplessness. She had witnessed Shion fight before, single-handedly defying a group of Romani horsemen and scattering them to the four winds. He did the same to the Boeotians, using his skill and his double knives to deflect any attack against him and preventing any of the warriors from reaching her. Behind them, she had seen the one known as Kiranrao exhibit a bloodlust that would haunt her dreams. He was brutal and efficient at killing and had the uncanny ability to disappear like smoke only to reappear nearby, ready to kill the next man.

Her father's curt command to gather had been promptly obeyed and none were left behind. None would have wanted to be stranded amidst a horde of ravaging tribesmen. She did not know where the Tay al-Ard had taken them until she saw a stunted, sickly tree and recalled having seen it earlier that day. Why she had remembered its lopsided shape from before didn't matter. She realized it was probably for that very reason it was chosen.

"And why did you spirit us away just then?" Kiranrao demanded, rounding on Tyrus. "We could have handled twice that number and left them all for dead."

Phae did not like his tone and how he always seemed to challenge her father. Instead of being angry, her father handled Kiranrao delicately.

"You may not have seen it," he answered softly. "They were the ones already starting to flee. Boeotians are quite superstitious. I have other tricks I could have performed that would have frightened them off at the beginning. They respect strength and now they have seen a measure of ours. I want their survivors to warn the Empress we are in her lands. She will draw forces to protect herself, which will leave fewer to face us. I did not bring us to these lands to slaughter Boeotians."

Kiranrao frowned, but he did not argue.

"What do you know of the Empress?" Baylen asked.

"Precious little," Tyrus replied. "She seeks no treaties, accepts no ambassadors, and she and her predecessors have repeatedly launched attacks on Kenatos. The Vaettir keep her at bay and occasionally the other kingdoms send forces to repel her attacks. They have no written language, no books, no history. Only the Druidecht are allowed into her realm unmolested."

"Why is she called the Empress?" Kiranrao asked.

"No one knows." He turned to Annon. "Seek spirits to watch over us as we sleep. There is no way they can track where we went. Also see if you can understand from the spirits how the Boeotians feed themselves. These lands have been rather inhospitable so far, and we'll need food to enter the Scourgelands. I hope to forage here, but we may not be able to without finding a settlement or one of their wandering camps. If you can, see if one of the spirits will guide us to one."

He turned next to Hettie. "Study the tracks that have come since we last crossed this path. See what you learn from them."

"Very well," Hettie answered.

"The rest of you—sleep while you can. Shion, you keep watch."

Phae saw the wisdom in the choice since the man did not ever sleep. Shion nodded, gave Phae a look that was enigmatic, and then the rest skulked to make their beds for the night, devoid of a fire that might reveal them. Phae was exhausted from the long march that day and promptly fell asleep.

They traveled three more days inside the Boeotians' country without meeting a single soul. Annon had learned from the spirits of the region where food could be foraged, and it was edible but not tasty, mostly consisting of roots and weeds. For meat, there were some hardy lizards that blended so well into the dirt and rocks that it took a keen eye to find them. Water was also scarce, and so when they found small streams or hidden pools, they would drink deeply and then fill their water skins. As they crossed farther north, the land became rockier.

The hard days of walking left blisters on Phae's heels, and the dust blowing in the air forced them all to wear makeshift scarves to breathe. The dunes were formidable and bleak, making Phae homesick for the lush valleys of Stonehollow. There were no Dryads in these lands, she could tell. Boeotia was a desolate place.

On the third day traveling north, the terrain changed. Instead of dusty dunes, the bones of huge rocks were exposed, changing the landscape dramatically. Jagged steps and bluffs, full of bumps and pockmarked rocks, cluttered the land in every direction. It was some misshapen mass, with strange gullies and cliffs. They entered warily, with Annon guiding them through the communion of spirit creatures. With the change of terrain came the opportunity for ambush, and so Tyrus kept them closer together.

Late in the afternoon of the third day, Annon stopped at the top of a rock ledge and pointed into a valley beyond. "There!" he said, waving the others to join him.

Phae was tired and her muscles ached. Her hair was caked with dust and she felt in desperate need of a stream to wade in. A stream had once carved the desolate canyons, but what she found was even more than she could have imagined.

"Well," Baylen said, pursing his lips. "That's a sight to be seen."

The others crested the small rise and Phae got a look at it and stared in surprise. The canyon below had been carved into a little city.

It was the strangest thing she had ever seen before. Her people, the stonemasons of Stonehollow, were expert builders, carving rock and building fortresses. These people, it seemed, were expert diggers. Spaces and chambers had been carved into the rocks. It was not primitive, but sophisticated. What surprised Phae was the size, probably no larger than a single castle with four or five crumbling walls erected and connected to the canyon side that loomed like mountains in front of it.

"What is this place?" Aransetis asked, staring down at the town embedded inside the base of the canyon. Chambers had been carved out of the rock faces. His black clothes were spattered with dust and dirt.

"It's abandoned," Khiara observed. "No cook fires. I see no one down there. Not a single soul."

"I think you're right," Tyrus said. "That is most likely. The Boeotians do not dwell in a particular place for very long. I was unaware of any towns built at all. This place appears to be ruins. As Khiara said, I see no signs of life."

"Why are we here?" Kiranrao muttered darkly. "I thought our journey took us into the Scourgelands?"

"It will," he answered patiently. "Annon, when you asked the spirits to show you a settlement . . . have they led us here?"

The Druidecht nodded. "This is where the spirits were leading us to. Maybe they did not understand."

"Or maybe something lives inside those caves," Aransetis added. "It is daylight after all and quite hot. They could watch us approach without being seen."

"We'll trust the spirits," Tyrus said. "It will be dusk by the time we descend to the bottom of the canyon."

"A good place for a trap," Baylen said. "If this is the only road in or out . . ."

Tyrus looked at him with a half smile. "We can't be trapped. But I appreciate you adding your voice of warning. Let us see what awaits us below."

A little city carved from living rock.

What a strange accomplishment, but it was eerily beautiful. Phae was the most grateful for the shade. The canyon floor provided shelter from the sweltering sun. They had wandered the forsaken streets and found no sign of inhabitants. There was nothing left behind, just the skull and bones of the abandoned city. A layer of dust covered everything and Hettie quickly deduced that there were no footprints and scant animal tracks. It truly seemed deserted.

Phae sat down along the edge of a low stone wall and tugged on her boot. A few sparse trees grew in the base of the canyon where an underground stream likely fed the roots. The stream had encroached along the edge of the forgotten city, but there were no trees deeper inside. Some of the walls had supporting buttresses, and each building was honeycombed with chambers and square windows. She pulled off her boot and poured out a fistful of sand from the inside. A scrawny lizard watched her from the base of the wall, its odd eyes examining her to see if she were a threat.

Baylen and Tyrus stood near a broken pillar, deep in conversation. The Cruithne towered over her father, but he seemed to be describing something to him based on the way his hands motioned toward the pillars and buttresses. Prince Aran sat in a meditation stance and Phae watched as Khiara came up to him and timidly offered a drink. He looked up, shook his head curtly, and then went back inside his thoughts. Khiara's shoulders drooped, just a little, as she departed. It made Phae sad.

Shion wandered up and crouched down next to Phae.

"Are we safe here, Shion?" she asked, peeling off her other boot as well.

He nodded curtly. "There are no signs of life. This place was abandoned long ago."

"An odd place to build a city."

"No, not really," he answered. He pointed to where the trees were, a little lower. "I imagine there was a time that gully was a swollen river. It probably floods here during the rainy season. It would be difficult for an army to march here. It's very defensible. The rocks we crossed were like a maze."

"Without Annon, we would never have found it." The pain in her heel made her wince. Gingerly, she rolled down her thick sock and then carefully peeled it away from her heel. The blister had doubled in size since she'd last checked but it had not ruptured yet. The skin was squishy and pale. She groaned.

"I have some salve from Khiara," Shion said, fishing through his pockets. "I noticed you limping and thought this would help. But we should puncture the blisters first. Do you still have that needle in your pack?"

She recalled it instantly, remembering the last time she had used it to stitch his shirt. Her pack was next to her against the wall and she rummaged through it until she found the needle. "Here it is."

"Give it to me."

She looked him in the eye. "I can do this, Shion. I've had blisters before. It's amazing you know what they are, since you obviously don't get them."

"What scars I have I will always keep," he replied, dragging the edge of his finger along the curve of his cheek. "Yours will heal."

He stared at her, his expression showing that he wanted to help tend to her, but he would not force it on her. She hesitated, seeing the polite entreaty in his eyes, and then offered the needle and he accepted it. Cradling her foot in his lap, he studied the size of the blister, running his finger around the dirty skin. He shook his head and removed his water flask and unstopped it. He carefully washed away the dirt. The feeling of the water on her skin was pleasurable and she found a memory floating into her mind.

One of her favorite things about living at the Winemiller vineyard had been crushing the grapes in the giant vats. There was no experience like it in the world. The grapes were soft and squishy beneath her feet, the cloying smell from the juices filling her nose. For several days after the harvest they crushed the grapes to make wine, and she had always found joy in the process, the useful act of tending the vines, culling the grapes, and then transforming it into a drink that could be stored for years to come. Having sticky, stained feet was a memory she would miss.

He pricked the edge of the blister with the needle and it brought her back to the dust-choked land of Boeotia. She hadn't realized she'd dozed off. Shion carefully pressed, draining the fluid from the blister, and then covered the clean skin with salve to protect it.

"You had a peaceful look on your face," Shion said, helping tug off her other sock to examine her other foot.

"A memory from back home," she answered. "I would ask you, but I don't think you'd remember it if you did."

"Ask anyway."

"I was remembering crushing grapes into wine after the harvest. Have you ever done that?"

He examined her other foot carefully and then nodded, satisfied. "I don't believe so. I have no memories from my childhood. But I enjoy the taste of Stonehollow wine. I wonder if I've ever drunk a cup crushed by these feet?" He squeezed her foot with just the hint of a teasing smile.

She felt a little flush rise to her cheeks. "Well, it may be. I don't know that any of our wine ever made it to Kenatos, but I can tell you that Dame Winemiller made us all wash our feet very thoroughly before standing in the vats." The memory was sweet but painful. The thought of never seeing Dame Winemiller again brought a lump to her throat.

"Cherish the memory," he said softly. "Even though it brings you pain. I would give anything to have mine back. I learned that recently . . . from a girl. I believe her."

She looked into his calm blue eyes, not seeing the menace or the danger there, but a thoughtful, caring man. His moods were mercurial. She wished there was a way she could keep him less dangerous more often.

"Thank you for treating my blister," she said, smiling at him. "There is something about this place." She stared up at the gaunt stone walls. "It has no memories. I pity it."

"It is your Dryad nature speaking to you. You live to preserve memories. Even the painful ones."

"Even the painful ones." As she stared at him, she realized that in order to restore his memories, after she gained access to her full powers, she would need to kiss him. The thought wasn't all that terrible in that moment.

"I can hear something coming, but I cannot see what it is," Khiara said. "It's coming down the road we arrived on."

"Prepare to depart," Tyrus announced. "Gather your bedrolls. Dawn will shortly arrive. Paedrin, can you determine if it is a threat? Report back quickly."

"I will, Tyrus." The Bhikhu gripped the pommel of the sword and rose into the air, flying away from their small camp at the edge of the city. Phae shook out her cloak before fastening it around her neck. Only the Vaettir could hear the trouble coming clearly, but she was just beginning to as well with the sound coming down the canyon wall. It was like the lumbering of a great beast.

They cleared the camp quickly after everyone rose, watching the pale orange of the dawn start to blush in the sky. Phae slapped the dust from her clothes and watched as Shion scanned the Bhikhu floating up toward the road. He seemed to hang, poised, and then came swooping down like a hawk, landing in front of Tyrus.

"It's no animal I have ever seen before," Paedrin said, much to everyone's amazement. "It is tall, like a horse, and has long legs with flat feet. There are these strange humps in its back and it has a long neck. There's a rider on its back, swathed in many drapes, but the face and head are covered. A single rider. The beast has a saddle of some kind and something to hold up a covering against the sun. It is strange to see, Tyrus. But only one of them comes."

"An emissary from the Empress?" Aransetis suggested.

"It would seem so," Tyrus answered. "One man or beast does not prove a threat. Perhaps the Empress wishes to treat with us."

"Or one of her bodyguards," Baylen said.

"I won't fear one man," Tyrus said. "We'll hear him out."

Phae waited with suspense as the masked rider slowly approached. They could all hear him now, the thud of the heavy, padded feet, the snort and grunts of the strange animal. Phae had never known its kind before and saw it perpetually chewing, like a cow. On its humped back crouched a rag-wearing rider, face and arms covered, swathed in tattered garments. The beast he rode was cream-colored with cute little ears on each side. It was a strangely beautiful animal.

The beast lumbered up the trail, approaching Tyrus's camp arduously, clearly in no great hurry. It approached and the rider gave a single command—"*Hup*"—and the beast slowly lowered itself on all four knees. The rider swayed slightly on the saddle.

Phae studied him carefully, looking for any sign of threat. She edged closer to Shion, who positioned himself in front of her. The man was breathing heavily, clearly winded and worn out with fatigue.

"Who are you?" Tyrus asked in a firm voice.

The rider slowly swung one of his legs around the beast's neck and slid off the slope to land unsteadily on the ground.

"He's sick," Kiranrao said in a low voice. "He may have the Plague. Don't let him near us."

Tyrus nodded curtly. "Stand there, friend. If you are a friend. Do you speak Aeduan?"

Phae felt a prickle of unease.

The stranger's voice was hoarse and scratchy. "Yes, we were friends once." With one hand, he began unwinding the cloth around his head, revealing a face hideously pockmarked and bulging with sacks and crusty skin. One of his eyes was milky white. The lesions on his face were grotesque, great putrid bulges of diseased flesh. His other eye was normal and looked at them with great intensity.

"Gather round me," Tyrus murmured softly, his hand grasping the Tay al-Ard.

"If my throat were not so parched, perhaps you would recognize my voice. You clearly do not recognize my face. I cannot blame you for that. We knew each other well as boys. I remember you . . . remember you *humbling* Sanbiorn Paracelsus when he visited the orphanage. I am still your friend, Tyrus. Even though you left me to die in the Scourgelands long ago."

"Revenge is a terrible tool, a dagger where the hilt is as sharp as the blade. I have heard the Arch-Rike wisely describe revenge another way. In taking revenge, a man is but even with his enemy; but in passing it over, he is superior. I thought he was the author of the saying, but have since found it written by one of the ancient scholars of Silvandom: To refrain from imitation is truly the best revenge."

- Possidius Adeodat, Archivist of Kenatos

VI

Annon recoiled in horror at seeing the man's ravaged face. The pustules were oozing, flecked with dirt, dust, and crusted blood. It was clearly a fatal disease, one that caused a wheezing rasp in his breath. All were silent following his announcement. All except Tyrus.

"Mathon?"

The cracked lips twisted into a smile. "You recognized me at last?"

"Not your voice, but the memory you described. Forgive me if I do not trust you. We have often been deceived by our enemy and even a man who looks like a friend turns traitor. The dead at Canton Vaud are testament of that."

"Ah, yes. Word of that has already spread to Boeotia, Tyrus. The Boeotians trust the Druidecht and so you have no small reputation in these lands at the moment." He doubled over and coughed fitfully against the ragged sleeve. Annon saw blood in the spittle. He felt Nizeera coiling next to his leg, her wariness mirroring his own.

"I did not harm anyone there," Tyrus said. "None of my company did."

"I know that," Mathon said, struggling to catch his breath. He wheezed, leaning back against the beast he had ridden on and hung his head. "I know you are innocent. I know this because I understand the full ruthlessness of the Arch-Rike we once respected and faithfully served. I wore a black ring on my hand. It gave the Arch-Rike access to my thoughts and it allowed him to control me. But I am talking too quickly. My message first." He took several deep breaths, steadying himself. "The Empress of Boeotia bids me invite you to her palace. Such as it is. I was dispatched three days ago and was guided by a vulture to this place where the spirit creatures of Mirrowen led you." He turned his gaze to Annon, his milky eye a disgusting sight. "You must understand that the spirits in this realm obey the Empress before anyone else. You were guided to a place of safety, as promised, but they guided you here where I could find you."

Annon's heart turned cold with fear. "They deceived me then."

He nodded curtly. "In a way. This is the way of the spirits in Boeotia. They are subtle. Many are cruel. Some would lead you to a scorpion's nest if you sought meat. Mortal pain amuses them."

Tyrus cleared his throat. "That is not much help in convincing us to accept the Empress's hospitality."

"Did she send you here to poison us with your disease?" Kiranrao challenged. "Shall I dispatch him? I can kill him from here."

Mathon began to cough again. After several alarming moments, it calmed. "The disease I suffer from is not contagious. You know my training, Tyrus. I was a healer first of all. I learned to my shock and horror that this particular illness comes from the mushrooms inside the Scourgelands. I was hopelessly lost and wandered for days without food, managing to elude the beasts sent to kill the rest of you. I think the Arch-Rike didn't care whether or not I survived. He used me to discourage you, to make you doubt yourself. I was helpless against his power, I assure you of that."

The ravaged face twisted with emotions, impossible to discern due to the craggy flesh. "In my absolute misery and hunger, I chose to eat some mushrooms to stay alive. Somehow I managed to wander out far to the north and west. There are fewer defenders along that side, but the terrain is more rugged and difficult to cross. I managed to escape the tricks and illusions that sought to contain me and I walked alone into Boeotia. I noticed the rash at first on my breast as my clothes were in tatters. The rash eventually deadened my skin. It is a fearful affliction, Tyrus. When I was discovered, half-dead, by the Boeotians, they would not kill me. They call it *leprosaria.* Men and women who are afflicted with it are pitied here, and they are feared. There are colonies of the weak and dying, hidden deep in canyons in the hinterlands. The Boeotians avoid the Scourgelands at all cost for fear of contracting this disease. Sometimes the winds blow the mushroom spores . . . but that doesn't matter right now. I must convince you. I must tell you as much as I can before that Vaettir killer next to you decides to separate my larynx from my esophagus."

"You will not be harmed," Prince Aransetis said, giving a baleful look at Kiranrao. "I will not allow it. You came peacefully."

"Of course *you* would believe this wild tale," the Romani said with a snort. "Let's be done with him."

Prince Aransetis turned to Kiranrao, his look stern and ripe with foreboding. The two looked as if they would strike each other. There was an unspoken challenge between them, a mounting threat.

Annon chewed on his lip, feeling compassion begin to mingle with the disgust.

Tyrus's expression was hard and interested, but he looked equal parts skeptical as well. "I will not try to prove your identity verbally. It seems the Arch-Rike can mimic even the memories of men we trust. So it would help your cause if you explained the

Empress's invitation. You cannot think we would willingly enter the heart of her domain."

Mathon chuckled without humor. "She does believe you will, actually. You must come, Tyrus."

"I can think of a number of compelling reasons why that would be unwise. I do not wish to delay our quest. I do appreciate the warning about the mushrooms, but we had no intention of eating anything in that cursed place."

"The entire forest is poisoned. But I must persuade you. Let me try. I was taken by the Boeotians to one of their colonies for those with leprosaria. That is her court, Tyrus. She is not an Empress like the Arch-Rike, with servants and valets and Rikes to do her bidding. She serves the weak and the dying. She is unafraid of contracting the illness. Her courage and fearlessness is what bind the Boeotians to her. She does not control them. She cannot give orders and expect to be obeyed. She rules through influence, and because none of the warlords in this place have the courage to face her in her stronghold for power. Their fear of the disease and her lack of fear are what give her power. When there is a dispute, fighting warlords will seek her wisdom and abide by her decisions. But they mostly leave her alone and she goes from colony to colony, serving those who are weak and dying. That is how I met her. I was one of the weak and dying."

Annon stared at the man in surprise. This was totally beyond anything he expected. He knew the Boeotians were cruel and merciless. He could hardly comprehend that their feared Empress was a woman who treated those afflicted with a disfiguring disease.

"You were taken to one of these colonies. Eventually she came. Go on." Tyrus continued to look doubtful.

"We became friends, Tyrus. She is a little older than us, a compassionate and educated woman. The history of their people is verbal, handed down like the Druidecht lore. While I was wearing the ring, the Arch-Rike continued to control me. He helped me gain her trust. He's quite good at that. I was to learn everything I could about her defenses. I was blindfolded when taken there, so I did not know where it was. The Boeotians treat her whereabouts as their greatest secret. Most do not know where she is at all. She leaves on camel when she travels between the colonies." Annon looked at him quizzically and he saw that others did as well. "The name for the beast I rode on. They are like horses of the desert and can go great distances without water. The Cruithne brought them from their original homeland before settling the Alkire. There are horses here as well, horses bred for stamina and strength. The customs here—I could spend days explaining the nuances to you. It is a savage land. They are cruel and desperate. But there is also beauty in these vast caverns and wastes. But I neglect to finish my tale."

"You realize this is incredible," Tyrus said softly, his lip quivering with revulsion and surprise. His emotions were rattled and he continued to gaze at his old friend with shock and distrust. "I am still amazed you are even alive. But I cannot recognize you. Even your voice is not familiar to me. This feels like a trap, Mathon. If that is who you are."

"Of course it does. That's because it is a trap, in a way. The Empress is wise. She knows the nature of men. She is very skilled at persuasion and manipulation. As are you, my friend. She reminds me of you in many ways. Now to the point. I remained in the colony for several years, the disease beginning to ravage my body slowly. I used every cunning and device the Arch-Rike planted in my mind to win her trust. It did not happen easily or quickly because she knew I was a Rike of Kenatos. But eventually, in time, she began to trust me. I felt the Arch-Rike's triumph." He gritted his teeth. "He was forcing me to betray someone I respected and admired, much as he had forced me to do with you inside the Scourgelands. It is torture. I could not remove the ring because I knew that it would destroy me. I lacked the courage and the will to surrender to death after having survived that far. I began to learn one of the consequences of my disease. The flesh deadens. The rash spreads. The victims, ultimately, begin to lose various parts of their bodies. Some lose their noses. Some a foot." He slowly began unwrapping the rags around his arm, exposing a diseased stump. "I lost my hand. And the ring with it."

Paedrin let out a whistle, his face a mixture of horror and delight. "That would do it," he said with a grin. "I believe him, Tyrus. He's telling the truth."

"As do I," Aransetis said.

Tyrus held up his hand to silence any others before they could add their voices. "What did you do when you became free of the Arch-Rike's influence?"

Mathon lifted his jaw. "I told the Empress everything. I confessed my treachery and the knowledge I had gathered, designed to destroy her kingdom. I told her the Arch-Rike already had the knowledge she had shared with me. I told her that I did not need to speak with him in order to share it with him." He shook his head, his eyes filling with tears.

"What did she do to you?" Tyrus asked.

The head lifted again, his lip quivering with emotion. Annon felt his own throat thicken. He stared at the afflicted man.

"She asked me . . ." he said hoarsely, "if I would agree to be her consort for life. She is my wife, Tyrus."

Hettie gasped with surprise, her expression showing disbelief that the Empress forgave him. Annon was amazed himself and wondered what sort of woman would do that, especially considering Mathon's disease.

"She trusts me completely. There is knowledge that she has about the Arch-Rike and who he really is. She will not allow me to divulge it and I will not. All I will say is that it is worth knowing.

It will benefit your quest to end the Plague. You will not expect or be able to deduce this information, Tyrus. It is an ancient secret. She sent me here, her own husband, knowing that you all might kill me because of my ravaged face. But it is vital that you know what she knows. It is crucial to you to understand the nature of our mutual enemy. When you vanished from the plains, she suspected you had a Tay al-Ard. Her Druidecht spies in Canton Vaud revealed as much. With a Tay al-Ard, and with my memory of the location, I can take you to her right now. She wishes to speak to you, Tyrus. You will not succeed without her knowledge."

Tyrus frowned, his expression solemn. "You could take us anywhere you chose, Mathon. Including right into the Arch-Rike's clutches."

"I know," Mathon replied. "So you will have to trust me."

The pained look in Tyrus's eyes made Annon hurt for him.

Mathon sat slumped against the side of the camel, resting, his arms folded. Tyrus's band huddled inside one of the abandoned structures, pulling close together in a tight circle. They were all seated on the ground, heads lowered.

"I seek your counsel," Tyrus said, looking at each of them. Annon felt the huge weight of responsibility and wondered what the decision would ultimately be.

"From all of us?" Baylen asked.

"Of course. I think I know Kiranrao's verdict already. Has it changed?"

The Romani snorted and said nothing.

"Aran and Khiara. I think you are like-minded on this issue. But tell me your opinion."

Prince Aransetis sat calmly. "Sometimes the simplest answer

is the most obvious. The man is clearly infected with a disease. His story rings true. There is an element of fate in this situation. As if a greater good drove us here."

Tyrus pondered the Prince's words. He nodded subtly. "Khiara?"

She looked almost startled. "His skin smells putrid. I do not believe it is a disguise."

Hettie motioned with her hand. "I have a charm, a necklace, with the power to assume the disguise of anyone I have seen or met. If he is a Druidecht, perhaps he wears such a charm. We cannot trust what our eyes see. He admitted himself that the spirits in this realm were cunning. I do not have a good feeling about this, Tyrus. I smell a trap."

Kiranrao gave her a pleased look, rose and began pacing around the circle. He seemed edgy and restless to Annon. He had changed much since their first meeting in Havenrook. Khiara watched him with wary eyes.

"Baylen?"

The Cruithne rubbed his forearm vigorously, pausing a moment. "I'm still thinking about this. Come back to me."

"Paedrin?"

The Bhikhu was squatting so low his heels touched the ground. He gave Kiranrao a challenging look. "His story rings true to me as well. He described perfectly the way one of the Arch-Rike's rings controls you. If we all go to see the Empress together, then the Tay al-Ard will be drained and we won't be able to use it again quickly. I'm not sure the Empress knows this, but let's assume that she does. If her intentions are evil, she brings us to her in a way where we are surrounded and in terrain we do not know without a way to escape. It seems foolish to me, therefore, to all go together. Just a few should be sent to claim the knowledge. The rest stay here."

"A thoughtful plan, Paedrin. Thank you." Tyrus picked at his beard. "Do you believe a trap is awaiting us?"

"After what you put us through in Drosta's Lair, I've come to expect them. If you go, you should take only one of us with you. I would suggest myself because of the Sword of Winds. It would be easier for a Vaettir to escape and I don't think Kiranrao even wants to go."

"You may carry the Sword," Kiranrao warned, "but you will have no idea what direction to go or how to make it back to us."

"It may not be easy to find, but flying above the land would be easier to spot this chasm than the way we came. Or if Tyrus gave me the Tay al-Ard, that would change the situation as well. Do you want to go, Kiranrao? I think you would fit right in to a colony with leprosaria. It would only improve your good looks."

"Enough," Tyrus said, glaring at Paedrin. "Annon?"

The Druidecht swallowed and struggled with his feelings. They had been deceived so many times by the Arch-Rike along the way that he found the past biasing his feelings. Like Hettie, he assumed there would be a trap as well. He was also uncertain whether to trust the nature of the spirit creatures in this realm. Were they obeying the Empress out of respect or compulsion?

"I'm struggling," Annon confessed. "My heart wants to believe him, but we have been fooled so many times. Even the Thirteen were betrayed by one of their own because of the Arch-Rike."

"We all see that, Annon. What does Nizeera think? She is wise to the ways of mortals."

Annon had not thought about that. He reached over and stroked her head.

Tyrus is considerate. There are some spirit-kind in Mirrowen that are not trustworthy. Those that are not are banished to this world. He does not reek of spirit magic. He reeks of death. I believe him.

Annon smiled at her, grateful for her presence. He turned to the others. "She trusts him. As do I. If you want, I'll go with you to see the Empress. I'm a Druidecht and have been taught that we are welcome in these lands of all the races and people. But we should all go together. Let's face this Empress with all of our knowledge and skills. If it's a trick, she'll regret deceiving us."

There was a subtle shift in the mood. Annon could see the others considering his words. He stared down at the ground again, absently stroking Nizeera's fur.

"Baylen?"

The Cruithne rubbed his bottom lip. "She sent one of your best friends to try to win your trust quickly. She sent her own husband, if what he said is true. I think we should hear what she has to say. But let's be clear. It's very likely we'll be fighting our way out of there. Though I'm frankly not afraid of facing men whose arms fall off."

Paedrin let out a loud chuckle. "I was thinking that very thing. Do we go together, Tyrus? I would vote for leaving Kiranrao behind."

Kiranrao gave Paedrin a withering look, but he said nothing. He looked at Tyrus, slowly shaking his head no.

"Shion?" Tyrus asked, turning to the quiet man sitting next to Phae.

"The Boeotians have always been enemies of Kenatos," he said simply. "The enemy of my enemy is my friend."

"Well said. Phae?"

"Does my opinion matter?" she asked.

"It does to me, Daughter. What do you think?"

She nodded firmly. "We should go."

"We know little of the Empress of Boeotia. No spies have been able to penetrate her domain. All embassies sent to treat with her have been savagely killed and grotesquely displayed on spear tips. They are at war with our society and civilization. They are, I think, the antithesis of what Kenatos was founded to become. And if Kenatos eventually succumbs to the midden heap of history, the Empress will rue her victory."

\- *Possidius Adeodat, Archivist of Kenatos*

VII

As the magic of the Tay al-Ard whipped them away, Paedrin's stomach churned with excitement as well as nausea. They arrived, moments later, and he searched the surroundings immediately, prepared for action, knowing the device would not be able to transport them again until it had regained its powers. They were in a chasm of some sort, in the shadows of a deep ravine with a thin river of light far above. The rock faces were crimson and orange, like fire, and the chasm was wide enough and deep enough to give him the sensation of being very deep inside a pit.

Paedrin inhaled and prepared to rise above, but Tyrus grabbed his arm and shook his head sternly. Instead, the Bhikhu gripped the hilt of the Sword of Winds tightly, searching for the sign of attackers or those who meant them harm. What he saw and smelled he could describe as a graveyard. Bile rose inside his throat.

"Don't rush off without me," Hettie whispered in his ear. He glanced at her confident expression, but he could also see the dread and loathing converging in her countenance.

The shadows were thick but they contained movement. The dead were walking.

"We are here," Mathon announced gruffly. "The colonies do not have names. There are seven in total, mostly zigzagging through these canyons. They are the only permanent dwellings in Boeotia. Remember—leprosaria is not transmitted person to person. Only exposure to the spores from the mushrooms will infect someone with the disease. This way. These people are crippled and harmless. They are merely curious about you."

Mathon began to shuffle toward one of the rock walls looming overhead. Paedrin craned his neck, staring up at the vast heights of stone wall, as deep and impenetrable as any fortress. He saw several ragged Boeotians staring at him. Some were missing limbs. One man was missing his nose, and the ragged features turned Paedrin's stomach. They muttered among themselves in a guttural language he did not understand. Khiara's expression was full of compassion as she gazed from side to side at the suffering people. Aran's attention was singularly focused on Tyrus while Baylen looked queasy at the various mutilated denizens. Kiranrao's look was full of open contempt and loathing, his brooding gaze enough of a warning to prevent anyone from approaching.

Hettie kept by Paedrin's side. "Stop baiting Kiranrao," she whispered to him.

"This is an interesting moment to begin lecturing me," Paedrin replied. "Stay focused and attentive. We do not know what we are facing here."

"As if every other man among us isn't ready to start spilling blood. We won't be taken by surprise, Paedrin. Not when we're all expecting a threat. I just wanted to warn you . . . something isn't right with Kiranrao. He isn't acting as he normally does. The loss of his fortune in Havenrook has unbalanced him."

"He was *never* balanced, Hettie."

"True. But you are not helping things. Your insults provoke him. A man who has lost everything is no longer reasonable. Please . . . stay away from him. Stay clear of him."

He gave her a piercing look. "Why?"

Her pause was poignant, her look intense. "Because of what he may do if provoked too far."

"This way," Mathon called, his voice pained.

Paedrin sighed. "I will try. I have no sympathy for his situation."

"I'm not asking you to show him sympathy. Just don't let your tongue cut your throat."

Paedrin nodded, his eyes adjusting to the gloom, and he could see the network of caves at the base of the chasm. Some were hollowed out, broken up by picks and hammers, but most seemed a natural interworking maze of warrens. The half-dead victims of leprosaria were everywhere. Small tents and shelters dotted the bleakness, covered in dust so that they looked almost like carved rocks themselves. Paedrin counted at least fifty afflicted with the disease along their walk to the rock wall, and he could not see far enough to judge how many tributaries of the caves went deeper. There were small pools of sluggish water, revealing how the population survived. It seemed to be the remnant of an ancient river, long spent.

"Why did we arrive in the middle of the ravine?" Tyrus asked Mathon, slowing his stride to keep up with his friend.

"To give the Empress time to prepare for our arrival. I left three days ago and agreed that if you came with me, I would have us appear where we did. Some were posted to watch for us, who are now running ahead to warn her of our arrival."

"I don't want to meet her in the caves," Tyrus said. "It gives her all the advantage. She should come out to us."

"She is the Empress, Tyrus. She does what she wills. I can only ask."

"Then do ask," he said.

As they reached a tunnel opening that was broad and deep, Tyrus stopped and waited. Paedrin and the others clustered around him while Mathon shuffled ahead into the gaping tunnel. The Bhikhu saw small stone urns placed before each tunnel opening. He did not understand the significance. He had expected an immediate attack. So far, Mathon's words had proven true.

"Do you sense any spirit magic at work?" Tyrus asked softly to Annon.

"I do," Annon answered gravely. He looked up at the tall walls. "The feeling is thicker than in Canton Vaud, but not in the same way. With the Druidecht, the spirits are generally very friendly, asking what they could do to help. These are . . . strangely . . . rather conceited. A few have brushed against my mind, but they are seeking information. Not a way to help. There is something . . . troubling the air. Like the smell of smoke from a distant fire. I don't care for it."

Paedrin craned his neck again, unable to see the spirits that Annon always seemed to be communing with. He squished his sandaled foot into the dirt and watched it puff with dust. The smell of death lingered in the air, reminding him of the Bhikhu temple after it was poisoned. Memories could be torturous sometimes. He recalled the face of Master Shivu, wasting away.

The sound of arrivals from the tunnel mouth announced the visitors. Paedrin could hear voices low in conversation, one of whose was a woman's. He was not sure what to expect, but he braced himself. Not in one of those hundred times he had perched atop the Bhikhu temple in Kenatos and stared out at the lake would he have dared imagine he would one day face the Empress of Boeotia within her own homeland. It was so absurd it nearly made him laugh outright.

Nor was he expecting the Empress of Boeotia to seem so plain.

She was simply garbed in layers of dusty desert clothing, rugged boots, and a long, jeweled necklace around her neck with a

Druidecht talisman in it. Her hair was dark brown with streaks of gold and gray showing the harshness of the environment as well as her age. She was slender but not in a vulnerable way and had a body hardened to the elements and the rugged country in which she lived. She could have passed for Aeduan except for the purple tattoos marking one side of her face. In the shadows, it was difficult to tell if her eyes were green or gray, but she had a smile that, when it appeared, was her most distinctive feature. She was holding hands with Mathon as they appeared up some steps from deeper inside the tunnel.

"You came," the Empress said, giving Tyrus a dazzling smile.

"You suspected I would," he replied, bowing his head deferentially. "Your bait was enticing."

"You expected a hook or the strands of a spiderweb here, Tyrus Paracelsus? I suppose that makes sense, but you have a reputation for treachery yourself. But I show my trust by bringing you here, knowing you have a Tay al-Ard. Well met, sir. My name is Larei. I am the seventy-second Empress of Boeotia. I am known by the people by a title instead of my name. As you can see, I am unarmed, though I do have many spirit artifacts that protect me. I am especially immune to fire. My demons affirm that four of you possess the fireblood. That is quite a collection, Tyrus. In your last foray into the Scourgelands, only two possessed it."

"You said you had information," Tyrus pressed.

"In due time," she replied, smiling again. "You are wary, which is what anyone would expect in such a situation. I assure you that no one here will attack you without express permission. Few of the many abandoned here are even capable of it. This is a place for the dying to die honorably and with grace. I tend them as best as I can alongside my husband." She beamed when she said this, her grip on Mathon's hand tightening. A shiver of revulsion went through Paedrin.

"I will not be delayed in my quest," Tyrus said. "The Druidecht of Canton Vaud attempted to waylay me. The Arch-Rike himself seeks my death—"

"I care nothing for that," she interrupted. "What I have to tell you, I am not going to speak in front of so many witnesses. I have gathered food and supplies for your journey. Fresh water in abundance to satisfy your thirst. And camels if you desire to use them. You will find none of this throughout my kingdom without great labor. My help will hasten your journey, not slow it down. Pick two whom you trust the most. They will join our interview. The rest can be near enough to see us as we speak, and you can determine whom to share information with at your discretion."

"Only two?" Tyrus asked.

"I do not debate or negotiate, Tyrus. I have been taught by the wisest minds in all the arts of rhetoric, logic, and persuasion. Believe me when I say that I have thought this through. Join us below when you are ready, or not at all." She turned and started back down the passageway.

Annon watched as the Empress and Mathon descended the carved steps of the tunnel entrance. He was awed at the aura of power that exuded from her, not from a weapon or an item she carried, but from the pure iron will she possessed—it felt as immovable as a mountain. Her face was pretty, if weather-beaten, and she had clearly aged well and lived a healthy lifestyle. But her exterior was a mask for a fiercely independent will. He hoped that someday he would possess such an attribute. She was stronger than any of the Thirteen he encountered.

As he stared up at the jagged, massive cliff face, it reminded him of the horrors they had faced at Basilides. He felt Nizeera tense by his leg.

I sense spirit beings inside the tunnels. They are aware of me. They are more ancient than I am. They bid me not interfere in this test.

Annon's skin crawled. A pit of dread opened up inside him. Should he warn Tyrus? *Is it a trap?*

Not in the way you think. It is a test.

Tyrus took a few deep breaths, glancing from side to side. "Annon. Phae. With me. The rest will follow behind. Be ready."

There was a collective intake of breath, Annon included. He had not suspected for a moment that Tyrus would choose him. A surge of gratitude thrummed, but he still thought Tyrus was making a mistake. Nearly any of the others would have been better suited.

Without brooking comment from anyone, Tyrus descended into the tunnels. Annon and Phae, glancing in shock at each other, followed behind. He felt the presence of Nizeera withdraw, as if something veiled her mind from his. He swallowed in a panic.

"Tyrus," he said, catching up. "There is something—"

"Say it quickly," Tyrus interrupted. His face looked intense and worried. "She's testing me. I need my wits at this moment. If you have something to aid my thinking, then do so, but do not trouble me about my decision."

"Nizeera can't interfere," Annon said. "There are spirits here that are older than her. Ancient spirits, probably banished from Mirrowen. I sense them, but they have not spoken to me."

"Thank you," Tyrus said. "That was useful. If you have any thought as to the nature of these spirits, you need to let me know. I chose you to accompany me because of your Druidecht lore and because you know my full plan. If I don't make it out of here alive, then you need to continue." The way he so casually talked about his own death made Annon tremble inside. "Phae, your abilities may also be called upon. Be ready. This is like playing a game where our deaths are the stakes and we don't know any of the rules. I apologize if I'm curt. I'm trying to keep us all alive."

"What do you want me to do, Father?" Phae asked.

"Nothing yet. Just be ready. I want you close to me."

The tunnels were lit by illuminated rock crystals with small oil lamps set inside them. The tunnels had a jagged nature with crevices of varying heights and depths, causing the light to spread at inconsistent intervals and conceal what lay ahead. The path was not straight but wound downward until it reached a vast chamber, the main living yard of those with the leprosaria curse. Annon could see it organized into kitchens, cesspits, and useful labor such as blacksmithing, tanning, and carving. Side tunnels branched off, revealing a honeycomb lattice of interweaving connections.

The Empress walked directly ahead of them, still holding Mathon's hand. "Each colony is organized much like a hive of bees," she said, drawing their attention with her clear, cheerful voice. "Each worker has a duty to perform. Some gather food. Some defend. We keep our waste separate. Have you noticed that among the cultures of lizards and ants and other creatures that dwell harmoniously together? My ancestors studied their habits and saw with remarkable precision how each breed handled their societies in similar manners. In a way, we have truly gone back to our roots. We thrive when we work cooperatively. Each does his or her part. It takes many bees to make a few drops of honey. Added together, however, and the comb is thick with it."

"Indeed," Tyrus replied with a neutral tone.

Annon surveyed the Boeotians staring at them, saw the blistering skin and rashes. Everyone he could see was afflicted with it. Some had lost the ability to even walk. It was a cruel fate to be sure. He wanted to cover his mouth to avoid breathing the air but recognized such an act would be insulting.

The Empress took them to a fire pit with logs blazing with assorted blankets and cushions. "Your friends may stay here. We will meet over there, by that stone. Within sight of each other, as I said. Agreed?"

Tyrus nodded, and Annon and Phae joined the Empress and Mathon at the base of a rugged boulder. There were markings on it—a face, actually. Annon stared at it, for the face had been worn nearly smooth. The nose had been chiseled off, it seemed. Strange runes adorned it. He felt his heart fill with warning as they approached. He touched Tyrus's wrist and nodded to the stone. He did not get a verbal response, but Tyrus did blink once before sitting down.

The Empress's face was very expressive. "I am pleased you chose to trust me. Observe those bringing food to your friends. Mathon will tell you the significance of which hand they are served with."

Annon turned so he could notice.

Mathon's voice was thick and wheezing from the walk. "There are many subtleties in Boeotian culture. If you are served food from the left hand, you must assume it may have been poisoned. There are certain rituals of honor in this land. It's considered perfectly just to murder a man who does not follow the culture. The left hand is used to . . . I'll put this delicately . . . cleanse the body after performing certain purging functions. It is the *shameful hand.* You greet a man with your right hand only. If someone does not observe that they are served with the left, then it is suitable to kill them through poison. Much is left to a person's ability to notice what goes on around them and interpret it."

"I see," Tyrus said. "And you lost your right hand along with the Arch-Rike's ring on it. You can only eat or greet someone with the shameful hand."

The Empress's eyes glittered with delight. "He is quick, Mathon. You did not underestimate him. We may survive this yet."

Tyrus cocked his eyebrow at her curious comment.

"Who you chose to accompany you is critical. You did not pick your most ruthless fighters. You did not pick your wisest Vaettir. You chose a Druidecht to aid you in some aspects of spirit culture you could not know or have been trained in. And you brought your daughter because you care for her safety above all others."

"You knew she was my daughter?"

"I have spies in Canton Vaud. Yes."

"Then would a father do any less?" Tyrus offered with a smile.

"My invitation to come here was not strictly duplicitous, Tyrus. When I learned you were in my lands, it gave me a glimmer of hope. I will soon be deposed. Not in all the years the Empresses have ruled Boeotia has a warlord gained the courage to unite all the factions and challenge one of us. Until now. Your arrival is timely. I do have information you desperately need and knowledge that should not be confined any longer to these forgotten lands. It is knowledge relating to our mutual enemy, the Arch-Rike of Kenatos."

Tyrus leaned forward. "Who challenges your rule?"

"That is not important right now. Let me deliver the knowledge I promised first. You don't understand what a treasure this is to speak to someone like you. In these lands, learning is despised. Knowledge is rarely sought. It is like that for a reason, and it is also why I fell in love with Mathon. I knew him before the sickness disfigured him. Outward appearances are deceptive. Sometimes the most beautiful people are the most shallow, corruptible, and feckless. Beauty conceals one's inner worth, the value of a heart and mind. Such is the case with leprosaria and Kenatos. The purpose of Kenatos is not to preserve knowledge." She leaned forward, her voice dropping. "That is a lie. They destroy knowledge. They mask the truth. It happens slowly and subtly. It has been happening even before Kenatos was founded. Instead of building libraries, we in Boeotia have built a culture that would preserve the most important knowledge we sought to maintain."

The Empress folded her hands in her lap, leaning forward, and studied Tyrus closely. "We live by a culture of honor. My ancestors found that it was the only way to preserve the knowledge of our enemy and to combat him. We have crafted this culture deliberately and its fruit has grown rather wild. In a culture such as ours, the smallest thing can give rise to mortal offense. The passions of this people run deep. They love deeply and they hate deeply. Enmity is the key emotion we foster here. Revenge is the butter to our bread. Again, this was done deliberately."

"Long term it seems an impractical strategy," Tyrus observed.

"On the contrary," she said, shaking her head. "Enmity is the only thing that endures. What you need to understand, Tyrus, is that the enemy you face is not the Arch-Rike of Kenatos. That is only the mask that he currently wears."

The choice of words the Empress used reminded Annon of something Erasmus had said. He sat up straight, leaning forward and listening intently. His mouth went dry.

The Empress's gaze met Annon's. "I think you begin to understand," she whispered eagerly. "Trust your intuition, Druidecht. There is magic in Mirrowen beyond our understanding and even our dreams. It is a realm where there is no death. Imagine if you understood how that was done. What if a mortal made it to Mirrowen, learned the secret of living always, and returned? That man would live in a world full of death. But he would never die. There is such a man. He has been purged from every history book, stripped away by generations of Archivists who did not know what they were doing or that they were serving an evil purpose. Every mention of this man was removed, copy by copy. Page by page. There are only a few references left, and they were so obscure and hidden that very few would even know what they were reading if they happened upon it. This is a great and terrible secret. Yet it must be told again for fear of it being shrouded if the line of Empresses fails." Her smile wilted; her eyes were like daggers. "You fight not against a mortal man, Tyrus Paracelsus. You fight against the first of your kind. The first who bore the fireblood. The father of your race. He is no more the Arch-Rike of Kenatos than he is the dead King of Stonehollow . . . or likely the King of Wayland next. He is already shifting his strategy, preparing a new guise, another metamorphosis. All the attention goes to Kenatos but he is preparing to alter his identity again and rule with another man's countenance."

Tyrus looked at Mathon, his eyes blazing. He said nothing, but his jaw was set.

"It's true," Mathon said, his voice throbbing with emotion. "We were both betrayed by the Arch-Rike, but not the man who he *was*. Not Band-Imas. We were tricked by the one who supplanted him and locked him away somewhere in the dungeons, and then took his place when he discovered that you were not to be dissuaded from entering the Scourgelands. This is the man, the *Intelligence*, who has unleashed the full fury of the Scourgelands upon us. And he is waiting for you to enter it again, Tyrus, with even more evil beings to do his bidding this time. You must understand this, Tyrus. You must understand that you are fighting a man who cannot be killed."

Annon noticed a twitch in Tyrus's cheek. It was a twitch that stopped him from turning his head and looking back. Phae, on the other hand, did not have the same self-control. Annon watched her head jerk and she stared back at the Quiet Kishion in shock.

"For what cannot be cured, patience is best."

- Possidius Adeodat, Archivist of Kenatos

VIII

Tell me what you know of this enemy," Tyrus said softly, eagerly.

Annon watched as the Empress's gaze tracked Phae's movement. Her eyes narrowed, just slightly. A sickening curl twisted inside Annon's stomach. The woman was observant, shrewd, and he could not know her thoughts or what she intended. Her attention went back to Tyrus.

"There is not much time remaining before they come," she murmured softly. "I will say what I can."

"Who is coming?" Annon demanded.

"Those who seek to destroy me. I will be quick." She leaned forward and put her hand on Tyrus's leg. "I do not know the name of our ageless enemy. In our tongue, he is called *Shirikant*—it means 'the Accuser' in your language. Let me describe the pattern to you, for it happened here in Boeotia and it has happened repeatedly since our fall. A wise man arrives, seeking to trade knowledge and wisdom that he has assembled in a vast book. He is friendly, considerate, rather charming. Some believe he is a Druidecht, for he wears a talisman. He has the fireblood but never uses it but to light candles or quench a flame. He is calm and works hard, winning trust easily. Such a man came to Boeotia long ago. He was given access to the records of the Empress, seeking knowledge about the history of the people. He jotted down his notes and studies, trading quips with the best scholars in the realm. He was fluent in many languages, but most importantly, the unspoken language of influence. When trust is earned, he brought several students to come as well. They are his disciples and help spread word of his fame."

She stopped, eyeing something deeper in the chamber. A small frown tugged at her mouth.

"Go on," Tyrus said.

"As the disciples pore over the records as well, they begin to steal snippets. They are covert. Sometimes they painstakingly copy a page or corrupt the text, changing the meaning of words. These deeds were done in secret, but the Empress Kosonin had them watched and observed. When she learned what was happening, rather than challenge the visitor, she began to study what the changes were and what things were being erased. Can you guess, Tyrus Paracelsus? Can you guess what information was being destroyed?"

Annon was growing more and more restless. The air felt tinged with dread and some lurking danger. He felt power emanating from the boulder behind the Empress, whispers in a language he could not comprehend. The hair on his arms pricked. He made a subtle signal to Tyrus, but the man's eyes were locked on hers.

"Information about the Scourgelands and its history," Tyrus said in a hushed tone. "Knowledge of Mirrowen."

"Of course. The Empress was wise and realized that the man was an interloper. She began to hide the records, one by one, to keep them safe. She prepared her servants to slay the man and his disciples for their treachery. But she was wise. She did not act rashly. She saw that the man was winning over the hearts of her people. Then his behavior changed, rather suddenly. Rather than seeking knowledge, he began seeking her affections. It did not matter that she already had a consort. His moods shifted. His information seemed limitless. She suspected that he was no longer the man who had arrived in Boeotia. He was an imposter, though he looked and sounded the same. She tested his knowledge, seeking to confound him with information, but although his responses were delayed, his information was accurate . . . as if he still had access to the *mind* of his victim."

She shifted uncomfortably in the dirt, her expression wary and full of loathing, and folded her arms imperiously. The purple tattoo on her face twitched with repressed anger. "Suspecting treachery, she summoned him to her chambers, bringing her most subtle skills. She tried to poison him. He did not die. She arranged for an accident where he was pushed from a height that would have broken any man." She shook her head. "When that failed, she suspected that he could not be killed. He retaliated, of course. He began to speak of holy signs, began to warn of the coming of the Plague. He predicted that it would strike the heart of Boeotia. His words caused a black fear through the people. He had seen the signs in other lands. He recognized them anew in our kingdom."

A low rumble of chanting began to swell. It was in the language of the Boeotians. The hair on the back of Annon's neck spiked up. It was a guttural, hissing sound, the chant of a war-like people. It slithered in the air like the snakes of Basilides. A bead of sweat trickled down the side of the Druidecht's face. Phae was trembling, her eyes wide like a child's.

"Say on," Tyrus prompted, leaning forward, seeming oblivious to the dangerous sounds bubbling up around them.

Annon noticed the carving of the face on the boulder—its eyes started to glow orange.

"Her consort was found dead. There was no mark on his body indicating how he had died. But fear began to crack the kingdom. Like an egg gripped too hard, it collapsed suddenly, all yolk and pus. The Plague struck with its devastation and fury. She sent her most trusted man to kill Shirikant. He returned, wounded, with a tale only a fool would believe. No knife could pierce the man. No fire could burn him. The Empress took her faithful servant, two books from her vast library, and fled. The Boeotian kingdom fell asunder. Her once-proud city was turned into a field of bones."

She reached and took Tyrus by the wrist with her right hand—right hand to right hand. "I am the seventy-second Empress of Boeotia. What I told you of occurred almost a thousand years ago. We have watched this pattern repeat over and over. The same pattern struck the Vaettir's homeland across the sea. The same pattern struck the Cruithne. There are races lost and forgotten, wiped clean as a sandstorm erases footprints. Beautiful races. Clever people. All of these have fallen to Shirikant."

The chanting grew louder. Annon saw Paedrin and the others were all standing, watching Tyrus to see what he would do. They gripped weapons nervously, feeling the tension in the air without understanding it. Annon shook his head, trying to steel himself against the dreadful emotions churning inside of him. Something was coming. A presence was awakening inside the boulder. His hand, uncontrollably, was trembling.

"The Plague has struck each kingdom in turn," Tyrus said sternly, ignoring the commotion around him. He pressed her for more, his eyes locked on hers. "Slowly they have been coalescing together, banding ever closer together to hold off the Plague. His goal is not to rule over us then. It's to destroy us."

She nodded solemnly. "There are times . . . occasions . . . when he has toppled the ruler and planted himself. The Plague does not come yet. The people unite under his rule, becoming his slaves. But in every case, over time, his oppression is finally unbearable and the people revolt and seek his overthrow. And when that happens, the Plague strikes again."

"Tell me of the Scourgelands," Tyrus said.

"You know more about that place than any other living person, save my husband."

"Tell me what you know."

"It has always been a forbidden place," she said. "Even in the records that have been handed down to me. It was forbidden even before Shirikant. It is the gateway to Mirrowen. There is the place called the Well of Plagues. To pass that place and go beyond is to seek eternal life. I surmise that Shirikant wishes to brook no rival. He has posted his sentinels to guard that twisted wood. He has corrupted the defenders to keep all others out. That is why you are his greatest threat, Tyrus Paracelsus. And our greatest hope of deliverance."

Tyrus's muscles were clenched, his eyes narrowed with stormy thoughts. "So what you are telling me is the man I thought betrayed me . . . the man who loved my sister . . . may still be alive? Our enemy is not truly Band-Imas?"

Mathon coughed fitfully and nodded in strong agreement. He was trembling as well, as if the power emanating from the rock unsettled him too. "Before we left for the Scourgelands, the Arch-Rike . . . Shirikant, to be clear . . . gave me a ring to wear. It was one of the Kishion rings. He said it would help keep communication with him while we were in the woods. He said that I could relay information back to him, which would be written down by the Archivists. I was not to tell you this, of course. Once I put the ring on my finger, he totally consumed my mind. I was trapped in my own body, unable to warn you. He used me to make you doubt yourself. That is his greatest weapon, Tyrus. That is how he gains power over someone. He put me there to poison your thoughts, because he knew that you trusted me, that we were friends. I can't tell you how it feels to be free of him. He is a monster, Tyrus. He seeks the death of everyone. It is my belief—"

"Our belief," she interrupted, releasing Tyrus's arm and reaching and taking Mathon's hand, squeezing it.

"Our belief," he agreed, "that he is drawing all kingdoms together. That he is pulling the remnants of all civilizations into a single place so that we'll be easier to exterminate with the Plague. I do not know if this is true, but what I have learned here these many years has convinced me. This may well be the last Plague, Tyrus. You must succeed. What we don't understand is how you will do it."

"My spies in Canton Vaud were not among the Thirteen," the Empress said. "We did not hear your conversation, but only saw the aftermath of it. This is part of Shirikant's pattern. He overthrows kingdoms, principalities, and powers. He seeks no one to rule but himself, yet he cannot rule wisely and destroys those he lures into obeying him. The pattern is sickening to watch. So I ask you, Tyrus, how do you plan to defeat him?"

Shifting, stumbling men emerged from the caves, surrounding them on all sides. Some carried crooked walking staves. Some carried spears. Wave after wave began to emerge.

"Tyrus," Prince Aransetis called in warning.

The Empress's mouth flattened into a firm line. "I am sorry, Tyrus. I have held them off as long as I could. I said that no one would attack you without express permission. Unfortunately, I will be killed shortly and my power to protect you will be gone. I have done what I could to aid your arrival. Food and water have been gathered for your travels. They are packed with camels at the top of the ridge beyond this chasm. There I have guides who will bring you as close to the Scourgelands as they dare go. You are on your own now. Farewell."

Tyrus seized her wrist like a snake strike. "Who seeks to overpower you?"

She did not fight his grip. Her eyes turned hard like flint. "His name is Tasvir Virk. He is a Druidecht, though one of the Black. He has corrupted the spirits with his madness, or perhaps they corrupted him. He has the fireblood too, so your powers will not harm him. He lost his right arm in a battle in Silvandom recently and came here to convalesce. When he saw the truth of things, he overcame his fear of the disease. He understood that I have no true power, only what my courage gives me. So he summoned his war band and he will unite the tribes under himself. The line of Empresses is ending."

Her words made Annon nearly choke with fear. Images flashed in his mind, of flaming torches whose smoke killed the spirits of Mirrowen. In his mind he heard the bite of an axe against Neodesha's tree. A gaunt man had arrived, speaking the Boeotian language, insisting that they hack down the tree and destroy the Dryad trapped inside. His goal was to purge the woods of all Dryad trees. Annon had fought him, wrestling with him by the oak tree. He remembered the sickening blow of the axe that had finally ended their struggle. He could still picture the severed arm amidst the smoke and ashes.

Tasvir Virk.

Tasvir Virk.

He heard the words now. The chanting growing louder and louder. The sibilant hissing. They had been saying his name all along. His soldiers had hidden among those afflicted with leprosaria. His followers had murdered Annon's friend Reeder. A cold, clutching feeling grappled inside the Druidecht's chest.

"He comes," the Empress whispered. She was sweating too. With her free hand, she reached for Mathon's arm and clutched it.

Tyrus rose to his full height, his face grim and brooding. Annon did not ask about the Tay al-Ard. He suspected that it would not be ready to transport them. They would have to face the situation without its magic.

"The far tunnel, the one we entered, will be blocked," Mathon said. "Behind us is another way out. There are spirit creatures there that will frighten all but the bravest Boeotians. Do you see the rune stones carved in the stone above the tunnel? Take your friends and go that way to escape."

Phae stood quickly and rubbed her arms as if a winter's chill had frozen the chamber. A crowd of shuffling masses began to straighten, revealing their deception as they drew nearer. All of Tyrus's band quickly clustered around where the Empress still sat, her face fearful but determined.

"Do we fight our way clear?" Paedrin asked, scanning the advancing warriors. There were easily two hundred or more, chanting the name of their leader over and over, drawing weapons from beneath their tattered clothes. Other faces were stern and impassive.

"You cannot face so many," the Empress said. "There are thousands more coming from the caverns. This is a war band, not a hunting party. Go!"

Annon saw him at last. The gaunt one. Tasvir Virk.

The look on his face was full of strength and glee. He was tall, thin as a rail, but Annon remembered his fierce strength. He detected the presence of spirit magic in a whorl around the man, as the Druidecht drew powers inside himself to aid against them. All the spirits in the room were drawn to Tasvir Virk like a whirlpool in a fast-moving river. None of them sought to aid Annon or the Empress. They harkened to one master.

"Ich chai velot grane!" Tasvir Virk shouted. The chanting hushed. His voice fell to a quiet, almost lilting, sound. "*Ich malor ich conen. Ich safar!*"

The Empress stood, her face going white. "It is time," she said, shaking her head. She looked at Tyrus in agitation. "Go while you can, Tyrus."

"Ich safar!" screamed Tasvir Virk. He raised an oozing stump high into the air. He switched his language to Aeduan, his leering grin triumphant. "I see the boy! I see the man. Oh, how I have longed for this day, Tyrus Paracelsus. Shedding the Empress's blood would have earned me the right to rule. Killing you will bring me renown and allow me to summon all the warriors to my creed. And there is the boy who left me with a shameful hand. You, pup, I will let live to be my slave. But I will take your hand, boy. I will take your hand! *Atu vast! Atu vast!*"

"We have, surviving over many centuries, a text written by an ancient Vaettir general on the art of war. It was written during a time when that race eschewed peace and spent many centuries embroiled in conflict. I heard the Arch-Rike quote it thus in our language: All war is deception."

- Possidius Adeodat, Archivist of Kenatos

IX

Phae's emotions roiled with the dread of the upcoming carnage. They were vastly outnumbered, the enemy poised to fight and growing more innumerable by the moment, and against a raving madman who reeked of the fire-blood. Part of her wanted to run. Part of her wanted to stand and fight and prevent the Empress from being overrun. The Empress had shared what little she could before her enemies arrived. She had not asked for help, and in fact was offering them a way to escape, to abandon her to her enemies. Part of Phae's soul shriveled at the sacrifice the Empress was making.

And yet, her ears were still ringing from the Empress's words about the Arch-Rike being invulnerable. The way she had described it reminded Phae so much of Shion that her mind had begun to spin possibilities she could not grasp. The claw marks on his face had been reminiscent of one facing the dangers of the Scourgelands. But what if he, somehow, had been granted the immunity and immortality that the Arch-Rike also possessed? Did they have, with them, the only weapon that would defeat the one called Shirikant?

The maddening maelstrom swirled around her, yet there was something in her thoughts, something just beyond her reach, which teased her. The Empress had directed them to the tunnel they could escape into. Or was it already too late?

Her father's expression was hardened with determination. He did not look frantic or agitated—just fiercely serious. Paedrin looked as if he were ready to spring into the air and start fighting. Hettie was looking at the doorway out, while Baylen glared at the gathering enemies and drew his twin blades. All of her fellow companions deferred to Tyrus, awaiting his decision. It happened in moments.

"We won't abandon you," Tyrus said, rounding to face the Empress. "Call a challenge. There is a blood debt here to satisfy. The boy will face Tasvir Virk. Challenge him in your tongue!"

Phae stared at her father in horror. Annon's face went white as milk.

The Empress blinked, startled, and then raised her voice into a scream. "*Itsun Golgotha!*" She strode forcefully in front of the group, raising both hands in the air and screamed it again. "*Itsun Golgotha!*"

Somehow those words managed to quell the turbulent fury of the Boeotians. The weapons raised were stilled, but they trembled with pent-up rage. The Empress stood like a lioness, chin jutting forward, her hair wild. "*A cochir. Tan vanu!* You are challenged to the death, Tasvir Virk. The Druidecht who stole your honor, who left you with nothing but a shameful hand, will finish what he started in the Vaettir woods. You are challenged for the right to lead this war band. Only blood will suffice."

Tyrus grabbed Annon by the shoulder and prepared to shove the boy forward. Phae quailed at the thought, but she trusted her father would not let the Druidecht die. Was there a weapon he would be given, something that would help balance the battle?

"What are you asking of me?" Annon asked hoarsely, his eyes blazing with naked fear.

"I will go," Paedrin volunteered, his jaw muscles tense. "Send me in there, Tyrus."

"No, Annon must go." He gave them each a hard look. "Annon must face him. Gather round me. Quickly."

Phae was already there and she saw the looks in their eyes. No one could tell what Tyrus was up to. Yes, the enemy Tasvir Virk was missing one hand, but in his other he clutched a wicked-looking club with a strange orange orb fastened into one end.

"You play games!" Tasvir snarled.

"You cannot defy this challenge," the Empress countered. "Or you stand as a coward before these men."

"It is trickery," Tasvir said. "They will flee. *Atu vast*!"

Phae felt a jumble and someone bumped into her and nearly knocked her over. When she straightened she watched Annon leaving the circle, walking toward the Empress. His face had a look of grim determination as he left the shelter of his companions.

"What are you doing?" Paedrin demanded. "He will be slaughtered!"

Phae looked for the cat-creature, Nizeera. She had settled down on her haunches, her tail lashing with misery as her pale eyes gleamed, staring at the Druidecht. She did not hasten to his side.

"Father?" Phae whispered, but Tyrus was already moving, bending low and whispering into Mathon's ear. The diseased face revealed no emotion, but the eyes were bright—a man being spared an execution.

The Empress turned as Annon approached. "He deserves a weapon. An equal weapon."

Tasvir Virk's horrid face twisted with the rush of glee and defiance. "*Atul!*"

From the press of bodies, someone hurled a club. Annon just managed to dodge the coarse object as it thumped into the dirty ground, bouncing a little before coming to rest. The wall of Boeotians opened around them, providing a small circle for the battle to happen. Chanting began, this time raw and full of triumph. *Tasvir Virk! Tasvir Virk! Tasvir Virk!*

Annon crouched and picked up the wooden cudgel. He slowly rose, holding it awkwardly.

The Black Druidecht suddenly reached out his hand and a jet of blue flames streaked at the young man, engulfing him in an instant. The heat and power knocked back many who were too close on the other side. She saw their skin smoking, the purple tattoos becoming livid, and then the flames died down. Phae stared in surprise. None of the Boeotians had been harmed by the flames. It seemed as if there was some magic in their tattoos that protected them. Their faces twisted with delight.

As the flames died, Annon stood steadfast, head bowed, unharmed. Of course the fireblood would not have harmed him.

Tasvir Virk nodded, as if he had expected to see that, and then he began to croon, speaking in the language of Boeotia, his tone taunting. He began to swing the club around in circles, faster and faster as he approached Annon. Spittle flecked from his lips.

Phae's heart raced with concern. Annon began to step back, his feet looking clumsy as he tried to time the Black Druidecht's attack. Phae squeezed her fists, biting her lip as she watched the duel. Then, like a cobra, Tasvir Virk lunged and his club whistled down the other way, aiming to crush Annon's skull.

Somehow the younger man managed to sidestep the attack in time and shoved Tasvir away with his own club. Nizeera growled in pleasure, if not relief. But the Black Druidecht brought an elbow into Annon's stomach and whipped the club around again.

Annon ducked and circled the other way, trying to keep out of the taller man's reach.

Phae was amazed. She was terrified for Annon, but it seemed his emotions had frozen in that moment of need, giving him clarity and strength. His eyes focused on his enemy, watching his movements and trying to determine his intentions. He dodged two more thrusts and then the gaunt man trapped Annon's boot with his. Suddenly Annon was lying on his back in the middle of the arena. Tasvir howled with victory and swung the club down, but the orb struck dust and dirt as Annon rolled to the side. He kicked out at Tasvir's leg, landing a strike right below the knee. The gaunt man grimaced in pain and tottered but did not fall.

The orb in Tasvir's club began to glow, sending off smoky tendrils of light tinged with green. The Boeotians who were packed tightly recoiled from the smoke and light and began to push against each other to back away, to clear more space for the combatants.

A wicked grin spread across Tasvir's lips. "You cannot defeat me," he said, saliva dribbling from the crook of his mouth. "My magic poisons you. You bear not the runes to defend against its power. Wither, boy. I will take your hand!"

Tasvir feinted with the club, sending its trailers of magic into Annon's chest.

Annon winced, his expression clouding over as if overcome with nausea. Phae began to tremble, wondering if she was going to watch Annon be murdered in front of them all. She looked for Tyrus and saw him bent over the ground near the stone boulder that the Empress had been seated in front of during her wild tale. It was the boulder with the broken face carved into it, the nightmare expression that would haunt her dreams. Tyrus put a stone on the ground near the boulder. She saw there were more already around it. What was he . . . ?

The sound of two clubs clashing drew her gaze back. The Boeotians were staring, startled. There was fear in their eyes—fear of what they had just seen.

Tasvir stared at Annon in surprise. Something had happened between them that Phae missed. She gazed at Annon as well, saw him standing a little straighter. Tasvir swung the club around again, hard as iron. Annon blocked it effortlessly, the cracking noise reverberating in the chamber. Tasvir screamed in fury and butted the ball into Annon's stomach. It was like striking a wall.

Phae's eyes widened and she realized what was happening.

Snarling with uncomprehending fury, the Black Druidecht pulled back and swung the club straight down. This time, his opponent did not step aside; instead he stepped in and caught the club with his own, which shattered Tasvir's weapon into fragments. Tossing aside the fragments, Annon—only it wasn't—gripped Tasvir Virk's wrist and flipped him onto his back in front of everyone.

There was a moment of pure mayhem and the crowd prevented Phae from seeing what happened. It was Shion, not Annon. Then she remembered the charm Hettie had—the one that allowed her to look like anyone else. Of course!

"Atu kolgren. Atu fesit! Bloch mondray."

The orders were said in a strong, piercing voice. She recognized it as Shion's, only somehow he was speaking in the Boeotian language. The crowd backed away even more sharply now and she saw Tasvir in a crumpled heap, his single arm twisted cruelly behind his back, his frothing mouth screaming in pain and rage in the dirt. He struggled despite the agony, trying to free himself from the vicious hold.

Annon's face turned to Phae; their eyes met. Somehow, despite the illusion, she recognized him. It was the expression, the studied serious look he always wore. It was strange on such a young man's face.

"You must kill him," the Empress said, striding forward. "It is the way of our people. He has failed and he must die. His honor demands it. You've bested him, Druidecht. Though I cannot say how."

Shion brought his arm around and hooked it around Tasvir Virk's throat, keeping his arm pinned all the while. Tasvir spluttered, trying to thrash his way out of the hold. He was untamable, completely mad, heedless of the pain. Blood trickled from his lips as he tried to contort his way free.

The Boeotians' eyes were full of battle lust, yet many set down their weapons, staring at the young Druidecht with awe.

With just a flex of his arm, Shion could have stopped the madman from breathing. Phae stared at them, wondering what the Quiet Kishion would do.

Then Shion's gaze met hers again. He nodded to her to approach. She knew exactly what he wanted her to do.

Phae rubbed her arms as she crossed the trampled ground separating them. She was vulnerable, she realized. Any of them could lash out at her, but somehow the power was centered on Shion at that moment. All eyes stared at him. She reached him in moments, feeling suddenly safer to be near him again.

"He's mad," Shion whispered, despite the moans and thrashing from his captive. "Take it away. Take it all away."

Tasvir's eyes bulged as he saw her. He tried to reach out with his stump to grab her, but there were not fingers to do the work. He shuddered with violent spasms, unable to break the iron grip of his captor. Phae stared into his bloodshot, maddened eyes. With her Dryad powers, she could steal memories of the last few moments or his entire life. All she needed was to look into his eyes.

She blinked.

Nothing happened.

A cool, prickling sensation went through her bowels. It was unpleasant—almost painful. She had felt her mind grip his memories, but they were suddenly slippery. She swallowed and clutched her stomach.

"Try again," Shion said, nodding to her with determination.

She looked into Tasvir Virk's eyes once more. The prickling sensation went deeper. She blinked again.

The magic took hold that time. In an instant, she had his memories, mostly dark and terrible and full of violence. She let them drain from her like sand.

All the fight went out of Tasvir Virk. He slumped, drool dribbling from his chin. His brows knit in concern, as if he were struggling to remember something, anything. Shion released him and stood straight, still wearing the mask of Annon's face as his own. The smoking light had vanished from the Black Druidecht's cudgel. Shion saw the club on the dirt, stepped over to it and picked it up with both hands. Then with a powerful downward thrust, he snapped it across his knee and tossed it aside.

The disguised Shion approached the Empress and dropped to one knee in front of her. Phae followed his example, also kneeling in front of her. Phae risked a glance, seeing a look of honor and tears of relief glittering in the Empress's eyes. Murmurs of celebration began to rumble through the huge chamber. All around, the Boeotians were shaking their heads, as if some bad dream had been dispelled. They too dropped down to one knee, bowing their heads to her.

The Empress turned and found Tyrus standing by the boulder, staring at it with grim respect.

"You defeated the stone carving," the Empress said in a hushed voice.

"No," Tyrus replied. "I merely silenced it. When I placed the last stone over there, the whispers all went silent. You noticed it, didn't you, for you wear a talisman."

She nodded eagerly. "Those whispers . . . have been so difficult to keep out of my mind."

Tyrus smiled grimly. "This kind of spirit is called a Greilich. They are dark ones banished from Mirrowen. Their whispers are very subtle. They tease you with peeks of wisdom. But the wisdom can spoil like fruit. You would do well to no longer listen to it."

"So it is not banished?" the Empress asked.

Tyrus shook his head. "It takes some time and means to trap a spirit such as this. I do not have either at this point. But if you keep those stones in place, they will quiet it. The spirit is angry, I assure you. Never remove those stones. Its influence will wane now that it cannot communicate with those who live in the caves. The Greilich's influence is best felt in the shadows."

"Your Druidecht surprised me," the Empress said. "I misjudged him."

"Indeed," Tyrus said with a smirk. But he did not explain to her what he had done.

Phae had the feeling she was staring at two masters of manipulation who had managed, just barely, to avert a disaster.

"It is said that even the philosopher cannot bear to endure a toothache. Words contain great wisdom, but it is only in the manifestation of these experiences that the wisdom settles into our bones and guides us to act. You see, the words printed here are but concepts. You must go through the experiences yourself."

- Possidius Adeodat, Archivist of Kenatos

X

Paedrin studied the Empress as he dipped his fingers into the bowl of mashed grain and scooped it into his mouth. The flavor of the mush was interesting and heavily flavored with a variety of ground spices. It was nothing he had enjoyed in Kenatos, and he found the dried fruit and figs sweet and pleasant to the taste. The Empress offered a steaming dish of some sort of sliced cactus to Hettie, who wrinkled her nose slightly and motioned that she was full. The Empress served each of them herself, bringing an assortment of trays and offering varieties, explaining what it was first before setting the remains in the center of the circle for all to enjoy.

He was impressed with her attitude of service. There was no throne she ruled from. There were no courtiers or banners or vats of spiced wine. She lived amidst a legion of suffering souls, and yet she tended to each of Tyrus's band personally, offering her thanks and gratitude one by one.

Paedrin was impressed, his experience here vying with the training he had received and his own encounter with the ruthless Boeotian horde. Deep in a flame-lit cavern in the bowels of the earth, he saw a leader more humble than a Bhikhu. And that was saying something.

The mushy grain was new to him. She had called it *orkair* and the taste was pleasing. There was little flesh with the meal, which was mostly an arrangement of things that could be preserved—olives, apricots, pickles, and an array of nuts and cooked beans. They were all subtly salted or dusted with sweet powder. It was delicious.

He ate silently, watching her serve, until the last tray was done before she seated herself next to Tyrus and Mathon. With her right hand only, she took some figs and began to enjoy the meal herself, the last to eat.

"How do you keep track of the time down in the caverns?" Tyrus asked, anxious to continue the conversation.

She shook her head. "We sleep when we feel like sleeping. Awake when it feels appropriate. There is no time in Boeotia. There are no crops to grow or tend. What we eat grows wild and replenishes itself. The seasons come and go, and the greater part of our people move from one place to another. What is time, Tyrus, truly?"

The Empress's gaze swept around the circle. "These are your accommodations. There are no palaces to sleep in. You can leave by Tay al-Ard if you desire, but I encourage you to ride the camels to the borders of the Scourgelands. As a caravan, you will least likely be disturbed. My word is not always obeyed outside this place. I prepared for you what I could."

"You are generous," Prince Aran said. He looked at her with grave respect. "My people have long fought against yours. Trust that I will remedy that when I return to Silvandom. We have never sought to kill, but I can see that it has given us the impression of weakness, instead of strength. Perhaps one day there will be peace between us."

The Empress bowed her head. "I thank you, wise Prince."

Tyrus left the food and turned to face her. "You mentioned that the culture of Boeotia was created to foster the remembrance of our mutual enemy. Help me understand."

Paedrin had a feeling that Tyrus already understood it, but that he was seeking to draw her out more, to explain some facets of her culture so the rest could be aware of it.

"We are all ruled by emotions. One of the most powerful is a state called enmity, which I spoke of earlier. It is irrational, deeply rooted, and can endure generations. It is fostered by a lack of trust in anyone outside our own culture. When there is enmity, we tend to see only the faults in others, and our own virtues. My ancestors realized that the knowledge they possessed about our enemy could eventually, over time, be compromised. Empress Kosonin saw one of the enemy's tactics was to mistranslate books, to deliberately cause errors in understanding or destroy knowledge to prevent it from being shared. She saw this in the pattern I mentioned to you, how he and his followers sought out any references to himself and eliminated them. References to Mirrowen were also destroyed to prevent those from seeking that place. One cannot seek it if one does not know it even exists."

Annon—the true Annon, Paedrin realized with chagrin—looked up at this and nodded. "The Druidecht do not inscribe our lore. It must be memorized and passed down verbally."

"Precisely," she replied with a tone of approval. "Well said."

Paedrin saw how Annon flushed with pride at her praise and realized she had done so on purpose. Even her tone of voice was calculated for effect. She was a charming woman, but he wondered if they were seeing her true self or an image she wanted them to see.

"To be clear then," Tyrus went on, "your aim is not to destroy Kenatos or its books?"

She nodded sagely. "Our aim has been to liberate its imprisoned people, including the spirit-kind trapped into service by the Paracelsus order. While I disagree with the philosophy behind harnessing spirit magic, I am grateful your knowledge helped liberate us from the influence of the Greilich. You can begin to imagine how tiresome it is having a being perpetually trying to influence your thinking." She grinned at him.

"A tiresome thing indeed. We have been doing that to each other since we met." He returned her shrewd smile with one of his own. "Thank you for your hospitality. While I do feel you manipulated me into helping you, it was deftly done and I was not coerced. You are wiser than any of the rulers in the kingdoms I have met thus far."

"Thank you," she said demurely, her expression betraying no hint of self-satisfaction. Paedrin was amazed by her.

"Tell me," Paedrin said, speaking up. "What has prevented you from sacking . . . I should say *liberating* Kenatos by now?" He meant it as a harmless joke and she seemed to take it that way.

"Our enemy's wisdom in founding the city in the middle of the lake. By the time we knew of it, the defenses were already formidable. The loyalty and honor of the Vaettir are also an effective shield. They can float over our armies and cross the lake ahead of us, no matter how hard we try to siege her. Attempts to build barges have failed. The navy of Kenatos is very efficient and lethal. Building a bridge is also impossible for we lack the skill and the patience. We are not a serious threat to the city. Nor have we been. If there was a way we could help you, Tyrus, I would order another attack on the city. If that would help draw his focus on us, it might be worth doing it, even if we had no hope of victory."

Shion spoke in his naturally quiet, stately voice. "There is a way."

Paedrin sat up straight, staring at the quiet man. Baylen looked at Paedrin in surprise, pursing his lips, and then turned to listen more closely. Everyone stopped eating.

"What do you mean?" Tyrus asked, his expression curious.

Shion brushed dust from his trousers. "Only the Arch-Rike's most trusted men know of it. Even the fleet commanders are kept in ignorance. At low tide, there is a band of ground that leads to the island, behind the Arch-Rike's palace. It is completely submerged, but shallow enough to cross the lake on foot."

Stunned silence fell across the group assembled. The Empress's eyes twinkled with the news, her expression slowly brightening like a sunrise. "Can this be true?"

Shion nodded. "I have used it to exit the city unawares. There are no ferrymen near it and very little shore to help conceal it. It was created in secret long ago, in case the Arch-Rike was ever deposed and needed to bring an army to reclaim the city. As I said, it is a carefully guarded secret." He then went quiet, bowing his head and picking at a bowl of figs.

The Empress stared at him, trying to discern something from his expression. She waited, letting the power of silence work against him. Paedrin covered a smile. She did not realize that Shion was known as the Quiet Kishion.

"What you have given me," she whispered in a husky voice, "is a treasure beyond any expectation. If there is a way we can interrupt his war and draw his forces and machinations back to the island, it will help you in your journey into the Scourgelands. I must away. Preparations must be made. I must summon the warlords. This changes everything."

Tyrus looked at her and then nodded. "And Mathon's knowledge of the city, the Rikes and their ways, will also be of assistance."

"I would not survive the journey there," Mathon said hoarsely. "Though I appreciate your confidence in me."

Tyrus turned and gazed at Khiara, who had been seated quietly all the while, but looked around at the individuals suffering from leprosaria with a pitying expression. She met his gaze, understood his meaning without any words, and nodded her acceptance. Slowly Khiara rose and went around the circle. Paedrin felt a prickle of apprehension run down his back, and he sensed a great power welling up in the Vaettir girl.

"This is Khiara Shaliah," Tyrus introduced. "Her way of healing, Mathon, is very unlike yours."

"I have long tried to discover a cure," Mathon said, his eyes turning almost wild with panic as she approached him. His scabbed face twitched with unsuppressed emotions that could not be deciphered. "I cannot even halt its progress."

Khiara knelt next to him. She gazed into Mathon's eyes, taking his measure, as if studying the depth of the curse that afflicted him. The tension in the air thickened, as all eyes—even Kiranrao's—watched the Shaliah healer. She did not speak, but she took several deep breaths, as if calming herself. Paedrin stared intently, forgetting the bowl of mashed grains nearby. He swallowed thickly, feeling a surge of emotion swell inside him. Compassion? Empathy? It seemed to be radiating from Khiara in waves, her hands clasped in front of her, fingers knotted together.

All were silent.

Khiara lifted her chin, her eyes wet with tears. She nodded once, to herself, and then reached out her hands and touched Mathon's face, her hands cupping his cheeks.

She whispered in the Vaettir tongue. Paedrin could only make out several audible words interspersed by gasps. *By authority . . . through the* keramat *. . . afflicted soul . . . lesions healed . . . be clean.*

A jolt went through Paedrin's heart and he found himself on his feet, backing away from her as if somehow she had slapped him across the face. He blinked quickly, confused and a little disoriented. He heard the sound of rustling wings. He felt the whisper of breath, like a great sigh in his ear . . . words he could not understand.

Paedrin stared at Mathon in shock. As Khiara removed her hands, another man's face was revealed. Not a puffy, pockmarked apparition, but a man—clearly Aeduan with a slightly bulbous nose, unkempt dark hair flecked with gray, and a look of complete shock and thrall over his face. As Khiara dropped her hands tiredly into her lap, Mathon stared at his hand, his left hand, and saw that it, too, was free of scab and taint. He still had the stump on his right wrist, but the haggard, wheezing apparition had been replaced by a hale man who looked to be Tyrus's own age.

Tyrus and Mathon stared at each other, in clear recognition of each other now, and they both rose and embraced fiercely. Paedrin felt his throat tighten into a knot and could not swallow if he tried. The look of gratitude on Mathon's face—it was beyond Paedrin's ability to describe. The Empress herself had risen, her hand stifling her own mouth as she stared at her consort and saw the man who had been stolen by the disease long before.

Paedrin felt a tear trickle down his cheek, the moisture surprising him. As he cast his look around, he saw tears in all their eyes . . . except for two. Shion, who bore a look of profound admiration. And Kiranrao, who was not staring at the two forgotten friends, but whose eyes burned into Khiara with a look that was almost unholy in its unbridled greed.

Paedrin, Hettie, and Annon sat together around the flickering coals of the cookfire. The embers were low but cast a dim glow across each of their faces. Nearby, Phae and the Kishion were talking softly together. Tyrus consulted with the Prince and Khiara well out of earshot. Baylen was snoring against a cushion, his big chest heaving with each breath. Nizeera lay next to Annon, her head resting against her front paws dreamily. Kiranrao paced further away, always on the fringe of the group, always restless as if he were ready to kill someone. The Empress and Mathon had left already, disappearing into one of the side tunnels.

"Remember the campfire we shared in the Alkire?" Annon said softly, poking one of the coals with his finger. It always unnerved Paedrin when he did that and was not burned. "When we were so curious about Tyrus's motives?"

"That was long ago," Hettie murmured. "We were all sitting there . . . with Erasmus, of course."

"Who can forget Erasmus," Paedrin said. He changed his voice to match the Preachán's. "There is a one-in-sixteen chance it will rain underground."

Annon stared into the fires, his expression haunted. "I think he understood. At the end of his life, I think he understood what the Arch-Rike really was. He penetrated the illusion."

"He was always making predictions," Paedrin said with a chuckle. "My favorites were the odds of surviving the night. He was not an optimistic man."

"He was realistic," Annon said. He rubbed his eyes and stifled a yawn. "There are these tombs in Basilides. Each was carved with a name . . . the name of a living ruler. It makes sense to me now. Perhaps the rulers are still alive, trapped in those dark sarcophagi until they die of old age." He snorted in disgust. "That is how Lukias deceived us so well. I remember seeing the Arch-Rike marching toward the lair of Basilides . . . and that was with Lukias at my side. It was all part of the deception, his attempt to win my trust and bring him to Canton Vaud and the Dryad tree."

"Sshhh," Hettie said, silencing him. "Do not speak of that here. Remember where we are."

He looked at her and then nodded. "You're right. Thank you." He patted her on the leg. "It is so strange to have forgotten so much. I wish I could remember everything Erasmus said."

Hettie covered his hand with her own. "You did the best you could, Annon."

"It wasn't enough," he replied. He sighed deeply. "I suppose I should not be terribly hurt that I was deceived by someone like Shirikant." He looked up into their eyes, each in turn. "We must bring him down, though. We must end this cycle of deception and lies. We must win. Think of how many he has murdered over the centuries. Over thousands of years. It is almost more than I can comprehend. How do you defeat a man who cannot be killed?"

Paedrin glanced over at Shion. "Maybe we don't kill him. But if we can subdue him, strip away his Tay al-Ard, hunt him down like he hunted Tyrus—"

"Have you thought about what our journey means?" Hettie asked. "We are going to the place that protects the portal to Mirrowen. Annon, what can you say about it? What can you tell us?"

He shook his head slowly. "There is no knowledge of the portal that was shared with me. Our lore is secret, though, and can only be shared by someone else in training. I will say what I can. It is a sister-world to ours. It is like a mirror to our own . . . which I believe is why it was named Mirrowen. In that world, beings communicate through thoughts only. With this talisman that I wear, I can hear them while you cannot. Even though the thoughts are not spoken, like we are speaking right now, it is much like hearing . . . whispers. Sometimes you can make out the words. Sometimes you can't, but you get a sense of the sentiments, the feelings. When we came into these tunnels, I felt the presence of the Greilich. I did not know what it was at the time, but once Tyrus named it, I understood and recalled learning about them in my studies. They are malevolent spirits, thrust out of Mirrowen. Those who will not obey the laws of Mirrowen cannot dwell there."

"I didn't know it was spirit magic at the time," Hettie said. "It felt dangerous, that we'd be killed if we did not escape. Once Tyrus put those stones in place, I noticed a difference then."

Paedrin scratched his ear, looking back at Annon. "How did Tyrus manage to . . . involve you in the duel? I know about the charm Hettie stole in Shatalin to disguise herself, but he did not *say* anything about it."

Annon smirked. "But Hettie caught his understanding. She's more used to subtlety than I am. He said that Annon must face Tasvir Virk. She figured out what he meant without being told."

Hettie beamed at Annon, then leaned over and gave him a hug. It left Paedrin feeling a little jealous even though Annon was her brother.

"I'm exhausted," Annon said finally, stifling another yawn. "I'm going to sleep right here. If you two stay up talking and trading insults, can you keep your voices down?"

Paedrin gave him a slightly amused smile, looking back at Hettie in the gloom. So much had happened between them since they had met. So many memories were yet to be made.

"Good night, Paedrin," she said, drawing out her blanket and wrapping it around her shoulders. Before she lay down, she hesitated a moment, then leaned over and kissed his cheek.

A flush joined his smile.

She was still madly in love with him. All was well in the world.

"The war with Havenrook was brief and ineffectual, as I reported earlier. The surrender was signed between the King of Wayland, the Nobles of Cruithne, and the Preachán hierarchy. It was an interesting truce between these mighty forces. I had expected the King of Wayland to claim the territory, but he graciously conceded it to the Cruithne, who will settle Havenrook and re-construct the ravaged city. I'm not certain what the King of Wayland gains from this, other than a cessation of hostilities against his trading caravans, which now operate unmolested through the lands. Perhaps that is what he was seeking in the first place. I do not believe the Preachán will appreciate the Cruithne overseers. It is said many are fleeing into the woods of the Alkire."

- Possidius Adeodat, Archivist of Kenatos

XI

Phae watched the firelight glint off Shion's dark hair. He stared down at the ground, his face inscrutable. She wished she knew what he was thinking, that there was some way she could pry into his mind and reveal the hidden secrets there. Part of her wanted to smooth the quill-tipped points of hair away from his brow. His gaze turned up to her at that moment, and she found herself blushing.

"When you stole Virk's memories," he said in a low voice, keeping their conversation intimate, "you . . . suffered. There was a look on your face as if you were in pain."

Phae recalled the sickening feeling in her stomach all too well. She nodded mutely.

"Describe it."

She looked around the chamber, trying to put in words a sensation that was beyond description. "I'm not sure that I can."

"Try, Phae."

She brushed a lock of hair behind her ear and then scratched her cheek. "It felt somewhat like the pain . . . the one that women have each cycle . . . except it was deeper. In my bones . . . inside my very being. I have never felt it before when using my magic."

"You did not feel it with Trasen."

"No. Not with him. I'm not sure if it was because Virk was mad . . . but why would that hinder it? I don't know." She stared down at her hands and wondered if some sickness was starting inside her.

He rubbed his chin thoughtfully. "It may be that you are drawing near the time you need to claim your birthright. As a Dryad-born, you need to bond with a tree. If that does not happen, you will lose your gift."

"You think it's a warning, then?" she asked. "That if I do not do so soon, I won't be able to?"

He nodded. "Are you ready for it?"

His words caused an avalanche of dreary emotions inside of her. The pinching feeling in her stomach was nothing compared to the roiling inside her heart. She missed Stonehollow, and the thought of never seeing the Winemillers again was tortuous. What about wee Brielle, who never spoke? Would Phae never hear that little girl's voice? What about Tate and Devin? What about Rachael? She missed them all, and the spasm of loss crushed her heart. Without wanting them, she felt tears prick her eyes.

"There is much I'll be giving up," she confessed, her voice so thick it came out as a whisper. "But each of us is making a sacrifice. This is my part."

He reached out and took her hand, startling her. Glancing up, she saw him looking deeply into her soul. "I will not force you to do this, Phae. You have a choice . . . even still."

She stared down at the rugged hand enfolding hers and felt another strange sensation competing with the rest. His touch was like the fireblood and made her warm inside. "How can I walk away now?" she asked. "We're in the middle of Boeotia."

"I'm not suggesting that you do. I'm telling you that you have a choice. You always have a choice." His expression darkened and he released her hand. "I choose to have my memories restored. I want to know them and face them. I want to remember, no matter how painful they are. I must know the truth about myself." His voice trailed off, his expression suddenly leagues away.

She waited in the silence, knowing instinctively that he wasn't finished yet. Both of their voices would not reach beyond them. She felt dirty and unkempt, wishing there was a place to bathe and get clean again. Not that it would matter. The land of the Boeotians was thick with dust.

"How does it work?" Shion finally asked.

"What?"

"How does a Dryad restore someone's memories? I know you take them with your eyes. Is it the same restoring them?"

An uncomfortable flush started up Phae's neck.

His look became perplexed. "I see by your face it troubles you. Will it hurt you?"

Phae bit her lip to stifle a laugh. She felt very warm at that moment, wondering how she could reveal the information without embarrassing them both. Uncertain still, she shook her head no.

"Tell me."

"Well, I could explain it this way. A Dryad steals memories with her eyes. They are restored . . . through our lips. It's called a Dryad's kiss. That is how it is done." She was surprised she got the words out without stammering.

It was Shion's turn to look uneasy. He stared at her, eyebrows raised with curiosity at her candor. He said nothing for a while, and she saw his jaw muscles clench.

"It only works after I've fully become . . . who I am," she said. "Then all of your memories will be restored to you. We . . . from the way I understand it . . . *share* them in a way. That is how it was with Annon and with my father. They could remember everything, even being an infant."

His look transformed from alarm to horror.

"I do not want you to share my memories," he said darkly. "You least of all. You are young . . . an innocent. I've done unspeakable things."

"You are not who you were, Shion," she said, reaching out and taking his hand. "People can change. You are helping defeat our enemy now instead of helping him."

"Nothing that I do can fix what I've already done. I accept that. But to burden *you* with those memories . . ." He shook his head with determination.

She knew it would not be wise to push him. "Well . . . we will travel that road when we need to. We are already bound together, you and I. Strange . . . I feel like it has been months since I've known you." She waited a moment, letting him brood in silence. "There is something I wanted to ask you." She nudged herself even closer to him. "The Empress told us that the Arch-Rike—that Shirikant—is immortal. That he went to Mirrowen and has blocked the portal. He cannot be killed. It made me wonder if you have been to Mirrowen also. In the past. How else to explain your invulnerability?"

"You think so?" he asked, staring down at her hand overlapping his. He looked confused.

"It makes sense to me. When the Empress mentioned this, I thought of you. You are not Shirikant. But it makes sense to me that you are one of his tools. Perhaps he has found a way to channel the magic and immortality into you that protects him as well. I don't know."

"I have no memories of my past, as I told you," Shion said. "I do not know what the truth is, but I wish to know it. We will learn that in time. But Phae, if my memories are as awful as I fear, I don't want to burden you with them. That is unfair to you."

She patted his hand. "It'll be all right."

"You don't know that."

"What matters more is not what you did in the past. It matters what you do moving forward. I wish I could return to Stonehollow. I would love to explain to them what happened to me. But I see now that I cannot. My future is different from my past. So it is with you. It is time that you put away the Kishion." She swallowed, her throat suddenly dry. "It is not who you *really* are."

"And who am I?" he whispered, staring off into the cavern. It wasn't a question seeking a reply.

She clutched his hand. Phae did not know how to answer that question for herself. She was Tyrus's daughter. She was the daughter of a Dryad too. She had the fireblood and all that it represented. But despite this history, she was a person—with feelings and ambitions. She had wanted to build a homestead with Trasen. Now her homeland would be a twisted thicket of disease-filled trees. She would never be the same again after this experience. There was truly no going back.

Still clinging to his hand, she thought about the Seneschal of Mirrowen, the being who would take her oaths and bind her to the tree with a Voided Key. She wondered if she would ever understand the mysteries shrouding the secrets.

"Thank you for being my protector," she said after the intense silence. "Whatever comes, I feel my courage grow stronger because you are with me. If my fear starts to outweigh my desires, please remind me of this. I don't want to quail when that moment comes."

His other hand cupped hers and he offered a warm smile, nodding. Then something caught his gaze and he let her hand go, nodding for her to look as well.

The voices were just starting to rise to the point where others could hear. As Phae turned her head to look, she saw Kiranrao speaking vehemently to her father. Both were standing apart from the others, deep in conversation. It was Kiranrao's voice that was rising.

"I will return immediately," the Romani said sternly. "You cannot deny me this request, Tyrus. My people are being butchered and I've learned something tonight that can help them. It'll take days before the Boeotians can attack Kenatos. I can have Romani there before tomorrow evening."

"I have no doubt that you can," Tyrus said, his brows knitting in anger. "But you can just as easily not return with it at all, and I cannot take the risk. It is vital to my plans for conquering the Scourgelands. I gave you the chance to leave earlier, Kiranrao, and you chose to stay. Have you changed your mind?"

"No!"

"Then why do you persist in arguing about this? I will not give you the Tay al-Ard."

"I can take it from you," Kiranrao said in a warning voice.

A surge of panic thrust inside Phae like a knife. Shion rose immediately and walked toward the two men. Prince Aran approached as well.

"I do not underestimate your abilities nor the powers of that blade," Tyrus said, seething. "I have a keen respect for both, or you would not even be here. If you attack Kenatos now, you may slow Havenrook's defeat, but it was ordained to be defeated when the Arch-Rike decided to alter the shipping charters. We seek to banish the Plagues. That will do the Arch-Rike more harm than anything else you try."

"Give it to me."

Tyrus shook his head. "Think, Kiranrao! You are seeing threats in shadows because your people are being hunted and persecuted. Erasmus once told me that when a man risks losing his fortune, or his health, or some other thing he feels entitled to, he will begin to think irrationally to forestall the event."

Kiranrao's face went black with rage. Phae stood shakily, worried for her father's safety. Shion closed the gap, approaching from behind the mercurial Romani.

"You're saying I'm a fool?"

"Of course not! You are the shrewdest man in Havenrook. Everyone knows it. But you are also the Arch-Rike's enemy and you know how implacable he is. He has been plotting your overthrow for several years. As I have been plotting his. We are allies, Kiranrao. This quest cannot succeed without you."

"Then give me the device," Kiranrao snapped. "I will give you the blade in exchange so that you know I will return as promised. You say you have faith in me, but your actions do not match." He turned suddenly on Shion, his face livid. "You may not be harmed by other men, Kishion dog, but believe me . . . this blade will kill even you."

Shion was unmoved by the speech. He stared at Kiranrao with cool disregard.

"I'm warning you—"

Tyrus interrupted. "Kiranrao, you must accept my leadership in this quest, or we cannot go on with you." He stepped even closer to the Romani, his voice pitching lower. "Don't be offended that I didn't send you against Tasvir Virk. You could have slaughtered the man in an instant. But that blade draws in the strengths of those it kills. Would you want your mind tainted by his madness? Think! You are the crucial part of this. There are dangers in the Scourgelands that only you will be fierce enough to confront. I count on that. Don't be petty. You are worth your price . . . worth the reward you will gain. You will redeem your people if you stay true to me. Believe in that."

Kiranrao's face was mottled with fury, but Tyrus's words were starting to assuage him. The look of murder in his eyes had softened. Phae believed that Tyrus was manipulating his emotions, trying to play the right chords to calm him.

Snorting with disgust, the Romani whirled and stalked away, his face twisted with displeasure. Phae approached Tyrus and only then saw his fist unclench. His hand trembled with emotions. She had never seen her father betray any sign like that before.

"Father?" she asked, drawing nearer to him. She sidled up next to him, grateful that he was still alive and worried that the Romani's wrath would snap like a taut bowstring.

"Thank you, Shion," Tyrus said in a low voice.

He was answered with a brief nod. Prince Aran's expression was black with distrust.

Paedrin approached them as well, his expression firm and mixed with anger. "Why do you suffer that man to be with us?" he whispered to Tyrus, his voice thick with rage. "He almost killed you, Tyrus. I swear he almost did."

Tyrus shook his head. "You exaggerate, Paedrin."

"You know that I do not. He is not as he was in Havenrook. His grip on sanity is precarious. Tyrus, this is not wise."

"We need him, Paedrin," Tyrus said with finality. "You will understand when we reach the Scourgelands. When we face the dangers there, it will become very clear to you."

"Will he even last that long?" Paedrin said with a puffed breath. "My instincts warn me that he cannot be trusted. He will betray us, Tyrus. He will bide his time—"

"Hush," Tyrus interrupted. His eyes were dark and stormy. "We play an elegant dance, he and I. Do not interfere with the timing."

Paedrin looked at Phae and then at Shion. "This is a mistake, Tyrus. It would be better if we left him behind."

Tyrus's expression began to smolder with anger. "Trust me, Bhikhu. It is likely that many of us will be left behind as corpses as we go on from here. Friendship is a driving emotion and is a powerful one. But against the threats that we face, it is not enough—as you have seen with my friend Mathon. It was not enough then and it is not enough now. Duty drives me, not friendship. This may be the last chance we have to stop the next Plague. Our way forward is dangerous beyond your imagination. You will see the wisdom of choosing Kiranrao later."

Paedrin's scowl was deep and distrustful. "You misjudge your allies as well as your enemies, Tyrus. I would not be doing my part if I did not warn you."

"I understand, Paedrin. Master Shivu was preparing you to join me on this quest. It was a tacit understanding, never spoken out loud. He never told you this. There is much you still do not know about the ways of men and ambition. This is the Uddhava. I learned it from the Arch-Rike. It is only a matter of deduction where he learned it from." Tyrus squeezed Phae's shoulder. "Get some sleep. We go in the morning."

"It was said long ago that the desire to be observed, considered, esteemed, praised, beloved, and admired is one of the earliest as well as the keenest dispositions discovered in the heart of man. All the great ones have ambition and all desire recognition for their efforts. More than most people, I knew Tyrus Paracelsus of Kenatos to be a man of deep ambition, which he cloaked with worthy goals. It has been said he's turned traitor and will unleash the barbarian hordes of Boeotia against us. I am saddened but not surprised. How are the mighty fallen."

- Possidius Adeodat, Archivist of Kenatos

XII

The group had assembled on the ridge top above the canyon. Annon had never met the king of his own land. Observing how Tyrus and the Empress of Boeotia conversed, he wished he had taken the time to do so. It fascinated him how leaders sized each other up, how they probed each other for weakness and strength in the comments they used and the short little phrases that tested one another. He had witnessed the Thirteen of Canton Vaud, the wisest of the Druidecht order, debate with Tyrus and seek to sway him away from his quest. He had observed the cruel machinations of the Arch-Rike attempt to do the same thing. The Empress was completely different. In every way, she sought to aid them—offering camels, supplies, sturdy men who could be trusted, and advice on how to maintain composure during conflict and to trust the inner voice that had guided him over the years.

Larei of Boeotia, Empress and servant to the lowest dregs of human life, amazed Annon, and he found himself overwhelmed by her wisdom and forethought. He was grateful to Tyrus that he was allowed into their private conversation. He knew it would mark him for the rest of his life.

A sudden gust of wind blew dust into his eyes and the camels snorted and spat, loaded down with casks and rugged sacks and bladders full of wine and oil. Tyrus stroked his own beast's neck, trying to soothe it as they spoke. Annon listened in eagerly.

"We will strike Kenatos from the docks," the Empress said, her voice low enough not to carry far. "Make them think that we are seeking to steal vessels to ferry our way across the waters. I will send Mathon and a chosen few to cross into the city from the bridge in the shallows. We will steal disguises and learn what we can from the inner defenses."

Tyrus nodded and gestured to Mathon. "Go to the Preachán quarter—it's on the western part of the city. Seek the aid of Bartimeus of the Cypher Inn. He will shelter you and aid you. He has no love of the Arch-Rike and I think he'll be loyal to me. You will not stay hidden long, for the Arch-Rike has his spies throughout the city. They watch the docks vigilantly. Coming in from another way will aid in the deception."

The Empress smiled with pure brilliance. "You have given us a spark of hope, Tyrus. If we can do nothing but interrupt Shirikant's plans, it may aid you while you penetrate the Scourgelands. I do not think it will be difficult to topple the city from inside her defenses. She was designed to withstand an interminable siege, not a coup. But I assure you . . ." she added, reaching and grasping his forearm to emphasize her sincerity. Annon noticed how she communicated with all parts of her body—voice, eyes, and touch—aligning all three to help deliver her messages. "I assure you that we seek the Arch-Rike's fall and will not harm the citizens of Kenatos if we can help it. We come as their liberators, though they will not see us in that light. Their minds have been poisoned against us. I have no desire to burn the Archives or purge knowledge from the city. Much of it is good and useful. As I told you before, his goal is to purge knowledge of himself from the land. If we are successful, I will add my records to the Archives personally."

"Thank you," Tyrus answered, his expression softening. "They are my people and they believe I've betrayed them. I will never be welcomed back to the city again. I knew this would happen. But the lead Archivist is named Possidius Adeodat. I do not believe he has seen through the Arch-Rike's web of lies. But he may be the most reasonable man you can influence. In fact, he may make a fair Arch-Rike himself if given the chance. He's never desired leadership, which probably serves him well."

"I will seek him out," she replied, lowering her hand. Annon noticed it was her right hand. "Is there anything else I can do to assist your journey?"

"You've already done so much," Tyrus demurred.

She shook her head. "Do not think of it like that, Tyrus. You are bearing the greater burden. When you faced the horrors there before, you barely survived." She reached over and took Mathon's hand, squeezing it tenderly. "Going back will bring a flood of memories."

"It already has," Tyrus said.

She nodded. "That is your greatest danger. Those memories will attempt to unman you. They will rob your courage. They will wilt your resolve." Her eyes burned with fiery determination. "Take with you my blessing. Take with you my strength. I know you can do this, Tyrus. I know that you can defeat the evils that roam that land. For all our sakes, you must. There has not been a man . . . not in a thousand years, who *can* do what you *must* do. Death will hunt you. Defy it. Hunger will threaten you. Defeat it. I have seen a man waste away for forty days without food and still not perish. When you are past the need for hunger, your mind will open to new truths. Expect it. Heed those truths. You are facing a horrible task. But you do not face it alone. My blessing goes with you. Should you need to regroup and heal, return here immediately. These caves will shelter you. What else can I do for you?"

Tyrus stared at her, his eyes shining with renewed determination. "Your faith in my cause was what I needed most to hear."

"It is all that I have to give you," she replied. "Bend your head. Let me give you my blessing."

Tyrus obeyed, dipping his chin. The Empress stood on the tips of her boots and kissed the crown of his head. "Fare you well, Tyrus Paracelsus. When next you come to Kenatos, all the spirits your kind have trapped will be set free. Think of it, Tyrus." She gripped his hands with both of hers. "Think of what that freedom will mean to the people. I long to loosen the bonds around the minds of my own people, to set them free of enmity and hate. In the end, that is the best we can do for one another. We set each other free."

Tyrus looked at her, his expression almost startled. "My friend Drosta shared such a conviction. He saw the imprisonment of the spirits of Mirrowen as a great evil."

"So it is," she added, nodding. "There is nothing we crave so much as truth. And what did the ancients always say? The truth shall set you free."

"Farewell, Dame Larei," Tyrus said, bowing deeply. "You are the wisest of women. You have earned my trust."

"You did not need to say it for me to know it," she replied gravely. "Thank you, Master Tyrus, for saving my life. I hoped . . . we hoped . . . that you would *choose* to do so." She took Mathon's hand, her smile dazzling.

With that, Tyrus mounted the stirrups of the great beast and swung up onto the huge leather saddle. Four Boeotian drovers had been sent to assist them in caring for the camels and bringing them toward the Scourgelands.

Annon's heart was afire with emotions and he stood staring at the Empress, unwilling to break the spell she had cast on him. Tyrus had won over his loyalty and trust. But the Empress had captured Annon's devotion. He stared at her until she looked at him, her eyes curious and thoughtful as she read the expression on his face. It only took a moment. Nodding to the Druidecht with a look of respect and honor, she hooked arms with Mathon and turned away.

Stars twinkled in the vast, cloudless sky, a garment made of countless tiny jewels. A small fire crackled amidst the camp they had set up. Annon stared at the broad expanse above, his mind lost in the magnitude of it. He wondered what those pinpricks of light really were—distant candles? The shroud obscuring Mirrowen from view? He breathed in the cool night air, unable to sleep. Nizeera nestled against him, her eyes open and glinting with the reflections. They had traveled by camel for several days and he knew they were nearing the dreaded forest.

You are restless.

I am, he answered with his thoughts. *We face death.*

I will protect you. With my last breath.

He scrubbed his fingers into her deep fur. *I should hate to lose you, Nizeera. Tell me of Mirrowen.*

She was silent, luminous eyes blinking slowly. *You would not understand it. When you were Dryad-kissed, you may have endured a glimpse of it. It is too much for a mortal mind to comprehend.*

Annon sighed, continuing to stroke her fur softly. A faint purring noise came from her throat. *Every Druidecht dreams someday of being welcomed there. I am young still, so I have not expected it. But we travel to the bridge between our worlds. What if we succeed? Would I be able to enter Mirrowen from Poisonwell?*

If you survive.

A knot formed in Annon's stomach. *Survive the Scourgelands . . . or survive entering Mirrowen?*

He wasn't sure he wanted to know the answer to that.

Nizeera was thoughtful, her ears lying flat. *No more questions, Druidecht. You must earn the privilege of entering Mirrowen on your own merits. A king may not be able to enter, yet a peasant might. Few wealthy men can shrink small enough to enter.*

Annon shook his head, baffled. *I should have no problem with that. I have nothing.*

Her head lifted, her muzzle turning to face him. *Possessions matter not. What you bring matters. You bring who you are. Are you worthy to enter Mirrowen? Are you willing to die to test that worthiness?*

Annon grimaced.

Nizeera laid her head back down on her paws, her tail beginning to sway like a serpentine thing.

Boots crunching in the sand approached. Annon turned to face Tyrus as he settled down next to the Druidecht.

"How are you feeling?" Tyrus asked him, which was an odd question. Tyrus had never seemed to care how Annon was feeling.

"Does it matter?" he replied. "I am well enough. I meant to thank you earlier . . . for letting me overhear your conversation with the Empress. She's a remarkable woman."

"I can see why the Boeotians worship her." He sighed. "She is deft at manipulating men. I'm not sure whether I should be insulted or pleased that she played us so well."

Annon's eyebrows lifted. "Do you trust anyone, Tyrus?"

A reserved smile appeared before the reply. "The Romani have a saying: It is no secret that is known to three. While the Empress told us a great deal about what she wanted us to know, she did not reveal all of her motives. Notice she did not ask for mine either. If she had, I would have lost all trust in her immediately. Sensing this, she did her best to coax me into revealing it voluntarily. I nearly did, so powerful was her persuasion. But I have a duty to all of you, to protect your lives the best that I can. There are some secrets we must not share." His voice dropped further. "Even from the others."

Annon watched as Tyrus withdrew, surreptitiously, a ring from his finger. With one hand, he reached out and gripped Annon's shoulder. As he did so, he dropped the ring into Annon's lap.

A cold feeling welled up inside Annon's heart. "What is that?" he whispered.

"A piece of Paracelsus magic," he replied. He glanced over Annon's shoulder, his eyes roving the camp. "I fashioned it myself. When you put it on, magic veils it and it cannot be seen, but you will feel it on your hand. It is connected to the Tay al-Ard, Annon. It will summon it into your hand directly. Do you remember when we faced Shion in Prince Aransetis's manor and I vanished with him?"

Annon nodded.

"I used the Tay al-Ard to bring us to the waterfall where the Fear Liath keeps its lair. Because of the water and the pressure, I dropped it into the churn and swam free of the waters. I let Shion think I was dead so that the Arch-Rike would not feel the urgency to kill all of you. But I used that ring to summon the Tay al-Ard back into my hand from the bottom of the waterfall. I'm giving it to you."

Annon swallowed, his eyes widening. Again he was struck by the amount of trust that Tyrus had placed in him—a boy. He breathed slowly, trying to understand what was going on.

"You would only give it to me if you felt you were in danger of losing it," Annon whispered. His throat tightened with fear.

Looking into his eyes, Tyrus nodded. "It is important that you know about the ring and what it can do." He bowed his head, his expression very grave, his teeth clenched with suppressed emotion. "Merinda went mad in the Scourgelands, Annon. She used the fireblood to save my life and keep me from dying. In return, she asked me to save your life. Yours *and* Hettie's, it turns out." He paused, building up his words. "If I must, I will do the same for you. Do you understand why I do this now? Kiranrao may kill me for the Tay al-Ard. If he does and slips away, you can bring it back to your hand with a thought. Be sure he is far away, though. And if I go mad in the woods—" He coughed, covering his mouth on his forearm. His steeled himself again. "If that happens to me and I'm holding the Tay al-Ard, then I will be too dangerous to confront. I must not keep the Tay al-Ard if that happens to me. The damage that I could do . . . I shudder to think on it. But if it happens, Annon, if I lose myself in there, I want you to send Shion after me. He is the only one of you who could do it without being destroyed himself. And I don't want to burden any of the rest of you with such an awful task. Let him be the one. I don't want to be left in the madness, Annon. Not like my sister."

Tyrus dropped his arm, his shoulders sagging. He hugged his cloak tightly about his bulky frame, shivering in the dark. Annon stared at Tyrus, shaking at the revelations given. His insides roiled with pain and sorrow. How could Tyrus expect him to do these things? To face such heavy burdens?

"I need you, Annon," Tyrus whispered hoarsely. "Promise me."

Annon wanted to weep. He wiped his mouth, trying to master his emotions. "If there is another way—" he started to say, but Tyrus brooked no refusal.

"There is none. The madness is irreversible. Even Tasvir Virk. His memories were taken away fully, but he's a babbling lunatic still. I do not wish that for myself, Annon. I saw what it did to my sister. I saw what it did to your mother. You must have Shion do it. It isn't murder. It's my will. Promise me."

Annon knew he could not escape Tyrus's implacable will. He felt the other's strength of mind bearing down on him. Annon could see he had already given this great thought, that he had delayed burdening Annon with the task until the last possible moment.

He sat shuddering under the starry sky, overwhelmed by the thought of ordering Tyrus's death. His own mother had faced that madness to save his and Hettie's life. Tyrus promised to do the same. Perhaps he had realized already that he would not return to Kenatos to seek fame for what he had done. Annon wished he had thought of this earlier.

"Promise me," Tyrus insisted, gripping his shoulder once more.

Annon stared down at his lap, looking at the round eye of the ring. He scooped it up and slid it on his finger.

"It pains me," Annon said, his voice choking, "but I will."

The look of relief on Tyrus's face made it hurt all the worse. He stared at Tyrus—a man who he thought was his uncle most of his life—and realized he could never be like him. A man of secrets. A man plotting to overthrow the strongest power throughout the kingdoms. He looked across the sheltered campsite, the kneeling camels and sleeping bundles. They were amidst a vast plain full of scrub and stones. The air smelled of dust and camel scat. Shion was also awake on the other side of the camp, staring up at the vast, starlit sky. What a pitiful few straining at the lever to overturn such a huge boulder. Would it even be enough?

"Thank you," Tyrus whispered. He squeezed Annon's shoulder and rose, slipping away into the shadows.

Annon stared down at his hand. The ring was gone, though he felt it still.

"One of the ancients once said that the face is the mirror of the mind, and the eyes—without speaking—confess the secrets of the heart. I think this is true of most people. But there are some who so carefully guard themselves and their emotions that you cannot imagine the deep inner workings of their souls, let alone feel justified in characterizing it in some shallow way. The Arch-Rike of Kenatos is such a man. The occasional sparkle of temper may casually reveal itself at times. But those times are rare."

- Possidius Adeodat, Archivist of Kenatos

XIII

Paedrin refused to ride one of the camels. The thought of perching atop a swaying saddle, strapped to a cud-chewing beast, filled him with deep disgust. He had no trouble keeping pace with the others—the fact was that he was faster afoot and with the Sword of Winds than any ride. He was grateful for the food and water skins, and he made himself useful by scouting the land ahead of the four Boeotian drovers who led them away from the maze-like canyons and toward the dark, haunted woods of the Scourgelands. It was from his lofty position, gliding through the sky, that he saw the danger coming behind them.

"What is that?" he muttered to himself.

It was the third day since leaving the Empress, and the drovers had led them in a northeast direction through the hills and scrub of their forsaken lands. The drovers were all suffering from the early stages of the disease and rarely spoke to them, for they spoke little Aeduan themselves, and were good as the Empress had promised, caring for the beasts and setting up the spacious tent each night for them to sleep in.

From his position above the others, Paedrin saw a wall of dark clouds and swirling dust approaching from the southwest. It was enormous, like a storm cloud that scudded across the desert, too swollen to rise into the sky. He swooped down immediately, using the blade to bring him straight to Tyrus.

"There is something a league or so off," he warned worriedly. "Some fog bank or storm. It will overtake us within the hour."

Tyrus chirped a command to the beast he rode and twisted in the saddle. Already the edges of the storm could be seen. Tyrus motioned for the drover near him and gesticulated toward the approaching front.

The drover stood tall, shielding his eyes, and then began barking orders to his fellows. "Make camp," he said urgently. "Make camp. *Ata! Ata vancou! Haboub!*"

The group quickly dismounted the camels and the drovers began to scramble to pitch the tent. Paedrin joined them and Baylen followed suit, for they had both watched the drovers before and knew the order for assembling the tent.

"What is coming?" Prince Aransetis asked.

"They call it a *haboub*," Tyrus said. "Paedrin saw it first. Some sort of dust storm."

The wind began to whip and ruffle their clothes. The camels were made to kneel and the supplies stripped from their backs and brought inside the tent. Everyone lent a hand, hurrying to bring the gear inside. The wind began to blast, and soon they could all see the dust cloud advancing. It was eerie and brown, longer than a forest wall and taller as well. Paedrin used the blade to shoot into the sky one last time, trying to get a sense of its vastness. The wind shrieked and pulled at him, buffeting him roughly as the monstrous storm advanced. He could not see the end of it as it bore down on them.

The tent pavilion was lashed to extra stakes, the drovers chirping and calling to each other to hurry. Paedrin nearly went end over end with the sudden gust of wind and quickly returned to the desert floor and joined the others as they entered the tent. They staked the camels to prevent them from escaping, but they were not allowed inside the tent.

As Paedrin entered, he saw that the gear took up a good portion of the space and that everyone was huddled close together, including the agitated drovers, who tightened the straps on the door ropes.

Paedrin did not like being in confined spaces and he glanced around nervously at the others. The haboub struck their camp like a blacksmith's hammer. Everyone instinctively drew closer together as the winds began thrashing the hide walls of the tent. Fine grains of dust began to seep in through the open spaces, swirling like smoke. The storm blotted out the sun, dimming their vision like an early twilight.

"The storm will rage a while," Tyrus said. "Rest if you can."

Most leaned against stacks of provisions, trying to find comfort in an uncomfortable setting. The wind shrieked and howled, rattling the posts that held up the tent. Everyone was subdued, the darkness deepening with each passing moment.

The tent filled with the smell of the dust, and some started coughing. Paedrin sat in a calm stance, trying not to let it impact his heart. The light grew dimmer and dimmer, reminding him of that horrid dungeon beneath the Arch-Rike's palace. He felt the prickle of sweat down his back and did all he could do to remain composed. That dungeon was his worst nightmare. He dreaded even the memory of it.

"Reminds me of the squall we faced by the cliffs of Shatalin," Baylen said. Paedrin realized the Cruithne had settled near him. "The fog was so thick."

Paedrin turned and looked at him, seeing the intelligent look in his eyes. He observed people. He had noticed Paedrin's disquiet.

"That was a dark night," Paedrin said softly. "We've been from one danger to the next."

Baylen nodded sagely, looking nonplussed by the storm. "Storms are unpredictable. They are vast powers that none of us can control. It's wise to be wary of them."

The light was now totally vanquished by the haboub. It had scarcely been past noon and now it was as dark as midnight. Paedrin had never seen such a transformation in so short a time. He shook his head in surprise, grateful he had his second sight. Closing his eyes, he could sense where everyone was sitting. It was like seeing ghost-shapes in his mind, and he could tell who was who by their posture and size. Hettie hugged her knees, resting her cheek on her arm. He wished he was sitting closer to her. She looked like she needed comforting. He was grateful Kiranrao was farther from her than he was.

"Of all the lands I have visited," Paedrin said, "I've decided that I don't want to live here."

"Where then? Silvandom?"

"No. Nor Kenatos either. I feel a duty to restore the Shatalin temple. There may be some Kishion to evict, but that craggy mountain is calling to me. The lessons must be taught again."

"Will you only allow Bhikhu? Or maybe I should be more precise. Vaettir-born?"

"I will teach any who wish to learn," Paedrin answered.

"I would be very interested," Baylen said. "I'm not sure I will ever be able to float . . . no matter how much I hold my breath."

"I'd welcome you there. You have no wish to return to Alkire?"

"I was orphaned in Kenatos. What I've heard is it's smoky, cold, and a place you'd get lung rot. They've always craved a better climate and offered to help rid the woods of the Preachán to claim a better land. They'll pay for it, over time. The Preachán won't stay defeated."

"I've been to Havenrook," Paedrin said distastefully. "It will take many years to make that place livable again."

"Cruithne are patient."

Paedrin found the conversation had helped calm his nerves. He was grateful to Baylen for instigating it. "You said that when you were a boy, Aboujaoude helped you. What was the situation?"

Baylen sniffed loudly. The air was thick with dust. The camels moaned with discomfort outside. "It's of no consequence."

"Tell me."

"You'll probably be disappointed. It's not much of a tale."

"Your reluctance to tell me only heightens my anticipation. It must involve a girl."

Baylen snorted.

Paedrin lowered his voice. "I hit the mark then. Tell me. There is nowhere else we are going to go."

"I'll preface it by saying that I was very young . . ."

"And she was higher than your station. Let me guess . . . the daughter of a—"

"Baker. Yes, the daughter of a baker." Baylen's voice was very low. "Not nobility, surely. I was one of the many urchins who roamed the streets. But there was this baker's shop. We would all smell it when we passed by. I could see her in the window. She was a tiny thing . . . probably six."

"Six?"

"I was eight. Don't let your imagination run wild."

"I'm sorry. Go on."

"She had long blond hair full of curls. She always had a serious look on her face. Aeduan girl . . . very pretty. She was the pride of the baker. You could see it in his eyes." His voice was still low, but

Paedrin could hear the memories seeping into the telling. "I was just a child, but I was hungry. Not just for the bread. I hungered for what she had. A family. I just wanted to be inside that bakery. I daydreamed that when I got older, I would carry sacks of flour for the family. I would sweep the stoop. I just wanted to be part of it, in some small way. I don't think that little girl ever noticed me staring through the window." His voice trailed off.

"The leader of my little band of urchins . . . he was a rough fellow from Stonehollow. His name was Drew. He was big . . . bigger than me though I was still stout for my age. I think he saw me looking in that window, over and over. He had a bit of cruelty to him, let's say. One stormy day, when we were hungry and hadn't found anything we could trade for bread, he suggested we rob that bakery." He sighed heavily. "We had done that now and then, when we were desperate to eat. But I couldn't stomach it. Not *that* bakery. Not where the little girl lived. To them, it was just another bullying. But I think Drew knew how I felt—at some level. He told me to do it."

Paedrin inhaled deeply. "I'm waiting for the part when Aboujaoude comes. This is even more interesting without him so far. What did you do?"

"I said no. I couldn't bring myself to injure that family, to taint what I saw behind the window glass. Drew was four years older than me. The others were on his side. I knew I wouldn't be able to win that fight. Drew knew it too. Let's just say that before I was on the ground being kicked in the street, I had broken one of Drew's teeth, knocked two others into the mud, and almost had my fourth before one of them hit my head. I just remember splashing in that puddle of mud while they were kicking me. It didn't even really hurt. I remember being so, so tired and wanting to sleep. That's when Aboujaoude found me." There was a grim chuckle. "I believe he dislocated Drew's shoulder. Something about pain being a teacher. Then he cleaned me up and helped me to one of the Rike's orphanages, where I learned to read, to watch, and to fight."

Baylen chuffed to himself. "I've never told anyone that story before. Now, I know what you're going to ask. Did I ever go back and meet that girl in the bakery. Yes. Her name is Marae and she runs the bakery herself now. Her father is a bit old, but he still helps out. Her husband's name is Drew."

Paedrin started. "Really?"

A chuckle sounded. "I made that part up. Sorry. She is married, and I don't know her husband's name. I don't really care what it is. I buy my bread from that bakery. She smiles at me when I come in, and I always buy the biggest loaves and pay a little extra. Before I left Kenatos to hunt you and Hettie in Lydi, I bought one last loaf. She had a little baby girl in her arms and introduced me to her. I knew that I would never be going back to Kenatos again. But if anything I do can help stop the Plague from returning . . . if that little baby can grow up in a world where there is no Plague . . . well, I'll take that instead of gold any day."

"So you never told her how you felt?" Paedrin asked, his emotions struck by the story he had heard.

"Of course not," Baylen replied. His voice pitched even lower. "For the same reason Khiara doesn't utter a word about her feelings for Aran. Marae's happiness is worth more to me than my own."

Paedrin could see that Baylen truly had observed his companions. He had been watching them all, and Paedrin wondered—a bit uncomfortably—what Baylen had concluded about Hettie and him.

"So it's not just about helping out Tyrus and a debt owed to a Bhikhu."

Baylen chuckled. "There are always two reasons we do anything, Paedrin. The real reason and the one that sounds good to everyone else."

"Well, since you can't return to Kenatos when this is finished—though I see no reason you won't be able to, since we *will* defeat the Plague and we *will* overthrow the Arch-Rike—you can visit Shatalin whenever you choose. It will take some time to get the temple ready for students. But you are welcome to be part of that family regardless. The strongest bonds come from families—those we are born into and those we choose."

The keening wind was growing even louder. "It sounds like someone is crying," Paedrin observed, more loudly. "It's almost human."

"It is not human," Khiara said in a warning voice. With his new sight, Paedrin saw her stand across the other side of the tent.

"Are we missing anyone?" Tyrus demanded. "Did everyone come inside?"

Paedrin glanced around, quickly accounting for everyone. "We are all here, Tyrus, even the drovers."

"The sound is coming from a beast . . . I can hear it," Khiara said. "It's been getting closer and louder. Sounds like no creature I have heard before."

Quieting everyone with a hush, Paedrin listened to the sound of the wind and sure enough he could discern a howling sound. It was like the yowling of a cat, though much deeper, and caused a chill through his heart.

"I hear it," Paedrin said.

"So do I," Prince Aran added.

"Do you want me to go out there and kill it?" Kiranrao grumbled from behind another stack of goods. "It may draw others toward us."

"Stay inside," Tyrus said, dropping his voice to a hush. "Draw near me. The storm blinds it. Be still."

The sound of the creature was now loud enough for all of them to hear it. It cut through the moaning wind that lashed at the taut ropes and canvas. It pierced the darkness, defying them to describe the creature by its howl alone.

"What kind of beast is it, Tyrus?" Paedrin asked.

"Hush," Tyrus snapped.

The drovers started to moan with fear. They were beginning to understand the danger, that they were much closer to the Scourgelands than they had perceived. "Away . . . we must away," one of them babbled.

"*Makapenrinee*," whispered another drover, his eyes widening with recognition.

Light filled the tent as Tyrus's hands glowed blue with flames.

"The scars of others should teach us caution."

- Possidius Adeodat, Archivist of Kenatos

XIV

Do you sense it? Annon asked Nizeera, reaching out and plunging his fingers into her fur. He did not want to reach out to it with his talisman, for fear of attracting the creature to them. *What creature is it?*

It is a Vecser, came her response. *They are vicious hunters and can smell blood and flesh. It is blind to us because of the storm. They hunt in packs.*

As if to reinforce her thoughts, the sound of another came, even farther away. The first was drawing near to the tent and they could hear the crunch of the sand as it approached.

Tyrus's face had a grayish cast in the flame light of his fingers, his eyes fixed on the tent door. Were their enemies already prowling the borders of the Scourgelands, seeking them? Would they even be able to approach the woods unseen?

A thought came to Annon's mind—a quick memory of his time in Basilides. He wore an iron torc around his neck, a device imbued with magic that had banished the serpents inside the lair. It repelled any animal, including his friend. Nizeera felt his thoughts and her hackles rose, her ears flattening, and she hissed at him.

Annon reached out and took Tyrus's wrist to get his attention without speaking. He motioned to the torc around his neck, offering it as an alternative to using the fireblood so soon. Tyrus examined his gesture and then nodded curtly.

Closing his eyes, Annon withdrew inside himself and uttered the word in his mind that activated the torc—*Iddawc*. The torc had jewels embedded into each end and he felt their warmth begin to flush his neck as they responded to the thought. Waves of mental blackness extended from him, and Nizeera squirmed away, her mind repulsed by the fear emanating from the torc. She skulked in the corner of the tent, as far away from him as she could, hackles raised.

The screeching sound of the beast outside changed instantly. The baying stopped. The ferocity of the sandstorm increased, but not because of the magic the Druidecht wore around his neck. He felt the twin orbs pulsing against his skin, becoming unbearably hot. Annon mastered the pain, determined to keep the dark creature at bay. He clenched his fists and hugged himself, exerting his mind to endure the heat. Sweat trickled down his face with the effort. He did not like the black shroud preventing him from feeling Nizeera's thoughts.

After several long moments, Tyrus signaled for him to stop. He gratefully relinquished control of the magic and the stones began to cool instantly. The shroud passed away and he felt Nizeera's mind again, quavering with fear and anger that he had summoned its power.

"Well done," Tyrus said.

"I would have killed it easily enough," Kiranrao said petulantly. "Next time, send me to do such work."

Tyrus turned and looked at the Romani solemnly. "That was a Vecser, Kiranrao. The plural is *Vecses,* as they hunt in packs. It was trying to get our scent. They are different from Weir . . . more like dogs than cats. Their hinds are lean, like a greyhound, but their chests are massive and their jaws lock tight. They have long tails with a pod-like sac on the ends. I did not want it getting our scent yet. Annon's suggestion avoided the confrontation."

Kiranrao leaned forward, his jaw jutting arrogantly. "Tyrus, you are as fearful as a child. I could feel it all the way over here. If you could only see yourself. We haven't even entered the Scourgelands yet and you are already trembling."

Annon felt a surge of anger at Kiranrao's words. He had noticed the tremor in Tyrus's hand as well, but he would never have stated it as nakedly as Kiranrao had.

"Of course I am terrified," Tyrus replied, a half smirk on his mouth. "I know what we are about to face. I know the dangers far better than you. Trust me, Kiranrao. Even you will face your fears when we enter. Even you."

The Romani snorted. "I fear nothing. You lacked the proper weapons when you last ventured in there."

"We will see."

Annon did not like the tension filling the tent. He watched the two men stare at each other, wrestling with their expressions instead of words, their faces illuminated by the flames in Tyrus's hands. Kiranrao rolled over against the pile of provisions, turning his back on them all.

Annon breathed easier when he did.

A firm hand jostled Annon's shoulder, rousing him from his sleep. "The storm is easing. We will go." It was Tyrus.

Annon rubbed his eyes, his neck stiff and his legs cramped from the awkward position inside the tent. The others were coming awake as well and the tent door flapped open in the breeze.

Annon stood and stretched and tried to speak to Nizeera, but she was still angry with him and skulked out of the tent ahead of him. Ducking his head to pass through the flap, he saw the air had a strange greenish cast to it, still full of dust, but the visibility was much improved. The wall of the storm was ahead of them now and the amount of sand that had built up around the tent wall was surprising. The camels were hacking and snorting, their hides thick with dust and sand, and several rebuffed the drovers who were trying to tend them.

Craning his neck, Annon stared up at the sky and saw that the sun had already faded into twilight.

Tyrus emerged from the tent and tossed a water bladder to Annon. "Fill your pack with provisions, as much as you can safely carry. There will be no other food inside the Scourgelands. We're going tonight."

"Why not wait until sunrise?" Annon asked, brushing the dust from his sleeve. The drovers were beginning to load the camels with burdens.

"A thought," Tyrus replied, approaching him. "That sandstorm is blowing directly toward the Scourgelands. It will lose its fury when it reaches the trees, but if we approach from behind it—"

"Then it will shield us from the gaze of those who watch the borders," Annon said, realizing it. He chuckled to himself. Tyrus was a cunning man. "You are right. And approaching by night will also help hide us."

"Precisely. I thought the storm would delay us, but actually it comes as a boon. It was impenetrable, remember? The darkness lasted for a long time before the storm blew past us. The drovers know we are close to the borders of the Scourgelands. The presence of the Vecses tells me that Shirikant is watching the borders closely for us. Let's take advantage of the storm to slip inside unnoticed."

"I didn't realize we were that close," Annon said nervously.

"We are," Tyrus said, and then motioned for him to return to the tent and fetch food for the journey. Annon did so, stuffing his pack with dried meats and fruits, nuts, and seeds. The Boeotians did not make things like cheeses or breads. Their fare was hunted or collected among the roots or other edible plants that were unfamiliar to Annon. He missed Dame Nestra's bread and honey, wishing selfishly that he could borrow the Tay al-Ard for just a moment to return to Wayland and fetch some for them. He longed for the simple Druidecht life he had left behind when he had chosen to answer Tyrus's summons.

Annon secured the straps of his pack and shouldered it. There was still plenty of food left behind, and Tyrus gave instructions to the drovers to take it back along the path they had come from. He described a rock formation that he had pointed out to them earlier, one with a distinctive tower-like structure that stood above the rest. He instructed the drovers to leave the food there and that it would be used after their quest was finished. The drovers glanced at each other and looked at Tyrus in wary disbelief. Annon could see that they did not believe any of them would survive. But they agreed to do as they were bid out of loyalty to the Empress.

Tyrus explained his plan to the others and they set off into the darkening night. The storm had left so much dust in the air that the stars were invisible. The heat from the day was still oppressive, even though the sun had set. Annon trudged through the sandy dunes and noticed Hettie scouting ahead. She stopped and studied the series of tracks left by the Vecses. Crouching by them, she gazed at the shape and followed the trail a short distance.

Annon approached her. "I wish I had your skill," he muttered softly. "Are those even tracks at all?"

Hettie looked up at him and nodded. "Heavy creatures, judging by the depth of the prints. These are still fresh. See how their tails drag behind it, like this? I've never seen such tracks before."

Her eyes showed her alarm and unease. He knelt and gripped her shoulder. "Be careful, Hettie. Just promise me you'll be careful."

She could have said the same thing in return, but she did not. They stared at each other, feeling a sudden surge of intense emotions. Their mother had been pregnant when she had ventured into the Scourgelands. Eighteen years ago, under a similar starlit sky. Annon and Hettie were children of the Scourgelands in a way. The thought sent a black chill through him. They both rose and Hettie gave him a quick, forceful hug.

Into the night they walked, keeping close, remaining silent. Like Paedrin, Annon preferred being on his feet instead of riding the truculent camels. He watched for signs of spirit life and observed nothing. The land was full of dead, wasted dunes. He had always envisioned the Scourgelands as a forest, yet he wondered what he would find when they reached there. Mapmakers were completely unable to chart the vastness of its domains and usually labeled the northern edge of their work with threatening words, as if to warn away curious adventurers. That was also likely Shirikant's influence, to make the place seem even more forbidding.

Annon's legs and ankles felt strong as he walked, hearing the soft tread of Nizeera's paws behind him. He was grateful for her presence, even though she kept her mind veiled.

The night was dark and lonely and the sweltering heat from the day had vanished at last and turned to bone-chilling cold. On they walked, deeper into the gloom. The dust cloud finally vanished, revealing a startlingly small sliver of moon. The night wore on as the myriad stars spun overhead. Often he had stared up at the vast heavens, wondering what lay deeper in that vast, jeweled expanse. Was it merely a screen that hid from view glimpses of scenes too wonderful to behold?

Yes.

Annon glanced back at Nizeera, grateful for the contact at last. He did not chide her for her reticence, for he was grateful to have earned her companionship again. Gazing back at the sky, he was overwhelmed by the sheer immensity of the horizon.

In a while, a touch of brightness began to thread the eastern horizon, though they were still marching northward. Annon glanced at each of his companions in turn, trying to commit the moment to memory. What a disparate group they made. Khiara spoke softly to Prince Aran in the Vaettir tongue, her look forlorn and nervous. Baylen walked with grim determination, gazing ahead periodically to judge the distance. Kiranrao skulked, keeping apart from the others. Hettie and Paedrin bantered with each other, the Bhikhu always ready with a quip. Phae and Shion were walking near each other. Neither of them spoke. So many differences. The only commonality really was Tyrus Paracelsus, the mastermind behind the expedition. Annon watched him more than the others, wondering why he always seemed to call out Annon to counsel with or position as potential leader. Annon felt the ring on his finger that would summon the Tay al-Ard into his hand. He kept that knowledge secret and wondered if there were other secrets to be learned.

The Scourgelands.

Annon nearly caught his breath when he saw them, appearing out of the gloom—a massive wall of unruly trees. The vicious sandstorm had slammed into the impenetrable woods and spent its fury out. Fresh sand was everywhere, clearing tracks or trails. Annon's heart lurched at the sight.

The Druidecht had always considered the twisted shape of oak trees to be a slightly frightening thing. The tortured limbs and branches often took on grotesque shapes. The trees of the Scourgelands were ancient, hulking and misshapen beyond anything he could have expected. Several trees were so huge and bent that their limbs were too heavy to hold up and sagged on the blighted earth. The trunks were wide enough that it would have taken all of them to join hands before managing to clasp the entire tree. The air had a rotten, decaying smell. Mixed with the sparse leaves were dense, shaggy moss and other growth, probably mistletoe. The colors were muted because of the glowing sunrise, but they revealed themselves in swaths of greens, grays, and mottled browns. Each oak was unique and there was no symmetry or pattern to the forest. Some had branches forked like towers into the drab sky. Others were so twisted and bent that they seemed to be crawling across the earth like fat spiders with too much bulk.

There were no ferns or shocks of crabgrass or other signs of plant life—only the presence of ancient, hulking trees. The woods had a presence, a majesty that went beyond his ability to describe. But it was a terrible majesty, a powerful force that scorned the approaching mortals. The Scourgelands seemed to bid them, in whispered, haughty tones, to enter its midst and die.

Annon heard a muffled intake of breath, a sob unable to be concealed. He turned and saw Phae, her lashes wet, as she stared at the Scourgelands. She stopped in her tracks, unable to calm her trembling. Tyrus joined her side, putting his arm around her. Shion was there as well, even his face betraying some deep emotion. Was he reliving memories of the place? Was this where he had earned the scars on his face?

"It's so sad," Phae said in a choked voice. "I feel them, Father. I can feel them even from here. This is a terrible place. Such terrible sadness." She coughed against her wrist, then buried her face against her father's cloak. "The memories. There are so many memories."

Annon's heart clenched with shared pain as he watched Phae suffer. His own heart felt as if it would burst when he saw the oaks and realized that he had lost Neodesha forever. Mortals were banished from Mirrowen because of these trees, the barrier preventing the two worlds from communing.

It reminded Annon, very briefly, of how the sick woods around Havenrook felt. Those had suffered from neglect and the relentless gambling and commerce of the Preachán. Wagons had carved ruts into the dirt. Axes had sliced a crooked path through the forest to reach its destination. No such road greeted them into the Scourgelands. The twisted, tangled oaks were a buttress—a fortress of colossal size that stretched across the horizon in both directions.

Tyrus murmured softly to his daughter, trying to help her steel herself. Annon saw a sick pallor on Phae's cheeks. She nodded at something her father said, but Annon noticed her arm clutching her stomach, as if her bowels troubled her.

"Why are we dawdling?" Kiranrao said with a raspy voice. His eyes glittered as he stared at the trees. "Let's finish this madness."

"The madness is only beginning," Tyrus said stonily. "Remember my warning. Come to me when I yell the word *Hasten*. I will not wait for anyone. We must act as one." His breath started to quicken, his eyes crinkling with worry. Clutching Phae to him tightly, he kissed the top of her head. Then letting her go, he began marching toward the maw of the wicked trees.

Annon stared at him, amazed at the courage. His own heart was teeming with trepidation.

Go, Druidecht, Nizeera thought, nudging his leg with her nose. *I fulfill my oath at last.*

"Why is it that we fear dark places? Even a place well trodden by us through time can arouse the greatest foreboding when un-illuminated. We tread carefully. Our ears strain at every sound. Darkness is but a pause in breath of a voice we do not wish to hear speak."

- Possidius Adeodat, Archivist of Kenatos

XV

Despite the limited sunlight, the Scourgelands were deep and impenetrable. The trees were huge and twisted, thick with moss and lichen. As they entered the shadowed realm, Paedrin felt his pulse quicken with dread. He scanned everywhere, gazing quickly at the trees but never lingering to stare at any one of them for longer than an instant, having been warned by Tyrus that doing so would jeopardize his memories by exposing them to the magic of the Dryad sentinels.

Phae explained that a Dryad could snatch away a single memory or purge a person's entire remembrance of himself. It was a fearful power and Phae warned that they should avoid the complete mind purge altogether by not looking directly at any tree. Which was difficult to consider since the size of the oaks defied belief—they towered over everyone, their warped branches braided to prevent him, or any Vaettir-born, from escaping the net of hooked limbs. The power of flight would be hampered, but there were pockets of space where he would be able to maneuver and use the advantages that his race and the Shatalin blade provided.

The ground was a whorl of desiccated leaves and twigs that snapped and crunched with every step. Even as light-footed as Paedrin was, he could not pass soundlessly through such a field. The sound of Baylen's boots filled his ears with the hissing noise of the thick ground cover. He searched from side to side, up and down, every muscle tense.

Hettie was chosen to take the lead, her bow drawn and an arrow ready in the nock. He watched her from behind, admiring her cautious gait, her deliberate movements darting from tree to tree. He would not let her slip too far ahead, for fear of the creatures waiting to ambush them.

Shortly after passing into the shadowed realm, they were met by a barricade of mossy stones, intermeshed with the trees to form a rugged form of wall that stretched endlessly in both directions.

"We called this the Fell Wall," Tyrus said, his voice betraying tension. "We were attacked as soon as we crossed it."

"Let me go first," Paedrin offered. "I can glide up to the trees and see if anything lurks on the other side."

Tyrus looked at him and then at Phae. "Are any of these Dryad trees?"

Phae's face was ashen. She shook her head no and pointed off to the west. "Over there. I can sense her. But this way is safe."

The Paracelsus looked back at Paedrin and nodded curtly. Grateful for the opportunity, Paedrin sucked in a steady breath. He swiftly rose, feeling the welcome giddiness that accompanied flight, and nestled on a huge, bent branch, almost forming a cradle amidst the boughs. The bark was rough with dabs of orange sap, which he avoided. Landing gracefully, he crouched and peered down the other side of the Fell Wall. He studied the ground for movement, letting his eyes linger on the gloom, trying to penetrate it.

The maze of trees went on in every direction.

From his perch, he saw no movement, heard no sound except for the rustling of the branches as the breeze fluttered overhead. This was no forest like he had seen. The hush was palpable, the dim, vague shapes of trees and shadows playing tricks on his mind. He studied the ground, searching both ways as well as up into the trees. He motioned for the others to start climbing.

Hettie came first, bounding up the rocks with agility, reaching the base of his tree in moments. The others were more cautious as Baylen brought up the rear with two huge broadswords clutched in his meaty hands. He faced the woods they had already crossed, forming a wall to defend the others as they climbed.

"It's so dark," Hettie murmured. "What do you see from up there?"

"Not much more than you can. This place is . . . I'm not even sure I have the right word. Loathing comes close. Dreadful."

"It is ancient," Hettie said, rubbing her gloved hand along the craggy bark of the oak. "The trees all feel like they are watching us. We are intruders here."

Paedrin did not want to be distracted by their conversation and kept staring down at the other side, crouching even lower and leaning over to grab a tree branch to steady himself. As soon as he did, an overwhelming impulse to jump seized him, jolting him with the suddenness of the emotion. Not to float down, but to let himself crash to the ground, face first, and die. The emotions were powerful, and he felt the urge to obey grow stronger.

"Don't touch the trees," Paedrin warned, releasing the branch and floating down to avoid the impulse to kill himself.

Hettie's eyes widened. "Are you okay?"

He reached her side, grateful that the terrible urge subsided. "That was awful," he confessed.

"What?"

"Touching the tree with my bare skin made me want to kill myself. I nearly did." He looked at her hands and saw her wearing her bracers and gloves. The same impulse had not come to her at all.

"Be careful," Paedrin warned to the others. "Don't touch the trees."

Khiara and the Prince joined them at the summit, and together the four of them ventured down the other side while the others finished climbing the stones. Something flickered on the edge of Paedrin's awareness and he shot a look to his left. Nothing. He ground his teeth, hating the exposed feeling that enveloped him. He saw the look on Hettie's face as she stared into the deep woods, a drawn, anxious look on her mouth. He wanted to hold her tightly so much, whisper reassurances into her ear. But those words would be lies. He was anxious himself, the dread pall of the Scourgelands settling across his shoulders and burrowing into his soul.

Kiranrao appeared off to the right, a swirl of shadow magic that made him substanceless one moment to the next. The Romani stared at the woods with contempt.

"Let's go," he said. "No traps here. Nothing defies us."

"A good omen," Tyrus said from the top of the mound. "But I have no doubt that the denizens of this place know we are here now."

The baying came from the woods behind them. They had passed into the lair of the Scourgelands unharmed so far, which Paedrin ascribed to Tyrus's brilliance of moving in following the dust storm. But the hounds had discovered their scent at last.

He looked at Tyrus and saw his jaw tighten. "They can communicate with each other at great distances. They'll surround us before attacking, so we have time still. Faster."

"Will you use the Tay al-Ard?" Prince Aran asked.

"Not yet. Only if the situation is dire. Stay together and move fast. We'll change directions often and see how they react. This way."

Paedrin's heart was hammering with anticipation. He was ready to fight, ready to kill. If Aboujaoude could master his squeamishness about death, then so could Paedrin. Strange, hulking boulders covered in moss stood in various points along the way, some sheared as if struck by lightning. The companions walked faster, trying to get away from the sound of the baying. Before much time had passed, the sound came again, also from behind them. It was answered by a call from another direction, ahead of them.

"That way," Tyrus said, changing direction suddenly, bringing the others into step with him. They plunged through the trees, heedless of the noise they made. Some of the oak trees had branches so low that they had to hurdle them to pass. The pungent air grew thicker, not with the smell of renewing loam but with the fetid stink of dying flesh.

Another chorus of bays started from another side, joined by the other two from different points around them. The beasts were responding to their movements fluidly and the sound took on an eerily human sound, like the cry of a child. It made Paedrin shudder to his bones.

Tyrus cursed softly to himself. "Ahead . . . keep going!"

"We should find a position to defend ourselves," Baylen suggested.

"The Cruithne is right," Kiranrao joined. "We don't want to be attacked on all fronts."

"You don't understand their tactics," Tyrus snapped. "The baying is to unnerve us. When they attack, they will attack after it has gone silent."

The sound was achieving its intended purpose, Paedrin realized. The howling came from every direction now and he thought he could see slips of shadows through the dark maze of trees.

"We're heading right toward a Dryad tree," Phae warned, pointing. "That way."

"Follow me," Tyrus said, altering the course immediately. They were going back the way they had come, circling the other direction. Paedrin was sure of it.

"We're heading back, Tyrus?"

"Trust *me*," he said. "Don't trust your senses. We've shifted directions multiple times already. Without the sun, you have no way to trust your bearings. Just follow me."

They plunged into the woods deeper and suddenly the baying stopped.

Everyone looked around in bewilderment and fear. The look on Annon's face was full of dread and Paedrin noticed his friend's fingers start to glow blue.

"Not yet," Tyrus ordered. "Follow."

"What about our defenses?" Baylen asked.

The Paracelsus turned on him. "You're about to understand it firsthand, Baylen. There are no defensive positions. You stay alive. That's all you think about."

"How many do you think there are?" Kiranrao asked.

"We only heard their pack chiefs. I counted probably eight."

"How many are in a pack?"

"A dozen to two dozen each," Tyrus said grimly. "They'll go for your throat. Be ready, but keep moving. We disrupt them by advancing and not waiting. Faster!"

Before they could go another step, black shadows sprang at them from the twisted line of trees. Paedrin whistled in warning, spinning away from the others to launch himself at the first ranks. They were dogs, but not dogs—huge hounds with jet-black pelts. The beasts were as tall as ponies and ribbed with muscle and short black fur. Paedrin saw the gleam of snapping teeth and realized in horror that each of the monsters had two heads. There was no growling or yowling, just charging fetid breath and snapping fangs.

Paedrin felt the whole earth slow into a syrupy haze. He vaulted forward, one arm aiming backward, his sword arm pointing out. He leapt at the first of the beasts with a rush of magic and launched himself like a spear. He impaled the beast right in the fork of its neck, plunging the blade into its heart. The impact of the thrust nearly buried the blade, so he quickly tugged it back and swung around again, for another was snapping at his legs and the other at his arm.

Paedrin could not describe the feeling of calm that centered deep inside his chest. All his life he had trained in the Bhikhu temple, sparring and conditioning his body to perform feats of delicate balance and harsh fury. There was no time to think or plan. There was no moment to analyze. A hundred Vecses had charged into their midst and Paedrin slashed and ripped at them with passion and lethal skill. He saw blinding flashes of blue flame and heard cries of terror and intense emotion.

There was pain. Certainly, there was pain. There was no way he could prevent injuries from such a flood of snarling, snapping monsters. He flung himself one way and then the next, not staying put long enough for the beasts to focus on him. He noticed that none of the Vecses had eyes, but deep sockets that were glassy smooth like teacups. Even though they had no eyes, each beast had two snouts that seemed to know exactly where he was, just as his blind vision could also see them. He recognized that their noses were sensitive and he could easily disable a beast with a sharp blow to the nose, or smashing the pommel of his sword against them. He felt gashes on his legs and knew he was bleeding. But none of them could pin him down or gain access to his throat, despite how many hurtled at him like darts.

Paedrin slashed and turned, spraying blood from another monster as he impaled it with the Sword. He was starting to tire. There was a constant rush of new beasts, each one hungrier to drink his blood than the one before it. He fought off his weariness, wondering how the others were doing but not daring to see. Yelps of pain came as fire engulfed some of the hounds in wave blooms of heat.

There was nothing but rage and determination inside Paedrin's veins. He would not back down. He did not want Tyrus to summon them to flee. He was determined to slay every last creature that came at him.

Just as fast as the charge had started, the hounds suddenly turned and loped back off into the woods. He was sucking in air to feed his lungs as quickly as he could, becoming aware every moment of the shards of razor pain along his arms and legs. He did not sway one bit, but stood poised in a stance, solid and firm as a mountain. He could feel the others behind him, sensing them through his blind vision and quickly tallying their number.

Smoldering leaves licked with flames from the plumes of fire that had been summoned to stave off the attack. The corpses of the doglike monsters were thick around them, bleeding black blood into the ground.

Paedrin glanced movement to his left, in the direction the Vecses had fled.

There.

There was a man in the woods.

He had no face.

Annon remembered defending Neodesha's tree from the Boeotian attackers. He had faced insurmountable odds at that time and had used the pain of Reeder's death to summon courage. The fireblood sang in his veins as he used it to shatter the creatures trying to rip out his throat. Nizeera was a fury of claws and muzzle, shrieking with rage at the monsters attacking them and launching herself into their midst with reckless courage. One had managed to snag Annon's boot in its jaws and tug him down, but fortunately the leather cuff had protected the Druidecht from the fangs. Another beast came at his head and Annon had to grab the animal by the throat and blast it apart with the fireblood. He kicked the other one loose from his ankle and rolled up to a kneeling position, launching fire two ways at once, sending streamers of flame into a massive arc to hold the others back. He felt the stirrings of giddiness inside him, warning him that he was drawing too deeply from the cup of magic.

Annon saw two of the beasts hit Nizeera at once, saw her fur glisten with blood as one snapped at her middle. He charged forward, screaming with fury himself, and launched himself on the upper hound, clutching its maw with his fingers and blasting it full in the face with flames. A heavy beast slammed into his shoulder, knocking him down, and he felt the fangs rip into his shoulder. He could not feel the pain through the flood of desperate emotions and rolled over and sent fire into the belly of the creature, causing it to explode in a plume of ash.

He saw Nizeera sink her teeth into one of the dog creature's necks and slash viciously with her claws down the length of its hide. Sweat streaked down Annon's face as the monsters suddenly yipped and began to escape back into the woods. He was so startled by the sudden change in action that he nearly stumbled as he turned around.

Baylen extracted one of his broadswords from the hide of one of the creatures, and Annon saw a literal harvest of dead around the bulky Cruithne. He didn't even look winded. Hettie shot several arrows after the fleeing hounds, dropping each one she aimed at. A slash of blood trickled down from a wound on her forehead.

"There!" Paedrin shouted, drawing their attention.

Annon looked where his friend was pointing but saw nothing.

"What is it?" Tyrus asked.

"There was a man. Now he's gone."

"A man?" Kiranrao demanded.

"Yes, I swear it. He had . . . there was no face in the cowl."

A shiver of dread went through Annon's bones. He felt a whisper of wind against his cheek, his stomach aching with fear.

"I saw nothing," Prince Aransetis said.

"It's the Shade of Aunwynn," Tyrus said, going pale. "He can't be killed. He leads the packs. We had to run when we faced him."

"There!" Khiara shouted, pointing in another direction.

Annon turned and caught a glimpse of a gaunt man in tattered clothes. There was a pale nothingness inside the cowl that turned Annon's blood to ice. Then he was gone.

"The fireblood?" Annon asked.

"Doesn't harm him," Tyrus replied. "We must go. The hounds will try to keep us here. We must break through their line and flee."

"No," Kiranrao snapped. "You could not kill him because you lacked the weapon that could. I have it."

"You don't understand his powers," Tyrus said. "When he breathes on you, your body will wither like dead leaves. Weapons do not hurt him."

"This one *will*," Kiranrao said, his eyes gleaming with bloodlust.

"There!" Phae shrieked.

They all saw him now. At the edge of the dead corpses stood the gaunt Shade. He was thin as a rail, a bony hand clutching the end of a barbed whip. The hounds began to bay again, their shrill sound grating through Annon's heart. Even Nizeera sensed the awesome, ageless power emanating from the Shade and limped near Annon, her throat gurgling with terror.

"Come to me," Kiranrao said, striding forward. Some of his clothes were torn and shredded from the melee with the beasts. "I will take him."

"As you wish," Paedrin said deprecatingly.

The Romani strode forward menacingly, not feinting or seeking to deceive. "Are you the lord of this land? I defy you, Shade."

The gaunt man faced the Romani. His bony hand suddenly jerked and the whip sailed out, wrapping around Kiranrao's throat.

"Terror is only justice: prompt, severe, and inflexible."

- Possidius Adeodat, Archivist of Kenatos

XVI

Phae's heart raced with the suddenness of the Shade's attack. She staggered backward, her bones cold from the presence of such a malevolent being. Kiranrao's face twisted with pain, the barbs in the whip digging into his neck. He jerked at the cords fastened around his throat with one hand and brought up the dagger to sever the length, but the Shade of Aunwynn yanked on the handle and pulled Kiranrao off his feet with inhuman strength, sending him flying into an oak tree. Kiranrao blurred, his body becoming shadow just before the impact, and the cord went loose. The Romani emerged from behind the tree, face contorted with hatred. The blade gleamed in his hand.

Blood trickled from the barb wounds on Kiranrao's neck, but he stalked forward.

Then the Shade was gone.

Kiranrao stopped, hesitating. He craned his neck to listen.

The whip lashed out again and the end snapped on open air as the Romani dove forward and rolled, avoiding it. He sprang up at once, and Phae saw the Shade had reappeared elsewhere, his bony frame and tattered cloak on the other side of the glen. The howling of the hounds picked up, their incessant baying making Phae cower with fear. Shion was near her, tracking the Shade with his eyes, keeping her just behind him.

Kiranrao launched himself at the Shade, his movement so fast she couldn't follow. As his dagger plunged down, the Shade vanished again, only to rematerialize right next to Kiranrao. She watched in horror as a dripping maw opened up in the blank, sack-like face. It wasn't a mouth. It was too stringy, like pulling through melted cheese. The void opened up where a mouth should be and a horde of black moths, tiny and quick like jiggering gnats, engulfed Kiranrao in a cloudy pestilence. There was a shriek of pain and the Romani staggered away, flapping his arms to ward off the cloud.

He stumbled backward, going down, and Phae saw with blooming sickness that his skin was shriveling like parchment just as her father predicted, the muscles of his arms desiccated and frail. The Romani tried to scramble, but his limbs were suddenly grotesquely thin.

"Khiara, save him," Tyrus ordered. "Shion, Baylen—help cover her."

Khiara's staff whirled and struck the Shade of Aunwynn from a distance, sounding like the clatter of wood against wood. She spun the end around and jammed it into his middle, trying to knock him away from Kiranrao so she could heal him. The cowl turned and faced her and then it vanished again.

"Tyrus," Annon pleaded, "we cannot kill this creature!"

Khiara looked swiftly and then rushed to Kiranrao's side, dropping low and placing her palm on his chest, her head bowed in determination. Her hand glowed orange and then bright, like a sudden glimpse of sunlight peeking through the clouds. Kiranrao's mummified skin was restored again, flesh and muscle filling out.

His eyes, though wild with pain a moment before, calmed as her powers swept through him.

Then the Shade was back, appearing nearby. The whip lashed out, wrapping around Khiara's neck, and he yanked her toward himself. She was choking, her eyes wide with fear, and she dug her boots against the exposed roots of the oak trees, trying to find a foothold. But his strength overmatched hers easily, and he drew her inexorably closer. The maw opened again.

Shion rushed forward, faster than a snake, Baylen just behind him. Phae felt instantly exposed, her protector gone to save the Shaliah girl. She wanted to scream, but she also wanted him to save Khiara. Would the Shade's magic affect him? Would he also fall to another immortal's power?

Shion reached Khiara, grabbed the taut whip with one hand, not heeding the barbs, and slashed against it with his dagger. The whip severed and Khiara tumbled backward, still choking for breath.

The dripping maw opened again and the Shade flung one of his arms wide, belching out another cloud of moths that surged into Shion and swarmed him. Phae stared, unable to tear her eyes from him. Shion pulled himself closer, wrapping the whip around his hand and wrist, binding himself to the length, pulling at the immobile Shade. The gnats vanished and Phae gasped with relief when she saw that their disease had not altered Shion at all.

Aunwynn pulled back on the whip and jerked Shion off his feet like he was nothing more than a small bag of flour. Shion did not sail loose like Kiranrao had because he had wound the whip end around his wrist and forearm. Instead he crashed into the forest floor with jarring impact.

Shion rolled to his feet and hurtled his knife at the Shade's body. It whistled sharply in the air and was deflected away harmlessly, clattering into the brush nearby.

The Shade heaved again on the whip and Shion flew up and over in a dizzying arc, landing with a bone-rattling fall onto the mess of roots and packed dirt.

"Go!" Shion said, wincing. Phae wasn't sure if he was hurt or not. "I'll catch up!"

The two were connected now. Phae realized that by holding on to the end of the whip, the Shade wasn't able to disappear and reappear again. Maybe his magic would not allow him to bring someone else when he vanished. Without letting go of the whip himself, the Shade was fixed to that location.

From the radius of the woods, the hounds attacked again, rending the air with their shrill barks, coming to the aid of their master. Tyrus shouted in warning and Phae summoned the words to tame the fireblood in her mind. Shion had kept her safe during the last battle and she realized she was unprotected. The dogs had no eyes and so her Dryad powers were completely useless.

Her fingertips glowed blue and she saw the ravening pack charge into them again, collapsing on all sides, howling and shrieking.

"The Tay al-Ard!" someone shrieked.

Not without Shion! Phae wanted to scream back.

The woods were teeming with the pack. How many were there? Another hundred? More than that? She unleashed the magic in her blood and sent it blasting into the front ranks as they rushed her savagely, barking and snarling. The flames scythed through them, turning their coal-black hide into ash.

Her father stood by her side, his arms raised, his fingers like hooked talons as he sent wave after wave of flame into the midst of the attacking creatures. Phae glanced over and saw that Shion had found his feet again and struck at the Shade with his free hand. He kicked and punched. Nothing swayed Aunwynn. With colossal strength Shion was thrown down, each time harder and harder, as if he were an unripe walnut refusing to be split open. Phae grimaced at the look on Shion's face. She saw not pain but determination.

And then she witnessed Kiranrao rising up behind the Shade, plunging the blade Iddawc into its back. A sound ripped through the forest—the squealing sound of metal rending wood. It was a haunting sound, a keening rip that made Phae cover her ears as her knees buckled. The Shade arched its back in agony, its jangled limbs contorting into odd angles. The maw on its face opened wide enough to fill the entire cowl and millions of black flecks jetted forth, spraying skyward and disintegrating.

In the end, Kiranrao was left gripping an empty, ragged cloak. Nothing else remained. He tossed the cloak aside.

The hounds turned and bolted, scattering like the moths, like windblown leaves, like the dew frost before a blazing sun.

Shion carefully lifted his head; he was covered in dirt and dried oak leaves. The whip was still lashed around his wrist and body. The handle rested nearby.

Kiranrao tossed the tattered cloak aside, his expression haughty.

"I could have killed it sooner, but I didn't want to stab you by mistake," the Romani said. He reached down and helped Shion rise. Slowly, her protector unwound himself from the deadly implement.

"I'm glad you didn't miss," Shion said sternly.

Kiranrao smirked. "I respect you, Kishion. You saved the Shaliah. We all need her to survive this place." He gave her a look of intense interest and gracefully bowed to her. "I am in your debt, Khiara. I look forward with interest to repaying it in the future."

Khiara's own neck was lacerated by the barbs of the lash, trickles of blood she tried to stanch. "I gave it freely. There is no debt."

Kiranrao shook his head. "A promise is a debt. I will repay."

Then he turned to Tyrus, his face full of mocking. "Is that the worst these Scourgelands can send at us?"

"No," Tyrus said flatly. "We've only just begun."

While Khiara tended to heal the others from injuries, Phae crept up on Shion and brushed some crushed leaves from his arm. "Are you hurt?" she asked him quietly.

He looked at her in surprise, then shook his head no.

She sighed with relief, and he seemed amused by her concern.

"The Shade was stronger than me, clearly. I had a wolf by the tail and dared not let go. He could not hurt me, nor I him. And while I would not die from it, the thought of being gnawed on for eternity by those hounds isn't pleasant."

He wandered over to the brush where his knife had landed and retrieved it, sheathing it back in the scabbard on his belt.

"If only you had Kiranrao's blade," she suggested. "That would have worked."

Shion shook his head, revulsion replacing his calm expression. "I don't want it. There is something malignant about that blade. Every time I am near it, I feel . . . whispers . . . in my heart."

"You feel whispers? You don't hear them?"

"No, that's not it. It's not voices in my head. They're in my heart." He tapped his chest with a finger. "They're familiar to me." He glanced around at the trees, a dazed look appearing in his eyes. "This place is familiar. I've been here before."

She reached for his hand and then patted it, nodding without understanding. In a strange way, it was the same for her. The presence of ancient Dryads was all around her, making her feel tiny and insignificant. Yet at the same time, their magic was familiar to her, a need . . . a longing inside her chest. It was a strange emotion.

"Come," Tyrus snapped. "We cannot stop for long. Other dangers will face us if we stay put." He started off into the trees and the rest gathered to join him.

Paedrin approached Shion. "That was brave what you did. You didn't know that its magic wouldn't harm you."

Shion shrugged and said nothing in reply. He took Phae by the arm and pulled her with him to join her father. The dead hounds were everywhere, marking the ground of the group's first victory. But instead of feeling joyful, Phae was sickened by the carnage. Would the Vecses hounds return with their master destroyed?

They walked for an interminable distance, craning low at times to pass beneath the huge, swollen limbs of the trees. Phae had a sense when one was occupied by a Dryad and warned her father to steer away from it. She could almost feel them brushing against her mind, trying to coax her to communicate. She shut them away from her thoughts, not wanting to heed them.

Tyrus paused frequently along the way, studying the land as if memorizing a trail or trying to remember if he had passed that way before. Sometimes he looked troubled, as if the memories were too awful. A series of strange clicking noises began to echo through the trees, as if defiantly chastising them for entering the forbidden domain. Some of the party members conversed in hushed tones. They paused after several hours for a quick meal from their packs and a drink of musty water.

As they paused to rest and eat, a sound came from far away—the call of some wild, catlike animal. Tyrus stiffened immediately, tilting his head and listening closely.

"A Weir," he said sullenly. "Not hunting. It's alerting its kind to where it is." He swore softly under his breath. "They are more vicious than the hounds."

"They're not two-headed as well, are they?" Baylen asked blandly, chewing on a heel of dried bread.

Tyrus shook his head. "No. But their claws are like daggers and poisoned."

"Wonderful," the Cruithne said. "Will we sleep?"

"No," Tyrus said. "Not unless we absolutely need to and never for long. Staying still is death. We must keep moving. Come." He rose and started off again, somehow knowing the way to go.

At least, Phae thought he did.

Not farther down the unmarked path, they encountered an unending row of boulders forming a low wall. It looked exactly like the row of boulders they had passed over while entering the Scourgelands earlier. She stared at it in shock. Had they come all this way only to be turned around and reach the beginning again?

Tyrus stiffened when the wall appeared in the shadow of the trees ahead. He stared at it, dumbfounded. "That's impossible," he muttered.

"We're back where we started?" Phae asked, her heart sinking.

He stared at it, his face suddenly turning pale. His jaw clenched, his fingers tightening into hooked talons again. She saw the tremor on his lips, the memories spilling into his mind with a thousand fears. She gripped his arm, stroking it.

"Father?"

He stared at the wall, as if it were some perplexing mystery that baffled him. The look on his face was fearful, almost like a child's.

"It's all right," she soothed. "You warned us this would happen. The woods are like a maze. They turn us around." She did not want the others to see her father like this. He was always so certain and determined. "It's all right, Father."

His breathing was quickening, but he closed his eyes. He nodded to her, reaching out and squeezing her hand with such intensity that it hurt.

"I'll be all right," he whispered. He swallowed and took a deep breath. He turned to face the others.

"We're back where we began?" Kiranrao said darkly. "I thought if you didn't look at the trees, you would find our way through?"

Tyrus held up his hand in a placating gesture. "I did. Bear in mind that these woods constantly shift and change. It is easy to lose your bearings without the stars or sun to guide. There is no horizon to fix on. I think we have veered eastward and circled back. This isn't the same place where we started, but we've run into the perimeter again. That means we need to head back away and try to do better at maintaining our bearings."

Kiranrao shook his head with contempt.

Phae saw the looks in the others as well. Their confidence in Tyrus was starting to weaken. It was easy to second-guess someone else's decision without carrying the brunt of the trouble oneself.

She put on a brave face, looking at the others and trying to smile confidently. But perhaps they, too, were seeing the fear in his eyes.

It wasn't the stone wall that had unmanned Tyrus. He had not expected to see it so soon, but he did not believe in his own infallibility so much to think that they wouldn't get turned around occasionally. As he had walked firmly toward the wall of stones, something caught his peripheral vision. Movement in the trees to the left. He glanced toward it, seeing nothing, and when he looked back he spied her.

Merinda Druidecht.

She was smiling at him, beckoning him to follow her up into the maze of stones blocking their path. She was not spattered in blood with a crooked arm. She looked as she had in the prime of her strength, her reddish-brown hair and expression so reminiscent of Hettie that his heart seized with unquenched pain. There was something . . . otherworldly about her. As he stood stock-still and stared at her, it was immediately clear that no one else could see her.

The fireblood.

Had he used too much of it during the attack of the Shade of Aunwynn and its hounds? Had he crossed the boundary of proper use and entered the boundary of madness? How many times had he suffered the hallucinations of his sister when she went mad? Or Merinda herself when she was afflicted?

No. Not yet. It's too soon.

He felt his daughter's grip on his arm, pulling him momentarily back from the brink of utter despair. But he realized with growing sickness that it was already too late.

The madness and hallucinations would only get worse.

"The night has already fallen and the city bells of Kenatos are still ringing. There is word that an army of Boeotians has emerged from the hinterlands northward and is hastening to invade our shores. It is the biggest army they have mustered against us in all the recorded years since the founding of this city. What purpose could they have to throw away their lives against our defenses? What incomprehensible motive drives them? There are even rumors, which I can scarcely give credit to, that the Empress herself leads this force. The gates are shut and the fleet is drawing in to the quays. We are quite safe."

- Possidius Adeodat, Archivist of Kenatos

XVII

There was an unsettled look on Tyrus's face that caused worry to fester inside Annon. Dusk settled over the massive depths of the Scourgelands, thickening the shadows and making every startling sound into a threat. He watched Tyrus from the corner of his eye, feeling his own sense of dread increase. The Weir had found their trail and begun the hunt.

"Why didn't you use the Tay al-Ard when we faced the hounds?" Kiranrao demanded suddenly, his voice full of enmity.

"I use it as a last resort, Kiranrao. Don't question my judgment."

"Your judgment has brought us around in circles so far," the Romani said coldly.

"If you know a better trail, by all means declare it. Otherwise be silent. They are getting closer."

Tyrus was normally more patient with Kiranrao. There was a marked change in his tone to what he had used before. With night drawing closer, their troubles would only increase against beings that could see in the dark—or did not require eyes at all.

Do you hear them yet? Annon asked Nizeera in his mind.

Yes.

Annon felt a sensation of coldness enter his limbs. He tried to check his fear, but it was not possible. Tyrus's story from his last foray into the Scourgelands conjured thoughts that were horrible to ponder.

How far away?

They are coming behind us on three sides, trying to converge their attack. They are fierce hunters, Druidecht. Stand ready.

He swallowed, glancing over at Tyrus and trying to meet his eye, but their leader was steadfastly focusing on the way ahead, dodging over crooked tree limbs and crossing the rugged terrain. The mesh of branches overhead would blot out the moon.

What kind of creatures are the Weir? Annon asked.

Nizeera was quiet.

Nizeera?

They are much larger than the hounds of Aunwynn, the Vecses. They are powerful and subtle, able to blend their coats with glass-like magic that can render them nearly invisible. They are strong and swift, natural predators. The dust from their pelt is poisonous to mortals, making wounds difficult to heal. They will often disable their prey and then drag them to their lair to feed.

Annon stumbled over a tree root, his mind filling with terror. *Truly, Nizeera?*

It is better to die quickly than be dragged off to their lair. I will protect you, Druidecht. I will protect you as well as I can. I sense your fear.

A loud wail came from the distance in the dark, discernible to all.

"They come," Tyrus whispered hoarsely. He stopped, straining to listen. The echoing sounds of their adversaries started up in a chorus as other Weir began to yowl and moan. "They were waiting for daylight to fail," he added angrily.

The sound of a cracking branch startled them. A huge limb crashed to the ground behind the group, as if some heavy animal had climbed into the trees. The sound of the crash was so near that they all started.

Mirrowen save us, Annon thought bleakly.

"Run," Tyrus ordered and plunged into the darkness ahead.

The sound of their pursuers rose up in a cacophony of yowling, mewling sounds, the cracked leaves crunching and hissing. Shapes loped into the shadows, gone in an instant. Annon was unable to see them fully, but he could sense them closing in from behind, and he stumbled after Tyrus in the darkness, dreading to face the creatures hunting their steps.

There was a sound of warning, a shout of surprise, and then splashing.

Annon's boots plunged into brackish waters. They had reached the edge of a pond, the surface covered with so many dead leaves that it hid the expanse of waters like an illusion of ground. Tyrus had stumbled into it first and warned the others, but Annon was quickly behind him and had plunged in next unwittingly.

"Hold!" Tyrus bellowed, his face dripping. "It's a swamp. They're herding us right into it."

"And we have played into their intentions," Kiranrao snarled. He wheeled back to face the pursuers. "They can't come at us from behind. Are we going to hold our ground here or use the Tay al-Ard?"

Annon felt something brush against his boots under the water. He took a wary step backward and used the Vaettir words to summon fire. His fingers glowed, spreading a cone of blue light over the dark waters. The pond was full of ugly black fish, their mouths puckering as their faces emerged from the waters, sucking the air. Little appendages of flesh stuck out from the mouths, and he saw many of them coiling around his legs, the faces coming out of the water to gasp on the air. The sight revolted him.

"There's some sort of fish in the wat—" he said as a huge, catlike beast landed on his back, shoving him face-first into the muck. He felt the claws digging into his muscles and he screamed soundlessly in the water in pain and shock.

"The trees!" Paedrin shouted, sucking in his breath and vaulting upward with the Sword of Winds. He could not see the Weir with his natural eyes, but he could see them with his blind vision and stabbed the first one he encountered right in the heart. The blade sliced through fur, skin, muscle, and bone, impaling the monstrous cat. He felt the shuddering weight of the creature as it slid backward off the branch and fell with a crash onto the ground.

Many more were slinking in the trees, maneuvering through the twisted limbs with grace and agility. One launched itself at him and Paedrin used the blade to go higher so that it fell short and also landed on the ground. But it was not disabled and struck at Baylen with a vicious scream.

Paedrin felt his blood respond to the noise and he wanted to fight. He wanted to avenge the death of Aboujaoude. He heard the ping of arrows and watched Hettie stick several into a single Weir, but the arrows did nothing to injure them. The creature vaulted at her and she managed to duck low so that it sailed over her head. Instantly fire streamed from her fingers, ripping into the creature's hide and turning it into ash.

The commotion of the battle stretched all along the edge of the pond. Snarls and ripping claws came in a rockslide of fury, the Weir bounding into the fray with supple grace and fluid motions.

Paedrin dropped down from above, stopping one with his sword, but another ripped into his side with its claws, opening up ribbons of flesh that stung and burned with heat.

He yanked the blade free from the carcass and whirled around, catching its throat before it could sink its teeth into his arm.

One landed on Hettie and she blasted it in the face with the fireblood, engulfing its entire head. He saw her face wrinkle in pain as its hind legs clawed her legs. Paedrin sliced it open just before the magic of her fire consumed it into ash.

He reached down and pulled her to her feet, seeing her pants stained with blood.

"Hettie!" he gasped in concern.

"Behind you!" she cried.

Paedrin whirled as two confronted him, their yellowish eyes locked in a feral rage. Baylen severed one of them in half with his huge broadsword. Then he went down on one knee and upthrust with the other sword, catching the second Weir in the middle and lifting it up off the ground before slamming its body back down. The look of rage in the Cruithne's eyes was more terrifying than the Weirs.

Everyone was fighting, struggling to keep from being shoved into the pond. Paedrin used his blind vision to search out everyone quickly, trying to sort through the gyrations and movements. The attackers came at them relentlessly. How many? He could see them mounting like waves, coming in ring after ring.

Where was Tyrus?

Annon was drowning in the brackish water. His back seized up with pain as he felt the claws raking him over. Desperately, he lifted his head to breathe air but could only inhale another gulp of swamp water. His panic reflexes were working and he thrashed, drenched to the bone, as he shoved himself up on his knees, heaving the heavy beast upward. His ears were ringing from the water-muffled screams and he realized Nizeera was fighting the Weir savagely. He had the weight of both cats on him and felt his muscles give. He splashed down in the pond again. The strange gasping fish were all around him and he felt burning pain as their suction-like mouths attacked his face.

The Weir toppled and fell over, and Annon was able to rise at last. He sat up in the water, grabbing the slimy bodies and yanking them off. Little teeth had attached to his skin, which he felt shred as he wrenched the fish away. His lungs were still full of water and he coughed and hacked, trying to expel it all. He doubled over and vomited violently.

Nizeera screamed, standing behind him, facing off against two Weirs who stalked him. He turned and saw them, their glassy pelts shimmering in and out of sight.

Pyricanthas. Sericanthas.

He was wracked with coughs again, still unable to breathe. He felt himself blacking out, his vision suddenly narrowing. The queer fish were all around him, faces emerging from the waters, puckered mouths gasping, hungry for his skin. The flesh of his back was in tatters. Nizeera screamed in challenge and launched at the nearest Weir, who caught her midleap with its massive claws and tossed her away like a doll.

Annon blinked, feeling himself starting to totter over. He was going to land in the water. He was going to die.

He saw Nizeera strike a tree and slump to the ground. Already she was twisting to come up and attack. The whole world moved slowly, like some terrible seizure had wrapped everything in mud.

A Weir loomed over Nizeera, its fangs sinking into the ruff of her neck. He could feel her panic and her pain.

Annon planted one hand into the muck, steadying himself, willing his eyes not to droop. He saw Nizeera's gold eyes blink once, connecting with him.

My master—

The Weir jerked its mighty neck, snapping Nizeera's. He felt the connection with her vanish. The Weir tossed her aside.

Thas.

Blue flames irrupted from Annon's hands. One of his hands was still underwater, causing a gush of steam and livid bubbles to rise up from the murky pond. Annon leaned forward, bringing both hands together, and sent a wreath of fire exploding out in front of him, consuming the two Weir instantly and ripping bark from the oaks. He rose in terrible fury, unable to remember the pain in his back or his lungs—unable to bear the pain in his heart at Nizeera's death. Another Weir hurtled at him in the darkness, nothing but two glowing eyes, and Annon snuffed it out with a savage yell. His lungs and brain were clearing from the sensation of drowning and he involved the torc around his neck, summoning life into the blue stones.

He had always dreaded using it because of what it did to Nizeera. He couldn't feel any black terror coming from her now. Nothing came from her now. Grief ravaged his heart. First Reeder. Then Neodesha. Now Nizeera. A blackness welled inside his soul, deep as a bottomless pit.

Annon could see the effect of the torc's magic on the Weir. Several snarled and hissed at him, but they dared not come closer, their ears turning back in defiance as they snarled and raged at him. Annon walked forward purposefully, sending blast after blast of fire into their ranks, walking away from the deadly pond and toward the rest, causing a ripple from the ranks of the Weir as they struggled to get outside the range of his twin magics. He blasted them apart, reveling in their destruction. Some part of his mind was aware that the torc's magic was burning his skin. He felt it like twin shards of pain, but he was beyond pain—he was beyond caring. He staggered forward and the Weir flinched back, some fleeing into the night, gone like smoke.

He sensed a creature of magic in the dark waters of the pond. He could sense it approaching, could feel its thoughts reaching out to his mind hungrily. It was aware of him. It was lurking beneath the waters, all tentacles and sludge and iron sinews. Its thoughts were enormous, like some giant toad the size of a boulder. He could feel it creeping toward the group.

Hettie grabbed his shoulder, shaking him. He could not hear her words. The look in her eyes was desperate. She was trying to say something, pleading with him. Tears streamed down her cheeks. Why was she crying?

Annon turned and saw the others. They were illuminated by the fire raging in his hands, most gathered around Tyrus, each one clutching his outstretched arm. In Tyrus's fist was the Tay al-Ard. Paedrin stared at Annon in shock, his eyes wide with desperation. He was nearby but he had not grabbed Tyrus's arm yet. There was Prince Aran and Khiara looking at Annon with concern as well. Kiranrao's expression was one of deep respect, but he also gripped Tyrus's arm. So did Baylen. Why were they gathered around Tyrus?

He saw Phae. She pushed away from Shion and her father and approached him, shaking her head no.

Then he understood.

Tyrus had uttered the command to gather, that he was going to use the Tay al-Ard to flee that place and the approaching danger. Annon had not heard it. The others had gathered but Annon had not, lost in his revenge and his inability to hear through the water in his ears.

Annon let the fireblood go, taming its magic instantly, and he grabbed Hettie around the waist and pulled her with him toward Tyrus. Phae reached for Annon's hand and all three rushed to join the others. Annon saw a spark of hope in Tyrus's eyes. Together, they gathered around Tyrus, each one clinging to another. With Hettie included, Paedrin joined his hand too.

One last time, Annon turned and stared at Nizeera's crumpled form, his soul grieving with the loss. Tears burned his eyes, blurring the image. He felt someone's hand grip his cloak. Someone patted his arm. Annon hung his head, knowing he was bereft of protection now.

With a whirl, the magic of the Tay al-Ard wrenched them away from the danger approaching in the waters.

"We are thunderstruck by the size of the Boeotian army. They have claimed the quays on the northwest edge of the lake and have begun to set up a siege of some kind. What they hope to accomplish is entirely uncertain. Strange tents made of animal hides surround the shores. The Bhikhu from Silvandom began to arrive immediately, but it will take some time to gather them in from the vast woodland realm they have protected. The citizenry are fearful but brave. We have faced these threats many times in the past."

- Possidius Adeodat, Archivist of Kenatos

XVIII

It took several moments for Phae to gather her senses after the Tay al-Ard spilled them back to the earth. The night was deep and foreboding, thick with clinging shadows. The hulking massive trees formed wedges to box them in, offering only a little bit of light, faint silver threads from a waning moon.

"Where are we?" Kiranrao demanded.

"Be silent!" Tyrus snarled at the Romani. He shook off their grasping hands and strode a few paces away, before whirling and facing them again. His face was nearly lost in shadows, but Phae could sense the tumultuous anger seething from his cowl. His hands glowed faintly, and she could tell it was taking great effort to rein in his fury.

The trauma from the Weir attack still raged in her heart. Despite all her imaginings, they were more terrifying than she had supposed. Thickset yet fast as quicksilver, cunningly intelligent and near invisible until they launched to tear your throat out. She shuddered at the memory, feeling her hands tingle with the fireblood she had summoned to defend herself. As she gazed around at the others, she saw that all were wounded in some manner—except Shion.

"Our attempt at unity is a complete and total failure," Tyrus said in a low growl, his voice betraying thick impatience and smoldering venom. "Annon, I nearly left you behind to face that demon in the pond all on your own. The torc drew it right to us and if we had not fled, probably half of us would have died back there."

Annon looked ashamed. "I could not hear, Tyrus. I was half-drowned—"

"I knew it was risky bringing you with us," he interrupted savagely. "If Nizeera hadn't died for you, you would have fallen for certain. You must *fight*, Annon! You must use your wits and your will. These are not human creations, with feelings and hesitancy. They are beasts born of ancient magic, and they are hunters. They are hunting us even now. You should have come when I called you!"

Phae quailed at the tone of her father's voice and she saw Annon's shoulder slump with dejection. She had never seen Tyrus this angry, this uncontrolled. Fear flooded inside her, witnessing this darker side of her father.

Tyrus took a step closer, his finger firmly pointing at Annon's chest, as if it were some spear ready to impale him. "The next time I will leave you behind. We don't have time for weakness."

Annon bowed his head, shuddering but silent. He nodded submissively.

Tyrus turned his fury on Hettie next. "And what was your excuse, Hettie? I warned you all we face certain death in this place. You left the circle to save him. I thought you were wiser than that."

Hettie would not take the chiding quietly. Her chin lifted, her eyes blazing in the dark. "He couldn't hear you, Tyrus. You feared he was lost in the fireblood, but he wasn't. He just couldn't hear!"

"That's *his* excuse. What is yours? Come, a pithy Romani proverb would be perfect."

Hettie took a step forward. "He's my brother. What better excuse is there? I don't regret it."

"Weak," Tyrus said coldly. "Pathetic. Look at us. Bleeding. Poisoned by the dust of those beasts. But if we do not act as one, if we do not fight under orders, this land will rip us apart, one by one. Only the strongest will survive."

Phae knew he was going to rip into her as well and she shrank thinking of the lashing she'd get. Her knees started to tremble uncontrollably. Her mouth was as dry as the deserts of Boeotia. She would be a slave for a drink of water. Her insides were full of twisting worms, and she nearly flinched when he barked at her next.

"You, Phae, are the linchpin. You are the key we cannot lose. I know you feared I would leave them behind, but you knew . . . yes, you *knew* that I could not leave you behind. That makes your betrayal even worse than the others. You cannot do that again. You must stay near Shion and myself. We must all be willing to give our lives to protect you, because without you, we cannot succeed. Even if we all die, you *must* be willing to go on. There is no other choice. There is no other way. There is no other hope. You must obey me, child. We risk all because of you."

His anger was exhausting itself. The blue glow around his tense fingers dimmed. He shook his head, as if waking from a reverie.

The tone of his voice was less hurtful, less raw. "Khiara—tend to their wounds. We will not rest for long. Sleep if you can. Shion—guard the perimeter."

After rolling up his sleeve, Annon saw the leeches sticking to the flesh of his arm. Their slimy black bodies were wriggling as they feasted on his blood. Hettie grunted in disgust and summoned the fireblood to her fingers and began plucking them off his arm, their bodies smoking and writhing as she pried them away. Annon clenched his teeth, struggling through the pain.

"On your neck as well," Paedrin said, bending close. "Ugly little pustules." He pinched away several and cast them aside. "You went face-first into that water, Annon. Hopefully there aren't any inside you."

"That's disgusting, Paedrin," Hettie chided.

He dropped into a low crouch, showing his vast flexibility. "I'm glad Tyrus didn't chide me as well. I may not have controlled my temper so well."

Hettie swore under her breath. "How could he say those things?" she muttered darkly. "It was unfair."

"But it was true," Paedrin quipped.

"You're saying we should have left Annon to die?" She was incensed.

Annon looked back at the Bhikhu. His heart was still raw with pain from losing Nizeera. A blast of white-hot heat went through him, but Paedrin held up his hands placatingly.

"I'm not saying that at all. Look how quickly we turn on each other. This doesn't bode well. I made a statement of fact. I didn't say that I agreed with it. See how complex the Uddhava is? There are too many actions, each causing other actions and reactions. I'm not sure Tyrus would have abandoned you, Annon. He may have been testing us to see if we'd obey him, and we failed."

"Testing us?" Hettie asked.

"Why not? We're in a difficult situation. Tension is high right now. We're wounded, frightened, and threatened. How we would normally act under normal situations is suddenly off. Tyrus needs to see how we'll react to this new reality. At least, that's my conclusion. He's using the Uddhava. By scolding us, he's trying to shape our future behavior."

What Paedrin said made sense to Annon, but there was another, darker motive. A thought that slipped insidiously through his own mind. "There's another possibility, Paedrin," Annon whispered in a low voice. The very thought of it made him sick.

Paedrin rocked forward on his heels. "Yes?"

"There is a risk when using the fireblood," Annon said. "If you do not think the words of power that tame it, prior to summoning it, then you can easily lose control of its use. The result is madness."

Paedrin scowled at him. "I know that's been a risk ever since I've met you two. Are you suggesting . . . ?"

Annon stared at him and nodded. "Our mother died using the fireblood to save Tyrus's life. His own sister lost her mind as well. Hasn't he been acting rather strangely since our encounter with the Vecses?"

"He knows the dangers we're facing," Hettie said, her voice guarded. "He also knows the risks of the fireblood better than anyone."

"I know that, Hettie. But he does not seem quite himself. We should be cautious."

Hettie nodded grimly. Then she gazed at his back and winced. "You're bleeding profusely. That Weir slit your back into ribbons. It's still bleeding. Khiara!"

The Shaliah finished treating Baylen's wounds and then hurried to them, her face pinched with exhaustion. She examined Annon's wounds, nodded with empathy, and then put her hand on his shoulder. Her healing magic suffused him. He was always impressed with the *keramat,* and its effects were instantaneous. Her powers had stopped him from dying at Neodesha's tree, earning him the boon of learning her name. A rush of warmth and relief descended from his shoulders, going all the way down to his toes. He bowed his head reverently, feeling the grace of her power washing over him in waves. There was a poignant feeling, a wishing for release from the coils of life. Then the emotion passed and he was healed.

"Thank you, Khiara," Annon said gratefully. In his mind, he saw Nizeera lying crumpled near the giant tree, tossed aside like refuse. Pain gnawed at his insides, replacing the calm relief with darkness. He clasped his knees, brooding. Glancing up, he saw Tyrus talking with Prince Aran, their heads low in deep conversation. Annon resented the scolding. Before he had been treated as the budding leader of the group. Even now, he wore a ring on his hand that could summon the Tay al-Ard to his fist. Being treated like an errant child was humiliating.

"Look at your legs, Hettie," Khiara said. "Let me heal them." Her gift was repeated twice, restoring Hettie and then Paedrin back to their full strength.

Khiara rose stiffly, swaying a little, and then walked back to Tyrus. "I am finished."

"Good," he said gruffly. "We go. Gather around."

There was no time to rest. Annon felt refreshed, however, his strength restored by Khiara's miraculous touch. He could not bear to meet Tyrus's eyes, but he stood firmly and waited for the words that would come.

"I see where you brought us," Kiranrao said blandly. "It's too dark to see far, but there are the boulders over there. It's the wall. You brought us back to the beginning."

"Yes, we will follow it a ways. Then we will plunge deeper into the woods. We need to reach the center."

"How do you know that what we seek is in the center?"

"You'll have to trust me," Tyrus replied, his voice suddenly gaining an edge of hostility.

"Ah," Kiranrao said. "Back to that concept again. I don't think you have any idea what we're looking for or where it is."

A cool wind rustled the trees, spilling decayed leaves. Tyrus stood firm, his face directly toward the Romani.

"Think what you will, Kiranrao."

"I do," he replied. "You've managed to bring us in circles so far. Forgive me if I find trusting you a little difficult right now."

"A good beginning is half the work?" Tyrus taunted.

Kiranrao scowled at the use of a Romani proverb. "Be wary, Tyrus. I may grow weary of you."

"Everyone who came here serves a purpose," Tyrus said icily. "I chose everyone with great care. Even you."

Kiranrao stiffened. "I serve no man."

"I didn't say that you did. You serve a purpose. You are greedy and you've lost your fortune. I helped arrange that, Kiranrao. I wanted you to be very desperate. After losing in gambling, the mind becomes twisted with regret and one cannot see things as they really are. You know this, having been master in Havenrook for so long. You count on it, the ability to trick a man away from his treasure because he's already lost so much. You've played right into my hands."

Annon stared at Tyrus, feeling his mouth go dry at the brutal words coming from his mouth. This was not like Tyrus. He had always been so calm and diplomatic. Now that they were inside the lair of the Scourgelands, it was as if he were taking off a mask and revealing his true self—a manipulative, ruthless man seeking power.

"You chose poorly, revealing yourself at last," Kiranrao said slyly.

Tyrus gave a curt nod to Prince Aran.

The Prince grabbed Kiranrao by the wrist and forced him face-first into the scraggy dirt. The awkward angle of the Romani's arm, the suddenness of the move, startled everyone. It was a Chin-Na technique and Annon watched in surprise at how quickly Kiranrao was subdued.

"Have I?" Tyrus said coldly after Kiranrao stiffened in pain, totally unable to move. "You're discovering that your magic obeys me and not you. I was the one who taught the Paracelsus who crafted it. I know the nature of the spirits trapped inside the sword and they will obey me. You also have a very dangerous blade, the Iddawc. I warn you right now that if you attempt to use it against me, you will fail. Everyone is here for a reason. Prince Aransetis is here to guard me from you. Trust me when I say that I've thought out all of your moves, all of your options. You can't flit away like smoke unless I let you. You cannot draw the blade Iddawc unless I permit it. And while you think you may be fast and can throw the dagger at me, I wear a charm that will send it hurtling back at you with the same force. I cannot be harmed by that blade, Kiranrao. But you can."

Tyrus stepped closer to the cringing Romani, his voice full of disdain. He loomed over the Romani like a hawk ready to pounce. "You think the boulders over there are the wall surrounding the perimeter. I've told you before, this place is like a maze. There are walls inside as well. If you think you can skulk away into the woods and then flee us, you are quite mistaken. Now that I have you here, you'll see this through to the end. You see, I need you here. There are some demons here that only you can kill. But we do this on my terms."

Annon stared at the unfolding scene with shock as well as frightened appreciation for how well Tyrus had mastered the scene. He stared at the man he once thought was his uncle.

"Are you agreed?" Tyrus asked thickly, his cheek muscle twitching with barely controlled contempt. His eyes glittered.

They all stared at the subdued Romani, seeing the murder flash in his eyes. His face was twisted with rage as well as cunning.

There was the distant cry of a Weir, a piercing whine that deepened the darkness around them. Annon felt a chill and brushed his arms.

"Yes," Kiranrao spat.

"Wise decision," Tyrus said. "Aran. Show him what you've been training to do."

The Prince hauled Kiranrao to his feet, but he did not release his grip. Then suddenly, he torqued Kiranrao's arm the other way and flipped him onto his back. He stepped in, turning again, and the Romani's back arched with agony, his fingers splayed. The edge of Aran's hand swept down against the side of Kiranrao's neck but stopped short of the blow. Then with hooked fingers, he mimicked digging into Kiranrao's eyes to blind him. With his mouth wide in an unfulfilled scream, the Prince grabbed his bottom teeth and mimicked jerking downward, as if to break his jaw. He swiveled Kiranrao's wrist again and brought him chest-down on the ground. The Prince landed two soft blows to his kidneys and then stepped on Kiranrao's back, grabbing the Romani under the chin and pulling backward until the thief's spine arched dangerously.

Aran then released the grip on Kiranrao and stepped back, folding his arms, looking imperiously down at the fallen man. "That is what I will do to you if you betray Tyrus."

Annon stared at them in fearful amazement, seeing the cold ruthlessness in the Vaettir's eyes. He had trained his whole life to injure and kill. He was not like a Bhikhu at all.

The look on Paedrin's face was a mixture of revulsion and respect. All of the maneuvers that the Prince had put Kiranrao through lasted only brief moments.

Tyrus's voice was full of warning. "Prince Aran has trained almost exclusively to disarm bladed weapons. I have seen him fight many times, wrestling his opponents in moments and flinging their weapons away. Even you, Baylen, would find it difficult to use your size advantage against him."

"I don't intend to," the Cruithne said with a gruff voice.

"I didn't think so," Tyrus replied. He stared down at Kiranrao and then bid him stand. "Pain is a teacher, Kiranrao. Learn from it. I promised you a reward if you were faithful to me. You will earn it. But I humiliate you deliberately to prove that I can and that I have the upper hand in this situation. Think twice before crossing me or challenging me. Now follow. All of you."

Tyrus turned and approached the wall of boulders. Annon thought he recognized the spot from when they had reached it earlier that day.

He wondered why Tyrus had not chosen to cross the barrier then.

"*There is a wise Cruithne proverb that says thus:* I need not fear my enemies because the most they can do is attack me. I need not fear my friends because the most they can do is betray me. But I have much to fear from people who are indifferent. *Their other kingdoms have not yet risen to our aid. Their indifference to our plight most troubles me.*"

- Possidius Adeodat, Archivist of Kenatos

XIX

A deep fog settled on the Scourgelands just before dawn. It blocked the first rays of day and wreathed the gorged oak trees in voluminous folds. All night they had walked, save a little while to rest, and Phae felt the chill settle deep into her bones. The mist left dew on her face and hair, and she wiped the trickling beads away from her lip, hunched over with fatigue. Only her fear went deeper than the cold.

Her father's sudden alteration in personality had unsettled everyone. They had trudged in the darkness, stumbling against twisting roots and uneven ground. There were no stars to guide them and for all Phae knew, they had walked in indeterminable circles all night long. The humbling of Kiranrao had altered the mood even more. The Romani was like a shade, aloof and silent, sulking beneath his dark cloak and cowl, his eyes burning with hatred. There was a palpable dread in the air, a silent vow of revenge.

Phae stumbled again on a wretched root and Shion caught her, keeping her from crashing into the gorse. The mist gave the woods a ghostly menace and brought out strange smells, dead leaves and bracken mixed with the ever-present stench of decay.

She wrinkled her nose, reviling the scent. Deeper than the cold—even deeper than the fear—a slowly twisting pain had begun to grow inside her bowels. It was as if she had some rough stone deep inside her that was trying to pass its way out.

Sister.

Phae shuddered as the thought brushed against her mind. The woods had been speaking to her since they had entered the Scourgelands, but always it was a distant shushing sound, whispers too low to be heard.

She ground her teeth and ignored the voice.

Sister—come to me.

Phae swallowed, hugging her cloak more tightly around her shoulders. Mud and dirt were caked into the seams and cracks of her skin. She glanced at Shion, seeing nothing but iron determination. He seemed to sense her look and turned his gaze questioningly at her.

She shook her head.

Sister—you must join us soon. I sense the change coming over you. If you do not bond with a tree, the magic will pass outside of you and you will lose all your gifts.

At that moment, it didn't sound like a bad idea.

Choose me.

Another thought interrupted the first. With the thought came a deep compulsion to look at a specific oak tree, shrouded in the mist.

"Be careful," Phae warned in a loud voice. "The Dryads prey on our minds right now. Look at the ground. There are many around us."

"Can we pass through them?" Tyrus asked, his voice stern and impatient. "How many?"

"I don't know," she answered. "I sense others ahead of us. They are . . . thicker in this part."

"Are we reaching the center?" Annon asked.

"Too soon," Tyrus rebuffed. "Don't look at the trees, any of you. Stay close to each other. Come in; tighten ranks. Now!"

The impatience of his voice only increased Phae's dread. What if something had happened to her father? Or what if this was his true self coming out at last, now that they were deep into the dreadful woods? What if everything he had done or said before was an act—a way to lull them into willingly joining his mad quest? A part of her heart went black at the thought and she shook her head angrily, hating the feelings that surged inside of her.

Join us, Sister.

You are the first Dryad-born to enter these woods. Where is your mother?

I will be your mother. Set me free!

Phae clenched her fists and tried to force the thoughts away from her mind. They continued to pass the enormous trees, ducking low to avoid drooping branches. A cold prickle went down her neck, as if an invisible hand had reached out to touch her.

"What is it?" Shion asked her, grabbing her around the shoulder and pulling her close to him. "You are flinching at shadows."

"I hear voices."

"I hear none."

"Perhaps they are only luring me then. When we first entered the woods, I heard them as whispers. Now I can hear their words. They're pleading for me to join them, to release them from the curse of this place." She kept stride with him, focusing her eyes on the ground and not the woods. There were Dryads all around them now. She did not understand how so many could be clustered together so closely. She had believed that each tree was unique and stood alone, protecting one of the portals to Mirrowen. How could so many have grouped together?

Speak to us, Sister!

You are Dryad-born.

You must swear the oaths. You must before it is too late.

"I hear the voices as well," Annon said in a strangled whisper. "They are truly all around us. Tyrus, it is madness going this way."

"Press on," Tyrus replied. "Keep their thoughts at bay."

"How?"

"Yank off the talisman, you fool." He muttered something else under his breath.

Silver light expanded the area's details as the dawn grew more pronounced against the skeletal boughs. Phae wanted to look up and feast her eyes on the light, but she dared not.

Look at us.

Be one of us.

Only you can free me, Sister. Please . . . I have waited so long.

You brought men. Thank you, Sister.

We will each claim one.

Phae tried to cover her ears, but that did not help in the least. She felt Shion squeezing her shoulder, digging his fingers into her skin.

"Can you not hear them?" she gasped in desperation.

"No—not a word."

He will betray you, Sister. We know him.

You cannot trust him.

He betrayed us all.

"Talk to me, Shion," Phae said, feeling desperate. The urge to look at the trees was maddening. "Anything. I can't stop the voices in my mind."

"Baylen!"

The shout came from Paedrin.

Phae turned and saw the Cruithne had stopped. He was gazing off toward the trees, his expression confused. They had nearly walked off without him.

"Baylen!" Paedrin shouted again.

The Cruithne did not seem to hear him. He took a step away from them, a hesitant one.

Paedrin swept into the air and landed near him, grabbing at his tunic sleeve. "Can you hear me? Baylen!"

The Cruithne turned and looked at Paedrin, his expression full of distrust and confusion. He shook his arm free, his face deepening into a scowl.

"What is your name?" Paedrin asked.

The Cruithne stared hard at the Bhikhu. "I don't remember."

"You are Baylen of Kenatos. You are my friend. Now follow me away from this place. Come!"

Baylen turned back and looked at one of the trees, a hulking shape with branches loaded with mistletoe. Phae averted her eyes, feeling the urge to stare at it gnaw inside her. The cramping became worse and she bent over, gasping.

You can hear us, Sister.

We've already taken his mind.

He is useless to you now.

Leave him to us.

To me.

Phae panted with pain. "They've taken Baylen's memories."

"Leave him then," Tyrus barked. "Come! We must get past this barrier. Further."

"I have an idea," Shion said. "Hold a moment, Tyrus." He helped Phae sit, which eased some of the stabbing pain inside her. She rocked back and forth, starting to moan. Looking up, she saw Shion withdraw the little golden locket. He opened it and laid it in his palm and the grove filled with the haunting music. She had forgotten about the locket. The memory of the first time she had heard the tragic song came rushing back. Almost instantly, she was transported back to the shell of the stone house that they had rested in. It was as if she could smell the dust and dirt, remember the taste of the pears she had plucked from the abandoned orchard.

The melody filled the air, swirling around them with its plaintive, beckoning sounds. It was the song of lost love, the death of a friend, the anthem of an old widow asleep in her grave.

The song banished the voices of the Dryads.

Phae could sense them withdraw, as if the melody were anathema to them. The compelling thoughts no longer troubled her mind, though the pain had not lessened much. Shion could see the effect it was having and quickly slung the locket around his neck.

"Now!" Tyrus ordered. "Before the music ends. We must go! Quickly!"

The giant Cruithne shook his head, his expression clearing. "What happened to me?"

"Do you remember who you are? What is your name?"

"I'm Baylen. I can't remember how I got here though."

"Later, my friend," the Bhikhu said with a grin. "You are fortunate not all of your memories were stolen. Come on!"

Shion helped Phae rise and pulled her with him as they started after Tyrus, trying to get through the maze of trees. Fog thickened somewhat as they walked, dulling the sounds of the wood. The smell of rotting flesh grew stronger, the scent making her gag.

"What is that carrion smell?" Hettie said. "Can anyone tell?"

"It smells like your cooking," Paedrin replied, trying half-heartedly to lighten the mood.

"It's over there," Hettie said. "Some kind of bird killed. Two more over there. Already dead."

"What kind of birds?" Paedrin asked her, approaching one.

"Don't look!" Khiara suddenly shrieked. "Annon! Calcatrix!"

Phae heard the flapping of wings in the trees above them, like huge crows bobbing from branch to branch.

The music of the necklace died away.

"One look in their eyes turns you to stone," Annon said. "They're roosting in the trees all around us."

Tyrus stood stock-still for a moment. Then his arm jutted out and blue fire exploded from his fingers as a hailstorm of Calcatrix swept down on them.

Annon remembered facing the Calcatrix—or Cockatrice, as the Druidecht lore called them—in the Arch-Rike's temple Basilides. How fitting that he guarded his inner sanctum with the same monsters that guarded his Scourgelands. He remembered their poisoned claws and how the light emboldened their attacks. It was daylight now and they would all be easily seen with no orbs to crush to bring on darkness as Khiara had done.

The gout of flame from Tyrus was broad and expansive, an impressive shield of fire that was more than anything Annon had ever summoned before. The first wave of Cockatrice was incinerated in the flames, but the attack came from all around them, dropping down with flapping wings and hissing beaks. Annon shut his eyes. *Pyricanthas. Sericanthas. Thas!*

He felt one land on his back and he reached up and blasted it away with the fireblood. Memories of the fight in Basilides hummed inside of him, bringing a panic of dreadful emotions. There was no way to call off the attack, no way to distract the birdlike monsters or keep from being found. Darkness was the only ally and that protection had ended with the new dawn. Surely Tyrus would call on the power of the Tay al-Ard, but would it work so soon? Had enough time passed?

"Hasten!" Tyrus called, answering his premonition.

Keeping his eyes shut, Annon surged forward, reaching Tyrus quickly but butted into by Baylen, who knocked him over.

Clawing back to his feet, Annon rushed forward and they all encircled the Paracelsus, much more swiftly this time. Dread filled Annon when he felt the grip of the Tay al-Ard around his middle squeezing him.

But they did not move. The magic failed.

"It's too soon still! Don't look at them!" Tyrus bellowed. "We must fight our way through this. Paedrin! You are our best hope. You have the Sword and can see without your eyes. This is your purpose. Direct us!"

"I will," Paedrin answered, stepping free from the others and vaulting into the sky, the Sword of Winds slicing a Cockatrice in half as he lifted. Annon felt one pecking at his shoulder, tearing away strips from his cloak as it tried to shred his flesh. He grabbed the flapping wings and sent flames into its body. Hettie was also using the fireblood, as he could sense her drawing deep into her powers.

"There are hundreds!" Paedrin shouted from above them. "Maybe more! Another wave is coming this direction. I'll meet them in the middle and try to scatter them. By the look, it's a swarm!"

Annon felt them all around him, flapping and hissing and ripping at him. He invoked the power of the torc and the Cockatrice fled from him. He needed to find Phae so that he could help be a shield for her. The frenzy of the battle grew hot and fierce. Cockatrice were everywhere. Dead ones littered the ground. There was nowhere safe to turn his eyes, so he kept them clenched shut.

He could hear the slashing of blades, the spray of blood. This was butchers' work.

"Phae!" Annon shouted.

"Over here!"

He listened to the sound and rushed closer to her, trying to endure the pain flaring at his neck as the magic of the torc seared his skin. His presence near her drove off the attacking Cockatrice and they flapped away, only to attack someone else. He could hear their wings beating over his head and sensed their will pressing against his to look up at them, to gaze into their terrible eyes and turn to stone. Annon raised his hands and sent up a whirlwind of flames.

"Paedrin, how many left?" Tyrus yelled.

Annon could hear the Bhikhu's weapon as it sliced through another one. His voice was panting with exertion. "So many still! So many!"

There was another sound. A huffing, coughing growl. A deep snort, gruff and thick and menacing. Annon heard the snapping of branches and felt something looming from the woods. Its breath he could smell from quite a distance, the cloying breath of an animal that had been devouring the Cockatrice.

The burn in Annon's neck was growing unbearable.

"Tyrus," Annon warned, turning to face the new threat.

He heard Shion's intake of shocked breath. "No!"

A new enemy had joined them. The beast let out a roar that turned Annon's legs to water. He opened his eyes, seeing the hunchbacked beast, its fur the color of storm clouds. Its eyes were gone, gouged out by some horrible blade. The scars on its face were livid as it revealed long, pointed teeth. It wasn't quite a bear, but had some resemblance to one. It was bigger than any creature Annon had ever seen. It rose on hind legs, its massive paws and claws swaying mesmerizingly.

The fear that shot down Annon's legs made him stand rigid.

The mist. The fog. Horror rooted into his bones.

It was a Fear Liath.

"There are rumors of food shortages throughout the city. The people obviously are panicking and hoarding what they can. Of course, the larders will be full, for I know the Arch-Rike has stores aplenty. I believe the Preachán are the source of this saying: When the stomach is full, it is easy to talk of fasting."

- Possidius Adeodat, Archivist of Kenatos

XX

Phae could hear the shiver in Shion's breathing. She dared not look up for fear of the Cockatrice, but the presence of this new enemy had changed the feeling in the air. The mist was colder somehow, knife-sharp, and caused her to tremble.

"What is it?" she whispered, afraid to grab his arm, for he had been slashing ruthlessly at the attacking creatures coming down from the treetops. One of the creatures had scored her arm and she felt her skin itching from the poison.

There was a deep huffing snort followed by a snickering sound at the back of its throat.

"A Fear Liath," Kiranrao announced, his voice suddenly thick. "Our blades will not cut through its hide. Fire will not stay it. Its only weakness is sunlight—the hide is vulnerable then."

"Bigger than a bear," Baylen said gruffly.

"Watch out!" Hettie screamed.

Phae heard the heavy paws crunch into the mat of desiccated leaves as it charged directly at her. She lifted her gaze, knowing instinctively that she'd die if she did not. In that moment, everything slowed, and it felt as if her arms and legs were plunged into mud. She saw the look of wild terror in Shion's eyes, saw the twisting snarl on his mouth as he seemed to relive a memory that, though shrouded, smashed against his feelings. She understood immediately what had given him his scars so long ago.

In that same terrible glance, she saw the Fear Liath charging them, its maw thick with fangs. It came like a runaway wagon, hind legs enormous and powerful, thick and shielded with soot-gray fur. Its claws were like silver blades. It was beyond huge, radiating a primal energy and horrible stench that blacked out every part of her brain except the desire to flee.

Shion shoved Phae aside and was struck by the full force of the Fear Liath's charge. She glanced off a tree, losing her footing and going down. She watched helplessly as the monster batted Shion away like feather fluff. He sailed across the grove before crashing into a thickset oak tree. The Fear Liath swiped its claws at Shion, gouging the bark of the oak with savage ferocity as the besieged man twisted away. Phae scrabbled to get to the other side of a different tree and heard its snout snuffling after her, drawn to her scent.

The Fear Liath roared, a sound so close and penetrating that she clamped her own ears with her hands, and still it pierced her. She tried to run but collided with the body of her father. She heard the crunch of the Liath's bulk in the twigs not far behind.

Tyrus's eyes were frantic. Grabbing her wrist, he pressed something into her hand, an uneven stone. His voice was harsh against her ear, short and curt. "If all fails, squeeze it. Squeeze it hard! Now flee! Get up a tree!"

He turned her toward the woods and shoved her to get her going. Phae stumbled and almost fell, but she managed to catch herself. Images flooded her mind of when she had fled from Shion in the mountains of Stonehollow. She had been terrified then. At this moment, she understood truly how deep fear went. The Fear Liath was immune to their attacks. It was hunting her. It would kill her.

"Shion!" she screamed in desperation, bolting into the mist-shrouded woods, leaving the others behind. A bear had attacked them in that abandoned house. His knife had killed it. This time, there was no weapon that could stop this creature.

A Cockatrice flapped straight toward her face, its claws slashing at her cheek. She ducked, feeling the claws shred through her hair, and ran deeper into the woods.

A blast of blue fire exploded from behind her and she heard the Fear Liath snort with derision and knock Tyrus aside. She could hear the sound of it savaging him, the shred of fabric, the grunt of pain from a man, not a beast.

Help us! Phae begged, running as fast as she could, sensing a Dryad tree just through the mist ahead. She didn't know why she pleaded for help, or to whom she pleaded. It was instinctive, born of desperation and terror.

And then she heard the Fear Liath snuffling after her into the mist.

Paedrin was blind, but he could see the massive shape of the Fear Liath in the shadow world of his second sight. It was an inky black blur, a being that sucked in life and light from all around. It was the incarnation of death, a predator to both man and beast. He remembered the fear of facing one outside of Drosta's Lair. This time, there was no Druidecht summoning them to a hollow trunk. He realized that if he had faced the beast that night, with a broken arm, he would have died almost instantly.

He whipped the Sword of Winds around, severing a Cockatrice in half. They were all around him, drawn to his presence as a challenge. Khiara had also risen, using her long staff to bat them away and scatter the rush. She was closing her eyes and so could not be effective, but there were enough that it was not difficult to hit one with almost every swing.

Paedrin swooped down, stabbing another from behind before flinging its carcass aside. The Fear Liath had left Tyrus in a heap and was turning again after Phae, who fled into the woods. Shion bounded after her, already trying to intercept it, fleet-footed and sprinting, but there was no way he could catch up in time. The monster was huge yet quick.

Snarling with frustration, Paedrin dived after Phae, surging through the trees to provide another obstacle. Suddenly Baylen struck the beast's pelt with one of his twin broadswords. It was like watching a blade slice at ooze. The mass quivered, but the edge could not penetrate the hide. Tossing aside the weapons, Baylen grappled the Fear Liath with both hands, using his own mammoth strength to forestall it.

The Fear Liath snarled and twisted, slashing Baylen across the back with its claws. The Cruithne shrugged the blow, dropping low, and tried to heave the monster aside. The two were a tangle of mass, full of muscle and bone and savage sinews. Baylen kept away from its slavering jaws, gripping the pelt and shifting his stance to try to undermine its energy. He was using the Uddhava, changing his attack constantly, cuffing its snout when it tried to bite him again.

Paedrin soared right at it, aiming the Sword of Winds at its neck. The blade slipped harmlessly off its pelt.

"Help me!" Baylen roared. "Aran! Kiranrao! All of us!"

The Cruithne was bathed in sweat, his face twisted with determination. Suddenly the Fear Liath snarled and heaved its bulk on top of the Cruithne, bearing him to the ground with a crushing weight. Paedrin heard the sickening sound of snapping bones. A groan of agony came next and Paedrin blanched with horror. The Fear Liath's jaws snapped at the Cruithne's head, digging into the hair and bone.

Paedrin's heart screamed in defiance. He hacked at the monster from above, trying to draw it away, but every slash was useless against its slippery hide.

The Fear Liath rose suddenly, slashing Paedrin across the middle. He felt the claws go through his skin, but he was beyond pain at that moment, too shocked to comprehend the damage that was possibly done.

He felt his life begin to leech out.

Phae gripped the object in her hand, not wanting to lose it, but also not wanting to squeeze it too tightly to activate its magic. She glanced down at her palm, saw the slender, carved stone with sigils carved into it.

"Phae!"

It was Shion's voice.

She looked back, but only saw the mist. The sound of pain and dying came from the billowing folds. She could no longer see the Fear Liath, but she could hear its coughing bark and sensed it coming.

To my tree, Sister! Flee to the tree!

The lure of the Dryad was clear in her mind. The monster would not be stopped by Dryad magic; she knew that. But if she could climb into the branches a bit, perhaps that would save her from the Fear Liath. She wanted to break down into terrified sobs, but she couldn't. Each step brought her closer to the tree.

The crooked branches appeared out of the mist ahead of her, a trunk large and gnarled, as if its entire frame were wracked with indescribable agony. There were no leaves, only thick clumps of mistletoe. The lower branches sagged to the forest floor. One had broken off, leaving a jagged wound in the trunk.

"Phae!" Shion called again.

She surged forward, closing the distance to the tree. After stuffing the stone into her pocket, she jumped over one of the low-hanging branches. Mist and sweat caused beads of moisture to trickle down her cheeks. Frosty breath came from her mouth as she gasped, feeling the cold even more pronounced.

This is its lair.

Phae swallowed with horror, seeing a darkened cave through the shroud of the mist.

Bond with my tree and I will save you from the Fear Liath. Release me, Sister, and you will escape.

Phae tried to close her mind to the insidious thoughts. She was not to bond with just any tree in the Scourgelands. How was she to know the right one?

She gazed up at the twisted limbs and quickly decided which ones to start on. She climbed and tried to keep steady as she approached the knotted trunk. Phae heard crunching in the leaves, the snuffling sound of the monster's breathing. She heard the clicking noise again in its throat, and she shuddered.

The next rung of a bough was higher up, very wide, and she could tell it would be difficult to climb. She started up the trunk and her boots slid, scraping against the bark. She winced with frustration and fear, knowing she did not have long before it reached her. She grabbed the next limb and began pulling herself up.

A black muzzle appeared around the side of the tree, its fetid breath grunting with the exertion of moving something of its size.

Phae screamed and jumped at the branch, pulling herself higher. She made it to the second branch, but the Fear Liath rose to its full height, easily as tall as where she was. Her body jerked convulsively with fear and she leapt away from it to another branch, landing on her stomach with a painful gasp. She felt herself slipping and grasped the limb's edge, her legs dangling. With her elbows she tried to pull herself up, but the tug of the ground beat her efforts.

She felt something grip her feet and it began pushing her up. Looking down, she saw Shion just below her, arms stretching up to catch her boots.

"Climb!"

He won't save you, Sister. He murders Dryads. You are not safe with him. No one is safe with him. Be grateful his memories are stolen or he'd kill you now.

The pressure at her feet made it easier to find purchase with her arms. She swung her knee up and around the limb and began scooting toward the trunk.

"Higher!" Shion shouted.

A blur of gray-black fur engulfed him. She listened to the sound as the thing's claws shredded Shion's shirt. The roar came again, deafening her with fear. Shion struck back, without weapons, grabbing the beast's tough hide, striking it from all sides ineffectually. He could not be killed by the Fear Liath, and neither could it kill him. But Shion was hopelessly insufficient to counter its brute strength. The Fear Liath sank its teeth into Shion's side, making Phae shudder as she watched him thrown aside.

You will die, Sister. Let me save you. Bond with my tree!

Are you the Mother Tree of this land? Phae demanded. *Where is the source?*

You will never make it that far, child. You will die here, amidst my roots, unless you bond with my tree. I will show you how. Take the burden from me. Please!

Phae tried to rise but felt a sudden rush of vertigo and nearly fell. She pushed herself closer to the trunk.

Can you take me to Mirrowen? Can you bring me to the Seneschal? Phae asked.

There is no Mirrowen. The gate closed long ago. The Fear Liath will kill you. It was made to kill you. Give me your promise and I will shield you from it. Quickly, Sister!

Phae brought up one leg, trying to steady herself, and reached for the next branch higher up. She saw Shion charge at the Fear Liath again, jumping at its head while pummeling its muzzle with his clenched fist. His look was wild with desperation. The Fear Liath snapped at him, snarling, wrenching him away with claws and throwing him away again. Phae balanced on her feet and coiled to jump for the next branch.

The Fear Liath shifted its weight and snuffled toward her, the clicking sound right near her feet. Phae heard a cracking sound. She tried to jump but suddenly was falling as the branch broke off and crashed to the ground with jarring force. She landed on her stomach, dazed, a sharp pain in the side of her head. Her ears were ringing with the impact and she felt dizzy.

The Fear Liath snarled, sniffing toward her amidst the debris of the shattered branch. It would be on her in moments. Phae reached into her pocket and squeezed the stone hard.

Annon sent another blast of the fireblood into the attacking Cockatrice, shielding Khiara as she tried to heal Tyrus. He could see Paedrin lying on the forest floor, his entire front soaked in blood. Hettie was trying to stanch the bleeding, her expression desperate. Paedrin was dying. Annon could not see the Cruithne's chest rising at all. He was probably already dead. He intensified the fireblood against the Cockatrice, spreading it wider and burning to ash all that swept down on them.

This was nothing like the test in Drosta's Lair. This was nothing like what they had faced previously. The Arch-Rike's defenses inside the Scourgelands were beyond anything he could have imagined, even with Tyrus's multiple warnings. The Fear Liath would hunt them down, one by one. Its only weakness was sunlight, but there was no sunlight in this place, only the frigid mist. His own wounds bled and itched, but he knew the others were a priority, that Khiara was the only one who could heal them.

Kiranrao appeared suddenly, emerging from the smokelike magic imbued in his cloak. "Is Tyrus dead?"

Khiara did not look at him, her head bowed in concentration.

"Leave him alone," Annon warned, his fingers burning blue with the fireblood.

Kiranrao snorted. "I don't need to kill him, Druidecht. This place will do that by itself. We should flee while we still can. Khiara, you are important. I will make you very rich if you come with Hettie and me. You can come too, Druidecht. I have no bones with you. The Fear Liath will keep hunting, I assure you. Best to flee now while it's distracted with the others. Come, Khiara. You're wasting your energy trying to save them. They're dead men."

Tyrus began to choke and cough, his head lifting. "I'm well enough. Save another."

Khiara nodded and rushed over to Paedrin, where Hettie was crouching, using her fireblood to join with Annon in keeping the Cockatrice away. The birdlike creatures scattered back to the treetops, cooing and rustling and escaping the devastating flames.

Hettie, panting, lowered her hands, though her fingers were smoking.

Kiranrao's eyes burned into Tyrus's. "You brought us here to die."

Tyrus sat up, his face still showing a chalky complexion. "I never lied about that, Kiranrao. You came willingly."

The Romani snorted. "I could kill you so easily. Your Prince fled into the mist to save your daughter, but what can he do? You've failed again, Tyrus."

Annon watched Tyrus wince as he rose to his feet.

"Give me the Tay al-Ard," Kiranrao demanded.

"You can't kill me with the blade," Tyrus said hotly. "I already warned you."

"I can kill you just as easily with my bare hands."

Annon straightened, facing the Romani, glowering at him.

Kiranrao smirked. "Boy, don't even think of unleashing the fire on me."

Annon knew that he was facing his own death. Deep down, he did not even care. Khiara was trying to heal Paedrin. It was as if they had walked into the deepest part of the Arch-Rike's trap deliberately. If only Erasmus had survived Basilides. He was the smartest man Annon knew. He would have probably solved the problem already.

Because the solution is so obvious, sheep-brains.

Annon blinked, his stomach lurching. Erasmus's voice was clear in his mind. The Fear Liath was invulnerable to blades. It was faster and stronger than a human . . . than all of them combined. But its weakness was sunlight. When he had encountered one in the Alkire, it had made its lair behind a waterfall so that there would be a perpetual mist. There was no waterfall here. So what was causing the mist?

Annon.

The voice in his mind came like a whisper, only it made his heart burn and tingle. It was a woman's voice. A Dryad? It sounded . . . was it Neodesha?

Annon turned the direction he had heard the voice. Through the mist in the shadow of a burly oak tree, he saw a small cave made from the exposed roots of the tree. Inside that cave, he saw two burning eyes carved into stone. Eyes carved into stone? He remembered Basilides, having seen larger monuments placed there to warn away intruders, also with glowing eyes.

Tyrus gripped Annon's arm. "Do you see her?"

Annon turned to look at him. "What?"

"What are you staring at?" Tyrus asked, his face awash with conflicting emotions. "Do you see her? The woman by the tree?"

Annon looked back at the tree, only seeing the glowing eyes.

Annon.

"Fools learn from experience. I prefer to learn from the experience of others."

- Possidius Adeodat, Archivist of Kenatos

XXI

The pain in Paedrin's middle was excruciating. Hettie had stuffed her cloak against the wound, but it was crimson and blood oozed from her fingers. He was so lightheaded that he collapsed in a swoon.

"No!" Hettie shrieked. "Paedrin, wake up. Wake up!"

He heard her voice and roused himself, opening his eyes. He felt Khiara's fingers pressing into his shoulder.

"I'm awake," he moaned through clenched teeth. "Hettie . . . I'm fading." He felt he was out of breath. Each gasp was painful. His vision swam with colors, but the edges were fringed in black and seemed to close in. His body convulsed.

"No," she said tremulously. "Stay with me. You can't leave me here. Khiara, hurry!"

Another set of flapping wings came from above, claws slashing at Hettie's shoulders and hair. She screamed in pain and rage and unleashed the fireblood like a shield above them, blasting the creatures to ash, keeping a steady stream of flame from her hands.

Paedrin's heart shuddered with pain. He wanted to speak to her, to soothe her. He blinked, trying to gaze at her one last time.

There were tears running down her cheeks. Her expression was fierce and full of wrath as she sent flames at the Cockatrice.

Khiara rocked back and forth, trying to remain conscious as she attempted to heal his mortal wound. She murmured a Vaettir prayer, singing to his soul as it began to slip away from his body. Her words were coaxing, pleading him to stay.

"Hettie . . ." he whispered, feeling his last breath slip away from his body, feeling the weight of his flesh sinking into the earth like a mother's embrace.

She turned to gaze down on him, her eyes widening with shock. The flames sputtered in her hands and died. "No," she moaned, shaking her head with disbelief. "No!"

Paedrin closed his eyes, unable to bear the look of her grief.

"I see no one," Annon murmured. "But there is a stone at the base of the tree. It causes the mist."

"Ah," Tyrus said. "A spirit trapped there. Free it, and the mist will depart and the beast will be vulnerable. Go, Annon. Quickly!"

"Give me the Tay al-Ard, Tyrus," Kiranrao said in a threatening tone.

"You cannot have it," Tyrus answered vehemently.

The Druidecht glanced at the Romani, his face screwed up with fury and rage. There was a look bordering on madness in Kiranrao's eyes. Annon backed away from him swiftly and then ran to the tree. He saw the stone, carved into a human face with a look of sorrow. The eyes glowed white against the rock, not brightly—he would not have even noticed it if the whispers hadn't drawn his gaze that way.

Annon hunkered down next to the roots and reached into the small cave. The stone was heavy, the size of a bread loaf but weighing enough that he struggled to lift it out. As soon as his hands touched it, he heard the Fear Liath's roar. The stone was suddenly cold in his hands, so cold it burned. He nearly dropped it and hissed in pain. His skin was turning gray before his eyes. Instantly, he summoned the fireblood and sent the flames pulsing into the stone, filling it with fire and heat. He struggled against its weight and the biting coldness. His hands were scorching with the cold, mixed with fire. Smoke rose from the stone and livid flecks began to seethe inside the rock. He channeled magic into the rock, trying to free the spirit trapped inside.

There was the sound of wild crashing in the woods. The Fear Liath was charging at him, undoubtedly aware that its defense was failing. Panic strained at Annon's nerves. He wanted to hurl the stone and run for his life, but he battled down his fear and increased the heat and pressure. Slits began to form. Orange flames engulfed the rock, surrounding it like a living orb, but the flame was not hot enough yet. Annon drew deeper into his power, feeling the urge and craving for it grow with wildness inside his heart.

Cockatrice suddenly plummeted around him, landing on his back and shoulders, slashing him with their hooked claws. He felt their beaks stabbing at his head, and he knew the pain and the itching would drive him insane if the fireblood didn't madden him first. He screamed in torment, sinking to his knees while clutching the rock to his stomach and filling it with fire.

"Annon, destroy it!" Tyrus roared.

The Fear Liath crashed into the grove, snarling with fury. Annon could not see it, but he felt the monster's awful presence, its insatiable hunger. In a strange moment of sudden calm, he understood the beast's nature. It fed on terror, literally. It was a cruel spirit that tormented its victims with shadows and roars before rising up terribly with claws and snout to eat them alive, creating a feast of fear that only sated its hunger a short while. Some of its victims it dragged back to its lair, where it nursed their fear with helplessness and misery, preying upon those terrible emotions.

The insight was quick, horrifying. But Annon understood its nature now.

Annon clutched the stone to his stomach, no longer having any feeling in his blackened hands. He drew deeper inside himself, using the fireblood to quench his fear. His grief at losing Nizeera and Neodesha was snuffed out. His rage at the Arch-Rike was extinguished. Calmness and peace flooded his heart.

The rock exploded inside his crippled hands. Burning chunks crumbled around his boots, snapping and hissing into the detritus of leaves. The blast sent the Cockatrice flapping again into the trees in full retreat.

Annon turned to face the monster as the Fear Liath's claws raked across his cheek, whipping him aside and toppling him. He still clutched a smoking fragment of rock in his hand. The pain in his face was horrible, but he was not afraid. Not afraid of dying. Not afraid of anything. He tried to sit up, to stare at the ravaged eye sockets of the Fear Liath, to face his death with courage and defiance. As he blinked through the pain, he saw the mist was receding away from the woods, draining like a ruptured sack.

The Fear Liath snarled at him, its breath too hideous to endure, and then it loped away into the woods, fleeing for the darkness of its lair.

"Kill it, Kiranrao!" Tyrus shouted. "It is vulnerable to you now. Kill it!"

"I know it's vulnerable," the Romani said. "I sensed it the moment the rock burst."

"This is the chance to be rid of it. It will hunt us again at night and finish the destruction it started."

"No."

Annon, face burning with pain, struggled to his feet. The finality in Kiranrao's voice was startling.

"You can't take the Tay al-Ard from me," Tyrus said. "Even if you stole it, I would get it back. You are trapped here with us until we finish the task we came here to finish."

"I'm not your puppet! I dance to no man's strings. Give me the Tay al-Ard!"

"I am not as defenseless as you imagine."

Kiranrao snorted. "Hand it over, or I will end your foolish quest right now."

Prince Aran appeared from the woods, his face haggard with grief. "It is over. Phae's dead, Tyrus. Shion's with the body. She's dead!"

Annon dropped the smoking rock, seeing the pain in Tyrus's eyes. He looked as if a dagger had been plunged into his stomach.

A single deep, full breath swelled Paedrin's chest and he opened his eyes again as his body began to rise off the forest floor. The soothing, peaceful warmth permeated his entire frame. The pain in his belly was gone, even though his robes were stained with blood.

Tears of relief streamed down Hettie's face as she embraced him, burying her face against his chest. He pulled her tightly to him, savoring the feelings and sensations that still coiled around him.

"Thank you, Khiara," Hettie whispered, her voice choked. "Oh, thank you! Thank you!" She released Paedrin and grabbed the Shaliah's hand, squeezing it tightly.

Khiara looked ashen, but she acknowledged the gratitude. She rose to her feet, swaying slightly when Prince Aran appeared with the dreadful news.

Khiara's eyes flashed with dread and she sprinted away, rushing in the direction that Phae had fled earlier.

Paedrin quickly made it to his feet, pulling Hettie up with him, and grabbed his fallen blade. He looked at Kiranrao with defiance, wondering what he would do after hearing the news.

"Dead?" Kiranrao said, his face twisted with surprise.

"I watched the Fear Liath sniff her corpse," the Prince said, his expression hardening from sorrow to fury. "Tyrus, there is no point in going on! She was the key to this."

"Khiara can revive her," Tyrus said, his voice choked. He marched after the Shaliah.

"She cannot bring back the dead!" Aran said flatly. "She cannot do that *keramat*."

Paedrin grasped Hettie's hand and pulled her with him after the others. Even Annon followed, blood streaming down his face from the Fear Liath's wound.

They arrived at a broken oak tree choked with mistletoe. One of the tree's massive branches had cracked off. Next to it, Shion knelt, holding Phae in his arms. He was stroking her leaf-strewn hair, shaking his head, the look of abject misery on his horror-stricken face.

Khiara knelt nearby, her hand on Phae's brow, shaking her head. "I cannot heal her."

Paedrin squeezed Hettie's hand, tears pricking his eyes at the sight.

Annon stared at the scene with mute grief. His heart ached, seeing the lifeless pallor on Phae's ashen cheeks. There was no breath. Her arms were limp in Shion's embrace, dragging on the earth floor. He took a tentative step forward, overwhelmed by his emotions—overwhelmed at seeing the grief on Shion's face, the quivering mouth contorted with anguish, the brooding and haunted look in the eyes. The eyes especially, Annon knew firsthand, revealed the true torture of someone's soul. Annon knew of that kind of pain personally and felt empathy overshadow him. Everything they had fought for was over. The quest had failed. It struck him so deeply that he felt like weeping. Tyrus shook his head in rock-hard determination, unwilling to submit to the brutal truth.

Kiranrao, almost in amazement, wandered up and stared down at Phae's body, as if not believing what he saw. "She is dead," he said tonelessly. Then he turned to Tyrus, his expression hardening with rage. "You failed again."

The impact of his words seemed to strike like thunder.

Tyrus looked haunted, his face a mask of blood, debris, and coalescing sadness and misery. They were all blood-spattered and exhausted.

"We go on," Tyrus announced, his voice cracking.

Kiranrao stared at him as if he were mad.

"If we find the center, we can use the Tay al-Ard to come out again. With that knowledge and with the Tay al-Ard, one of us can . . . in the future . . . we can come back . . . if we know . . . if we know where it is." He was stuttering, his words blurring together.

Kiranrao spat on the ground. "I am not spending another cursed moment here! We flee and when the Tay al-Ard is no longer spent, we leave."

"We go on," Tyrus stammered. "I will not . . . there will be no . . ."

Suddenly Kiranrao moved in a blur, grabbing Khiara around the neck and dragging her to her feet, holding the dagger to her side.

Annon was startled, staring in horror as the Romani backed away from them, taking Khiara with him. Her eyes were calm, not frantic, which surprised him.

"Stop!" Hettie shouted. "By the Fates, Kiranrao, let her go!"

"We're leaving, Hettie," Kiranrao crooned. "The three of us are leaving this cesspool right now. Come, girl. I know you've stolen the device already. I saw you snatch it. We depart now."

Annon stared at his sister in shock.

"Leave her with them then, Kiranrao," Hettie said. "I will go with you, but leave her with them."

The Romani clucked his tongue. "Who pays the piper, calls the tune. Come, Hettie. Now."

"Kiranrao, you won't escape here," Tyrus said. "The trees will subvert you. Let her go."

The Romani laughed disdainfully. "I'm tired of playing your games, Paracelsus. You betrayed me. Vengeance is the price. You will die here as you should have died before."

"You won't make it out of here alive," Tyrus said.

"Come, Hettie!" Kiranrao snarled.

She hesitated, her head swaying no.

Kiranrao frowned with a look of hatred and then stabbed Khiara in the side with the blade Iddawc. Annon watched her life snuff out and she crumpled to the forest floor. Kiranrao turned and fled.

"We are betrayed. The bells of the city are tolling. We do not know how, but the barbarians are inside the city. Fires burn in the western ports. Ships have been stolen and sail across the lake to ferry across more invaders. The citizens are fleeing to the Arch-Rike's temple for protection. I've tried to summon a guard to defend the books but none are coming. The Bhikhu fight in the streets. All is madness."

- Possidius Adeodat, Archivist of Kenatos

XXII

When Paedrin saw Khiara fall dead to the ground, stabbed by the blade, something broke inside of him. She was an innocent victim, had done nothing in the world to provoke or insult Kiranrao, yet she was the one who had been murdered. And the reason was brutally clear. Kiranrao knew they would not survive without her healing powers.

A well of grief opened up inside of him, unimaginable in its depths. Khiara had suffered alongside them, never complaining. Her knowledge and compassion had brought great benefit. She was quiet and shy, always glancing with unacknowledged love at Prince Aransetis. She did not deserve such a fate.

A feeling of raw hatred blazed up from a deep, deep well shaft in his soul. The feelings that exploded inside him drove all thoughts from his mind except one—Kiranrao must die. His treachery could not go unpunished.

He invoked the power of the Sword of Winds and rushed after the murderer.

"Paedrin, no!" Hettie shrieked.

She would not be able to keep up with him, nor did he want her to. This revenge was for him to exact. He would hunt him down. He would chase him to Havenrook or farther. Kiranrao was a dead man. There was no way he could outrun Paedrin.

"Hasten!"

He heard the word barked with a loud, commanding voice. It was clearly Tyrus's warning to come back. What did it matter now? The Tay al-Ard hadn't worked when they were attacked; it wouldn't work now. What point was there to obeying him? They had failed. All was lost.

He heard Hettie screaming, but he dodged through the massive oak trees, rushing past them like a breeze himself, the sword held poised, his body spread like a hawk. He saw Kiranrao sprinting ahead and began to close on him.

The screaming went silent.

Paedrin felt a branch slash his cheek as he ventured too near it. The boiling fury inside him began to subside.

What had happened? Was the Tay al-Ard working after all? Why had Hettie's screaming stopped?

The woods were dark and menacing, each way looking like the one before, interspersed with ravines and stunted stumps. As he swooped down on Kiranrao, the Romani suddenly vanished in a plume of shadowy smoke.

Paedrin plunged forward, pointing the sword where he had last seen the Romani, and it struck into the earth harmlessly. He stopped his flight, kneeling on the ground, breathing fast, beginning to feel the first vestiges of panic. His heart thumped wildly in his chest and he tried to calm it. He listened, trying to hear the sound of fleeing boots. Nothing. He realized that he had never really heard Kiranrao's movements when he was engulfed in his shadow-cloak. Closing his eyes, he reached out to discern the Romani through his blind vision.

Nothing.

Wild panic began to throb inside his mind. What had he done? Crouching on the rugged earth, he began to gasp with fear and dread. He lacked Hettie's skills, could not track a man through the woods. His decision to hunt down Kiranrao was purely born of hatred and raw emotion. He had never trusted Kiranrao—had never understood why Tyrus insisted he come along. Murdering Khiara had been the ultimate betrayal, the ultimate sign of the lack of Tyrus's wisdom. Their whole world had been shattered, and he had felt such a raw surge of hate and vengeance that it made him forget everything a Bhikhu ought to be.

With mounting agony, he could almost see Master Shivu's scolding eyes, his look of disappointment and disapproval. This was not how he was trained. This was not what he had determined to be. And even worse, he had left Hettie behind screaming.

Paedrin regretted his decision immediately. He felt the shock of the abandonment. They had left him. Turning, he launched back the way he had come, shooting past the trees, hurrying to return to the place where the group had huddled near the broken Dryad tree. After several moments, he nearly went mad with panic, wondering if he was already lost. Which way was it? The trees all looked the same.

Movement fluttered in the trees ahead. He could hear the coos and clucks of the Cockatrice, fidgeting in the tree line. What had he done? What stupidity, what recklessness! He cursed himself a thousand times, wending through the trees, trying to find the place of the massacre.

His robes were still damp with his own blood. He touched his skin, feeling not even the trace of a scar. But inside his heart, the wounds were deeper, bleeding, ravaged. How could he have been this foolish? How could he have lost himself so utterly?

There.

He saw the broken Dryad tree. Skeletal. Abandoned.

Dropping down to a low crouch, he saw where the others had been standing before they vanished, drawn away by the Tay al-Ard. His mind whirled to make sense of it. If the Tay al-Ard was working, why hadn't they escaped the fight with the Cockatrice and the Fear Liath? Tyrus had summoned them to him and it hadn't worked. Was that real? He realized how little he understood about the operation of the device or its limits.

Blackness swam in his vision. Or was Tyrus mad? Had he lost control of himself? Had he lost himself to the madness of the fire-blood? He remembered the warning that Annon and Hettie had shared with him about using their magic. He remembered seeing the look in their eyes—like a craving.

Paedrin knelt, plunging the blade into the ground, and rested on its hilt, breathing heavily. The others were gone. There was not a sound from any of them. With a swallow, he realized the Fear Liath's lair was nearby, probably a cave where the sunlight would not penetrate.

The fluttering of wings sounded in the treetops above him. Spasms of agony pierced his mind. He was alone in the Scourgelands. He had forsaken the quest and his companions in a fit of blind rage. And when the dark came, the Fear Liath would emerge from its den and begin to hunt him.

What have I done?

There was a noise behind him, the crack of a twig.

Closing his eyes, he drew on his blind vision, expecting Kiranrao to be sneaking up behind him with the dagger. He readied himself to swing around and cut the Romani in half.

No one.

He whirled, swinging the blade around in a broad circle. He stood still, poised, a bead of sweat dripping from his nose.

He heard a voice, a little distant and full of pain.

"Help."

Baylen.

When Phae had squeezed the carved stone in her fist, she had felt its magic begin to swell. With the Fear Liath snuffling over her, the stone's magic had drawn part of her—the living part of her—inside its peculiar facets. She lost all connection with her body, but strangely out of all her senses, she still possessed her hearing. The pain from her wounds was gone. It was strangely blissful, like a deep yawn that went on forever. There was no breath, yet everything had an airy quality. She sensed the Fear Liath sniff at her, smelling for a sign of life, but there was none. Then its snout sniffed against her arm and began nudging it, trying to loosen her hand from her pocket.

"Get back!" Shion threatened. She could not see him, but she sensed his presence, like a shaft of light in the dark, too bright to even look at. The Fear Liath snarled in savage anger and the two collided again. She could hear the huffed bark, the snarl of anger, and Shion was thrown again, smashing into the tree next to her.

Then the monster roared with desperate fury and charged away, its massive legs churning through the detritus and scrub.

Shion grunted and knelt near her body. She could hear the crackling of the leaves. She tried to speak to him, but there was nothing she could do—no way she could form any words. She floated inside the crystal, trapped like one of the myriad spirit creatures of Kenatos.

"No," Shion whispered, his throat catching with agony. She was aware of his presence, squinting at the light and how it refracted within the prism of her prison. She heard the ragged intake of breath, the quaver. "No . . . no . . . no . . ."

I'm all right, she thought to him. *Shion, I'm all right!*

She experienced a strange disorientation, as if her body were being moved. The brightness intensified, but there was no way she could blink or shield her eyes. He was glowing so brightly. Part of her retreated deeper into the gemstone, trying to avoid the stabbing glare, but another part of her was curious and she drew toward the light.

"No," he whispered with soul-crushing despair. "Not again."

Shion! she screamed at him. *I'm alive! Do not despair, I am alive!*

He started to weep. The sound ripped through her senses, plunging her into depths of sorrow. She wanted to scream, to shake herself free. If she could unclench her hand, she knew she would awaken—to comfort and reassure him. But she could not control her body. She listened with pain as he wept for her. His words were so soft, yet they pierced her like swords.

"I failed you. I failed you. Not again. Please, not again."

Shion! I'm here. I'm here. Please . . . don't despair. I'm here. I am here!

"Too late," he moaned. "I failed you. I failed you again. My darling. My love."

There was another sound, the sound of a man approaching.

Phae's soul stretched with suffering and anguish. His words . . . what did they mean? He loved her? What could he mean? Why was he saying he had failed her again? What was the source of such despair?

Shion! she screamed at him in her mind.

She heard Prince Aransetis's voice, muffled. "She's still alive. But you must appear to mourn her. She clutches a stone, the same one Tyrus used to deceive you. Her spirit is trapped inside it. When we leave this place, Tyrus will revive her. Courage, friend. Courage."

Shion's shuddering breath resounded through the sob. "Truly?" he gasped.

"It's part of Tyrus's plan. Stay. I'm to tell the others. Hold her close. We leave by Tay al-Ard."

Phae could hear as Prince Aran left. She did not hear what happened to the others. Instead, she could hear Shion's breathing begin to calm. The disorienting feeling came again. The stone moved. She felt the lurch and swirl of the world and it dizzied her.

"Are you . . . are you truly alive?" Shion whispered to the stone.

Yes, I am! I want so much to tell you—if only I could speak. She wished she could relieve his suffering. She yearned for a voice to assure him. It made her suffer seeing him suffer so much. It was a shared torment.

All was quiet. "They come," he said, his voicc deadening, shrouded again with the mournful sound of a sorrowing soul.

⁂

"*Vitess Morain.*" The words were Vaettir-born, but spoken by Tyrus.

Annon stared at Phae's ashen face. Suddenly, her skin began to flush with color and she began to breathe. Hope surged inside him, lifting him from the despair. They crowded around her as her eyes fluttered open.

"Amazing," Annon whispered, covering his mouth. Phae winced, suddenly aware of the pain through her body. The cut on her head began to drip small beads of blood. She looked up at each of them, wrinkling her nose, but when her eyes finally locked on Shion's, she rose up and hugged him, burying her face shyly against his chest.

Annon's heart burned inside him, soothing the pain from his slashed face. His hands were throbbing. He dared not look at them for fear of what he would see. They had survived the ordeal. Somehow, they had survived it, but not without its victims.

Hettie stifled her own tears and turned away from the scene, her eyes glistening with pain, her expression contorted with the rush of emotions. Annon went and slung his arm around her shoulders, pulling her to him, holding her close.

Hettie shook her head sadly, brushing the tears angrily from her eyes. "The fool," she stammered, her bravado masking her worry. "The pigheaded fool. Paedrin, you really have sheep-brains."

Annon wanted to chuckle, but another part of him wanted to sob. "My heart hurts right now. I'm not sure what to feel."

He glanced over at Prince Aransetis, who knelt alone, stone-faced, his mouth curled down in a dark frown. He closed his eyes and bowed his head, uttering a Vaettir prayer under his breath. Tyrus stood solemnly, patting Aran's shoulder, his gaze brooding but controlled. The half-wild look in his eyes was gone. He turned to Annon and motioned for him to approach.

Annon studied the woods, seeing the weave of trees around them. There were strange skeletal oaks, stripped of leaves and mistletoe, blackened and stubby. All around was gorse. They were standing thick in it, vibrant and colorful. The air smelled fresh and clean. Farther away, surrounding them on all sides, were more vast, shaggy oaks, like gnarled sentinels all around.

"What is this place?" Annon asked, his voice hoarse. "Are we still in the Scourgelands?"

Tyrus nodded gravely. "This is the place . . . this is where your mother, Merinda Druidecht, went mad saving me from the Weir." He raised his arm and swept it across the grove. "She burned everything to ash all around here. Look how it is grown and revived. Fire renews a forest over time." He dropped his arm and sighed deeply.

"Was this all part of your plan?" Annon asked, feeling conflicting emotions competing inside of him. He wasn't sure what he should be feeling.

"I had not meant . . . for Khiara to die," Tyrus said heavily. A flash of dark emotions rippled in his eyes, but his iron will contained it. "That was unexpected. I thought Baylen would have lasted longer as well, but no man faces a Fear Liath unscathed. I could not predict how Kiranrao would react in every situation." He pursed his lips, still trying to master himself. "I expected he would try to kill me or Phae. That left Khiara unprotected." He sighed. "Gather round me. Let me explain."

Tyrus knelt in the gorse by Phae and Shion and motioned for Annon, Hettie, and Prince Aran to join them. He had a pained look on his face, but not the anger or madness he had shown earlier. "My heart is heavy," he admitted. "I'm disappointed in Paedrin's choice. I'm not surprised, but it pains me. However, it serves a deeper purpose."

"What purpose?" Hettie demanded, her look fierce.

"I will say what I need to say. You won't like it, but it's the truth." He gazed at each of them, his eyes meeting each in turn. "I did not fully disclose all of my plan to anyone. It is no secret that is known to three. I've deliberately held back pieces from each of you. Don't expect me now to share it all either. I will say what I can. Hettie—you warned me that Kiranrao had asked you to steal the Tay al-Ard. You were part of the deception, making him think that you had stolen it. I was trying to force his move. A problem facing the dangers of the Scourgelands is that our enemies can overpower us when we stay together. The Arch-Rike marshals them against us, using the forces at his disposal to kill us and weaken us. When I learned about the blade Iddawc, and understood that its power would even kill spirit creatures, I recognized it would be a potent counterspell."

He breathed out deeply, caressing the green fronds growing near his lap. "Kiranrao's purpose in coming with us was to be set loose inside the Scourgelands, to help draw away from us some of the Arch-Rike's minions. His magic attracts the notice of the spirit creatures here as if he were holding a firebrand while walking in the dark. My plan was to bring him deep into the Scourgelands and convince him that our mission failed, for I knew he would abandon us as soon as he saw the right opportunity. I even gave Annon a way to summon the device in case Kiranrao did manage to steal it from us. That was part of my plan."

Annon stared at him in shock. He shook his head, amazed. "You've been provoking him deliberately? When you had Prince Aran . . ."

"Precisely," Tyrus said. "In order to be convincing, I needed to appear that my judgment was flawed. That I was doomed to repeat the same mistakes of the past. Only Aransetis knew my ruse. My goal was to trick Kiranrao into believing we would fail. It appears I also convinced some of you. And Paedrin too. Let me be clear. My motives are what they have always been. I've employed subtlety and deceit to further my aims, but I do intend to carry on this quest to the end. Losing Kiranrao with the blade inside the Scourgelands was part of my design from the beginning. He will draw many of the defenses after him and hopefully that means fewer will face us. But deceiving a master deceiver isn't easy. He needed to believe, from looking at all of your faces, that you also thought I was out of control. I apologize for the deception. Now you know its intent."

Hettie screwed up her face. "That comes with little solace, Uncle. You've managed to leave Paedrin alone in the woods too."

Tyrus looked at her shrewdly. "I did not know he would chase off after him like that. I admit that he surprised me. We cannot always predict what others will choose to do. He failed to trust me. If there is a way I can bring him back, I will. Let me think on it. We all need some rest. When the night comes, we will pursue our destination again."

"Now that there are fewer of us, can the Tay al-Ard be used more frequently?" Annon asked.

Tyrus nodded, smiling. "Another benefit of my deception. Now that we have lost Kiranrao from among us, we can speak more freely. One of the things we need to do next is understand where the Mother Tree is in this forest. I have my suspicions, but I believe Phae can lead us there more quickly. I've deliberately had you avoid speaking to the Dryad trees, for I believe that the Arch-Rike is connected to their minds. It's a risk, but one we may need to take to get to our destination faster. We will mourn those we've lost. We will rest a little while and tend to our injuries. We cannot stay here for long."

Annon stared at Tyrus, not sure what he should feel about the situation. His heart ached for those they had lost, yet he knew the risks had been great from the beginning. Hettie's face showed a frown of bitterness, but she was skilled herself at duplicity. Phae stared at her father sadly and said nothing.

Tyrus rose, his presence looming over them. His voice fell soft. "There is one more thing I must confess." He looked at Annon and Hettie gravely.

Annon stared at him. Hettie grabbed Annon's forearm, her look unsettled.

"I may have overused the fireblood already. Since we entered the woods, I've been haunted by a shade. The shade of your mother, Merinda. I've seen her several times already, including at the Fear Liath's lair. She was pointing to the stone hidden in the tree. I heard her whisper your name, Annon."

A shiver went down Annon's back. "Maybe you aren't mad, Tyrus. I heard it too."

"We are reinforced by the King of Wayland. The Arch-Rike's defenses within the city are formidable. Without ships, the soldiers are arriving somehow. It is some arcane power from the Paracelsus Towers that allows this. The fighting in the streets continues. The gutters overflow with blood."

- Possidius Adeodat, Archivist of Kenatos

XXIII

Phae watched her father blanch at Annon's words. He shook his head as if dizzied by the news. "I don't know what this means. Does she watch over us? Is this a trap? Have we all gone mad?" He coughed roughly against his forearm, then shook his head with consternation. "Let me puzzle this through. We should tend to our injuries while we can. Hettie . . . I must rely on your healing skills."

"I will do what I can," she said, scrunching up her face. "I can make a salve that will draw out poison. I have some needles and thread for more serious wounds."

"Work quickly," Tyrus said, smiling gratefully. "I don't know how long we can rest before the Weir find us again."

"I can also help," Shion said. "I've been trained." He gripped Phae's shoulder and nodded toward her blood-soaked sleeve.

"I will stand guard," Prince Aransetis said. "Even I must grieve. In my own way." His dark eyes hardened, his jaw clenching with buried anger. He stalked away from the little grove a short distance and began to pace the perimeter, gazing into the dark woods as he made the circuit.

As Shion knelt before her, Phae watched the daylight glint in his hair. She was awash in surging and conflicting emotions. He had thrown himself against the Fear Liath over and over, even though no weapon or blow could injure it, yet he hadn't quit in his efforts to protect her. He had shoved her feet to help her climb the branch. He had been tossed aside multiple times, but returned persistently, trying to draw the beast's attention away.

But she was unsettled. As her spirit had been trapped inside the stone, she had heard his mourning, and his words had ripped open feelings inside her that she had just begun to suspect she possessed. Her heart wrenched with powerful emotions when he had whispered to her, and she had no idea how to handle them. *My darling. My love.*

What did he mean by them? Why did they awaken in her such tenderness? She had cared about him before. She realized her feelings had moved further.

Shion examined the torn sleeve, looking at the wound. His lips pursed and he muttered under his breath. Taking out his water flask, he uncorked it and slit some of his own cloak to form a cloth, which he soaked and began washing the wound. It stung and she gritted her teeth. The wound was dirty and could get infected, so she bit her tongue and endured the pain, studying his face as he worked.

She noticed that he refused to meet her gaze. It wasn't the companionable silence that she was used to with him. He was brooding. It amazed her that she could interpret his mood, that she could almost see the feelings whirling inside him.

He soaked the cloth, wrung it out, and then began dabbing at her forehead. She flinched with pain, but he continued to wipe away the blood on her face. Memories flashed in her mind, of a meadow in Stonehollow, where he had chased her down and then tended to her as well. Was he even the same man? Back then, his look was dark and violent, mercurial between savage instinct and compassion. While she still saw a remnant of the killer, what struck her more was his humanity, his reluctance to cause her pain yet desire to restore her again.

"There's blood on your neck," he said next. "Those winged beasts clawed at your scalp too. Let me part your hair."

She nodded mutely, feeling her throat swelling with gratitude for how tender he was being. The Dryad in the tree had warned her about him. Was he truly a man who murdered Dryads? She didn't think so. The Arch-Rike used doubt as his deadliest weapon. Shion was not random in his violence or mean-spirited. He was ruthless, but not savage. She felt his fingers delicately part her leaf-strewn, clotted hair and wished there was a pond or a stream. But there was none. His touch was featherlight as he pressed the sopping rag against the forming scabs on her head. He picked away some of the leaf debris and scattered the fragments.

She could not see his hands, but she could feel the heat coming from his body, and it made her shiver. His shirt was in tatters again, his cloak clawed through. But he was unharmed.

Meticulously, he bathed her wounds with water and patted them dry. Hettie finished mixing an herbal concoction and brought some of the salve for Shion to apply. It was pasty and smelled fragrant. He dipped his fingers into the mixture and gently applied it to her many cuts.

"It smells nice," she murmured.

Shion nodded, saying nothing.

When he came back to tend her wounded arm, he slit some of the sleeve to open wider and applied generous dabs of the salve. It caused a little warm tingle on her skin, but no pain. After smearing the wound over, he cut another long strip from his cloak with his dagger and bound her arm several times to protect it.

As he worked, she stared at the claw marks on his face. Someone had tended those wounds—had stitched them closed and applied salve. How long ago had it been? Were they tokens of violence he received from the Scourgelands? It seemed so. The dreadful place conjured many possibilities.

With precise hands, he dabbed salve on the crown of her head, parting her tresses to reveal the skin of her scalp once more. She felt his breath on her neck and blinked, trying to subdue the conflicting emotions churning inside of her.

He finished the ministrations, brushing his hands together briskly to remove the doughy salve.

"Thank you," she told him.

He shrugged, sitting down across from her, clasping his wrist over his knees. He would not look at her.

The painful mix of feelings prodded at her. She could not pretend she did not know. More importantly, she felt she needed to understand what they implied.

"Shion," she whispered, glancing over her shoulder. Hettie was still deeply involved in tending Annon's wounds, stitching the cuts on his face. His hands were coated with the salve. Tyrus sat farther away, eyes closed as if in a trance. Prince Aran was farther still, wandering the edge of the grove.

Shion's eyebrows lifted in curiosity.

"You've been quiet," she said timidly, trying to find the courage to broach a tender subject. "More than usual," she clarified. "What's troubling you?"

He shook his head, his expression darkening with discomfort. She swallowed, trying to overcome her hesitation, and then reached out and touched his hand.

"You need to understand," she said, keeping her voice very low, "that while my spirit was trapped in the stone, I could hear . . .

I could hear and sense everything around me." She bit her lip. "I heard you, Shion."

She felt a small quivering in his wrist. His gaze lifted, his deep blue eyes finding hers. She was a little startled by the depth of emotion pooling there.

"I'm sorry," he whispered breathlessly. "I didn't know that."

She shook her head. "You have nothing to feel sorry for." She swallowed again. "This is difficult to say. I don't know how you came to feel those things for me, but it is soon . . . my heart is . . . conflicted."

A self-mocking frown tugged at his mouth. "Don't . . ." He seemed at a loss. He shook his head. "I don't, for even a moment, expect you to reciprocate my . . . my sentiments in any degree." He looked at her, his eyes burning with a surge of emotions. "I know what I am. I harbor no illusions. I expect nothing from you. I admire your courage in coming to this place. If I can protect you, in any way, I will. If you bid me take you back to Stonehollow, I will." His lower lip trembled. "It *pains* me to see you hurt."

His words calmed her deepest fears and she was grateful she had found the will to speak to him, even when the topic pained them both. "I'm not saying that I couldn't feel . . ."

He lifted his hand warningly, breaking her touch. "No. Say nothing. I will never speak of it to you."

She frowned, feeling the discomfort bubbling up again. "But we must, Shion."

"No good will come of it. I am a monster. For some reason, I have immunity to the evils of this place. But I am a monster still, like the beasts we have faced here. Somehow . . . somehow you've tamed me. But I feel it writhing inside of me, a terrible darkness that I'm afraid will be revealed." He looked her straight in the eye. "I don't think . . . I don't think I want my memories back now." He shuddered.

Phae realized she was shivering. Her eyes flicked with tears. "Whatever they are, we will face them together."

"No," he said in a clipped tone. "I dare not. I don't want to hurt you."

"You're afraid," Phae said, edging closer to him. "What are you afraid of?"

"I'm afraid of the truth," he said, with a hint of exasperation. "I quail before it. I must ask myself, were my memories stolen? Or were they surrendered? Have I murdered babies? Have I slit the throats of the innocent? Would I loathe myself beyond any form of pity if I knew who I truly was?"

She grabbed his wrist. "Stop it."

"I don't *want* to know the truth."

"Stop doubting yourself," she commanded. "That is the Arch-Rike's weapon. It is his best deception. While I was climbing the tree, the Dryad was flinging doubts at me like stones . . . trying to knock me from the safety of that perch. Enough lies. Enough doubts." She took both of his hands in hers, drawing so close their knees touched. "When you thought I was dead, you said something."

His face went crimson with mortification.

"Trust me, Shion. I'm not trying to embarrass you. I'm trying to help you. You said . . . *not again*. I heard it distinctly. What did you mean by that? I've never died before. What did you mean?"

The haunted look on his face brought a surging swell of compassion into her seething heart. She squeezed his hands. "Tell me," she pleaded.

His breath was so shallow, she could barely hear it. He struggled with his emotions, his face turning into a rictus of pain. She waited patiently, trying to lure the words out of his mouth with her quiet. It always seemed to work with him. A blob of a tear crept from his eye and trickled down his cheek. He mastered himself though, holding his neck rigid to the point she could see his tendons straining.

Shion closed his eyes, his voice full of self-loathing and despair. "When I saw you lying there . . . dead . . . it struck me with great brutality that it has happened to me before, long ago. Even though I could not remember it, the feeling was so . . . familiar . . . that I thought the grief would murder me. I had been in that situation before, in my past." His breath became a pant. "I mourned someone . . . who I loved." He gasped for breath, nearly choking on the pent-up sobs. "A blackness . . . unlike any blackness I've known threatened to swallow me. A girl . . . dead in my arms. Was she my first victim? Was she my wife? I can't remember her. I can't remember her face or the sound of her voice. But even still, I remembered how it felt to lose her." He hung his head, his shoulder shuddering.

Phae's throat was clenched. She struggled to speak. "You fear the worst. You fear that you killed her."

He nodded, exhaustion sagging his mouth.

She squeezed his hands anew. "Whatever it was," she promised, "we will face it together. If it truly is beyond hope, then I promise I will snatch the memory away from you again."

He looked at her, startled. "That means you will carry it alone." He shook his head violently. "No."

"Then we will suffer the burden together, Shion. I can see that those . . . feelings . . . those memories . . . have great power over you." She reached out and smoothed a lock of hair from his brow. "These are chains you've bound yourself with. It's time to unlock them. Face them. You have come here, into this dreadful lair, to help me banish the Plague. When we succeed, we'll have saved the lives of thousands yet unborn. Surely that gift of life will help compensate for some of the darkness in your heart."

"You mean *if* we succeed."

Phae shook her head. "No more doubting. No more despair. We *will* see this through." She felt heat inside her blood, a fiery resolve that put steel in with her muscle. With the edge of her hand, she tenderly stroked the claw marks on his cheek. "What sorrows you have known," she whispered sadly.

Her caress made him shudder once more.

She clasped his hands between hers again. "I am very young and this place is very frightening. I'm glad you are here with me, Shion. Thank you for facing your fears. It helps me face mine."

The mask of pain that had ravaged his face was slowly softening. He stared down at her hands and then lifted them to his mouth, pressing a small kiss there. "Thank you," he said hoarsely. "You saved me from despair. You are the most compassionate soul I have ever met."

She smiled at him. "I've always been a good listener," she replied. "Which is difficult, because you are not much of a talker."

A stab of pain burst inside of her, making her double over and wince, her fingers digging into his. Nausea accompanied it and she felt a spasm travel down her spine.

"Phae?" Shion said worriedly, sitting up and putting a hand on her shoulder.

She struggled to breathe through the pain.

"Same as before?" he asked.

She nodded, whistling through her teeth as the shard of agony intensified. Her knuckles were white from her tense grip, but she knew she wasn't hurting him at all. She rocked back and forth, trying to find a way to breathe again.

Hettie approached. "What is it?" She put the back of her hand on Phae's brow.

The pain began to subside, bringing relief. Phae wanted to curl up and moan, but she clenched herself and tried to anticipate the blissful calm that was coming.

Annon and Tyrus approached as well. The young Druidecht's eyes were blazing with alarm. Her father, however, looked knowingly at her.

"What's wrong?" Hettie asked. "Is there another wound?"

"No," Tyrus explained. "It's a twisting in your bowels, a pain like a needle poking inside of you. Each time it happens it gets worse."

Phae nodded, feeling her brow damp with sweat now. He knew what it was as well.

"It's the Dryad seed," Tyrus said. "It is the magic she was born with that allows her to bond with a tree. If it passes outside of you, then we have failed." His meaty hand gripped her shoulder. "How many days have you felt it now?"

Phae bit her lip. "We need to hurry, Father. We need to find that tree."

"I'm in shock that the Archives are still unprotected. A handful of Archivists have barricaded the doors against the invasion. Food is running scarce and all is in confusion. We need Bhikhu to guard us, but they are all engaged in fighting the invaders in the streets. What use are the streets if the knowledge protected here is undefended?"

- Possidius Adeodat, Archivist of Kenatos

XXIV

They left the vibrant grove and entered the skeletal woods once again. Immediately the mood became somber and Phae watched the strain gradually appear on the faces of her comrades. She wiped her face, hardly believing how few of them were left already. *So soon*, she thought gravely. *We've lost them so soon.*

Where were the sturdy Baylen and his twin swords? Where were Paedrin and his constant jesting? Khiara was murdered. Nizeera fallen. Kiranrao—she was grateful he was gone. She glanced at Annon and Hettie, recognizing that neither of them were the strongest fighters. They had the fireblood, which would be a great defense against some of the beings in the woods. But not against them all. Tyrus, Aransetis, and Shion were her champions. In the end, who would survive?

She flung the dark thoughts from her mind. The pain in her belly had subsided, but she felt it on the fringes of her awareness, ready to strike her again. She brushed hair away from her ear, annoyed by her damp clothes, the itchy feeling in her blistered feet. Mustering her determination, she pressed on.

Very little light managed to penetrate the interlocking boughs. The Scourgelands felt like a cage. Strange clicking noises intruded sporadically. Pungent smells lingered in the air. The woods were dark and foreboding, void of life and crumbling into ruin. It was an ancient forest—probably as old as the world itself. She gazed down at the spindly twigs snapping beneath her boots.

"Do you sense a Dryad tree yet?" Tyrus asked her, his voice low and guarded.

Phae nodded and pointed to the left. "Through those trees. I sense her and she senses me. She has not communicated with me yet."

"Let's go closer then."

Phae nodded, following his lead until he suddenly stopped short, gripping her arm.

Her heart quickened. "What is it?"

The others stopped, turning to look at him. Tyrus's face was ashen. "I see her again."

Phae saw nothing, not even the glimpse of a shadow.

"I see nothing," Annon said. "I hear nothing."

"Neither do I," Hettie added. She had her bow ready and arrow at the string.

"She's not speaking," Tyrus said. "Only shaking her head. She's pointing another way."

"Why can't we see her?" Annon said, frustrated. Phae could sense the emotions roiling inside of the twins. Neither of them had memories of seeing their mother. If the shade was real, it would be cruel not to reveal herself to them as well.

"It may be the madness," Aran suggested, his voice stern.

"I accept that," Tyrus said. "I don't feel any different. But I can't dismiss what I see in front of . . . she's gone. Vanished." A frustrated sigh escaped his lips.

Hettie swore softly. Then she looked back at Tyrus and asked, "What direction was she pointing?"

"That way," Tyrus said, gesturing.

"Do we trust it?" Shion asked.

"She led me to the stone," Annon said, his expression dark. "It robbed the Fear Liath of its protection. I heard her voice, Tyrus. I don't think it's the madness."

Tyrus sighed deeply. "I'm not fully convinced. To protect you all, I must be open with what I am thinking. If my behavior seems unnatural, then you owe it to yourselves . . . and you owe it to Phae, to carry on without me. If I cannot go on leading, then you should look to Annon for guidance. I've given him sufficient information to guide you. He is young but he is also wiser than I was at his age. That way then."

Phae followed her father into the new direction. The light was beginning to fade, signaling the approach of dusk. Wandering in the dark again was not her first preference, but there was no safety to be had.

Mewling howls sounded deep in the woods. The Weir—she recognized the sound now.

"They're hunters," Hettie said. "Did they catch our scent?"

"Not yet," Tyrus answered, gripping the fabric of his cloak more tightly around his throat. "They are communicating across great distances. When they stumble across that glen, we'll know it."

Phae's legs were tired from the long walk. Her knees throbbed. She hooked arms with Shion, allowing her to draw on some of his unflagging strength. She remembered when he had chased her through the mountains of Stonehollow and had pushed her, relentlessly, toward Fowlrox. The terrain inside the Scourgelands was rugged and brittle. Each step became a blur and she felt weariness stealing over her as the sun faded.

Welcome, Sister.

The voice in her head snapped her awake. She sensed the tree, could almost feel the dense mesh of roots beneath the earth under her boots. A sliver of knowledge came with it. The voice in her mind was . . . unfriendly.

"I found another," Phae whispered. "That way, beyond those trees."

"I don't see it," Tyrus said, craning his neck. "How distant?"

"A hundred steps maybe," she replied.

Tyrus looked up at the sky, seeming to judge the time before it was fully dark. "I want you to speak to her, Phae. You need to draw out from her what you can. How far are we from the mother Dryad tree in these woods? What defends it?"

"How can we trust what she's told?" Hettie asked.

Tyrus looked at her. "Beings from Mirrowen cannot lie. They may trick and deceive. They can veil what they know and reveal what is useful. They often mislead you based on your own false assumptions. But they cannot lie. You are here to set them free. Remind them of that. If we go with you, she won't appear, so we will stay behind . . ."

"No," Shion said flatly.

Tyrus gripped his shoulder. "She must."

He shook his head. "Too vulnerable."

"It won't be for long," Tyrus said soothingly. "If she won't listen to reason, then we'll continue on our way. Above all, Phae, you must not look in her eyes. She will tempt you to. You must not give in or all is lost."

The scowl on Shion's face showed that he did not approve of the risk.

"Trust me once again," Tyrus said. "She has the fireblood. She is not defenseless." He squeezed Phae's arm. "We must remain out of sight, or she won't appear to you. Do what you can to persuade her."

Phae nodded. She took Shion by the hand and pulled him with her toward the Dryad tree. The others ventured after them, walking slowly. A raven cawed somewhere in the distance.

You dare bring him *near my tree?* The thought had a sneer to it.

I would speak with you, Phae replied, edging closer. The shadows thickened quickly. She could just glimpse the mammoth oak ahead. The trunk was straight and rigid, but the branches seemed a tangle of snakes.

Come alone then.

Phae squeezed his hand and then disengaged, motioning for him to wait nearby. With cautious steps, Phae approached the enormous Dryad tree. There were no longer any leaves crowning it, but thick clusters of mistletoe garnished the branches. It was almost beautiful, but it smelled of rot.

I'm here, Phae thought to her. *What is your name?*

You think I'm a fool and will reveal it so easily?

You're not a fool, Phae replied. *You are ancient and powerful.*

Flattery.

As Phae drew closer, she averted her eyes and kept them on the ground. Her ears were keen for the sound of an ambush. She did not want to summon the Vaettir words yet, but she was ready to. She was nervous and edgy, wondering how she could persuade the other.

You are a child. An acorn. You think you can persuade a Dryad-born who has seen the ages of the world come and pass?

Phae bit her lip. *What have you seen of the world trapped in this forsaken place?*

I saw Tyrus Paracelsus. I saw him fail. My memories are deeper than the roots. Deeper than your timid imaginations. I have supped with kings. I have tasted the forbidden wine. You are nothing compared to me.

Phae reached the trunk and tentatively reached out her hand. *Show yourself.*

To what purpose, child? You are a sister, yes. But you are not here to claim my tree and free me. You spurn our kind.

Phae touched the bark. It was hard and cold, like stone. The wood was ancient beyond anything she had ever experienced. Her fingers played across the rugged grooves, imagining the memories trapped deep inside. What secrets were hidden there?

Many secrets. Deep secrets. You will die before you claim your birthright. Already your seed is failing.

Phae heard the snapping sound of twigs from the other side of the tree. Her heart began to race. She steeled her courage.

If I could free you, would you let me? Phae asked her.

A flutter of emotion blew across her feelings like a breeze—full of disdain. *You did not come here to free me.*

Do you yearn for freedom? Let me help you!

Another snapping sound. Phae closed her eyes tightly, listening to every movement.

You cannot help me. You cannot free me unless you bond with my tree. Save your breath, acorn. You are only a tool wielded by another's hand. We are alike.

Phae sensed the presence of the Dryad around the side of the massive trunk. Immediately, her mind was besieged with the impulse to look at her. It was a craving, a hunger much deeper than the want of thirst for water. The urge buzzed inside her mind with immense force, the curiosity like an itch that could only be scratched by looking.

Look at me, the Dryad whispered to her. *See what you will become. See the curse in your blood with your own eyes. I wish I were never born.*

Phae hugged the tree, pressing her face into the hard seams and cracks in the stone-hewn bark. She shivered uncontrollably, trying to resist the imperious urge that blackened her mind.

You think you can resist me forever? You will look at me, Sister. My will has been honed on the whetstone since the woods were first lit by dawn. Look on me!

Phae shuddered, feeling sweat streak down her forehead. The force of the thought was like a huge thunderhead, making her feel as insignificant as a field mouse. How could she defy such a presence?

I exist. See the cruelty of it. The portal to Mirrowen is closed. There are no whispers. The Seneschal has abandoned us. Look and see!

Phae began to sob. She squeezed the tree so hard that her cheek burned. Tears dripped down her chin, but she refused to look, refused to give in despite the fury of the Dryad's thoughts.

Suddenly the Dryad's thoughts turned to hissing and fury, a woman spurned. Phae felt her father's strong hands on her shoulders as he pulled her away from the tree.

"You've done enough," he whispered to her. "You did your best. Shion, take her."

Her emotions were still reeling from the brunt of the Dryad's thoughts. She felt Shion grip her arm and she hugged him as tightly as she did the oak, pressing her cheek against his chest, willing the pain inside her mind to stop. The feelings of futility still staggered her. The madness inside the Dryad's mind—being perpetually trapped inside the husk of a tree, with no one to relieve her, bound for a thousand lifetimes because there was no man willing to come and be her husband and forge a daughter to take her place. The wasting sickness of the Dryad's mind was beyond reckoning.

"Shion," she gasped with shock. She shook her head, trying to quell her emotions.

He soothed her with a whisper, stroking her hair and leading her away from the tree.

Blue fire lit the dusk, sending a piercing glare into the woods. Phae was startled and then looked back, seeing her father standing before the tree, his arms widespread, his hands cupping lashing blue flames. His head was bowed in terrible solemnity.

"Father?" she gasped, then realized what he was going to do. He was going to burn the tree. "No!"

She tried to shove away from Shion, but he held her tightly.

"Let me go!" she demanded, struggling to free herself. His grip was like iron. He had her wrists and continued to pull her away from the tree. "Shion! No! It's not her fault!"

The flames in Tyrus's hands continued to build brighter as he summoned more and more power into his hands. Waves of heat emanated from his profile.

"Father, no!" Phae shrieked, twisting and jerking to free herself. Shion clasped her like iron bands, pinning her arms and hoisting her back.

Tyrus raised his arms and sent the flames blasting into the rocklike trunk.

Phae heard the scream of torture in her mind. The Dryad's shriek joined her own and suddenly she was gibbering with madness. *No, Sister! No! The memories! He's burning the memories! No! He'll kill me! I can't go back to Mirrowen! I'm trapped on this side! He'll kill me!*

The thoughts made Phae go wild with despair. She tried kicking Shion, wrenching him, shoving him. He seemed to move with her like water, absorbing her efforts with almost too much ease. He didn't hurt her, but she was powerless against him. Even her fireblood would not harm him.

"Shion, please! Please! Don't let him do this! She can't escape. He's murdering her! Please!"

The flames from Tyrus's hands burned brighter as he unleashed the raw fury of the fireblood against the Dryad tree. She watched in horror as the bark blackened and began to sizzle and burn, as streamers of fire started to race up the long shaft toward the huge, snake-like limbs.

"Please, Shion! Please!" Phae pressed her face against his chest, sobbing again. "Please!"

He's burning me! He's burning me! Help me, Sister! I beg you!

"*Attenvost-thas!*"

The words were in the Vaettir-tongue, but it was Annon who uttered them. Suddenly the flames in Tyrus's hands surged and then vanished, and he collapsed to the ground.

Annon strode into the grove deliberately and approached the tree. He opened his hands, which also glowed blue, and began drawing the fire from the tree into himself. His face was a mask of determination and Phae wanted to hug him for saving the tree.

He looked down at Tyrus's body. "Drag him away," he ordered.

Shion released Phae at once and without saying a word, walked over to Tyrus's body and hoisted him beneath his arms.

Phae stared at him in shock, trying to understand what was going on.

"Phae," Annon said, gripping her shoulder. He gave her a small smile. "Make sure your father is unhurt. You've done enough." He went back to the tree and sat against the trunk, his back to it, and bowed his head. What was he waiting for?

She hurried after Shion, who had dragged her father's body back behind the screen of trees. Aran and Hettie were both waiting there, looking unconcerned.

Tyrus raised his head, looking up at Shion, and nodded.

Phae began to shake with fury. "What is going on?" she demanded hotly.

Tyrus rose to his feet, brushing off his hands. He reached to smooth aside some of her hair, but she knocked his hand aside.

"It is Dryad lore," Tyrus said softly, ignoring her rude swipe. "I explained it to the others while you were distracting her. If someone threatens a Dryad's tree, she will do anything she can to defend it. But if a person, especially a man, defends her tree, she owes him a boon. That boon is her Dryad name. With that name, she can be commanded." He smiled slyly. "Annon is going to collect the boon from her."

Phae's jaw opened. "You weren't going to hurt her?"

"A little fire can't destroy a tree that size," he told her. "But I needed to convince her that I was a real threat. And since she can speak to your mind and you can't deceive her, you needed to believe it as well." He reached for her again, and this time she didn't rebuff him. He stroked the side of her cheek and wiped away a trail of tears.

She wanted to glower at him but at the moment felt so relieved she was mostly just grateful.

"You are too clever," she said sternly. "I wish it didn't hurt me so much."

Tyrus nodded knowingly and patted her shoulder.

She turned to Shion, feeling ashamed at how she had tried to injure him in her panic and failed. "Does nothing hurt you?" she asked, exasperated.

Wisely he said nothing, as he usually did.

"Darkness falls across the city. Fires are burning in the Preachán quarter. I am restless this twilight. Heavy despair blankets Kenatos. There is no pain so awful as the pain of suspense, the Bhikhu say. I agree."

- Possidius Adeodat, Archivist of Kenatos

XXV

Blood smeared Baylen's face with little flecks of tattered leaves. There were gashes in his scalp too hideous to look at, and Paedrin experienced a rise in his gorge yet willed himself not to vomit. Baylen's eyes were blue, amidst the dark, clotted blood, and they were awake and quite alive.

"I can't move my legs," Baylen said with tortured breath. "I passed out from the pain. Where's Khiara?"

Paedrin stared down at the giant Cruithne, his emotions roiling with conflicting feelings. He hung his head, ashamed of himself, ashamed at the questions that were coming. "Dead."

Baylen closed his eyes, panting with shallow wheezes. "That's . . . unfortunate."

The word was inadequate to describe the desperate situation that hung as a pall. She was dead, Tyrus had abandoned them, and Kiranrao was loose in the woods with a dagger that could slay any living thing. The Fear Liath's lair was still nearby, and then there were the—

As summoned by his despair, he heard rustling in the branches overhead. The sound of flapping and hissing descending from the boughs. Yes, the Cockatrice were still there as well, gathering back to their roosts now that the violence had ended.

"Paedrin."

The Bhikhu sagged to his knees next to the bleeding man, powerless to save him. He rested his elbows on the hilt of the Sword of Winds, pressing his forehead against his arm. What a disgrace he was to the Bhikhu order. What a failure.

"Where is Tyrus?"

"Gone," Paedrin muttered. "Baylen . . . they're all gone. We failed. Phae was killed by the Fear Liath. I saw her body. Then Kiranrao grabbed Khiara—" A shudder passed through him. "He murdered her. The only thing I could think at that moment was killing him. He went into the woods, Tyrus shouted the word, and then they were gone and then so was Kiranrao. This is . . . this is bad."

Anguish twisted inside of him, shredding his composure and nearly making him sob with despair. He hung his head, feeling the full brunt of his stupidity and failure.

Baylen's hand brushed against his leg. Paedrin opened his eyes, stared down at him, and saw the determination in the Cruithne's eyes. "Go," Baylen said flatly.

Wings flapped as more Cockatrice arrived. He could hear them scuttling along the oak branches. Closing his eyes, he extended his blind vision and felt them rustling, preparing to swoop down and attack them. He was so weary. Fighting them off would take time, precious time he didn't have. He needed to escape the Scourgelands. Once it was dark, the Fear Liath would come out of its lair and begin hunting. He knew it for certain.

Paedrin reached down and gripped the Cruithne's hand. It was massive, and there was only a glimmer of strength left.

"Go," Baylen repeated.

Paedrin rose, staring down at the crippled man. Baylen was on his back, arms spread wide, his legs at a crooked angle. The Cruithne began to whistle with suppressed pain. Paedrin could see the agony in his eyes. He would not survive the night. Which was worse, being turned into a statue of stone or savaged by the Fear Liath? Either way was death.

What have I done?

He knew the answer already. What would it matter if he left Baylen to die? There was no way he could transport a man of Baylen's size, let alone contend with the suffering it would cause since he was obviously broken beyond repair. Paedrin ran his hand over the stubble on top of his head, wincing at the feeling of a long scab, not realizing he had been clawed.

He remembered Tyrus's story about his failure in the Scourgelands. How his friend, a Preachán named Declan Brin, had been mortally wounded and was left behind to die. He comprehended, just a little, what that must have meant. Leaving a man to die was terrible business. But what could he do? How could he save him?

A Cockatrice began to flap downward, hovering in the air above. He could sense the beast's will press against his, demanding he look up at it and turn to stone. They would come in a rush as they had before. If he fled now, with the Sword, he would be able to escape them. It meant leaving Baylen alone.

What else can I do about it?

He stared down at the Cruithne, hearing his little moan of pain. Baylen's body trembled with shudders of agony. The thought came into Paedrin's mind that it would be most merciful to end his suffering. Don't leave him to die. Kill him. Death will be a mercy.

The compulsion stunned him. Paedrin stared down at Baylen, saw the open flesh of his neck. A quick slice and the pain would end. But he realized that it would haunt him for the rest of his life. It would disavow every Bhikhu oath.

You're not a Bhikhu now. You're really just a Kishion. A killer.

Paedrin stared down at his hands, trying to hold against the tide of feelings sweeping over him.

"Go," Baylen said darkly. "Just go."

Paedrin prepared to summon the blade's power. He took a breath and started to float, rising from the ground. But something compelled him to let it out again and drop to the forest floor. Tyrus had said that he had failed the Scourgelands when he had quit. He had always regretted leaving Declan behind. The failure had taught him about himself, had taught him about his enemy, and had inspired his heart to continue the quest. Tyrus never knew what would have happened if he had only pressed forward instead of quitting. How could Paedrin know?

Something began to spark alive inside of Paedrin's chest. It was difficult to describe. Stubbornness? Determination? Courage? All his life, Paedrin had compared himself to Aboujaoude, the mightiest Bhikhu of his generation. When Aboujaoude had found a beaten Cruithne on the ground in the streets of Kenatos, he had intervened and saved him.

Paedrin swallowed, mustering everything inside himself.

He would not abandon Baylen.

At that moment, the floods of Cockatrice began to fall from the tree limbs, screeching and hissing. Paedrin sensed the wave and he leapt into the air to meet them, swinging his blade in reckless fury, striking at the mass as they came at him.

A single thought struck his mind, an idea that bloomed from the far recesses of his memory. He invoked the blade's power to fly, but it also contained another power. The hilt stone had magic of its own.

"Shut your eyes!" Paedrin yelled to Baylen, flipping the blade upside down. He held the sword by the blade and invoked the stone embedded in the hilt. A searing flash of green light erupted from the pommel, and suddenly the air was full of commotion. He watched, using his blind vision, as the Cockatrice flailed and batted away from the relic in his hands, rending the air with their screeches of pain. All of their gazes had been fixed on him and the magic of the stone had caught them, rendering each of them blind and full of searing agony.

A thrill went through Paedrin as he realized what was happening. The Cockatrice's magic was in their eyes! The Sword neutralized their power by blinding them. They would not be able to turn him or anyone else to stone. Their power had been broken.

Some of the Cockatrice pummeled into him as they desperately sought to escape the maelstrom of pain. Many flapped helplessly to the ground, writhing and hissing in debilitating agony. Others rose for the trees, seeking their roosts for safety.

Paedrin lowered himself back to the ground and then sheathed the sword. He grinned with triumph, watching the remnants of the creatures scuttle away or twist wildly with pain.

He walked back to Baylen's side and knelt next to him. "I'm not leaving you."

Baylen coughed with a gurgle. "I'm not going to last much longer."

"I'll stay with you then."

Baylen whimpered. "While I appreciate the gesture . . . it's not going to work."

"Don't argue with me," Paedrin snapped. "I'm not abandoning you."

"Is the Fear Liath . . . dead?"

"No, it went back to its lair."

Baylen started to choke. He struggled to catch his breath. "We both know that we can't beat it."

"I'll think of something. Maybe I can get you into one of these trees with the Sword. If we're high enough, it won't be able to climb."

"No!" Baylen barked. "It hurts just lying here. If you move me, it'll kill me."

"Let me think of something. Quiet and be still. I need to think." He gazed up at the mesh of trees and the shadowy Cockatrice writhing up there.

He sat down, setting the blade in his lap. He closed his eyes and began to meditate, focusing on his breathing, trying to clear his thoughts. He felt better already. Yes, he had made a terrible mistake in going after Kiranrao, but he had saved Baylen from the serpent-birds. Saving a life brought a flush of warmth to his bruised heart. *Good. Savor the feeling. Think. How do you move someone this large? What are the options?*

He calmed his breathing, letting his inhalation through his nose be followed by a deep exhale from his mouth. He felt his body rise slightly with each breath, and then sink. He delved inside himself, trying to sort through options. Some thoughts he tossed aside. Others he mulled. If not a tree branch, what about a cave? Was there a place Baylen could hide where he could escape the Fear Liath's claws? Or was there something he could use to block the Fear Liath's den and prevent it from coming out at night?

He sat cross-legged, hands resting on his knees, his fingers pinched softly together, his arms forming a hoop. Ideas went through his mind, quickly and calmly.

He thought about Baylen's injuries. His head had been gashed by the Fear Liath's jaws. He had slashes across his body as well, but the main damage happened when the beast had crushed him. Broken bones, likely his spine. His breathing showed that his ribs were probably broken as well. Paedrin lacked healing abilities and doubted even Hettie would have been able to repair the damage. Only Khiara would have been able to save him.

Khiara.

How did one become a Shaliah? Where did the *keramat* come from? He didn't really understand it. Was it some kind of faith? Was it an inherited power or one that could be learned? Was it similar to the Druidecht ways that Annon had demonstrated?

As he plunged deeper inside himself, he lost track of time and where he was. The dangers of the Scourgelands seemed to melt away. Annon had described communing with the spirits like being able to hear whispers. When they had first met, Paedrin had scoffed at the idea that there were spirits flitting about. But he had seen manifestations of them with his own eyes. He remembered one being trapped in a dagger he had taken from a Preachán in Havenrook. Annon had freed it with the fireblood and it had healed Paedrin's wound.

It had healed Paedrin's wound.

Was there another way to heal Baylen? Was there some spirit magic that would heed his call? He wore no Druidecht talisman. He wasn't even sure he believed in the Druidecht ways. What had Annon taught him? That there was a world that coexisted alongside theirs.

Mirrowen.

Just thinking the name brought a tingle of gooseflesh down his back. Was there a way he could tap into the powers there? Was there a way he could save Baylen that he was not thinking of? Could he learn the *keramat* without being trained by a Shaliah? He regretted that he had not thought to ask Khiara about it. She was so quiet . . . so sad. She deserved better than to be murdered by such a man as Kiranrao.

He sighed, remembering seeing her ashen face. She deserved better.

Bury her.

Paedrin blinked his eyes open. Where had the thought come from? He felt a tingle across his neck. What a peculiar thought. It was so small, almost a whisper. Yet not really a whisper . . . just the pulse of an idea. A flash of insight. Surely it came from his mind, didn't it?

He glanced around the darkening woods, then watched Baylen breathing fitfully, eyes closed in rest.

Bury Khiara. He had no idea why that thought had come into his mind. It seemed out of place, as if it had come to him unbidden. He waited a moment, experiencing the stillness, but there was no repeat of the thought. He breathed in deeply, floating up, and used the blade to direct him toward where he had last seen Tyrus.

There was Khiara's body. Her long staff lay nearby, neglected. Her body was already stiff, her face pallid. She didn't even look like herself anymore—the part of her that was *her* was gone somehow. All that was left was an empty shell. He knelt by the corpse, feeling a prickle of disgust skitter through him, but he ignored it. He touched the dark hair, clogged with dead leaves. He should say a Vaettir prayer over her. That's what was needed.

A bulging pouch tied to her waist caught his eye. It was made out of leather and was small in size, large enough to hold a small piece of fruit. Perhaps there was something she had that might help ease Baylen's pain? He did not know how he would recognize it, but he thought it was worth exploring. Gingerly, he removed her travel pack and explored the contents, finding an assortment of herbs, but mostly food and an abundance of water skins. He gratefully drank one of them empty. He hadn't realized he was so thirsty.

He smoothed the hair from her brow and then maneuvered her limbs into a reposing position.

There was the pouch at her waist, catching his eye again. Was it full of money? As a Bhikhu, he did not care for money and the trap that it was to people. He stared at the pouch, wondering what was inside. He undid the strings fastening it to her belt and then unwound the knot closing it off. The pouch was squishy and did not clink. Pulling on the edges, he opened it.

The pouch was lined with oilskin, making the bag quite thick. It had a fragrant aroma. Paedrin probed the insides with his fingers and felt a sodden pulp inside. Even more curious, he wriggled his hand inside the small opening and scooped it out.

It was a small clump of green moss, with little buds of blue and violet. It smelled earthy and vibrant, and it was dripping wet. The moisture trickled through his fingers. What was it? He stared at the colorful moss, raising it to his nose, and smelled. The scent was intoxicating. He shook his head to clear it. Perhaps it would help ease Baylen's pain. After dipping the moss back into the pouch, he closed the bag and cinched the strings.

He lacked the tools to bury Khiara properly, so he decided to rake dead leaves to cover her. There was a fallen oak branch nearby, one that had split from the Mother Tree. He slid her body until it pressed against the tree and then set to work. Before long, he was done and mopped the sweat from his brow. He took her white oak staff with him back to Baylen and then set it down nearby.

Baylen's eyes blinked awake. "Thought . . . I thought you'd finally left. It's getting dark."

"I found something while burying Khiara. It looks like moss . . . maybe it's some sort of salve. I'm going to dress the wound at your head first. It looks like it's stopped bleeding anyway."

Baylen sighed and didn't reply.

Paedrin examined the torn scalp, the matted hair, and open wound. He winced at the sight and hoped the salve would not hurt too much. He opened the drawstrings again and dumped the mass of dripping moss into his hand. As gently as he could, he pressed it against the injury.

The Cruithne's body arched as soon as the moss touched him. His eyes shot wide with startled surprise, his slack expression filling with indescribable joy. The look on his face was transfixed with pleasure and Paedrin nearly jumped away from him in shock. Paedrin stared at the wound and watched the scalp close, the flesh knit together and heal. Baylen's body continued the arch, rising off the ground, and his muscles seem to flex and contort on their own. Paedrin heard the bones grinding, mending, snapping back into place.

"Guhhh!" Baylen groaned, his chest expanding to fill with air. He took several deep breaths, which became more rapid and pronounced. Suddenly, inexplicably, the Cruithne sat up.

Paedrin dropped the pouch in surprise, staring at him.

Baylen extended his arms, twisting his wrists, bending his elbows, flexing his fingers. He looked overjoyed, grinning broadly.

Paedrin looked for the moss, watching it shriveling before his eyes. When it was only a little tiny nub, it fell off into the dirty leaves.

"What . . . was . . . that?" Baylen chuffed, patting his chest, then reaching and touching his scalp, running his fingers through the tangle of bloodied hair.

Paedrin stared at him, overwhelmed. "I . . . found it . . . with Khiara."

Baylen stood, no look of pain or injury on him. In fact, he looked hale enough to sprint. He cast around the grove for his twin broadswords and inserted them into the scabbards on his back.

"You sure this isn't a dream?" Baylen asked, looking around the deserted woods. "I never saw her use that plant before when she healed someone."

Paedrin rose, a foolish grin on his own face. "Neither have I, Baylen. But I noticed the pouch just now." He sighed. "It came when we needed it most. Maybe it is the *keramat*. Maybe it is ghosts. Either way, we should press on and find the center of this maze. Even if Phae is dead, if we can penetrate the center, it will help Tyrus succeed next time."

Baylen smirked. "Next time?"

Paedrin nodded, grabbing the Cruithne's arm. "We'd better get going. I don't think that Fear Liath is going to stay in his den forever. But I like our chances of climbing a tree much better now."

Baylen nodded. "Which way?"

Paedrin shrugged, looking around. Then he pointed. "There. And if we happen to run into Kiranrao . . . so much the better."

"My spirit echoes the mood of the city. It is dusk. Tumult abounds. My heart frets. As we are, such are the times."

- Possidius Adeodat, Archivist of Kenatos

XXVI

Annon leaned back against the rough bark of the massive, bending oak. He drew the cowl over his head and sat in the stillness, listening to the stuttering clicks from some unknown insects, the sway of the heavy branches, the nearly audible sigh from the earth. The air smelled of acrid smoke from where Tyrus had unleashed the fireblood into the Dryad tree. Brittle leaves and twigs were his only cushions and he sat in fear that another enemy would crash through the woods. His energy was drained and his body ached from dozens of cuts and puckered wounds. He fidgeted with every crack and snap, worried about being attacked again. He shifted his thoughts to the moment, to face the test of will that was about to happen at the tree. Shadows thickened with the twilight, plunging the grove into darkness. He knew the others were nearby, listening for danger. He was not certain how long he would need to wait until the Weir found them.

Memories wafted through his mind, from another time—another tree. He had saved Neodesha's tree from the ravages of an axe. He had stood against a raiding party of Boeotians. Reeder was dead now. So was Nizeera. Even Neodesha's life may have been snuffed out. He folded his arms, huddling deeper inside himself, uncomfortable in the presence of such painful memories. Back then, he had waited by the tree until Neodesha had revealed herself. He remembered, with growing dread, how she had tempted him to look at her. If he had succumbed, she would have snatched his memories away and he would have forgotten all knowledge of her or why he had gone to protect that tree. His resistance to her alluring words had earned him the right to know her Dryad name, and with it—the ability to command her, as Tyrus had instructed him to do now. By claiming a Dryad's obedience, he would be able to learn where to find Poisonwell. Annon had the suspicion that Tyrus had known he would need a Druidecht on the journey for this very reason.

He glanced up at the ancient boughs above him. In his mind, he imagined the oak tree being a giant mushroom and he just a tiny crawler nestled at its base. Thinking of mushrooms reminded him of Mathon's warning not to eat the mushrooms in the Scourgelands. The thought made a gurgle of bile rise in his throat.

Far in the distance, he heard the fierce howl of a Weir. The sound was answered by another, coming from a different direction. A third joined the chorus, the sound piercing the tree against his back. If he was judging the sound correctly, they were coming in from three different sides. His heart began pounding.

"They know you are here."

Her voice was so soft, so faint and so sudden that Annon nearly jumped out of his skin. Her voice came from his right and he immediately shielded his eyes, burying his face on his forearm.

"Did you tell them?" Annon asked, hoping his voice wasn't too muffled to hear.

"Yes, Druidecht. The Weir are swift. You must flee them."

"I claim my boon," he answered.

He heard the small crunch of a twig and felt her presence near his side. He could feel the heat radiating from her, could hear the soft breathing. His mind began to go mad with anticipation. He wanted to look at her. Was she like Neodesha? What race would she be?

"Look on me," she said, her voice beautiful and intoxicating.

"I will not. Give me the boon."

"What boon do you seek, Druidecht? I know the way out of the woods. With my help, I can free you from the maze."

"I don't believe you will help me. What is your name, Dryad? Tell me."

Her voice became husky. "My name is ancient. It has already been claimed by another. But do not believe I have grown old and am withered. I cannot age. I cannot die. Would you bind yourself to me, Druidecht? Shall I kiss you? Would you like that?"

He felt a spasm of dread and longing rush through his blood. Tyrus had warned him not to accept a Dryad's kiss. While it would unlock his memories again, which he craved, it would also bind them together in a way in which she could follow his thoughts, reveal their presence to Shirikant. He kept his head bowed, his cowl to protect his face. He would not let her kiss him.

"I seek your name. I preserved your tree from harm. You must give it to me."

"It is given to another."

"And where is he that was supposed to protect you?" Annon challenged. "Why did he not stop the flames?"

"How do you know he isn't already here?" she whispered wickedly.

A shiver of fear went down his back, bringing on a cold sweat. He realized he was not just speaking to the Dryad. Through her voice, he was confronting Shirikant himself. He quailed at the thought.

"Come, Druidecht. I have no defenses left. What do you really seek? Revenge?" Her hand touched the crown of his head and he flinched. "Companionship?" She stroked the back of his head, gliding her fingers down to his neck. A mad gush of insanity flooded his mind, making him reel with images of what she might look like. She smelled like loam, rich and earthy . . . yet hinting of decay. The urge to look at her was nearly unbearable. Sweat dripped down his cheek.

Another series of howls started, much closer. The Weir were loping through the woods, rushing toward the Dryad tree. He would not have long to outwit her. To outwit them both.

"If I look at you," Annon said, "would you take my memories? You are a spirit creature, you cannot lie."

"If you looked at me, you would desire me. Such is the way of men. You are greedy and seek to possess us. I have no defenses against you. You flinch as if you were the prisoner. I am a slave to this tree. I have nothing left. Not even a robe. All is tattered and gone. Have pity on me, Druidecht." Her hand touched the edge of his cowl. "Look on me."

There was a feeling in Annon's heart, a cruel blackness that swelled up like a giant shadow. He felt desire so intense that it nearly drove all thoughts from his mind but the desire to see her, to pledge himself to her, to stand as a guardian in the sickly woods for the rest of his days. One look at her was all it would take. Flames of heat pulsed inside his heart, rending his composure. He started to tremble, unable to keep the shivering from his body, feeling the yearning intensify into sordid and unclean emotions. It was like the blade of Iddawc, a gnawing demand to defile and betray. Somehow she had unleashed a terrible shadow into his being. He felt his will begin to crumble.

"Look on me," she repeated, her breath brushing against his ear.

"I will not," Annon answered, nearly choking.

"You will," she mocked. "No man can resist that part of themselves. All succumb eventually."

"Even you, Shirikant?" Annon snarled. He grabbed her by the wrist and pulled her off-balance. She stumbled into the brush, twigs snapping, and exhaled with a gust of surprised breath. Forcing his eyes to remain closed, he felt along her wrist to her fingers and there, fastened to her skin, was a cold iron ring. She began to thrash and pull away, but Annon clamped her arm against the side of his body, shifting so that his back was to her. He grabbed the ring and pulled it off, just as he had freed Paedrin. He released her instantly and hurled the ring into the woods. For a moment, he wondered if the ring would explode, killing them both. He had gambled, though, gambled that a Dryad had not stained herself with murder. She could not remove the ring herself, but another could free her.

Annon stood cautiously, whirling to face her, yet kept his eyes closed. He unfastened his cloak. His heart pounded with heavy thuds. Swallowing, he extended the cloak.

"Take this," he offered. "Cover yourself."

He breathed heavily, unnerved by the silence.

More leaves crunched as she rose. Her fingers grazed his and she took the cloak from him. Annon tried to calm his breath, focusing on the task at hand. His heart sorrowed for the girl, wondering what prison she had experienced and how long she had endured it.

"You . . . you freed me?" she asked, her voice wavering.

Annon collapsed against the tree trunk, bending over to calm his rattled nerves. "Yes. That is my purpose for coming. I seek to set you all free. What is your name, Dryad?"

She did not hesitate. "Ruhamah."

A thrill of success trembled inside his stomach. "I charge you, Ruhamah, to speak the truth. Is your mind your own?"

"Yes, Druidecht. You have severed his thoughts from mine. I am truly free. I did not lie about the Weir. They are coming. He seeks to force you to flee again."

"I would speak with you first," Annon said. "But I cannot trust meeting your gaze. May I blindfold you? Then we can speak briefly. I will not tarry long."

"You may compel me in all things, Master."

"I am no master," Annon replied. He knelt and opened his travel pouch, keeping his eyes averted from her, but he saw the hem of his cloak and her toes poking from beneath it. He rummaged through the contents and withdrew a strip of linen for bandages.

"Turn around," he bid her. "I will be quick." She obeyed him and he cautiously peered through lidded eyes to be sure. She had long black hair, wavy and clotted with leaves. With care, he wound the linen strip around her eyes.

Another set of howls came and he felt his heart pounding. Time was running short. There was specific information Tyrus had charged him to get. He turned her by her shoulder to face him. Her mouth was drooped in a frown, as if she were experiencing great pain.

"Are you hurt?" he asked.

"I am weary of my life," she whispered.

"You are free," Annon said. "You may go where you wish."

She shook her head gravely. "I am bound to this tree. All is lost, Druidecht. All is lost. Even if you agreed to be my husband, it would not free me from this bondage." She sagged to her knees and began to weep bitterly.

Annon knelt near her, putting his hand on her shoulder. "Why do you cry?"

"What happens to me is no concern of yours, Druidecht. Ask me your questions. Quickly, they come near."

"Where might I find Poisonwell? It is the heart of this forest—it is the bridge to Mirrowen."

"Mirrowen is destroyed."

A rush of gloom went through Annon's heart. "Why do you say that?"

"I saw it," she replied mournfully. "The garden is ruined. The walls of the keep are all broken down. It is a myth you seek, Druidecht. A myth that is no more."

Annon stared at her expression, wrestling with his feelings. "Who told you it was fallen? Was it Shirikant? He is a deceiver."

"I saw it through his *mind*, Druidecht. He destroyed it. The bridge must remain closed or the Abyss will flood this world. He keeps the gate shut. He is the Seneschal now. His name is not Shirikant."

Annon stared at her, perplexed. "I don't understand what you're saying. But Mirrowen is not fallen. I am a Druidecht from another forest. There are spirits there, Ruhamah. This place is cursed. These woods are cursed. But I am come from far away, where the forest is healthy and there are many gardens." He pressed his hand against the side of her head. "Where is it? Where is Poisonwell?"

She took his hand between hers, gripping it as if his fingers were a rope and she were drowning. Her mouth frowned even more, stricken. "Is it true?"

"I swear it by the talisman I wear. It was given to me by the spirits of Mirrowen. Feel it—it bears the symbols."

Her fingers traced over the pattern on his talisman, following the curving lines. She gasped with recognition. "A lie? What he showed me . . . was a lie?"

"He is no longer your master," Annon said. "Where can I find it? The bridge must be opened again. Where is it?"

"Are you certain? The floods of the Abyss will drown this world if there is no Seneschal at the gate. You risk killing everyone, sending all into chaos. Are you certain?"

"I am," Annon replied, though he felt more uncertain with each passing moment. "Where can I find it?"

"That way," Ruhamah said, pointing directly with her finger. "It is a league from here. In the middle of the forest, there is a promontory of stone jutting out from the earth. The ruins of a keep are there. But the bridge between the worlds is hidden in caves beneath the promontory. It is a vein to the core of the earth. There are fumes and heat. Be wary. I cannot guide you to it. Only the Mother Tree guards that secret. She guards the secrets of the bridge and knows the word to pass between the worlds." Her hands clasped Annon's tightly. "She is mad with suffering and grief, Druidecht. Her daughter was stolen. Long ago. She was stolen and killed." Her voice dropped to a whisper. "The man who travels with you is not mortal. He is disfigured by scars. He is the one, Druidecht." Her fingers touched the side of his face. "He is the one who killed her."

Dread flooded inside Annon.

Shion.

"Where is the Mother Tree?" Annon asked hoarsely. He gripped her shoulder. "On the promontory?"

"No," she answered. "It is an ancient tree, even more ancient than this one. It no longer bears the shape of a tree. The heaviest branches fell off years ago and new ones have grafted. It's pockmarked and misshapen, like the soul of the Dryad mother who is bound there. The trunk is split into two legs, forming a small archway, almost like a cave, between them. That is the Mother Tree. Her will is stronger than mine, Druidecht. She knows you are coming. Her roots run deep and touch nearly every tree in the woods. She knows you are here. She will summon all defenses to protect the tree. Hidden there are secrets held since the beginning of time."

"Thank you, Ruhamah," Annon said. "Can you not return to Mirrowen through your tree?"

Ruhamah shook her head. "I am no longer worthy to enter. I was taught this by the Seneschal when I made my oaths. May I have your true name as well?"

"I am Annon of Wayland," he answered.

Tyrus's voice boomed from the stillness. "Hasten!"

“Will the dawn never come? Yet I dread its arrival. How much of the city of Kenatos has fallen during the night? The barbarians are shrieking in the dark. One cannot sleep through their howls.”

- Possidius Adeodat, Archivist of Kenatos

XXVII

Weariness from the run enveloped Phae like a cloak. Tyrus had used the command to summon Annon back from the Dryad Tree, but instead of using the Tay al-Ard, they had fled through the woods on foot to escape. She huddled in the dark, arms crossed over her knees, her shoulder pressed against Shion's. They found shelter in a small gully, bone-dry and thick with smooth stones. Not even the deepest level was damp, but the dirt was soft and provided some cushion. She felt her head bobbing and longed to sleep. After brushing her eyes with her forearm, she tried to make out the shadows of her companions.

Prince Aran guarded one end of the gully, about a stone's throw away. Hettie protected the other end, bow resting on her lap. Annon and Tyrus spoke in low tones nearby as he related what he had learned from the Dryad tree. For some reason, he had insisted on speaking to Tyrus privately.

A keening wail rose over the black woods, haunting and thick with strange rhythms. The sound was unnerving and kept Phae from sleeping. Scuttling sounds came from the trees far overhead and the already-dim light prevented them some seeing what passed through the trees. The moon had not risen yet and the forest grew colder with each passing moment.

"Try to sleep," Shion whispered.

"Not with that dreadful noise," she answered darkly. "It cuts right through sleep. Are they getting nearer? I can't tell."

"I don't think so. The calls are random."

She hung her head, feeling miserable at the lack of sleep and growing fatigue. Her muscles ached, as did her feet. Warmth radiated from Shion's body and she shifted to press herself closer to him.

"I wish you hadn't frightened me," she said after a pause. "Back at the Dryad tree."

"I'm sorry."

"Remember that evil tree? The one when we were fleeing through the woods of Silvandom? I was drawn to it by all those blue butterflies. I was sure it was a magical tree—one that would shelter us. It deceived me, yet I could not see it."

"I remember," he said simply. He turned to look at her, but she could not see his face. In her mind, she thought of the scars, his brooding eyes.

She rested her head against his shoulder. "I struggled against you, trying to wade into that brackish water. I was so certain you were wrong. It's difficult to trust emotions. Sometimes they betray you." She sighed. "I can see why you all deceived me. It still hurts though."

She felt his fingers graze her hair. His touch caused a shiver down her back. He hesitated and then caressed her again. "I'm sorry," he repeated.

"It's all right. I understand now. I just wish I had figured it out on my own. But I suppose that's a rash thought. Who can outpredict my father?"

"Phae?" Tyrus called to her.

"Yes?" She sat up, smoothing the hair over her shoulder.

"Annon has uncovered some interesting information. We must see how it compares to what you learned from the Dryad in Silvandom. Come closer, all of you."

Hettie and Aran quickly joined them, huddling in the shadows of the ravine. The wind shook the heavy tree limbs overhead, sending dead leaves spiraling on top of them. Phae hunkered down.

"He learned that at the center of this forest is a promontory."

"What is that?" Phae asked.

"It's a mass of stone . . . like a hill that hasn't worn down over time. The rock is older and suited better to withstand the elements. There are ruins of some sort there, but it is not our destination. Annon also learned where the Mother Tree is and its description. What we are looking for is a single tree, or perhaps two trees that grew into one, for there is a space at the base inside the trunk. A gap. This follows the Mirrowen lore that I've heard, where there are portals to that world through fallen trunks or natural gaps. The tree we search for is very old, very squat with many limbs protruding. It is ancient beyond our reckoning and probably very sick and diseased. That tree is at the base of the promontory, so we will need to travel around to find it. It would best be done during daylight, else we could walk right past it."

Phae felt a stirring of hope at the words. Just at the edge of her senses, she also felt the pain in her abdomen threatening to rouse again. She stiffened with the thought, remembering the agony of previous onslaughts. She needed rest!

"That is good news," Phae whispered. "What else? Do we know where to find it? What direction to go?"

"Yes. It was not far from the Dryad tree we were at earlier. When the Tay al-Ard refreshes, we can go back there again and head the right way. Roaming the woods at night is too dangerous right now. But we should go at dawn and see if we can reach the promontory before night ends. The longer we stay in these woods, the more hunters the Arch-Rike releases against us. This has been my strategy, to keep them hunting us away from the center. To draw his forces away from protecting the tree. If we can jump over his lines, so to speak, we can rush to the center and there will be fewer guardians."

"He will not leave it unprotected," Prince Aran said. "A sizable host will be waiting for us. How many Fear Liaths does he have chained in his service, do you think?"

"I cannot even guess," Tyrus replied. "Which is why attacking during daylight is critical. Those creatures are vulnerable in the day. Every foe we have faced bears a weakness. I suspect that we will be vastly outnumbered. I have brought certain magics with me to help in such a case." He gave a quick look to Annon, which Phae noticed. "The sooner we find the tree, the sooner Phae can enter it. Now there is something else you need to know."

Tyrus put his hand on her leg. "The Dryad warned that Mirrowen is destroyed and that venturing there will be lethal. I doubt this is true. It sounds like just the sort of deception Shirikant is famous for. But I had to speak it regardless. She also mentioned a being called the Seneschal. It means some sort of steward. A protector, maybe. Have you heard of this before, Phae?"

"Yes," she answered softly. "I don't think I'm supposed to speak of it though. I was told I must seek him in order to make my oath and be bound to the tree. I learned that the Dryads here are fallen. They have forsaken their oaths."

"I believe that is so," Tyrus said. "Even a Dryad can steal another Dryad's memories. Something happened at the Mother Tree. Some betrayal. I'm certain Shirikant is involved and that he has usurped the memories of the trees. Annon said that the Dryad he just met wore a ring like the Kishion have. They are forced to obey him. When you reach the tree, Phae, you must be very careful. The Dryad will probably try to kill you."

Phae's heart shriveled. "Even though I have come to free her?"

"Even so. The Arch-Rike would lose his grip on the Scourgelands if he lost control of her. Shion—you *must* protect Phae when she approaches the tree. He may even try to destroy the tree. I'm not certain what he will attempt, but we must expect every trick and cunning. If we do not succeed in finding it before the sun sets again, I fear we will be too late. All of our efforts, all of our thoughts must be focused on succeeding. Courage, my friends. We are so very close."

He reached out and took Phae's hand, squeezing it firmly.

A catlike shriek sounded from the lip of the gully and a Weir hurtled down at her.

Shion sprang like a crossbow and vaulted over her, slamming into the beast and knocking it aside. The Weir hissed and howled, raking Shion with its hooked claws, but Shion drew his twin daggers and slammed them into the beast's throat to end the savage cry.

"More!" Hettie warned, rising into a low crouch and readying her bow.

Phae's heart was hammering with fear from the sudden, savage attack. Tyrus grabbed her by the arm and motioned for Hettie to lead the way down the gully throat. Another Weir loped into view along the ridge.

Hettie sent one arrow into its hind and had another out as it dropped.

"They have the high ground," Aran warned. "We must scale the side . . . watch out!"

Suddenly the Weir were leaping into the stunted ravine, snarling and gashing. Phae watched the fireblood bloom from Annon's hands as he sent it racing along the edge of the brush. She thought the words to tame fire herself, and her fingers began to burn blue. One of the cats swiped at her middle, but she lunged to the side and burned the creature to ash. Shion caught up with her again, pulling her to the other side of the gully. He scrambled up first and then reached down and seized her wrist, pulling her up after him. The companions fought in the gully below and Phae could see the glowing eyes of the Weir as they advanced in the dark woods.

Shion tightened his grip on the daggers and planted himself in front of her, his neck muscles bulging. Prince Aran joined them and also positioned himself in front of her. Phae gritted her teeth, feeling nauseous with the sudden onset of pain in her belly. She winced and groaned, her knees beginning to weaken, but she kept herself upright.

The Weir snarled and charged, loping through the woods. Shion sprung into their midst, slashing viciously with his blades. Aran hammered at the Weir with his bare fists and palms, striking at their eyes, the soft flesh around the throats. Though he did not carry a blade, he struck with a force that injured them, and he could not be budged from his stance. She heard the shred of fabric and felt blood from Aran's sleeve spray her face, but although he was wounded, he did not back down.

Tyrus joined them next, his arms spread wide as he unleashed the fury of his fireblood on the attackers. Flames began to spread through the dried leaves, causing plumes of smoke and snapping twigs as they caught fire.

"Come!" Tyrus shouted. "Before they surround us."

Annon and Hettie were the last to leave the gully and together they smashed into the ranks of the Weir, leaving a fog of smoke in their wake.

Dawn crept over the tangled woods of the Scourgelands. Phae walked with leaden steps, one hand fastened to Shion's tattered cloak. She was sleeping while she walked, she felt, and the ground passed in a dreamlike state. Her other hand clutched her stomach. The pain was persistent now, coming in faster and faster bursts. All night it had tormented her, receding for a short while before returning with a vengeance. She was too sick to eat, but Tyrus made her choke down some dried strips of meat. Their water skins were drying up and the small sips did little to slake her thirst.

She cast her eyes around the dull light, seeing the haggard and worn expressions on all their faces. Purple bruises stained the eyelids. Annon walked, clutching his shoulder, and she could see the blood staining his tunic. His face was a mask of determination and foreboding. Hettie's hair was tangled with snarls and brush, her look sorrowful. Prince Aran was wounded too, his black jacket shredded from the Weir attacks. He walked with sternness, his face hard and without compassion or suffering. Phae mourned when she looked at him, remembering the secret looks that Khiara had given the solemn man.

A preternatural silence hung over the air and Tyrus stopped short, holding up his hand. Something creaked in the trees, something massive and hulking. They all halted. Tyrus motioned for them to draw near him and withdrew the Tay al-Ard.

A chuffing cough sounded in the gloomy dawn. It came from above their heads. Branches snapped and crashed down. A tree groaned, coming up by the roots, and started to fall toward them, its huge branches sweeping down like an avalanche.

Phae clung to her father's arm as the Tay al-Ard swept them away from the danger. When the spinning ended, Phae found herself on the ground, vomiting violently into the turf. It felt like the world was still spinning, even though the magic had already deposited them. Her ears rang and she wheezed and choked as every bit inside her stomach came out. The spasms clenched hard and painfully and she trembled with the efforts. Soon black bile was all she had left and she planted her palm on the ground, feeling a trail of it cling to her lip.

Shion knelt next to her, mopping her face with the edge of his cloak. She was so exhausted, so spent, she tottered against him, knowing she'd faint if she tried to stand.

"Drink," Tyrus whispered, handing her his own flask.

She shook her head, waving it away.

"You must," he said. He knelt beside her as well and pressed the flask against her mouth. She took a small sip and nearly gagged. It was awful, acidic. She waited a moment, hoping the pain would recede. It did—barely—and she took another drink. When she looked up, she saw the worried faces clustered around her. They were not looking at her, though.

Lifting her gaze, she stared at the woods, not recognizing anything. She knelt in a small grove of ancient oaks, but the limbs were glittering with freshly spun spiderwebs, thick as linen strands. The entire forest was covered in a veil of webs, from the trees above and between each.

"Where are we?" Phae whispered, stifling a moan.

Tyrus looked around, his face betraying his alarm. "Where we were yesterday. The Dryad tree is over there. I think I can make it out. But these webs were spun last night. By what, I do not know."

"If you only believe what you like, and reject what you don't like, it is not truth you believe, but yourself."

- Possidius Adeodat, Archivist of Kenatos

XXVIII

The webs clung to every tree, forming an impenetrable mesh. Back at the Winemillers, Phae had often marveled at the webs spiders could weave during the night between the grapevines and the trellises. As a child, she had touched the strands, which caused vibrations down the lengths, summoning the small spiders—tricking them into believing they had snared some prey. These web strands were thick and haphazard in formation, almost like cobwebs in dusty corners. But these were no silken strands that could be torn with a breeze.

"You don't know what caused these webs?" Annon asked, his voice grave and tremulous.

"No," Tyrus answered. "I never encountered them. We didn't make it this far."

Hettie lifted her boot and sticky strands came up with it. "They are everywhere. We can't use the Tay al-Ard again. What then?"

Phae struggled to regain her feet and leaned on Shion to stand. The webs were frightening, shrouding the view in every direction. What army of spiders had created it?

Tyrus frowned, stroking his beard. "The Arch-Rike knew we might return this way. This must be a direct path to the promontory, so he's encircled the area with a net of webs. We must be cautious, for the spinners are probably still near."

"There is a legend in the Druidecht lore," Annon said. "A race of spirits that is half-human, half-spider. They're called the Raekni." He swallowed. "They're quite large—the size of one of us. We should watch the trees above. They can move faster than us through this barrier and have stingers that paralyze their victims—" He turned around abruptly. "I heard something."

"It was the wind," Hettie said, touching his arm. "Let's use the fireblood to burn our way through."

Tyrus nodded, scanning the ground and then the trees. Hettie reached out toward one of the thick strands, and blue fire burst from her fingers. She held it against the strands, but nothing happened. She summoned more heat but the webs resisted its burning. The flame in her hand snuffed out.

"Of course," Tyrus said darkly. "It is enchanted against flame. He means to hold us here until the Tay al-Ard refreshes or force us to cut our way through and reveal ourselves. We don't have time to dally. Try your blade, Hettie."

The Romani girl nodded and slung her bow across her shoulder and drew her knives. She slashed at the first cord and it severed, but there was an eerie reverberation in the woods, like a plaintive discordant chord from a harp.

"Quickly," Tyrus said. "Shion and Hettie—lead the way. Do you have a dagger, Annon?"

The Druidecht nodded and produced a small hunting knife.

"I have one," Phae said, but Tyrus waved at her not to draw it. He put his arm around her and went with her into the gap carved by Shion and Hettie. Prince Aran took up the rear, searching the heights of the trees for a sign of the Raekni.

As they cut their way through the thick barrier, Phae felt the stirrings of pain begin again deep inside her. She breathed rapidly, taking little gulps of breath, and hugged herself to endure the pain and still walk. She was lightheaded after vomiting and still felt no hunger. As more of the strands were severed, a strange music seemed to linger in the air, wafting unseen as strands of different length were snapped. It was a ghostly hymn, a funeral dirge. It made Phae shudder.

Hettie and Shion struck down the webs that blocked their way. Sometimes the nets were so thick that it took both of them to clear the path so that they could pass single file. Annon craned his neck, staring up at the trees.

"Shadows," he said, pointing upward.

Through the veil of strands came the outsized shadow of spiders, skittering in the trees above them. These were huge, man-sized, and easily outpaced them. Phae saw only three, no more.

"If their webs are immune to flame," Tyrus said, "it is likely they are protected as well."

"The webbing is thicker ahead," Hettie said. "How did they work so quickly?"

A low-hanging branch blocked the path, and Tyrus helped Phae duck. Glossy strands stuck to her face and she brushed them away. Their boots crunched in the leaves and twigs. Anticipation coursed through her veins, mixing with worry and dread. The shadows of another spider creature passed overhead, making her shrink.

Sweat began to glisten on Hettie and Annon's brows as they continued to labor. Only Shion could work with unflagging strength, his expression dark and brooding. The pace was slow and tedious, and it became apparent that the spiders had been more than thorough in securing the way against intruders.

"At least the Weir won't be able to reach us here," Hettie murmured. She raised her arm to slash another strand. A spurting sound occurred just then and Hettie was hauled off her feet by her outstretched arm.

"Hettie!" Annon yelled, lunging forward, but Shion was faster. He grabbed her by the belt and pulled her back.

"Cut the strand!" Shion barked, yanking as Hettie squirmed.

Annon managed to slice through the bond that had snared her and she fell to the ground with a thud. Her legs began to kick and twitch and when Annon rolled her over, he saw her eyes had rolled back in her head as she convulsed in heavy spasms. A bloodstain bloomed from the front of her shirt.

A discordant chittering sound filled the air and new lines of webbing began to streak down at them. Tyrus drew a blade and fended off the webs as they came for him. At that moment, Phae doubled over in pain, seized by a violent cramp in her abdomen. She crumpled to the ground, pulling in her legs, groaning with anguish. The pain wracked her, blurring her vision as the web strands began to stick to everyone. She heard voices cry in alarm and felt something land next to her on the ground. A furry, stout spider leg was next to Phae's cheek, and she writhed and twisted away. Another pain struck her on the side as she rolled, and she saw the large black stinger protruding into her shirt. It withdrew immediately, dripping crimson.

"Shion!" she screamed, experiencing a surge of fiery pain.

Looking up, she saw him slashing wildly, beset by four spiders at once, a mass of quivering furry legs and spindle sacs that shuddered and bobbed in the fight. In horror, she watched another twisting Hettie into a bundle of spindly webs, wrapping her in the strands with effortless ease. Phae tried to sit up but the spider that had stung her batted her down. She felt her legs lashed together and suddenly the world was spinning, faster and faster, whirling round and round, her stomach so tender that she blacked out.

Paedrin pushed aside the branches, parting them enough to squeeze through. Inhaling again, he lifted free of their clutches and breathed in the cool morning air. The sun was just peeking through a long mane of puffy clouds, coloring it such a startling shade of pink that he gaped in wonderment. He drank in the rays of the light, feeling it on his face. He inhaled again, rising even higher, floating over the sea of treetops. It was such a strange sight, like a vast plain of rolling hills, except he was looking at the rounded caps of skeletal oak trees, some still clutching dying leaves or clumps of mistletoe. The view of the sky was intense and he felt tears prick his eyes at the beauty and majesty of the dawn and the gratitude for life.

"What do you see?" Baylen called from far down below. Paedrin had almost forgotten the Cruithne.

"A glorious sunrise," he said. He invoked the power of the Sword to keep his height as stable as he could and began to cast around in each direction. He wasn't sure what he was looking for until he saw it. "I see something! That must be the center of the woods."

"How can you tell?"

"There's a big hill made of stone. It's not that far. It rises above the rest of the forest."

"A mountain?"

"No, not that big. It's a cleft of rock. There are . . . ruins. I see ruins. Looks like a castle keep was once built there. Some broken stairs leading up from the woods, facing us. It's really not that far."

"How big?" Baylen asked.

"It's probably the size of the Arch-Rike's palace in Kenatos. Now that I look at it . . . it seems very much in the same style. The parapets are all fallen and broken, but there are segments of wall still standing. Some archways that haven't collapsed yet. It's overgrown with brush, but I think it's the way. If we can get there before turning back, both of us, then maybe that will help in the future."

Even though the sky was beautiful and radiant, the woods were still cracked and diseased. The smell in the air was moldy and sick. He looked around in each direction, wanting to make sure he had seen everything.

"I'm glad I came up here," Paedrin called down. "I see some huge spiderwebs over that way, blanketing an entire section of forest. If we keep the way we're going, we'll miss it entirely."

"I don't like spiders."

"I agree with you. Best to stay clear if we can." A series of black shapes rose from the trees and began flapping toward him. "Ah, looks like more Cockatrice are coming this way. They see me. I'd better come down."

Paedrin maneuvered through the branches again, hearing the sound of the coming creatures. He dropped down to the forest floor quickly, motioning for Baylen to follow him in the direction he had seen the ruins.

The Cruithne was dirt stained and weary. They had been walking all night long. The sound of the Fear Liath had made sleep nearly impossible, but Paedrin felt like they had to keep moving, even if they were walking in circles. Standing still meant death. With the dawn arriving, he knew the Fear Liath would go back to its lair again, unwilling to meet its own death from their blades in the daylight.

"Do you think we're going to make it out of here alive?" Baylen asked as they started to march toward the ruins.

"Anything is possible, my friend. Do you have the feeling

that the Arch-Rike isn't very concerned about us? Maybe the Boeotians are attacking Kenatos right now and that's drawn his attention over there. Or maybe he doesn't believe we can escape because the trees will steal our memories. I don't know what he's thinking, actually."

"He's probably trying to track down Tyrus. I pity him. But as you said, if we can get close enough to the center, it'll help whoever comes after us."

The sound of flapping emerged from above the treetops. Paedrin kept his eyes on the mesh of branches and wondered if the Cockatrice would wriggle down and attack them. He had the perfect weapon to scatter them again and would not hesitate using it a second time. But strangely, the creatures flapped further away, paying them no mind.

A strange exhilaration filled Paedrin's chest. They were very close to the center of the Scourgelands. He was convinced of it. Somehow, he had managed to go even deeper than Tyrus. Perhaps deeper than any two men had ever gone before. What a wild and forgotten place. Even the dark, brooding trees had a strange, ancient beauty to them. The sunlight could not quite penetrate the cowl of the oaks, but the light was evident and felt strangely reinvigorating. Some of the oppressiveness was gone from the air.

He glanced back at Baylen, chuffing along next to him.

"Do you want to stop and eat? Rest a while?" Paedrin offered.

"Right now, I'm wishing we had that device Tyrus carries. I'd be tempted to vanish back to Kenatos for fresh bakery bread. Apple butter is very good too. I'd lather it on right now."

"Stop," Paedrin complained, his stomach growling. "Don't talk about food right now. I'm almost tempted to eat the mushrooms."

"Not worth the disease. I'm sure they taste like bark."

"Well, you'd better get thoughts of Kenatos out of your head, Baylen. Neither of us will ever go there again. I'd still like to purge the Shatalin temple, but if the Arch-Rike cannot be killed, I may need to change my plans." He sighed. "We do our best. It's probably better not to assume too much."

They continued on the long hike, wending through the trees at a brisk pace despite the fatigue of having walked all night. He wondered where Kiranrao had ended up. Had he made it free of the Scourgelands yet? Paedrin had the sinking feeling that their paths would cross again. A frown creased his mouth at the thought.

Before midday, when the sun was beating down on the woods from directly overhead, Baylen and Paedrin emerged from the tangled thicket. Great trees had been uprooted and toppled, the tangle of roots exposed. A small clearing had been made, the earth freshly churned. Past the clearing, another stretch of woods led up to the mound of stone that rose over the Scourgelands like the shell of a tower. Great stone clefts stood proudly in the noon sky. Nestled on the clefts were the bones of an ancient fortress. A few saw-toothed walls still remained, but most had crumbled into dust. Several black shapes swirled in the sky above the mammoth hill, vultures or something even worse. A grayish-brown mist, like a dust cloud, hung in the air above the woods.

Baylen and Paedrin stood still, watching the ominous mound, feeling a silent whisper of dread. The broken trees were strewn about haphazardly. Paedrin was about to step onto the turf when Baylen held him back with a stiff arm.

The dull clop of a horse became evident. They waited, passively, as a single rider emerged into view in the midst of the churned ground. The steed was dark brown, thick and heavy as if carrying a weighty burden. On the horse sat a solitary rider, garbed in earth-colored tones, hood shielding his head from the sun. The rider was half-bent over the steed, one arm bunched crookedly, the reins nearly slack.

A chill went through Paedrin's heart. The horse trudged across the turf, picking its way slowly. The hunchbacked rider was quiet, the strange crooked arm drawing Paedrin's eyes. Something felt . . . unnatural about it. An eerie call, like the early morning cry of a heron, sounded. It made Paedrin start with dread and fear.

"It came from the ruins," Baylen muttered.

Paedrin swallowed.

The horse stopped sharply, stamping its front hoof, kicking up a plume of dust. The brown-garbed rider turned on the saddle and faced them.

Phae's skull was pounding. She blinked her eyes open and saw nothing but a sheath of white silk. A swaying sensation made her stomach uneasy and she realized with a throb of panic that she was upside down, suspended by her feet. Her side hurt, as did her throbbing head. She swallowed, trying to control the spasms of fear that wracked her.

Her arms were bound to her sides so tightly it was difficult to breathe. The strands covered her face, her neck, her entire body with their stickiness. As she tried to twist her neck, she saw small gaps in the strands, revealing more of her surroundings.

See how he struggles still.

The voice was feminine and struck her mind like ink blotting a page. She shivered at the metallic edge to the thought-whisper.

Struggles, yes. Save them, he mustn't. It was a different voice, slightly deeper, but still a woman's.

He has no blood to sip. Useless.

Phae wanted to see what the creatures looked like, but she could not from the angle. She struggled to twist and sway her cocoon.

He will stay until the Master comes.

The Master will slay him.

The Master will.

Phae tried to stretch against the cords. When she was wrapped up, she had been bent over, and so she was nearly like a spindle ball. Trying to flex her legs, she felt the strands flex, but they did not break. The exertion made her side burn with pain from where the stinger had stabbed her.

The Master will slay them all.

A little drink of blood. The others will be sweet. I long to taste it.

Wait until the Master comes.

Phae tried pushing her arms apart and felt the wrap strain, but not burst. The effort made her sac begin to sway.

One is awake. The girl.

She wriggles. She struggles.

Phae saw shadows through the gossamer threads, huge, eight-legged shadows that drew nearer to her. She stopped moving, trying to suppress the shudders of horror. Were they all captured? Had none of them survived?

Can you hear us? whispered one of the spider-creatures.

Can you hear our thoughts?

"I hear you," Phae whispered.

Pretty thing. Sweet thing. Just a sip. Just a taste. Your blood smells warm.

Would you see us, pretty thing?

Would you see our faces?

Phae stifled a horrified scream. She wrestled against the strands, trying to wriggle her way loose, but the stickiness only enmeshed her more.

One of the spider legs began to bat her gently, twisting her around. From the gap in the strands, she saw the others similarly suspended. She counted five other sacs, all wrapped in cocoon threads, suspended upside down from the oak trees. One of them, she recognized as Shion, was bound tightly and suspended from multiple strands to prevent him from moving. Several huge, dead spiders lay on the ground near his sac.

Only they weren't exactly spiders.

Phae peered closer, trying to understand the double image she was seeing. The jostling sac disoriented her. As it slowed, the image of one of the dead spiders on the turf took form. It was the shape of a woman, lying on her back. Instead of skin there was shaggy black fur, but Phae could see the mound of breasts and the abdomen that connected to a large, bulbous spinneret. Six legs grew from the woman's body at the sides, each like a giant tarantula's. Most spiders had eight legs, but the last two on this creature weren't legs at all, as the woman's arms lay limp. Where the mouth of the spider should have been, a woman's head thick with tangled black hair lay still, her lips deformed in a death cry of mute pain.

Pretty thing, whispered the voice, and a feminine hand stroked the side of Phae's face. It had fingers, just like hers, except the skin was covered in dark, black fur. She felt the other legs coil around her and she started to buck.

Just a taste, my pretty. Just a sip.

She felt teeth sink into the skin on her shoulder.

"No one is left to defend us. Boeotians are ascending to the Archives.

We've barricaded the doors the best we can, but I have little hope.

It is the end of the world. I cannot write for the tears."

- Possidius Adeodat, Archivist of Kenatos

XXIX

The Raekni's fangs sank into Phae's skin, deep into the flesh. There was pain and the bloom of blood and Phae screamed. Struggling was useless; the creature's strong legs held her bound. Her temples throbbed with pressure, but she twisted and heaved, trying to wrench herself free of the strands. Her arms were bundled up at her side and she managed to lower one arm and felt, amazingly, the pommel of the dagger still tucked in her belt.

"Phae!" Shion roared in unremitting fury.

He cares for you? the spider thought gleefully. The fangs left her shoulder, leaving it itching and burning. The strands around her face parted. *See him squirm. The Master comes for him. The Master comes.*

Phae saw him stretched out, suspended above the ground, as if the spiders had intended to pull him apart with all their strength. One of them scuttled over to Shion, stroking him through the sticky strands. *Be patient. Your end will come soon enough. Mayhap the Master will let you watch her die?*

Shion let out a groan of rage, the entire mass of strands quivering with his pent-up emotion. The strange harmonics sounded again as the vibrations took hold.

The Raekni toying with Phae turned back to her, mouth smeared with Phae's blood.

Their eyes met.

Phae stared hard into the Raekni's eyes, gripping her fast with her Dryad magic. The Raekni's mouth contorted with agony, but she could not look away. The magic inside of Phae trembled, nearly failing as the core inside her filled with pain again. But Phae refused to let go of the glance, knowing it to be her final chance. She blinked, severing the connection, dragging all the Raekni's memories with it, stealing every part of her except the mindless instincts of her nature. The memories flitted through the aether, lost forever.

The Raekni's face twisted with confusion. She looked around, befuddled, and Phae managed to slip the dagger from her belt.

He comes. The Master comes.

Phae sensed a presence enter the woods. She could not hear any steps, but it was as if a quiet chill had breathed into the grove. Phae twisted the blade, bringing the edge against the strands at her belly and slit them open. They parted easily, opening her shoulder for broader movement. Hastily, she bent herself double and slashed at the webs tying her ankles and keeping her suspended. The ground met her back with a violent jolt, dazing her.

"Master!" hissed a chorus of Raekni in unison.

Phae saw the shadow in the curtain of silk and watched with horror as the Arch-Rike stepped through the gauzy mesh as if it were nothing more than air. She recognized him from Canton Vaud, when she had last seen him following the murder of the Thirteen. His eyes were cold and relentless, his lips pulled back with exertion and a bitter grimace, which suddenly turned to a smile when he saw her lying on the ground. He was about the same height as her father, though there was very little hair on his scalp, just a dusting of gray stubble. His complexion was like uncooked dough, but it was his eyes that terrified her. He glanced at her face, not her eyes, and then looked away and observed the scene.

"I wasn't totally certain," the Arch-Rike—Shirikant—muttered. "Some trick perhaps? Another feint? Well, it was a merry chase to the last, Tyrus. A bold effort. You've come closer than any man ever has. However did you persuade the Empress to throw all her forces against me? I'm almost tempted to let you live . . . just to hear the tale. But alas, I warned you. And I will keep my promise."

Phae struggled to her feet, dagger gripped in her hand. Her heart thundered inside her chest. Who was she to face such a man all alone? If she could meet his gaze, she was certain she would win. If she could force him, somehow, to look at her.

"It's quite a story," Tyrus said in a muffled voice. "Before I die, tell me one thing. Is Band-Imas still alive? Is he trapped in one of the sarcophagi in Basilides?"

"I *am* Band-Imas," the Arch-Rike said blackly, his face curling with disdain.

"Even in victory, you cannot utter the truth. Why is it you fear the truth so much?"

"What is truth?" the Arch-Rike replied, chuckling with malice. "Your efforts here are wasted, Tyrus. Even now I'm preparing to unleash the Plague inside Kenatos. The Boeotians will fall and it will spread to every kingdom. They will all die. Nothing will stop it this time."

One of the Raekni hissed at Phae, sending a streamer of webbing at her. She jumped and rolled, landing closer to Shion. As she came to her feet, she looked hard at the Raekni's eyes and blinked, snatching her memories too. The creature's eyes went blank and then she began to scuttle around in a continuous circle.

"Stop that!" the Arch-Rike commanded. "Don't look at her eyes! Depart!"

"You fear the truth," Phae said, walking toward him, chin jutting as the Raekni began scuttling back into the trees. She felt a presence brush against her mind.

Sister?

It was the Dryad from the tree nearby.

Help us, Phae begged.

Will you free me from the Master?

I will, Phae thought with hard certainty. *It is why I came here.*

Suddenly the strand holding Shion up snapped and he came tumbling to the ground.

"No!" the Arch-Rike snarled in fury. He charged at Phae, gripping the Tay al-Ard in his hand. He groped to reach her, but she spun away. He missed her, but had already turned and lunged for her again.

"Shion!" Phae called, watching him thrash against his bonds, trying to free himself from the strands.

There was a ripping sound and Hettie tumbled out of her cocoon, landing a short distance from Phae. The girl's face was smudged with bruises and flushed red from hanging upside down, but she launched herself at the Arch-Rike, dagger poised in her hand.

The Arch-Rike looked at her with disgust and dodged as her dagger spun end over end toward his head. Only, Hettie was not aiming at his head. The dagger severed another line, freeing Tyrus as well, who began thrashing through the loosened threads to free himself.

Phae watched the Arch-Rike's hands catch fire, his face contorted with rage and hatred. His eyes were wild with madness, his mouth gnashing as he lunged at Phae again, trying to seize her. She ducked and dodged, twisting around to keep the Arch-Rike at bay.

Then Shion was there, colliding into the Arch-Rike like a battering ram. A spasm of glee shot through Phae as she watched them both smash into a tree. Then both were heaving and fighting, legs and arms a tangle of kicks and blocks.

"Hold him, Shion!" Tyrus yelled in desperation, his eyes blazing with triumph.

Suddenly the Arch-Rike vanished in a plume of smoke and Shion landed on the ground, startled. He lifted his head, looking around.

The Arch-Rike appeared again, his shadow-self materializing, away from them all, well out of arm's reach. His face was twisted with displeasure. "You cannot bind me or trap me," he snarled. "I invented the Uddhava! I have more ways of escape than you can ever imagine. I taught the first Paracelsus my ways. I trained the first Kishion in the art of murder. I am death. I am the Plague. You will not escape these woods."

"Take him!" Tyrus ordered, charging himself. Phae scrambled to her feet, rushing at the fearsome man.

Everything went black. All light was suppressed. It was as if a thick vapor had suddenly appeared, so thick that the air was heavy with a metallic taste.

"I can see you all well enough." The Arch-Rike's voice ghosted through the vapor of darkness. "I can see you too, Phae."

"Say nothing!" Tyrus shouted. "Aran, are you free?"

"Your eyes won't harm me in this," he said menacingly. "Hold my hand, girl. We will go far away. I am the true Seneschal. I will take your oaths."

I'm here, a woman's voice whispered to Phae's mind. She could feel the Dryad's presence behind her.

Phae began to tremble all over, feeling the blackness coil around her, threatening to smother her in darkness. She could not breathe. She could not call out to anyone. The Dryad stepped in front of her. Phae heard the swish of an arm, a blade, and she felt the Dryad stiffen.

The darkness vanished, drawn back into an obsidian gem fastened to a clasp on the Arch-Rike's cloak. The clasp had opened and the cape tumbled to the ground. As it left his shoulders, the Arch-Rike's countenance changed again. It was as if a peel had been removed—a flower bud opening in the spring dawn to reveal the truth. It was a man's face, young in years but stern and serious, handsome and rugged with swirls of gray through the tufts of thick hair. His look and bearing, even the line of his jaw, was Aeduan, except his features were stronger, nobler. Though he was comely and tall, the face was pocked not by scars, but by a deep, deep anger—a blistering fury that was both savage and composed. One of his hands bore a knife, which he had just plunged into the Dryad's heart, thinking she was Phae.

Their eyes met. Phae gripped his gaze, clung to it with all her force. There were so many memories in that gaze, a thousand lifetimes. It was vast beyond reckoning, but somehow her Dryad magic encircled it, billowing to the edges of infinity to snare them all. His eyes widened with panic.

And then the man was gone, pulled away by the Tay al-Ard before she could blink.

The Dryad turned to Phae. Not a mark was on the woman's skin where the dagger had struck. She was visible for only a moment after the darkness had dispelled, and then she vanished. Tears of gratitude sprang to Phae's eyes when she realized the knife wound from Shirikant had almost killed her. If the Dryad had not stepped in the way . . .

Tyrus reached and closed his hand on Phae's shoulder. He hung his head a moment, and then struggled to speak. His face was ashen with worry. "Almost we failed," he whispered hoarsely. "Who freed you from the webs, Phae?"

"I got myself loose. It all happened so fast."

"We must flee," Tyrus said. "Quickly, before the Arch-Rike arrives with others to destroy us here. We know what he truly looks like now. We know how not to be deceived."

"But did you notice," Annon went on, "how much he resembles Shion?"

Tyrus gave Annon a bemused look, and then turned to Phae. "I think we all noticed that."

Shion stood still, his expression already hard with earnestness. "I've seen that face before," he offered. "Where, I cannot remember. But when his mask fell, I knew I had seen him. And loved him." He sighed. "The truth comes in spurts, it seems. This is the land where all the secrets will be revealed." He hefted his knife and then slid it into his belt. "I long for it now." He gave Phae a dark look, one full of brooding and intensity.

With daggers in hand, they slashed through the strands of the Raekni webs, marching firmly toward the direction of the Mother Tree. Phae joined in the effort, knowing that each thrust, each cut, brought them nearer to the heart of the Scourgelands. After confronting such vivid darkness, she no longer feared it. Yet Phae's insides were twisting and wrenching with growing agony. Using her powers had only awakened the pain again. She hunched over, breathing quickly, trying to master herself. They were so close to the end. She could almost hear the faint echoes of unsung music.

Shion charged ahead, slashing viciously at the strands to carve open the path ahead. Prince Aran and her father stayed at her side, each with a hand on her arms to help keep her moving quickly. Her shoulder burned from the savage bite of the Raekni, but that was the least of her problems and not as debilitating as the seed moving inside of her.

"This is the end," Shion said, emerging into the dense woods into an area free of the Raekni webs. Phae felt relief at first, but her father's expression forbade her from rejoicing.

"What is it?" she asked him, clutching his arm and bending double.

"It's later than I thought," he murmured. "We have to find the tree, even if it's dark. Even by the light of fire." He sighed, shifting his grip on her arm. "We don't have much time left."

"These are the last words I may write. The barricades are breached. I've concealed the most important records, the copies of the works of the Paracelsus order, within a hidden chamber known only to the Arch-Rike. These secret works may be all that will survive the carnage. Learn from us. Be wiser than we have been. I bid you, dear reader, farewell."

- Possidius Adeodat, Archivist of Kenatos

XXX

Any sign of the rider?" Baylen asked as Paedrin floated down from the uppermost branches. From the vantage point, Paedrin had searched long and hard for a sign of the dark horseman, but he was not to be seen. A sick, gnawing feeling had entered Paedrin's bones. He felt danger lurking in every shadow and wondered what sort of guardians had been stationed to protect the cleft of rock in the center of the Scourgelands.

Crouching next to Baylen, Paedrin rubbed his chin, chafing the stubble and staring at the bulwark of stone and the ramp carved into rock to provide the single pathway up the side. He did not need to use the ramp, being a Vaettir, but his instincts warned him that it would be the most useful decision to walk up it himself, since a Tay al-Ard could only transport him back to a place where he had physically been. Seeing the ramp would not be enough.

From the base of the promontory, he could see the skeletal remains of an ancient keep, black with lichen and dark moss—crumbling to dust.

"No. I can't even hear the sound of the hooves. There is a storm closing in from the north. It may rain before nightfall."

Baylen stared hard at the stone ramp leading up to the deserted fortress. "The Arch-Rike wouldn't have left it unguarded."

"Obviously. With that single approach, it won't be difficult to defend."

"How far to the ramp? It's open ground, so I don't like it."

"Not far. But with the trees pulled down, there isn't any cover." Paedrin sighed. "We're heading into the jaws of a trap. I hate this."

"Spring the trap then? See what happens?"

"What if it's a bear trap?"

"We came this far, Paedrin. I feel . . . foreboding. No man has walked this land in centuries."

Paedrin heard the crunch of twigs in the woods coming from behind them. He gave a curt gesture to Baylen to silence him and shut his eyes, sensing the presence of three riders approaching them from a flanking position. The jangle of harness and tack followed, and Paedrin could feel dark eyes flash malevolently. He was acutely aware that if he had looked on them with his natural eyes, he'd be dead.

"Run," Paedrin said, rising and holding out the Sword of Winds. "I'll hold them here and join you on the ramp. Go!"

The giant Cruithne tore free from the brush and bounded into the torn earth, rushing across the small clearing toward the stone ramp.

Paedrin's heart was in his throat as the three horsemen charged through the brush. Two of them closed on the Bhikhu and one circumvented, heading after Baylen. Paedrin heard the clink of chains and sensed dark weapons coiling to strike . . . great spiked flails whipping around as the horsemen charged him.

Paedrin took to flight and arced away from the horsemen, swooping away from the riders. His heart hammered with fear, as wave after wave of unease and terror flooded his mind. He could sense the magic from the beings, and he only had his courage to draw on. He knew he had to open his eyes or risk smashing into the tree branches, so he opened them into slits and changed course to strike the horse of the rider charging after Baylen. His blade slashed at its withers and it screamed in pain. The spiked ball came at his face and he thought for an instant it would smash his nose, but Paedrin managed to twist sideways and felt the sharp tips just breeze past his mouth. He took a long loop inside the clearing to build up speed and came at the next horseman. With that one, he came head-on, sword aiming for the horse's nose, and the beast shied from him, exposing its neck. Paedrin knew a crushing blow would be waiting for him, so he did not follow through with a lunge but banked in the other direction. The horses gained speed, bearing down on Baylen as he chuffed toward the ramp.

Paedrin went skyward next, feeling the first traces of mist on his face. He opened his eyes and found the clouds bearing down hard. Distant pops of thunder came from far away. He tucked and then re-directed the Sword back down at his foes, aiming for the back of one of the riders. He heard a hissing sound and an arrow suddenly lanced by him, missing. One of the riders held a blackwood bow and reached his crooked arm to string another.

Paedrin frowned with concentration. Closing his eyes again increased the speed as he plunged the Sword through the rider's back, impaling him, knocking him from the saddle. He had buried the sword to the hilt in the rider's back and the rider twisted sideways as he fell from the saddle. Paedrin released the blade to avoid being trapped in the fall. He felt the magic release him and landed in a low stance, one arm extended for balance, striking a pose.

The rider stood, still bearing the blade inside his body. No blood came from the wound. In one hand, he gripped the chained weapon, swinging it around toward Paedrin's head. The Bhikhu ducked even lower and did a quick forward roll, then tried to sweep the rider's legs from under him. But it was like striking a rooted tree. He felt the jarring impact, the immovable presence, and realized with dread he was facing a being that was not mortal. The chain came around again, and he barely managed to dodge it. The rider faced him, the blade sticking from his chest, and Paedrin felt his stomach lurch with the loss of his blade.

The other horse and rider still bore down on Baylen, and Paedrin saw there was no chance the Cruithne could reach the ramp in time, not against a charging beast.

The distraction nearly cost Paedrin his life. He arched backward, felt the sting of one of the ball's spurs cut his chin and realized it had nearly knocked his head off. He flipped over and backward, landing on his feet again, his face burning with pain.

Paedrin charged the dark rider, inhaling, and felt himself soar up above his enemy. His momentum would have carried him far over, but he puffed out his breath and came straight down on him, landing on the shoulders. Paedrin slid down his back, found the hilt and pulled the blade free. He was backhanded by a gauntleted fist and an explosion of light danced in his eyes as he realized his cheekbone had been broken. Pain rocked him backward, but he had no time to think. Invoking the weapon's magic, he sailed up and away, arcing toward the final charging horseman from behind.

Baylen had turned to face the attacker, squatting low and holding one of his broadswords in two hands to slash the beast's legs out from under it—or get crushed himself. Paedrin infused the Sword with his need, increasing speed, and watched as Baylen executed his bold maneuver, lunging away from the steed while slashing at its forelegs with his sword. The rider had anticipated his intent and leapt free of the saddle as the horse was cut down. As Baylen rolled to his feet, the spiked ball struck him full in the chest, throwing him from his feet at least a dozen paces, where he landed on his back.

Paedrin swore under his breath and sailed past the horseman, banking slightly to pass him, and landed where Baylen had fallen. The Cruithne's face contorted with pain. The front of his chest armor was caved in where the ball had struck him and red stains appeared around the gashes.

"Up," Paedrin urged, grabbing Baylen's hand, and helped pull him to his feet. "Hide in the ruins up there. I'll find you."

"Better than standing and fighting these things," Baylen said, huffing and grimacing with pain. He massaged his massive chest and winced anew.

"Run," Paedrin said, dragging him toward the ramp. The three enemies advanced relentlessly, one of their steeds thrashing in agony on the turf. An arrow was loosed and Paedrin knocked it aside with his blade.

"It's the only way up or down," Baylen said, nodding toward the ramp.

"I can get us down again another way. Getting up is the hard part. Go!"

As Baylen worked his way up the steep slope of the ramp, Paedrin left him and flew up to the top of the rock cleft. The promontory was a maze of tumbled stone walls and fallen buttresses. There were no surviving structures in place. Paedrin hurried in a full arcing circle around the entire structure, trying to quickly size up the dimensions of the ruins. It was as large as the Arch-Rike's palace in Kenatos, except there was no city on an island beneath it. Every wall had crumbled to ruin, every bailey and rampant had been tossed down. At the center of the promontory, a dozen or so buttresses still stood, holding up a portion of a roof that had not caved in yet. Streamers of mist from the descending clouds began to smother the cleft, and Paedrin knew the visibility would be hampered shortly. He did not feel safe touching down on the ground yet, not without a chance to search for enemies, so he alighted on the top of the buttresses, on the apex where the stones joined to lend their strength to the roof. He touched it with featherlight weight, testing to see if it would give way, but the stone had survived despite the winds and storms of previous generations and it held him up well.

Mist crept in streamers along the stones, feeding down into the lengths below. How strange it was that mist should appear so suddenly, obscuring things when the day earlier had been . . .

His eyes widened when he realized the mist had been summoned. It had been summoned to blot out the sun, summoned to protect the hide of the Fear Liath. In crushing anguish, he realized that this was the final lair, this was the place most heavily protected. Perhaps not by one Fear Liath but several, and he was violating the sanctuary with his presence. A chill swept down to his toes and he felt the violent urge to fly away and leave Baylen to defend himself. They needed to get off the promontory immediately. The peril increased with each moment.

He scanned the grounds quickly, looking for a place to set down—a place where his memory might be used at some future moment to bring others deep inside the Scourgelands. Was this the right place? Broken walls littered the promontory. Derelict chimneys and skeletal archways still existed, but they protected nothing. In his mind's eye, Paedrin could imagine a sprawling courtyard, grander than the Paracelsus Towers in Kenatos. A few ragged trees, bereft of all foliage, had grown in seams and cracks in the rubble. The mist swept down as a veil, chilling him.

Low chanting sounded from just below where he was perched. To his surprise, he saw black-robed Rikes ascending from a gaping maw of stone in the floor just beneath him. Many held staves with glowing stones embedded into one end. A few carried smoking brands, reminiscent of the ones carried by the Boeotians to drive away helpful spirits. The Rikes were chanting in some ancient language, words that Paedrin did not understand. They emerged from hidden crypts within the bowels of the ancient fortress. A dozen men . . . then another dozen . . . wave after wave of Rikes emerging into the misty gloom, humming and chanting, some glancing fearfully at the shelves of rock and crumbled walls. The sound of clopping hooves approached and more riders appeared in the debris, their hoods concealing their faces. One raised a crooked arm and pointed, directing the Rikes with sibilant hisses in some ancient language.

Paedrin screwed up his courage, knowing he would need to leave before the Arch-Rike himself arrived. Fear raged inside of him, threatening to spoil his courage forever. The mist was thick and heavy and Paedrin gently inhaled, coming off the roof and floating away from the apex of the buttresses he had perched on like a gray dove.

Baylen was heading into a trap. This was not a battle they could win. The mist would help conceal them if they fled—hopefully. Paedrin quickly explored the ruins, seeing riders throughout the maze. He went around the complete perimeter, looking for a place to land, a small shelf of rock where he could bring others back with him—a place away from the deadly ramp and the deadly guardians there.

Around the base of the promontory, the woods of the Scourgelands pressed against the rock, giving it the impression of an island rising in a lake of oak burs. All the trees looked alike, of course, as they typically did to a young man raised in a crowded city. But as he glided along the far end of the promontory, there was a single tree that struck his attention and caught his gaze.

What struck Paedrin was the hideousness of the tree. He wasn't sure if it was even an oak tree at all, because it was so misshapen and distorted. At first look, it didn't even look like a single tree but as if twelve other trees had all grown together into a single, contorted mass. It was not the largest tree he had seen in the Scourgelands either. But it was singularly grotesque, and the trunk seemed to split in the middle, revealing a cave-like maw at the base that showed light from the other side, as if the tree had two massive legs and it were squatting. A variety of gnarled branches had grown from the hulking shape, most stick straight like the quills of a porcupine. Rotten foliage hung in clumps around it.

Paedrin stared, his heart burning with fire as he saw the mist descend and shroud the image of the tree below. He felt an overwhelming urge to fly down to the misshapen behemoth for a closer look, but a wave of sudden dread soured his mind. What would be guarding it? He thought it wise to land atop the promontory and watch it a moment, to see if he could discern any guardians. He knew it likely that a Fear Liath was hunting in the mist. He could sense them, their foreboding presence and darkest evil. Had Baylen reached the top of the promontory yet, and would he meet the Rikes and soldiers soon? His mind twisted itself in knots with all the possibilities.

At the edge of the promontory, just below him, Paedrin saw a fallen wall, broken to crumbled bits. He lowered himself down, breathing out softly, and decided to make his watch there, amidst the rubble. It was near the queer-looking tree, a place he would remember and be able to describe later. It was away from the escarpment where the Rikes gathered and would provide a good view of the tree below.

A horrible dread filled Paedrin's stomach. He had to be away, had to try to escape while he could. How would he find his way back to the ramp in the mist? He could not worry about that. He needed to position himself on the promontory. This was the legacy he would bring back to Tyrus—the atonement he would offer for his failure.

As Paedrin's feet touched the uneven stone, black roots shot up from the cracks of moldering stone and fastened around his ankles and up to his calves. They felt like iron and began squeezing with ruthless intensity, causing wrenching pain to shoot up his legs. He had barely noticed the solitary shell of an oak tree nearby. The clutches of the roots tightened further and suddenly he saw something dark materialize from the shadows. It wasn't the bulk of a Fear Liath—it was made of snatches of night that coalesced. Paedrin saw the dagger gripped fiercely in the man's hand. He saw the expression of hate on Kiranrao's face.

The fear in the Bhikhu's chest was a razor.

XXXI

Utter exhaustion had finally driven Kiranrao to tempt sleep in the crook of a shattered tree. He leaned against the rugged bark, trying to stifle the ribbons of pain on his arms and legs and across his shoulders. The last attack from the Weir had almost destroyed him, but he had managed to slay each one of the beasts. He could still smell their fur and blood, and the scent made him nauseous. His head drooped and he caught himself, listening keenly into the darkness. He was nothing but a shadow smudge himself, but he knew he could not rest for long. He knew the forest was still hunting him.

So was the memory.

A wave of self-loathing threatened to smother and choke him. Alone, in the darkest night of his life, he shuddered at the memory of murdering Khiara. Why should the death of one person be the rack on his conscience, one that threatened his very notion of himself? He was Kiranrao, master of Havenrook, lord of the Romani, father of all greed. He had swindled men and then left them dying in puddles of their own blood when they attempted retribution against him. He knew about suffering in all of its shades. He remembered a madwoman in Kenatos who used to sing before the wealthiest citizens and was reduced to living in squalor and bird droppings. He had faced the gallows and not flinched. Why was murdering Khiara so different?

But it was different. In the dark, his conscience accused him. She was a Shaliah, someone whose very existence was one of self-sacrifice and honor. It was cloying, actually, and he found himself despising the woman despite needing her gifts to stay alive himself. He had promised to repay her. Was it that broken promise that haunted him now? Why should it—when he had broken so many?

Somehow, Kiranrao realized deep inside that he had crossed a new border of ignominy. He had done it almost on a whim, to hamper Tyrus's efforts more than to help his own cause. Yet now, he was lying to himself again. He had thought about killing her before. The power she possessed . . . the ability to heal and restore was completely anathema to his own power, the power over death. The blade Iddawc had whispered to him to kill her. He closed his eyes, resting his forehead on his wrists, still holding the stained blade in his hand. He had not sheathed it since coming into the Scourgelands. There was something in its power . . . something in the way it whispered to him.

He shuddered again, trying to banish those murky thoughts. He could have retreated into the woods without anyone to stop him. He *should* have done that. Yet he had not, and there was no way to undo the death he had caused. Why had he succumbed to that impulse?

When had he lost control over his own mind?

He rubbed his bleary eyes, trying to listen for the telltale sound of danger. He had to survive the Scourgelands. Tyrus would not be the only man to have succeeded. Kiranrao was hungry, but determined to preserve his dwindling supply of food. He dared not forage for sustenance, knowing the diseases inflicted on those who ate. Khiara had removed that disease, a *keramat* of tremendous power. He coveted power. What power he could not have, he wanted to destroy so that others could not. He gritted his teeth in anger and frustration. He would kill Tyrus, of course. He would kill them all. Even that Quiet Kishion was weak compared to the power of the blade. Even an immortal could be killed.

Even Shirikant.

Kiranrao smoldered in silent fury, thinking on the Arch-Rike's face, wishing his hatred could summon the man in person. What a puppet master the Arch-Rike pretended to be. Well, Kiranrao would sever the strings and let the entire play collapse in a heap of wooden parts.

Even with his eyes closed, he saw Khiara in his mind, her eyes accusing. A stain of brown blood was on her tunic front. He could almost feel her standing near him, her eyes full of pity as well as condemnation.

"Leave me," Kiranrao muttered. "Begone."

The silent eyes continued to bore into his skull. Was that a whisper of breath? He opened his eyes, gazing in shock, fully expecting to see her shade kneeling by him. He saw nothing, but he still felt that she was there . . . or some other malevolent shade.

He looked furtively into the blackness, craning his neck to listen. Was that a sound? His imagination?

He started wildly, trying to calm his tattered nerves. No one could know. That was the end of it. That was why his thoughts were sloshing back and forth like a barrel of beer on a wagon. He would kill them all then. Every one of the band who had seen his shameful act, he would put them to death and silence their accusations forever. The Archivists of Kenatos would never scribe down what he had done.

He would destroy all of his enemies, including the Arch-Rike . . . or Shirikant . . . or whatever name he sought to call himself. And when he was done, he would rid his conscience of the stain. He would go to a Dryad tree and he would force the Dryad to purge the guilt. He would be free of all responsibility then. No one would know, not even himself.

He had spent his energies trying to escape the Scourgelands. He realized that he needed to stay . . . to find a Dryad tree and to make sure the others had perished. Perhaps he could find the Mother Tree itself? Perhaps that tree would unchain him from his conscience.

He would kill Prince Aran first. A cold certainty began to seep inside his inner parts. One by one, he would hunt them down. One by one, he would kill them.

Kiranrao fell asleep with thoughts of murder toying in his mind.

When the smoky shape emerged from the mist as Kiranrao, Paedrin stared with shock. He doubted his senses then, for he had been deceived by imposters before. He struggled against the tangling roots fastening to his legs, but it was like swimming with chains.

"Pity you're not Prince Aran," Kiranrao said with a sulky tone. "I had thought to kill him next, but you will do, Bhikhu."

A spasm of terror shot through Paedrin at the words, at the total lack of humanity in Kiranrao's dead eyes. He tried to squelch it, but it was like commanding his heart not to quail in the midst of a lightning storm or a shipwreck.

"I also pity that," Paedrin said flippantly. "I wish he were here too."

Kiranrao sauntered closer, the blade poised and ready. Paedrin's mind worked furiously. Should he start sawing at the roots? Would they yield like normal plants, or was this some sort of magic that was trapping him?

"I've wanted to kill you for a long time, Bhikhu. Hettie isn't here to stay my hand. Not that she could this time."

Paedrin shifted his hips, trying to ignore the squeezing pain in his legs. If he were flat on his back with the ague, he couldn't be more helpless. But he was not defenseless. He had trained his entire life to prepare for such a moment. The Uddhava would help him. Kiranrao looked almost trancelike. His inner spark was gone. His personality had been bleached away. Delay him—make him react to you.

"I always knew Hettie controlled you. So, Kiranrao, are there any Romani proverbs for such an occasion? Any words you say to the man you're about to murder? A good beginning is half the work?"

A weary expression came over Kiranrao's face—almost a smile, but not quite. "A postponement till morning . . . a postponement forever."

Paedrin held up one hand, palm facing Kiranrao. "I recall one that Hettie told me. It is no secret that is known to three." He slowly brought the sword behind his back with the other, watching the Romani advance.

"Fair words, Bhikhu. At least you understand now why I'm killing you."

"I propose a bargain," Paedrin said.

"There's no stopping the force of a going wheel by hand," Kiranrao said, starting to flank Paedrin on his left.

"I have a new one for you. The youngest thorns are the sharpest."

Paedrin brought the Sword of Winds to his chest, pommel up, and summoned the power of the stone in the hilt.

It was the same trick that the imposter Kiranrao had used against him in Shatalin. The magic of the stone went out in a flood of greenish light and Kiranrao screamed in pain and began slashing the air in front of him, his eyes blistering with the magic. Paedrin ducked low and began slicing through the roots with the blade.

Kiranrao roared with hatred and agony, the blade dangerously close to Paedrin's shoulder as he maneuvered away from the random sweep. The Bhikhu sawed at the roots and one came free, releasing the crushing grip on his right ankle, and he dropped to the lowest stance he could muster, feeling the weight of Kiranrao looming above him.

Paedrin didn't have time to swing the sword around, but he struck Kiranrao's abdomen—his liver, to be precise—with his open palm and the Romani tumbled backward, thrashing on the ground. Paedrin resumed sawing on the other cord of root and managed to sever its grip as the Romani made it back to his feet again and lunged at him, slashing wildly with the dagger.

Paedrin took in a sharp breath of air and used the Sword's magic to vault into the sky, above the danger. He stared down at Kiranrao, feeling the temptation to flee. But no, he had to face Kiranrao now. There would not be a better time to fight him, with his eyes burning in pain and his wits scattered.

Paedrin exhaled sharply and came down hard, landing on Kiranrao's shoulders, knocking him to the ground. He swung the sword against Kiranrao's neck, but Paedrin's legs were kicked loose from beneath him and he struggled to keep himself up.

Paedrin scurried backward as Kiranrao charged him again, his face a mutation of savagery. The Bhikhu twisted sideways as the dagger was thrust at him once, twice, almost grazing the fabric of Paedrin's tunic. He could not think about the risk he was taking. One cut from the blade . . .

Paedrin jumped and did a reverse circle kick, smashing his heel into Kiranrao's cheek. That also staggered him, but just for a moment and he was back again, coming down with the blade against Paedrin's shoulder. Reflexes saved the Bhikhu. He caught his enemy on the forearm with a block and their arms became tangled as both sought to wrestle the other into submission.

Kiranrao's knee came up into Paedrin's groin, a merciless blow that sucked his breath away and sent his body into convulsions of agony. He sank to one knee and whipped the Sword around, slashing through Kiranrao's front and spraying blood. Paedrin saw the cut wasn't deep and regretted it immediately.

If the Romani was debilitated by the pain, it was only slightly. Paedrin went at him again, trying to use the reach of the Sword to greater advantage. Kiranrao twisted sideways to defend himself, keeping out of the blade's path through uncanny reflexes. They collided again and Paedrin grabbed Kiranrao's wrist, trying to twist him around and put a hold on him that would disable him, but Kiranrao knew the ways of escaping such methods, and the grip faltered.

"Have I lasted . . . longer than you expected?" Paedrin huffed, trading blocks and kicks.

The dagger passed just a hairbreadth from his chest, and Paedrin swallowed as he jumped back, realizing that he was being foolish still. He was nearing the edge of the cliff and began retreating toward it.

Kiranrao's face was mottled with pain and anger. He deftly pursued Paedrin, feinting with the dagger, listening keenly for a sound that would trigger him to lunge at the Bhikhu.

"I thought you had fled the woods," Paedrin said, reaching the edge. He could feel a gust of wind on his back. "You seemed in a hurry to leave the Scourgelands."

"I'm not afraid of Shirikant," Kiranrao huffed. "Even he will fall to the blade. Even he fears it. I came here to spit on his ruins. *I* am the master of the Scourgelands now."

"You are nothing but a thief and a coward," Paedrin said. "You are a murderer, a common criminal. You will die here and no grave will be dug for you. Your only hope of being remembered is if a Cockatrice turns you to stone."

Kiranrao gave a throaty laugh. "It is more than you will get, Bhikhu. What glory awaits your kind? What comes from the briar but the berry? Reputations last longer than lives, Bhikhu. Even Tyrus craves this. It is his weakness. It is the weakness of all men."

"When people remember you . . ." Paedrin said, feeling his heart begin to churn with emotion, feeling words come into his mouth, words that rolled out in a forceful gush. ". . . they will sneer. They will chuckle behind their hands. Is this the man who made kingdoms shake? Is this the man who made the earth tremble under the weight of all those burdened wagons? All the kings lie in glory, Kiranrao. The Kings of Wayland, and Stonehollow, the rulers of Alkire and Silvandom. Every one of them. But not you. Your name will be said as a curse."

As he said the words, Paedrin knew—somehow—that they would be true. He felt a queer sensation, as if he had uttered a prophecy.

Kiranrao rushed, slashing with the blade of Iddawc, his mouth churning with rage and spittle. Paedrin stepped off the edge of the cliff and let himself fall before kicking off the mountain and veering upward to meet the Romani in the air. A blur of motion caught his gaze.

He watched Kiranrao plummeting toward the forest floor before vanishing into a gasp of smoke.

XXXII

It was Annon who spotted the riderless horse first, and he hissed for the others in warning. The mount was lathered and plodded through the grove, its reins dragging on the turf. The nostrils flared and it shook its mane. The group hid behind oak trees, each one claiming his or her own, except for Shion and Phae. The steed huffed past them, oblivious to their presence, skulking deeper into the woods. Annon looked at Tyrus, saw the baffled expression, and knew he could not make anything of it either.

From the wilderness where they had come, the howl of the Weir picked up again, causing repeat cries from several sides. They were getting closer and Annon felt the worry gnawing at him. He was tired beyond imagining, aching for rest and sleep, but there was no stopping now, nothing but the fear of being hunted, realizing that if night fell again before they had found the tree, it would be too late. He had the numbing premonition that they wouldn't live to see the dawn if that happened.

"There wasn't a rider," Prince Aran said. "What do you make of it?"

"I have no idea," Tyrus replied. "Shirikant must be pulling in all of his defenses." He gazed through the trees at the dwindling sunlight. The shadows grew darker with each passing moment. "Hurry. This way." He pointed.

Annon swallowed hard and they traversed the twisting woods. Hettie stayed close to him, her breath ragged from the long and tortuous walk. Her face was ashen with fatigue, but she managed a quick smile to him and patted his shoulder.

The woods broke away not far ahead, and Tyrus raised his hand. He picked out the widest oak, the most imposing barrier, and directed them all to cluster behind it.

"Hettie, what do you make of the ground?" Tyrus asked her.

She came forward, crouching low, and studied the land in front of them. The earth was churned and trees had been pulled up by their roots and dragged away. It was haphazard, disorderly, but it created a wide space between them and the base of the massive promontory jutting ahead. Annon craned his neck, seeing the ribs of craggy stone rising like arches into the sky. At the top, he saw the ruined battlement walls of some fallen citadel. The sky to the north was roiling with clouds and he saw the vivid flash of lightning coming from the distance. A rumble of thunder followed it shortly.

"We made it this far," Annon said, gazing up at the fallen fortress. Part of him didn't believe it was possible. Would he snap awake and realize it was only a vision? The bark of the oak was rough against his palm and he stroked it, wondering if the tree had been there when the foundation stones of the ruins had first been laid.

Tyrus breathed heavily. He stared at the gap between the woods and the ruins, a gap that would open them to the view of anyone on top of the cleft. "We will be seen advancing," he muttered darkly. "And who knows what pits and traps are waiting there. There is a reason the trees have been broken down, though I cannot figure what it is." He wiped his eyes, shaking his head with weariness. He passed over to another tree, examining the view from another angle. "What do you make out, Hettie?"

She stayed within the protective brush of the woods. "The ground has been churned recently. Possibly today. I see hoof-prints, but I need to get closer to see anything." She craned her neck, staring up at the promontory. "Soldiers patrol the top."

Tyrus sighed. "He'll keep beasts below to hunt us and intelligent men above to shoot arrows or catapults from above. I think he razed the trees to help them see us coming. We have to go around then." He turned to Annon. "Remind me what the Dryad told you. Where is the Mother Tree?"

"It's not on the promontory, but somewhere here around it. Do you think Shirikant razed her tree?"

"He may want us to believe so. I think if he were going to raze it, he would have long ago. There is no benefit to delay. What about the bridge to Mirrowen? Remind me of that."

Annon cleared his throat. "She said it was in the center of the promontory, in the midst of the ruins."

"Heavily guarded," Tyrus observed. "The Mother Tree gives us the word, I believe. The word needed to pass the worlds. Did you not say that?"

"Yes, Tyrus."

"Forgive my memory. I'm dreadfully tired. We can't stay here or the Weir will catch us." He stroked his chin, pondering deeply. "We don't have the men or the means to fight off a garrison. But we can confuse them. We don't know where Shirikant is, but I would guess he is closer to the tree. If only we knew." He rubbed his forehead briskly. "Time for another deception. We should divide our numbers. Here is my plan, but we don't have long to argue it." The keening of the Weir sounded much closer. "Time eludes us. Hettie will use her charm and disguise herself as Phae. She will come with me into the clearing. We will draw their attention to us, providing time for you to slip through the woods. I'll announce we're surrendering and see if I can draw some of them off the ridge to arrest us. If they come, we'll use our fireblood to make smoke and confusion. When I start, you do the same, start setting fire to the woods around us, just enough to cause some smoke and add to the confusion. If they charge at Hettie and me, we'll use the Tay al-Ard to come back to this spot and then circumnavigate the promontory the opposite direction as you . . . or track you if that seems more appropriate. Whichever of us finds the tree first, we'll wait for the others there and then attack the promontory together after Phae has gotten the name." He looked quickly at each of their faces. "Any suggestions or improvements? Speak them quickly."

"Will they be deceived by the surrender?" Aran asked.

"Not Shirikant. But if I can confuse the guards posted on the promontory, that will be well enough. Shirikant can't be everywhere at once. He has set his forces in motion and they will respond without him. He's dependent on living beings doing his bidding. Any other thoughts? Quickly!"

Shion frowned. "Once we separate, it will be difficult finding each other."

"True. More difficult to find us as well. We know our goal and must *act* with the best knowledge that we have." Tyrus looked deep into Annon's eyes, reaching out and squeezing his shoulder. "We are truly a mastermind. You know my goal. Get Phae to the Mother Tree at all costs. That tree has the knowledge we need. If dividing will improve our odds of success, even slightly, we must do what must be done." His hand gave a subtle squeeze on Annon's shoulder, unseen by the others.

Annon stared into his eyes, realizing what Tyrus intended. If he had to, Tyrus was prepared to unleash the full power of the fireblood and invoke his own madness to save them. He had given Annon a ring that would summon the Tay al-Ard into his hand, to stop Tyrus from using it while enraged. A sickening feeling crept into Annon's stomach.

Hettie approached, only she looked exactly like Phae now, her magic providing an exact duplicate of the Dryad-born's appearance. "Let's go, Tyrus. Before my courage melts."

Annon looked at her, feeling the urge to hug her. His pulse quickened with dread. "Watch yourself," he said hoarsely.

She gave him a quick hug, planting a kiss on his cheek followed by a pat.

Tyrus looked at the real Phae, his expression heartbreakingly tender. He seemed unable to speak, nodding to her in farewell. Phae shook her head, unwilling to accept that, and gave him a fierce hug, burying her face in his chest. His expression shifted from pain to sadness to ferocious determination.

As the Weir howled again, even closer, Annon watched the two leave the shelter of the trees and approach the promontory.

"I think I should limp," Hettie murmured, suddenly clutching Tyrus's arm and feigning injury. Her heart was pounding with fear at their exposed position. The calls from the Weir were drawing closer and she knew it would not be long before they bounded after them from the screen of trees.

"Good thinking," Tyrus said, fidgeting with his collar. She noticed a small strand of leather around his neck and he freed it, withdrawing a small leather pouch, very small and slender, as if it contained a single leaf.

"What is that pouch?" she asked, seeing him free it but letting it dangle over his shirt. "More Paracelsus magic?"

The sky seemed to be boiling, the clouds coming down like a blacksmith's hammer on an awaiting anvil. How fitting a storm was threatening to break on such a moment as this. The wind whipped up, blowing her hair in front of her face, and she brushed it back.

"Not magic," Tyrus replied.

"What is it then?" she asked, always curious, not willing to let him be evasive in such a moment. She saw the Tay al-Ard in his left hand, gripped tightly. The veins on his fingers were pronounced. He exuded a calm self-assurance, but she could see the tension in the crinkled skin around his eyes. He stared up at the massive bulwark with defiance.

"Romani poison. Monkshood."

Her heart went cold at the words. "Why?" she gasped.

He refused to look at her. "If this ends badly, Hettie, I'm determined it will end. I told Annon earlier that I was willing to sacrifice my mind to succeed. What I did not tell him was that I had no intention of spending the rest of my days insane. I picked a poison that would kill me relatively quickly, but allow me to do some damage to them first. I make this sacrifice willingly, Hettie. Your mother spared my life so that I could save you. Allow me, after all these years, to do what I can to save yours."

Her throat became thick. "Do you think we'll fail?"

He stared ahead at the promontory. "I didn't come here to succeed. I came here so that Phae would."

They were halfway to the promontory, two figures in the midst of a broken clearing. Hettie's heart raced with dread and anticipation. She looked up again, seeing the small figures of soldiers lined up along the fragments of the battlement walls. Some held spears and others had long bows. A few carried torches.

Tyrus put his arm around Hettie's shoulder and stopped, staring up. Were they in range of the archers? Probably. None of them had raised their bows to fire yet and no one had shouted a challenge down at them either.

Tyrus stooped slightly, and then lifted up his chin. He called out in a clear, firm voice. "I am Tyrus of Kenatos and this is my daughter. We surrender!"

There was a ripple of murmurs from the crest of the promontory.

Hettie saw the Weir emerge from the ring of trees, at least forty, if not more, stalking toward them, hides bristling. She felt a shiver go through her. *Pyricanthas. Sericanthas. Thas.*

"We surrender!" Tyrus yelled. "Is there a healer? My daughter is injured!"

Hettie felt her mouth go hot, watching the baleful glares of the Weir as they padded forward, their hides vanishing before reappearing moments later, much closer. Strange dust glittered from them as they moved, paused, moved again, bearing down on them and increasing speed.

From the cluster of soldiers emerged a black-garbed Rike with pale hair. "I am Lukias," he shouted down at them from the top of the promontory. "And I am ordered to watch you both die."

Annon's muscles burned as they ran. As each oak tree whipped by, he stared at it, trying to find the telltale description the Dryad had given him. With the storm clouds, it seemed that night was falling even earlier and he was afraid they would run right past it in the twilight. He was worried sick about Hettie and felt the danger and threat rise in a suffocating tide. Even though she was with Tyrus, he feared for her. He had pushed himself beyond his normal limits, and each step made his joints ache and brought a numbing fatigue.

Snarls from the Weir came from behind as the first of the beasts overtook them.

Annon whirled and raised his fists, repeating the Vaettir words in his mind and unleashing a blast of fire, turning the beast into ash. His heart went giddy with excitement at the power, and he felt the desire to let it loose throughout the woods, to consume the ancient forest in a blaze of triumphant glory. Another Weir launched at him from the left and he managed to sidestep it. Shion stabbed the beast as soon as it landed, plunging his daggers into its neck with perfect accuracy.

A third hissed in fury and raced toward them, bounding at Prince Aran, who met its charge as an immovable stone. The two collided and the Prince was scored by the Weir's claws but managed to strike its eyes himself, viciously blinding the feline with his hooked fingers. The beast wailed in pain and attacked in a frenzy but was put to death by Shion's blades in an instant.

"Go on!" Shion ordered, beckoning them to keep moving, for undoubtedly there were other Weir coming after them still. With hands still burning with unspent flames, Annon resumed the sprint, dodging past trees and keeping his wits as sharp as he could despite the thickening fog inside his head.

"Wait!"

The voice came from above, startling them.

The branches overhead were snapping as something battled through the foliage high above. Shion grabbed Phae's arm and pulled her after him, trying to flee the voice, but she dug in her heels. "It's Paedrin!" she shouted.

Annon had also recognized the voice. The branches broke loose and the Bhikhu came soaring down from the heights of the trees, his eyes wide with excitement and desperation. He plummeted to the ground, landing in a Bhikhu stance, one hand forward with several fingers up, the Sword of Winds tucked back behind him deferentially.

"Paedrin!" Annon shouted, rushing toward him, but Aransetis blocked the way.

"Hold, we don't *know* it's him!" Aran warned.

The Bhikhu straightened, searching their faces. "Of course you suspect me, with all we've been through together. You're still here. Phae, you're alive!" He laughed with surprise. "I thought you were . . . of course not . . . a trick of Tyrus. I know where the Dryad tree is!" His eyes were so thrilled with excitement, he almost looked deranged. "I know where it is! I've just come from there. It's surrounded by guardians, but I've been there . . . my feet have touched the ground by it. I can take you there, right this moment. Tyrus?" He seemed to have noticed finally that Tyrus was not among them. "Where's Hettie?"

"How can you confirm our trust in you?" Prince Aran warned.

"Look at me!" Paedrin said, impatient. "I'm bleeding, exhausted, and half-mad with delirium, but it *is* me. If I had leprosaria would you think I was Mathon? If I called you sheep-brains, would you think I was Erasmus? I'm Paedrin Bhikhu," he said, beginning to float, bringing his feet straight up into the air and balancing himself on the sword pommel with one finger. "I can take you to the tree *right now* with the Tay al-Ard." He came down suddenly, his eyes fierce. "Now I ask again—where are Tyrus and Hettie?"

"They're at the base of the promontory," Annon said. "Trying to buy us time to find the tree. He has the Tay al-Ard."

Paedrin's face wrenched with pain. "There are too many to fight, for them or for us. I've been atop the promontory and seen the ruins. He has five hundred men up there if he has fifty." Paedrin wiped his face. "The tree is ringed by creatures on every side, Weir mostly, but there are some brown-cloaked creatures too with bows as well. They shot at me the moment I came down, but if we had the Tay al-Ard, I could bring us right there in the middle. Some of them were trailing me and will be here shortly." He screwed up his face and let out a Romani curse. "We are so close!"

Annon stared at Paedrin, believing he was who he said he was. He had just the right amount of frantic energy and bravado. There were no rings on his hands either and his impatience and desperation were common to everyone at the moment.

"Which way is the tree?" Shion asked, grabbing Paedrin's arm. "Point it out."

"That way," Paedrin said, motioning the direction they were going. "But we're outnumbered. You're strong, Shion, but if enough Weir pounce on you, even you'll get pinned down. Maybe if we go around and try to flank them? But they won't go far from the tree, I don't think. They know we're coming for it. They just need to wait."

Annon saw the awful dilemma. Maybe Tyrus had suspected it too. He stared down at his hand, at the invisible ring on his finger. With it, he could summon the Tay al-Ard. He could let Paedrin use it to bring them to the Mother Tree. But doing so would trap Tyrus and Hettie in the midst of the clearing without a way to escape.

There was a flash of movement in the trees coming from both sides. The Weir from the tree had joined the ones stalking them from behind. The forces were converging on each side.

"We're surrounded," Phae warned in fear.

The Weir rushed at them, howling with vengeance as they charged through the maze of trees. Annon stared at his hand, frozen with indecision. Tyrus had laid the burden on his shoulders. Somehow, he had known. Summoning the Tay al-Ard would have consequences. Without it, Tyrus would probably use the fireblood and go mad. Hettie might die. Staring at his hand, he wondered what fate he would unleash and what guilt he would suffer as a result of his decision. He did not have time to think it through. He did not have time to reason it out.

Closing his eyes, he invoked the power of the ring. The object he desired appeared in his outstretched hand, still warm from Tyrus's own grip.

What have I done? he thought bleakly.

Paedrin stared at him in shock.

"Hasten," Annon whispered, extending the Tay al-Ard out so all could reach it. He met Paedrin's gaze, who seemed to be realizing the implications himself by the widening of his eyes. Annon nodded curtly, steeling his emotions. "Take us there, Paedrin."

XXXIII

Phae's insides wrenched as the magic of the Tay al-Ard hurtled them through the span of woods, arriving in a moment in a different location. Queasiness mixed with the dizziness of the power, and she grasped Shion's arm to keep from falling. What had been the subtle murmur of Dryad magic permeating the woods became a roar that flooded her with its presence. She sensed that she was standing on a vast web of interlocking roots that furrowed deep beneath the earth and whose tendrils expanded not just around the perimeter of a single tree, but seemed to connect in small and vast ways to every other tree throughout the impenetrable maze. It took no more than a single instant to realize they had arrived at the proper place. And it took less than an instant for the defenders of that lair to be aware of their presence.

Fire exploded from Annon's hands as massive, frenzied Weir began to appear. Their fur and hide expelled that strange dust-like hoarfrost as they moved, powerful sinews bounding, claws tearing up the ground. The blast from the fireblood struck them full, scattering and destroying the creatures, but another wave was coming from behind.

Phae's heart spasmed with terror at the immediate threat, knowing they had plunged into the center of the hive, that their survival against such a host of foes would be short-lived if she did not make it to the tree quickly.

The Bhikhu sprung like an arrow, his sword slashing through the nearest Weir, who came at him with savage ferocity. Shion grabbed her shoulders, ready to plunge into the thickest part when Annon caught her wrist. His eyes were blazing with intensity and despair. He thrust the Tay al-Ard into her hands. "To Mirrowen," he urged her desperately. "Save us!"

One of the beasts landed on Annon's back, its claws shredding through his previous injuries, and he screamed in pain. He raised his hands and seized the beast by the ruff, turning it into ash with a single burst of his magic. As he turned away from her, she saw the red stains on his shredded cloak and watched his face turn chalk white. She stuffed the Tay al-Ard into her belt.

Shion pulled her after him, but she saw a multitude of Weir bearing down on them. He could not stop such an onslaught himself, and she knew it. Hunching her shoulders, she dug her boots into the ground to stop and shoved her wrists forward, letting her own fireblood sear into the ranks of maddened creatures.

Come, child! I feel your presence. Come to me, lost daughter!

The voice in her mind was full of suffering and despair. A caged one, a victim, a being so thirsty for freedom she was desiccated. Wave after wave of emotion broke against Phae's mind, a pleading and yearning deeper than the ocean. She looked past the charging Weir, past the other sentinels guarding it, then saw the tree.

She could sense its unfathomable age deep down into the core of herself, the part of herself that was aching and trembling and that had nearly expelled the innate magic that was a part of her since childhood. She felt her Dryad magic throbbing, causing a wave of painful wrenching that tore through her violently. Phae gasped at the swell of it, at the insurmountable agony of being so close to a tree that was already part of her very essence somehow.

The tree was thick and twisted, not majestic as she had imagined, not a towering thing but a stunted one. It seemed as if limbs had been broken off or cut down and other limbs grafted on. The trunk was full of gnarled bulges and scabs, grotesque and hunchbacked. The trunk was split in two, showing a small gap between and a shadowed crevice inside. No other tree grew directly around it, as if its leaves and mistletoe were poison to anything else living. The tree seemed to sway, the spear-like branches defying her, warning her that she'd be pierced through if she ventured near.

One of the Weir slashed through her cloak, ripping the skin on her side into grooves of blood. She turned and blasted it away along with four others charging her from that side. There was no time to think, only to act, to unleash the heat inside her and endure the pangs that tortured every breath. Shion slashed at the wall of Weir with his twin blades, bringing them down with brutal efficiency.

There was a whisper on the wind, a cry of warning from Paedrin. Phae watched Kiranrao materialize out of nothing but smoke and stab Prince Aran in the back with his malevolent blade. The Prince's face went slack and he dropped like a stone. Phae nearly wept.

Paedrin roared with fury but the Romani vanished as quickly as he had appeared, his cold sneer fading with him.

Annon blasted where he had been standing with a stream of blue fire, spinning in an arc to cover the area. Paedrin's grief was terrible, and Phae could not watch it. Too many beasts were coming at her, too many enemies, but suddenly the Bhikhu's voice lifted in warning.

"The sentinels!" Paedrin shouted. "They have bows. From behind us. Do not look into their eyes. It is death to do so! They cannot be slain!"

With the warning just past his lips, an arrow hissed and struck Annon's shoulder, spinning him around and knocking him down.

An arrow shot at Paedrin, but he twisted and it sailed past, embedding into a tree. Annon scrabbled at the ground, groaning with agony, and she saw the tip of the arrow that had struck him protruding from his chest. Half-bent, he raised one arm, fingers hooked, and sent off another blaze of fire, spraying it wildly around them, setting fire to the trees and brittle brush. Soon flames were crackling and smoke obscured everything. Another arrow pierced Annon in the middle and he sagged to his knees.

Shion yanked on Phae's arm, drawing her with him toward their goal. Annon's face, twisted with excruciating pain and black with soot, was etched in her mind, his mouth gaping with an unfulfilled scream. She felt every rushing beat of her own heart. She could not hear Shion's words, though she saw his lips moving. He slashed the throat of one of the Weir hurtling at him, ducking the heavy body as it sailed past and killing the creature in a stroke. The fire was spreading. Paedrin stood in a maelstrom of Weir, his blade spinning in lethal arcs—in front, behind, in front, behind.

Suddenly Kiranrao appeared again, right next to Shion, and Phae tried to scream in warning. The blade lifted and fell just as an arrow pierced Phae's leg, shattering the bone. The pain engulfed her and she went down, unable to breathe through the torture of it, watching Shion evade the lunge and kill another Weir after rolling to his feet. He slashed at Kiranrao with his blade, but the Romani vanished again. Shion saw she had fallen and even though she couldn't walk, she clawed her way closer to the tree, pleading with the Dryad to aid them. *Help us! Please!*

Another arrow struck right by her breast, sticking into the dirt where a moment earlier she had collapsed. Shion scooped her up. She heard another arrow hit, only it struck him instead. She felt the jarring force of it stagger him, but he did not fall. Nor did the arrow stick. With a grimace of determination, he began to run toward the tree, and every movement made the pain in her leg more violent. She saw more Weir skulking by the tree, waiting for them, their eyes hungry. Where was Kiranrao? Swallowing the taste of bile in her mouth, Phae knew Shion could not carry her and fight them. There were still too many. She shot forth her hand and let loose another stream of flames, incinerating Weir.

The tree was unguarded.

Smoke and crackling heat pressed through the woods as Shion staggered up to the misshapen split trunk. The ground was uneven, the base of the tree lumpy with roots that made each step treacherous. She could feel the wild hammering of Shion's heart, she was pressed so tightly against him. He cradled her, taking another round of arrows in the back that nearly made him stumble and pitch her. But he did not, he would not give way, he would not relent from his purpose. In her mind, she remembered on the mountaintop near the cabin where Trasen's arrows had failed to bring him down. His ruthless determination to hunt was part of his character, was part of who he was. A moment of panic began to grow inside her, a fear of what she might learn when she came to know him fully. She stared up at his face, at the claw marks that had always been there . . . sealed into his skin as part of his immortality. The seed of her Dryad self was beginning to bud. She felt it responding to the Mother Tree, unfolding, beckoning to join the roots and earth and light, to drink the rain and taste the fragrances carried on the wind. To be trapped in this horrible place—a prisoner herself if she took the oath. Part of her longed for freedom, a chance to return to Stonehollow, to seek out Trasen and remind him of the feelings she had stolen from him along with his memories.

All these thoughts and feelings bubbled inside of her, tremulous and raw. But as she looked up, it wasn't Trasen's face she found comfort in. He would have perished during the first attacks in the Scourgelands. This man, Shion, whatever his history, had been forged inside this horrible forest. This was his home. His essence was tied to the roots. She could sense his memories seething inside the tree in front of her, clawing desperately to get out.

She stared at his jaw, his chin, his blazing eyes that ignored every threat. His face was so familiar to her now, so comforting. She wished she could tell him how much she needed him, how his steadfastness to her was the only source of comfort left. Her father and Hettie had been abandoned. She wondered if they were even alive. One by one the company had been brought down, all save her and Shion. In his arms, she felt a spark of hope . . . a sliver that perhaps they might survive the horrors together.

Shion pitched her with all his might toward the gap of the tree. She fell short, of course, landing with startled surprise and agony as the arrow gouged deeper. She spit dirt from her mouth as she lifted her head, shaking it. Looking over her shoulder, she saw Shion locked in combat with Kiranrao, holding the dagger at bay by a strong grip on Kiranrao's wrist. Suddenly the Romani vanished, only to reappear again on the other side, dagger midstroke. With blazing reflexes, Shion deflected it, stamping on Kiranrao's foot and bringing an elbow around to crush his nose . . . but again, the Romani disappeared, a phantom impossible to trap and catch.

Phae watched the desperate duel for a moment, not knowing how it would end. She could not wait a moment. Clawing the ground with her nails, she pulled herself closer to the shaded gap inside the trunk. Her right leg was totally useless, but she dug her left boot up and pushed herself forward, moving as quickly as she could. She reached the edge of the trunk, saw an army of ants groping along the base, oblivious to the carnage raging not far from their spot.

A cold hand clasped her wrist and she almost looked up, but realized it would be unwise to stare into another Dryad's eyes. She was pulled up to her feet, but kept her gaze averted, seeing only the Dryad's bare feet and legs.

"The name of the bridge," whispered the Dryad-born, "is *Pontfadog*."

Phae heard the word with her ears, but in her mind she could understand it, could sense the deepness of the meaning. It was an alien language to her, a language long forgotten. But she could sense what it meant.

Poisonwell.

That was how her father had translated it. That was how he had attempted to define an idea, a concept that defied explanation. A bridge between two worlds, separated by death. To hear it spoken in its original tongue brought a surge of triumph into Phae's heart. It sounded . . . familiar—as if it were a word she had learned in childhood but only forgotten.

"Thank you," Phae said, gripping the fragile hands that had raised her. She saw the iron ring fastened to one of the fingers.

"Tell him," the Dryad pleaded, her voice full of sadness, regret, and fringed with unshed tears, "I am sorry."

Alarm struck Phae's heart when she saw the iron ring. She knew it had the power to explode, to devastate her as well as the tree. She stared at it, expecting her life to be snuffed out, yet somehow it wasn't. Could the Arch-Rike—Shirikant—not bear to destroy the source of his own Dryad's kiss? To destroy his own ability to master memories?

Yes, came the thought to her mind. The hands folded on hers squeezed. *Go, Daughter. Tell the Seneschal I am sorry. I betrayed my oath. I am banished from Mirrowen forever. I grieve for all I have lost.*

The grip tightened on her hands.

Never forsake your oaths, child. Never. Now go!

Phae turned and looked back, seeing Shion backing toward the tree, daggers back in his hands. Three brown-cloaked archers were advancing, the hoods shielding their faces, gliding through the smoke of the fires Annon had started. A sense of dread and desolation exuded from their presence. Their tattered brown robes were full of decay. They were deathless beings. Phae could sense that from the tree.

Go!

"Where can I go?" Phae pleaded. "I cannot walk."

Through the portal in the trunk. A Dryad may enter Mirrowen this way. You must go there before you seek Pontfadog. You must swear your oaths. Go, Daughter. I cannot hold off his will much longer.

The hands clasping hers were trembling. Phae raised them to her lips and kissed them. "I will free you at last, Mother."

Phae took all the pain, all the suffering, all the hopelessness and stuffed them in a cocoon inside her heart. She released the Dryad's hands and pulled the Tay al-Ard Annon had given her from her belt and clutched it to her bosom. With her leg throbbing, she stumbled between the gap in the trunk and found herself in another world.

XXXIV

Hettie and Tyrus backed away from the bounding Weir, drawing closer to the rugged wall of the promontory. Lukias and the Arch-Rike's soldiers were up on the promontory above them. Both ways led to death.

"It wasn't much of a chance," Tyrus muttered darkly. "Grab my arm. The closer they are to us before we vanish, the longer it will take for them to find our—"

He stopped speaking, his eyes widening with shock as the Tay al-Ard disappeared from his hand.

A rumble of thunder sounded overhead.

Hettie's stomach twisted with the realization that they were stranded. What had happened? She saw the fury in the eyes of the Weir, their teeth bared and ready to shred.

As one, they both unleashed the fireblood on the charging beasts. Hettie's heart nearly exploded with fear and desperation. She let the whirl of emotions sweep her up in the temporary euphoria that always accompanied the power. Gushes of blue flames came out as a vortex, blackening the churned earth, igniting the mass of desiccated leaves within, and tearing through the

Weir. The thrill almost surpassed her terror, but not quite. They stood shoulder to shoulder, spreading the net of flames through the ground in front of them, trying to create a barrier of flames to hold back their enemies.

Where dozens fell, dozens more came out.

Plumes of smoke stained the air with a brown haze, and the flames began to spread across the ground. The Weir darted through the pockets, snarling and howling for their blood.

There were too many to stop. The next wave was already nearing them.

"We are defeated!" Tyrus shouted with panic in his voice. "Spare my daughter at least. Let me die, but save her!"

Hettie's insides churned as she watched the malevolent looks from the Weir. Their sinews and muscles were bunching, their stride increasing as they loped forward. The wind tousled her hair and she felt another moment of pure panic.

"Lukias!" Tyrus bellowed in desperation.

"You murdered her when you chose to bring her here," Lukias said coldly. "It's a trick, Tyrus. We both know it."

One of the Weir vaulted through the ring of flames and tackled Tyrus, its teeth snapping viciously into his shoulder. He wrestled it around, sending fire into its belly, dissolving it into ash. Hettie ducked as one hurtled over her, dropping into a low Bhikhu stance. With one hand, she sent flames surging into the next row. With her other, she destroyed the one that had gotten past her. Movement surged from every side as Tyrus made it back to his feet. His fingers were like claws themselves as jets of blue flame erupted from his hands, catching several of the Weir.

Hettie stayed near Tyrus, her face damp with sweat. A hopeless feeling swelled with the panic and she realized they were both going to die or go mad with the fireblood. Already she had used so much of it in the Scourgelands that she was giddy with the notion of unleashing the power fully. Annon had always been more self-controlled than she with the flame. She remembered using it alongside her brother on the road to Havenrook. This was not even a shade in comparison. The guilty relish filled her heart, demanding she push the limits further. What was the point? With the Tay al-Ard gone, they were both doomed. The Arch-Rike suspected a trick. The trick was on them.

One of the Weir managed to sidestep her attack and its claws ripped into her hip, slashing through the leather pants she wore. She almost didn't feel the pain when its teeth sank into her knee next, but she slammed her fists down on its head and channeled enough flame to destroy it. Pain and dizziness began to surface, threatening to break past her desperate struggle to survive. Pain and blood and smoke filled her lungs and she found herself screaming in challenge, delving deeper into the magic of the fireblood, drawing on its infinite power and infinite danger.

"No, Hettie!" Tyrus warned.

She heard his words but they were meaningless to her. Another Weir landed in front of her, and she grabbed it by the ruff of its neck and ripped it apart with her magic. *Let them come! Let them meet their death!* She was enraged, feeling her mind begin to totter over the brink. She no longer cared. If she were going to die in the Scourgelands, she would ruin it. It would be reborn in fire.

"No!" Tyrus shouted, striking her hard across the face, just as Annon had. While he was turned, two Weir knocked him down, ripping into his flesh. He groaned in pain, twisting quickly and shielding his face from their claws. Fire bloomed again, shattering them both, and he made it up just as another round advanced.

"Climb, Hettie!" he begged her, retreating to the promontory wall. "That way! Climb!"

He stood between her and the Weir, his expression full of hate and rage. He took the leather pouch around his neck and put it in his mouth, beginning to chew on the bag. It contained monkshood, the dose she did not know. He would chew on it, dissolving it with his saliva until it entered his system. It would kill him, but not until after he had released the full power.

Her heart spasmed with sadness, seeing the desperate look in his eyes. "Please!" he begged her, imploring her to abandon him to the madness. To save herself as he could not do.

Tears stung Hettie's eyes. He had always been so hard, so implacable. But she saw at the end that he had been preparing himself for the moment. That he had truly come to the Scourgelands to die and save her and Annon if he could. He wanted to repay the debt owed to Merinda. Hettie rarely wept. She experienced a surge of forgiveness so powerful that she nearly started sobbing. Through the hard shell of his emotions, she saw him as he truly was and she pitied his loneliness, his solitary life, his determination to sacrifice all to save the world.

Abandoning him was the hardest thing she had experienced. She hurried onto the rocky edge, clambering swiftly to find handholds and footholds. One of the beasts snagged her boot, but she kicked free of it and clawed her way higher, leaving the Weir down below to surround Tyrus on all sides. He was hunched in pain, his arms crooked as they spread out, unleashing flames.

The rocks scratched her fingers as she pulled herself higher, fighting off exhaustion and despair. The smoke from the fires made a haze that was difficult to penetrate. Before long, she lost sight of Tyrus below and the darting shadows that converged on him. A few drops of rain pattered on her head. Thunder boomed right overhead, splitting the air with its deep coughs. She struggled to find footing, maneuvering up a cracked lip that made her muscles ache and wither. There was no Paedrin to catch her if she fell this time. No rope or harness to secure her to the knobs and crags. Painfully, span by span, she climbed toward the crest of the promontory, listening to the barks and snarls below.

A wave of heat and light rushed from below, blinding her. She pressed herself against the rocks, scraping her cheek against a spur of jagged stone. The fire was white-hot in intensity, exploding in a pillar of devastation that scorched the ground all around. The wall of flames was almost as high as she had climbed and it made her reel at the power he had delved into to unleash such an inferno. The light made her shadow against the cliff wall, and she hung her head, drenched with misery as she realized what he had done. He had sacrificed his own mind and his life to save her, a poor Romani girl who had never studied the Paracelsus tomes, had lived a life of thieving and deception since she had been stolen at birth. Of the two of them, she had deserved to die.

The flames roared and spread across the wasted land. But amidst the roar of the flames, she heard Tyrus's mad laughter ringing out louder still.

Annon's eyes felt as heavy as stones. He lay crumpled in the clotting mass of dried leaves and sharp twigs. His blood seeped from his body, spilling from the wounds and soaking the ground. His feet tingled with the loss of feeling. His fingertips experienced the same sensation. As a strange memory, he recalled the Rike Lukias speaking clinically of these sensations where Khiara had revived him back in Silvandom. What a curious memory to have in such a moment. He swallowed, experiencing the effort it took to complete. His vision began to swim, but he tried to focus his eyes. Was that music he heard? What strange memory had been unlocked in his mind? He lay prostrate, one arm flung out ahead of him. The burn of the arrow in his shoulder that had pierced him through was fading. The one in his stomach had wrenched when he had collapsed, ripping his skin wide open. He felt numbness now. Water—just a mouthful of water would have been worth a thousand ducats.

He tried to move his neck, to see the gnarled limbs of the great Dryad tree. He could not see Phae but thought he had spied her entering the gap in the trunk. That was good. A part of their quest had been fulfilled. With all the death and suffering he had experienced, he was ready to lay aside his grip on the mortal coils. He had hoped, secretly, that he might catch a glimpse of Mirrowen when Phae entered it. A glimpse was all he desired.

Shion backed up against the great tree, fighting off the soundless guardians robed in brown. Annon could do nothing more to help him. His strength was ebbing, draining from his body. It was close now. He could feel his consciousness wavering.

Paws crushed the twigs near him as the Weir approached. He let out his final breath and shut his eyes. He began counting his last heartbeats.

There was a ringing in his ears that drowned out the sounds and he felt himself slipping away. His final thought was not of his sister. It was not of Tyrus or Reeder or the many people he had encountered.

Neodesha, he thought.

He imagined he heard a whisper—far, far away. *Annon.*

Paedrin's soul was wracked with sorrow and anger. Hettie was with Tyrus, abandoned without the Tay al-Ard. He desperately wanted to flee to her, to make sure she was safe. To be sure she had survived. But he could not leave Shion alone, not with so many enemies surrounding him. Not with Kiranrao and that wicked blade trying to kill him. Annon was sprawled on the turf, his eyes closed. It was another cause of grief. Was the Druidecht dead? It would haunt Paedrin for the rest of his life. Phae had vanished inside the tree, but would she emerge soon, needing to be taken to Poisonwell? If so, he had the ability to take her there. His memory could transport them to the spot he had visited earlier. He had to remain behind. He had to wait for her to return from the bowels of the tree. How long it would take, he had no idea.

Weir approached the tree, hissing and spitting but staying away from the three brown riders who sought to destroy Shion. Their gaze had no effect on him. Neither did their arrows. But he remembered how exceptionally strong the riders were and knew that eventually, the three would bear him down and subdue him. He could not win the fight. He could only delay the inevitable conclusion.

Unless Paedrin interceded. He was a Bhikhu by training, well versed in the Uddhava. Paedrin clenched his fists, readying himself. Each moment delayed added to the torture. His mind was frantic for Hettie. Would she survive? Was there anything he could do to save her? Or was her fate already spelled out in some bloodstained portion of earth farther away? The thought brought a cruel agony to his heart. Focus—he had to focus. He had to be ready.

Paedrin waited, watching for the moment. He knew it would come. He knew that Kiranrao would strike at Shion again.

The Romani appeared on Shion's blind side, the blade tucked underhand . . . like the Preachán who had tried to kill Paedrin in Havenrook. The memory was like a flicker of thought. Paedrin hissed out his breath and plummeted from the tree branches above.

Hettie swung her leg up around the edge of the rock and pulled herself up onto the ridge of the promontory. She lay still to rest a while, breathing heavily, pressed against the crumbled stone of the moldering ruins. Fearing capture, she had not climbed straight up but had moved sideways at an angle. The clouds had brought fierce winds and occasional bursts of rain that made the footing treacherous and cold. Her fingers were bleeding, as was her cheek, but she had made it to the crest alive, despite several moments when she had felt her footing slip and then suddenly catch on something firm. The thrill and worry of the climb had taxed her strength and abilities. She was on the ridge now, amidst a crew of soldiers and Rikes from Kenatos. What was she supposed to do next? Her heartbeat slowed.

From down below, she saw occasional bursts of heat and magic as Tyrus destroyed the attackers. The fires raged across the ravaged earth and had caught the outer rim of trees. The towering oaks were blazing and the fire was spreading, making her choke as she had climbed. Her lungs felt raw and ravaged. After a little rest from the difficult climb, her strength began to return.

"This way."

The voice came from beyond the shattered wall and she listened carefully, trying to block out the other noises, hearing the sound of a sputtering torch and boots walking.

"Are you sure?" came another voice.

"Lukias ordered all the edges to be searched in case they tried to climb. You go there. You go there. Check behind that wall too."

Her heart filled with dread as she heard the boots approach. Were there only three? She looked along the edge of the wall and the debris of stone that would make sneaking away treacherous.

One slip and the shuffle of bricks would give her away. She did not have time to think.

Keeping low, using the wall fragments as cover, she started off away from the approaching soldiers. The gap between the edge of the promontory and the wall narrowed until the footing disappeared entirely, dropping straight down. The corner had already given way, providing a small gap that she could leap through.

"I see someone!"

The voice was right behind her. She pulled herself over the gap and climbed up on the edge of the wall, using it as a crumbling walkway to get herself farther away. The soldiers shouted in warning and charged after her and Hettie stumbled off the edge of the wall, landing crookedly on her ankle. She went down in a heap, cradling her leg, rocking back and forth and whining with pain.

A sword cleared its scabbard with a metallic swish.

"Hold there, girl!"

"It's Tyrus's daughter," one of them whispered.

The three approached her, two soldiers and a Rike. She stared up at them, gripping her ankle tightly, cowering.

"Be careful," the Rike warned. "Don't look in her eyes or she'll bewitch you. She has the fireblood too." He held out a hand coaxingly to her, his gaze averted. "Give yourself up, lass. The Arch-Rike has ordered us to take you alive. Will you come?"

"Do I have a choice?" Hettie said darkly.

The world was made of fire.

Tyrus staggered through the crackling blaze, feeling wooden and confused. His bowels were on fire as well, all needles and pain and agony. He spat out the leather in his mouth, not aware of what it was or how it had gotten there. He snapped the twine keeping it to him and tossed it aside, watching with relish as the flames consumed it instantly. The fire was everywhere, even inside of him. His belly hurt. Why? What had happened?

Looking up, he saw the cliff of stone. A buzzing in his ears became annoying and he knuckled at his left ear hard enough that it hurt. But it could not hurt worse than the fire in his belly. He bent over, wincing and writhing. Where was this place? He could not remember the details. There was a fog about his mind, almost as thick as the plumes of sooty smoke billowing all around.

There was a rampway leading up the cliff. Anger drove him to it. The anger was terrible and roiling, hotter than the flames. There was someone to punish on the mountain. An enemy to destroy. He started to laugh, feeling giddy with the thoughts of revenge. His hands were glowing blue, swathed in flames. He stared at them, excited by the swirling colors. Blue, violet, even a tinge of green. He stopped walking, mesmerized by the flames gushing out of his hands. His arms were trembling. It made the flames dance.

Another spasm of heat and agony went through his middle. It was insufferable! He groaned loudly and let loose a string of blistering curses. Spittle flecked his lips. Up. He had to go up. Vengeance was required. Punishment given. Clack, clack, like a rod to unruly children. He remembered fragments from his life. An orphanage. A tower. Hatred drove him up the steep ramp, despite his wayward legs. There was a song in his mind, something he had heard from long ago. He remembered a golden locket. Why did that matter? He had lost the locket. He had to find it. Someone had stolen it. Yes, that's why he was angry. Someone had stolen his locket. Someone had stolen his music.

Tyrus bent over double, the clenching so painful he vomited bile. There was a sharp taste in his mouth. A bitter taste. He started walking again, moving up the ramp in a daze of pain and anger. Someone had stolen his song. He would kill the thief.

Ahead, up the slope, he saw a group of soldiers in the haze, forming two lines. They all had crossbows. Crossbows were made of wood. Wood burned.

Tyrus smiled, willing the wood to burn.

The crossbows exploded into flames and the soldiers began shrieking, fleeing into the haze.

Tyrus staggered up the ramp after them.

XXXV

Phae entered Mirrowen and dropped to her knees with pain shooting up and down her injured leg. The ground was soft, yielding. Her fingers dug into the cool grains as she gasped and moaned, hoping the agony would subside. Instead of suffering with the pain, she tried to focus on the sensation of the gritty dirt between her fingers. But it wasn't dirt. It was finer, like river sand. She squeezed it, feeling it give away, but firm as she compacted it in her fists. The throbbing in her leg began to subside.

Strangely, she did not experience any sense of danger or imminent threat. There was the murmur of a gentle brook somewhere on her right. In the distance, she heard a sound she had never experienced before. It sounded like thunder, but it didn't come from the sky. The rumbling noise built up and then exhaled like a long sigh, only to build up and again, release into a sigh. The sound was vast, not one of a creature—unless the creature were larger than the world. Smells struck her next. The air was crisp and fresh, with a slight saltiness filled with pleasant aromas from flowers. The scent was distinct, blended in a way that struck her so much that she let it linger, focusing on breathing it in and exhaling.

She realized the throbbing inside her, the budding seed of her Dryad powers, had settled. She straightened, wincing with the pain in her leg, but felt her abdomen was no longer clenching.

Phae heard steps approaching in the sand and she opened her eyes.

At first, it seemed as if the sunlight blinded her, but there was no sun in the sky. All was light and warm and pleasant, but she saw no trace of sun or moon. The sky was a rich blue, full of enormous billowing clouds.

A woman approached her, barefoot. Phae averted her eyes, not daring to meet anyone's gaze and risk losing her memories. She saw the feet first and noticed the bracelet around one ankle. It was shaped into the coils of a serpent and wrapped around her ankle. She was a Dryad.

"Who are you?" Phae asked tremulously. "Is this Mirrowen?"

"Phae," replied the woman.

The voice sounded . . . familiar. Her heart began to pound inside her. "Neodesha?"

The woman knelt in the sand in front of her, wearing a beautiful but plain woolen dress after the manner of Stonehollow. It was a deep orange color, like a sunset, with trim along the sleeves.

She felt the woman's fingers in her hair. Her voice was thick with emotion. "Daughter, do not fear to look on me. I won't steal your memories. I am your mother. Who else would the Seneschal have sent to greet you?" She stroked Phae's tangled hair. "My child . . . my lost child. I see you at last!"

A well of longing opened up deep inside Phae's heart. She was desperate to believe this woman's voice. So desperate to embrace her, but how could she be sure? Phae felt tears sting her lashes and she dropped her head, beginning to weep, confused.

"Phae, there is no deception in Mirrowen. You come from a brooding world where people cheat, deceive, and murder each other for ducats. I lived long inside the prison walls of Kenatos. I saw it all. This is a place of rest, a place of healing, a place of unalloyed truth. Believe me, Phae. I *am* your mother. I was sent to heal you and prepare you to meet the Seneschal. He is a kind master, Phae."

The words were a balm to Phae's heart. With tears streaming down her cheeks, she looked up at the Dryad's face, scarcely hoping to believe.

When she saw her, Phae's heart leapt with joy. She looked so much like Phae's father, as if she had taken part of his essence inside of her. Her hair was dark with natural waves, similar to Phae's own, except without the amber tint. She resembled Dame Winemiller, with eyes expressive of a mother's love and care. Phae hugged her fiercely, ignoring the pain in her leg, and her mother embraced her, kissing her hair and stroking it tenderly.

"Mother," Phae panted, trying to quell the sobs that threatened to choke her. All her days she had wondered about her mother—who she was, how she had lived or died. She had always imagined someone like Dame Winemiller . . . not a girl her own age. Though she was young, her eyes were full of wisdom and deep understanding.

In the distance, she heard the deep grumbling sound followed by the sighing reply—an endless rhythm and cadence.

"Come, Phae. Let me heal you first. Lean on me while you stand. We're going to the brook over there. It isn't far."

Phae felt her mother's strength help pull her to her feet. She winced and gasped as the pain shot through her again, but she managed to hobble on one leg, supported by the Dryad until they reached the shallows of the brook. The waters were tranquil, full of life. Little colorful fish darted through. Insects skimmed the surface with beautifully hued wings—dragonflies and butterflies and ladybugs. Her mother reached over the brook to a mossy rock protruding from the waters and tore a fragment of it away. The moss was flecked with blue and violet flowers and smelled of honey. The Dryad gently touched the moss to the arrow protruding from Phae's leg.

Phae's blood began to sing with spirit magic. She shuddered, feeling the cuts and bruises mend and fade. The Dryad pulled the arrow free and it did not hurt. The arrowhead emerged silver, untarnished. Phae watched as the gaping wound in her leg closed and felt her bones fuse together whole. She gasped with delight, the magic flowing through her, healing every ailment and injury. It was over in moments, but the feeling was blissful and swift.

"What is that?" Phae asked, staring at the shrinking nub of moss. Her mother reached down and put the remains back on the rock. It immediately began to brighten again, the shriveling buds blooming once more.

"The vegetation is called by different names in different worlds. It is plentiful here in Mirrowen. It can cure any disease. Even the Plague." She gave Phae a knowing look.

Her heart began to hammer. "Can I take some with me?" she begged. "Those who brought me, who helped me, they are injured and dying. Mother, if I save them—!"

"Child," her mother said soothingly, interrupting, "this will not be easy to understand. You must try, though. There is no time here. There is no need to rush or to hurry. In the mortal world, time flows in one direction . . . like a brook of water." She motioned her hand over the rippling waves. "But we are not in that brook, nor are we subject to its laws or constraints." She rose and pulled Phae up with her. "You can enter the brook at any point, before or after. There is no rush. The dangers you faced in the woods cannot follow you here." She squeezed Phae's hand. "Come, let me show you Mirrowen. Walk with me."

Phae did not understand it, but she trusted what she was told. As she looked around, she saw deep foliage on the other side of the brook, covering her gaze. Tall fronds appeared on each side of the sandy path, and from the sand grew a hardy green plant that she did not recognize at all. It had large violet flowers blooming amidst it. Beautiful trees appeared deeper behind her, enormous redwoods that almost formed a wall the way she had come. The sandy trail led away from them, toward the murmuring sound she had heard since arriving.

They walked side by side, hand in hand. The trail was crooked and finally opened to a broad expanse of beach. Phae stopped, staring in amazement. The sights filled her eyes all at once and she almost quailed from the majestic images revealed to her.

The first thing she saw was an ocean. She had never seen it before, but it was the source of the shushing noises she had heard since arriving. The waters were vast and grayish-blue, and white foam churned as the waves hammered against the glassy shore. There were many others on the beach, walking back and forth, some in deep conversation, others looking silently at the crashing surf. Some were Vaettir-born, others Preachán. Some races she did not recognize at all because of their skin color or the shades of color in their hair. She blinked, trying to understand.

"They have all earned the right to live in Mirrowen," her mother said, as if reading her thoughts. "Many are Druidecht, but not all. Do you see the city?"

Of course Phae did. The beach was several miles wide, crescent shaped. Huge towering rocks and boulders were in the waters, and the waves crashed against them with enormous sprays. The boulders were of different sizes but they seemed to form some sort of border or boundary. There were hills on each side of the beach. To her right, the hills were full of enormous redwoods and eucalyptus trees, and amidst these towering trees was a city that filled the hillside.

Phae gasped, her eyes trying to absorb the enormity of it. There were multiple levels within the hills and she could see streets and garden, archways connecting separate buildings. The levels were all interconnected through a series of intricate stone structures, polished to a glassy shine. Some of the hills had waterfalls, showing cascading rivulets that caused a gray mist to emerge where the fountains struck the ground. Lights zigzagged throughout, reminding her slightly of Canton Vaud. Vaettir-born floated between the levels, and she wondered how many thousands lived in the palaces built into the vast hills. The structures even extended into the sea, with balconies opening up over the waters.

Phae's knees became weak as she stared at the beautiful land. Lights and color, trees and gardens, music . . . the music! She could hear the strains even from the distance, and its echoes were haunting and mystical, reminding her of the charm Shion had taken from her father. The Paracelsus had captured part of the music of Mirrowen, but it was only a shadow in comparison to the real experience.

"Look at the sea," her mother whispered. "This wave is massive."

Phae broke her gaze from the dazzling city gardens and watched as a wall of churning water came roaring at the beach. It was ten times larger than any she had seen since arriving, a vast monster of churning foam that advanced like an army. She could see the wall of waves coming in, thundering in, high enough to submerge the entire beach and drown half the city. Phae clutched at her mother's arm, staring in horror. Seeing it made her want to flee, but her mother stared at it with unconcern, but respect.

"It cannot harm us, Phae."

The wave seemed to build in height and intensity as it drew closer. There were people near the edge of the surf, walking blithely, as if unaware of the looming danger. Phae stared, her mouth agape as the waves gathered to a ferocious height. As if there were an invisible dome shielding the beach, the waters crashed against the rock sentinels in the shallows, but the rocks *repelled* the sea. Phae blinked in amazement, as the waters seemed to hang poised over them, unable to penetrate the bubble. Then all the energy seemed to fade from the rushing waves and the waters slid back. Some of the waves had been high enough to feed the upper fountains of the city and thus the waterfalls began to churn more energetically, draining away the spent fury of the waves as they receded.

Her mother patted her arm. "We are safe here," she murmured softly. "So long as our thoughts remain vigilant. The Seneschal will explain it all better than I can. He is over there with the children. Do you see him?"

Phae followed her gaze and she saw the Seneschal. His back was to her, but she recognized the description she had received from Neodesha. He was easily two heads above her own father, and Tyrus was a tall man himself. His hair was dark and long, like a Vaettir's, except brown and not black. He wore an interesting mix of robes and armor and Phae saw twin blades strapped to his back, crosswise. A supple golden cloak fluttered in the breeze. A small diadem crowned his head. At his feet were several children digging with shells, creating a castle out of the wet, compact sand.

"Come with me," her mother said, pulling Phae closer.

As they approached, Phae cast her eyes to the hills on her left. They were not full of buildings or structures. Small footpaths had been carved into the hillside and slender stone steps helped travelers ascend to the various heights. Sculptured stone benches sat at various places and Phae could see many people sitting on them, some gazing and pointing out to the sea. Some had even seemed to notice her walking and she thought she could spy one of them waving at her.

Everyone she saw was dressed in elegant robes. Not ostentatious, but each of a variety of color and design, marking a different era or country. There were people from every race she could tell, and again—seeing some that were new. The beach was not full, but neither was it empty. She saw other Dryads as well and felt a kinship with them.

"Is Neodesha here?" Phae asked her mother.

"You want to know if she survived the blast that destroyed her tree?"

"Yes."

Her mother nodded and smiled. "The blast destroyed our link to the mortal world. But it did not destroy us. She is here, if she is not off on a task from the Seneschal. There is no time here, as you remember. There will be opportunity enough to see her as well. But first, you must make your oaths. You are Dryad-born, Phae. It is a choice you must make alone."

"I feel so dirty," Phae said self-consciously. Her clothes were filthy and her hair a tangled mess. She rubbed her arm, gazing at the others on the beach. None of them looked at her askance, but she did feel different, singled out.

"You will receive a robe when you take your oath," her mother said. "With it, you can look like anyone or appear wearing anything you desire. My ancestors came from Stonehollow, and so I fancy their attire the most. Deep down, our childhood impresses us most significantly. I have watched you grow up, Phae. I knew you were coming, which is why I let your father take you away from me." A mix of sadness and pride crossed her face. She touched Phae's cheek. "You are the one who can correct the wrong that was done. And in so doing, give rebirth to your fallen world. But I speak of things I ought not to. It should be the Seneschal who explains this to you and the oaths you must take."

"Am I doing the right thing, Mother?" Phae asked, squeezing her hand strongly.

"Soon you will know enough to answer that for yourself," came the enigmatic reply. They approached the children digging, and one of them looked hauntingly like Brielle. Phae stared at her in surprise. No, it *was* Brielle, from the Winemiller orphanage.

Her mother smiled and stroked Phae's hair again. "Not her. Not Brielle. Her twin sister who died. They are still connected. That is why Brielle does not speak. She can see shades of Mirrowen in her dreams and longs to be here." She smiled, squeezing Phae's hand, and faced the Seneschal, who began to turn to greet them.

"My lord, I have brought Phae as you bid me to. I healed her injuries and have taught her a little portion of Mirrowen, which you instructed me to. She is here to learn about her oaths so she may decide by her conscience whether she will or not. Thank you, my lord, for sending me. You are kind and thoughtful." She bowed deeply.

Phae saw the massive swords strapped to his back with intricately carved leather sigils. Each buckle was precise, each cut of cloth the work of a deep master. She could not see his hands, for they were folded in front of him. But something struck her attention immediately. From his wide belt, he bore a series of ancient keys, the metal so pitted that they seemed older than the stars. The shape of the keys was nothing like she had seen before. The head was rectangular with a strange cross embedded into the top, but it was hollow in the middle, and that hollow part was fastened by a ring to other keys of similar design. The shaft of each key was thick and solid. The end was shaped into a circle with two nubs pointed from the side of each. The circles were also hollow. The metal looked to be iron, raw iron, but old and pocked. The Voided Keys. That's what Neodesha had called them.

The Seneschal turned, and Phae looked up into his face.

She recognized him.

"I write these words in dread of my own safety. Forgive me the gap between entries as much has happened of great concern in the interval. I have hidden my journals and some of the more crucial manuscripts in a secret vault here in the Archives. What I must write here is perilous and may cost me my life. I have just come to learn a tale that has astonished me beyond measure. I have secretly met and been tutored by the Empress of Boeotia and her consort, who was once a Rike here in Kenatos by the name of Mathon. I now understand the legend of the being known as Shirikant. Words cannot express the depth of my feelings of outrage, shock, and sense of doom. We are in mortal danger. I am perfectly convinced that his current manifestation is now the Arch-Rike of Kenatos. I have been a puppet. I have been a pawn. I have been a fool.

Unwittingly, I have aided in the destruction of certain knowledge. The Archives do not exist to preserve memory as I once believed but to sponge away all references to this malevolent usurper. How many civilizations have perished as a result? How many cultures will never be known? I weep at the enormity of this injustice.

I must make amends and restore what I can when the time is right. I will be killed because of this knowledge. The Empress and I have agreed that secrecy is utmost since no one has seen the Arch-Rike in several days. The Empress fears that he is preparing to unleash the Plague on the citizenry of Kenatos, and that if they are infected, the population will flee the city and transmit it through Stonehollow, Silvandom, Wayland, Havenrook, and Alkire. Even Boeotia. We must act wisely if we are to preserve our civilization. I understand now that Tyrus is not a traitor nor ever was. His quest may indeed be our salvation."

- Possidius Adeodat, Archivist of Kenatos

XXXVI

That she recognized the Seneschal startled Phae. He looked ageless, with smooth skin that marked a man barely middle aged. His hair was long and dark brown. His eyes were blue, a striking color that matched the jewel she had worn around her neck throughout her life. He was somber, with a hint of sadness in his eyes, but when he smiled at her, she felt a thrill go down to her toes. He wore a Druidecht talisman on a chain around his neck.

"Welcome back, Phae." He greeted her with a rich, melodious voice. "It is wonderful to see you." He reached out and took her shoulder, his grip firm but excessively gentle.

She felt as if he had grown up in the orphanage with her or had been wandering the Scourgelands alongside her. His presence was striking, causing emotions to bubble and surface as if the two of them had sat around a warm hearth, drinking tea and sharing stories for ages gone by.

"We have and we will," he said, his eyes crinkling. "If you accept your charge, that is. Phae, I can hear your thoughts. I have followed your life, hidden in the shadows where you sensed me, but you could not see me. I was there when you first used your Dryad powers in an empty wine barrel." He smiled at her again, caressing her cheek. "But you have many questions. I feel them bubbling inside of you."

Phae stared at him, no longer feeling soiled or a stranger. There was no strangeness at all about the Seneschal. He was so familiar that she wondered why she could not remember having met him before.

"How can you hear my thoughts?" Phae asked, not certain she understood what he meant. "Is it your magic?"

He smiled and nodded. "As the Seneschal, I have all the gifts bestowed on the races. But before I explain that part to you, let me first explain what Mirrowen is. What you see is a beach. You hear the surf. You see a city full of gardens and waterfalls. You live on a world. It's a sphere, round like an orange. There are many lands and oceans and peoples you have not met yet. There are many worlds like yours. More than can be counted, yet I know of them. If you were to count the grains of sand beneath our feet across this wide beach, it would not begin to number how many other worlds there are. Some are inhabited. Some are not. I am the guardian of this one, its protector and defender. Huge chunks of rock beyond this sphere hurtle through the expanse. Sometimes, you've seen them at night, streaking through the sky, at certain times of the year. You remember them?"

The images came to her mind immediately and she nodded. "We call them falling stars."

"Yes. It's not what they are, but it's what they appear to be. Some are larger than mountains. They hurtle through space and sometimes threaten a world like this one, as the sea tries to unmake the earth. Two forces are at work in this grand, infinite expanse. There is a force that destroys. It is called by many names. Some call it the Abyss. Some call it the Deep Fathoms. Some the

Void. It is also called Decay. It is inexorable, like the waters of the surf on the beach."

He put his arm around her shoulder and expanded his other arm toward the surf. The edge of the beach was glassy smooth, the frothing waters rushing back down at an incline into the waves until the next round came crashing again. The force of the waves was powerful, yet not frightening. She wondered if the water was cold.

"It can be," he said, answering her thoughts, startling her again.

The Seneschal extended his hand to Phae. She glanced at her mother, who smiled.

His hand was warm and strong. They started walking toward the grassy hill on one side of the beach, an area carved with steps and paths. There were many people about, each walking along, and she wondered how many people lived in Mirrowen.

"Many," he replied, squeezing her hand. "Some visit from other worlds."

"How do they come here?" Phae asked, wondering. "I'm not sure I understand what you meant about this idea of being on a world."

"Not yet. You will begin to understand such things later. When someone visits from another world, they come from the sea. Not in a boat, as you'd expect. What happens is a great wind blows and the waters along the beach part, opening up a pathway into the ocean. It's an impressive sight, Phae. When the waves part, everyone gathers on the beach to greet the newcomer and learn about their travels. So many places to visit. I never tire of meeting them."

Phae looked up at his face. "Do you ever leave?" she asked, but she thought she knew the answer. "No, you can't . . . can you? You have the Voided Keys. They must . . . stay."

He smiled and nodded to her. "Your wisdom is quickening already, Phae. Trust those insights. Mirrowen teaches you about herself all the time. She whispers to you."

Phae nodded, feeling thoughtful. "Why does she whisper? Is Mirrowen a person? No, that doesn't feel quite right."

"Why should one scream when a whisper will do?" the Seneschal asked her, answering her first question. "The Decay is about noise. It's about distraction. Notice the sound when the waves recede off the beach. It's a shushing sound . . . like a whisper. All the rumbling fury of the surf, but contrast it to the sound when it strikes the shore of Mirrowen. Now, let me show you something on the hilltop. We could take the path, but you are with me, and so you will travel as I do. Hold tightly."

He inhaled and suddenly he was floating upward, Phae with him, her body suddenly weightless. As they rose into thc air, like the Vaettir, she was thrilled beyond belief, experiencing a gentle tickle in the middle of her stomach as they began to soar up toward the hilltop. She watched the sandy beach disappear beneath her feet and then watched the flowing grass streak beneath her. She coughed in surprise and then started to laugh, unable to contain the delight. She thought of Paedrin and felt a surge of jealousy for his gift. A soothing wind tousled her hair and clothes. They ascended rapidly and then gently eased down on the crest of the hilltop as the Seneschal breathed out. His eyes twinkled with mirth at her reaction.

"That was amazing," Phae said, turning around and looking from the view atop the hill. The expanse of the ocean went on as far as she could see. Leagues of blue-gray water extended all across the horizon, forming a flat line that met the sky. Suddenly the clouds were roiling, going from white to black. The waves began to churn restlessly, drawing back from the shore as they mounted and rumbled.

"The children are safe?" Phae asked, worried about them playing down at the shore. She could see them kneeling in the sand, digging into the moat, heedless of the waters rushing at them.

The Seneschal patted her hand. "The bounds are set. The waters cannot pass. Despite their fury, despite their power, they will yield to the will imposed against them. Watch the stones in the water. Did you feel them last time? Those rocks in the waters have sigils carved into them. Faces. They will repel the waters."

Phae shuddered as she watched the furious waves reach the guardians of stone. She could feel power coming from those stones and they broke the charge again, as she had witnessed before. The children still played, oblivious.

"I am the Seneschal of Mirrowen," he said, turning to face her. "My duty is to protect the mortal world from destruction. If Mirrowen did not exist, the waves you saw would come crashing into your world. We keep them at bay. I mentioned there is a force that makes things decay. There is another force at work too, Phae. One even more powerful. It is called by many names too. But its essence organizes and brings order to chaos. If those children stopped working, the castle they built would succumb to the Deep. If they halted their efforts, it would wash away in no time at all. Remember the derelict homestead you found in Stonehollow? Where you both were attacked by the spirit creature?"

"Yes," Phae answered, the memory vivid in her mind. "It felt like it was a spirit creature."

"It was. I sent it."

She looked at him in shock. "You did?"

"Don't you remember all of the creatures that tried to get your attention? You were so afraid that you could not hear the whispers from Mirrowen. I was with you the whole time. I'm always with you, Phae. I can be everywhere. I follow each person's life. I know them by name. I've ordered things to achieve the outcome I desire."

Phae shook her head, confused. "You sent that spirit creature to its death?"

"Death is part of the fallen nature of your world, Phae. Of course it would naturally die going there. But Phae . . . I have the power to restore life again. I can reverse death. The Vaettir call it *keramat*. I am the source of that power through these keys I wear, the Voided Keys. They hold dominion over the Deep. There must be suffering in your world. It serves a purpose, Phae. Your struggles prepare you for greater things. I've looked forward to you coming to Mirrowen. You endured what you were meant to in your world. You can leave the mortal coil forever. Being bound to a Dryad tree makes you part of the essence of Mirrowen. You preserve wisdom and knowledge. A Dryad cannot die nor can she be killed. When your season is finished, you will be freed from the bond, free to travel to other worlds. Freedom beyond anything you can yet imagine."

Phae's heart pounded with excitement. "How does this work? I was told, by Neodesha, that there was a tree. There was fruit from that tree."

"Yes. The tree is in the city, over there. Do you see the river that you were near when your mother found you?" He pointed along the beach toward the overgrown area where Phae had emerged. "Follow the river with your eyes and you'll see it leads to the heart of the city. There is a tree there. The river comes from the tree. There are twelve different fruits growing from the branches, each fruit granting a different power. One of those fruit will make you like me."

"Immortal?" Phae asked.

He shook his head. "That is not what we call ourselves. We are the Unwearying Ones. We do not tire, nor thirst, nor grow fatigued. Our combined will keeps the Decay away from your world. Our thoughts hold it at bay. The thoughts of mortals in your world attract the Decay. Thankfully, our thoughts are higher than your thoughts. Our ways are higher than your ways. I invite you to become one of us, Phae. To become an Unwearying One yourself."

Phae's heart leapt at the thought, her eyes blinking in wonder. "Like Shion!" she gasped, understanding flooding her. "It's not the Arch-Rike's magic at all that protects him. He is part of this, isn't he? I know he is!" She thrilled at the thought, beginning to see and understand, and it was all jumbling together in her mind.

"Yes," the Seneschal replied. "Only he has forgotten who he is."

"Will you tell me?" she said, taking his hands and looking at him pleadingly. "I promised I would help restore his memories, if I could."

The Seneschal clasped one of his hands atop hers. "It depends, child, entirely on you. Would you know his history? Would you free his memories if you could?"

Phae nodded vigorously. "I would. Must I swear an oath first? Is it possible to stop the Plagues? By coming here, must I abandon my father and my companions?"

"Phae," he said quietly, his eyes twinkling. "You will understand it all. But you must fulfill your destiny first. You must make your oath and you must honor it always. As you learned from the Dryad whose tree you will liberate, there is a heavy price in forsaking the oath. Do you do it willingly?"

"I do," Phae said, nodding, her heart nearly exploding with emotions. She felt tears on her lashes.

"After you have accepted the oaths, you will be allowed to eat one of the fruit from the tree. Each kind bestows a power. For example, the fruit of ambition causes the fireblood. One of the fruits bestows the Vaettir gift of breath. You are also Dryad-born and possess a gift through your faculty of sight. Not only can you take in experiences through your eyes, you can also take them away from others. You can draw memories from someone else. Or restore them, once the power is fully consecrated. What you will learn is knowledge that you cannot share within the mortal world. Possessing it will make you different from others. It will give you great wisdom, Phae. However, in much wisdom is much grief. And they that increase knowledge also increase sorrow. As you learn the truth, you will grieve. But I promise you that the fruit of that knowledge, while bitter to the taste, is also most sweet too."

He turned away from her, looking out at the vast expanse of ocean, the teeming waves crashing down below. The wind whipped the fringe of his robe, gliding through his long, dark hair. She saw the double swords strapped to him, realizing that he had many skills and played many roles.

The Seneschal turned back to her. "A Dryad protects knowledge, Phae. She helps prevent the Decay from destroying knowledge from the mortal world. She is bound to a tree for a period of service. It means she coexists between Mirrowen and the mortal realm. When your service is complete, you will be allowed to dwell in either world or in a new world entirely. The family and friends you know now will not be there when your service is complete. Not many mortals earn the right to be part of us. Most are distracted by ducats and how to acquire them. When your time is growing near, you will need to choose a husband in order to bear a daughter who can replace you. You will teach her of Mirrowen and her responsibilities. When she is nearly sixteen, you will bring her to me in Mirrowen, where I will bind her with the Voided Keys to your tree. That will free you from service."

"I understand," Phae answered. She exhaled deeply. "Unfortunately, the Dryad tree I seek is in the midst of the Scourgelands. Not many mortals will be able to seek it."

The Seneschal smiled. "It has always been thus, because that tree guards the portal to Mirrowen. A Dryad can visit here through a tree. If a mortal seeks to become an Unwearying One, he or she must pass through the portal. The last man to have done so made the journey very long ago. His name is not Shion. He was known by another name then."

"Will you tell me?"

"Do you accept the duty of your race, Phae? Will you accept a new name with these powers I unlock inside of you? Will you serve the mortal world and help those living there to remember Mirrowen and seek to attain it?"

"Yes," Phae answered, bowing her head.

The Seneschal gripped one of the Voided Keys in his left hand. He put his right hand on her shoulder, bent down, and kissed the top of her head.

"My name is Melchisedeq. I give you your Dryad name—Arsinowe. I bind you to your tree by the Voided Keys."

A feeling of warmth and strength began to suffuse across Phae, from the crown of her head, spreading down to the nape of her neck, all the way down to the soles of her feet. She shuddered, feeling her mind opening, blooming, her memory quickening. The seed of power inside of her, the part of her that was truly Dryad-born, expanded, filling her with compassion and empathy.

She looked up, tears streaking down her cheeks, and saw the Seneschal smiling at her with tears in his own eyes.

In the stillness, amidst the caress of the wind, she heard his thoughts as if spoken audibly. The voice was the sound of rushing waters. It went deep into her marrow, and she was fairly certain that every being in Mirrowen could hear the thought as well as she—that distance meant nothing. It jolted her with its simplicity, yet also with its penetrating quality.

Neodesha—come

"The Arch-Rike's temple is under heavy guard. Any attempts to breach its walls are repulsed with devastating magic. The Rikes hold power there, and some of the citizenry were turned away when seeking shelter. There are Bhikhu there as well, but mostly Kishion guard the walls. The Empress is agitated, worried about the lives of the populace. If the Plague strikes now, the situation will become desperate. She has suggested we anchor the fleet away from the piers. But will doing so cause a riot? I wish I had the wisdom to foresee what would happen."

- Possidius Adeodat, Archivist of Kenatos

XXXVII

"There you are," Neodesha said, peering over Phae's shoulder into the polished silver mirror. "Goodness, Phae, but you are beautiful."

Phae saw the reflection of herself and was hardly able to recognize the image. Her hair was still damp but the tangles were brushed free. The dirt and grime of the Scourgelands had been scrubbed away. Her torn and filthy clothes were gone, replaced by a beautiful wool gown made in the style of Stonehollow. It was a deep amber color with blue-and-gold stitching along the sleeves, cuff, and hem.

"I don't think I've ever worn a gown before," Phae said, stroking the fabric along her arm and feeling its comfort and softness. "They're not very practical on a homestead." The robe had a wide fabric girdle and she had put the Tay al-Ard into one of its folds.

"Remember what I taught you," Neodesha said. "This is no ordinary garment. It adapts to your needs and to your location. Think about the vineyard, Phae. Hold the thought firmly in your mind, and then think the word of power."

Phae's memories were vivid and complete. She could remember every word she had ever spoken, every conversation, every emotion. She would be able to pass along this gift of perfect memory to someone else if she kissed him. It was not one of her Dryad powers, but a gift from the Seneschal's kiss on her forehead. Bringing up the Winemiller vineyard came to her as naturally as breathing, for she could remember every detail and knew the place as if she were right there.

Scield she thought.

The image on the mirror wavered and suddenly she was wearing her tunic and pants with comfortable boots and worn leather belt. The Tay al-Ard did not transform but remained in her belt. The transformation was not just an illusion, though. The Dryad robe could become anything she needed. She could appear as a Bhikhu or even a Rike. The magic would transform her instantly.

"You must always keep this robe," Neodesha said, looking into her eyes seriously. "If you surrender it, you cannot return to Mirrowen."

Phae turned and looked at her, feeling grateful the Seneschal had sent Neodesha to help her bathe and make the final preparations that would separate her from her past life. The look in Neodesha's eyes was full of warning.

"Is that what happened?" Phae asked, gripping the other girl's arm. "To the Dryads in the Scourgelands?"

Neodesha shook her head. "We do not know what happened, Phae. It was long ago and the Seneschal does not speak of it. I only understand that they forfeited their right to return to Mirrowen, and that I was warned, as I'm warning you, never to part from it. You now have your Dryad name, which you must give as a boon to someone who protects your tree. Be very careful whom you trust with it, Sister. Better to steal their memories than to be subjected to them." Neodesha smiled and patted her shoulder. "Do you like the city?"

"It's beautiful," Phae said, staring at the bathing chamber with its marble tiles and gauzy curtains. Every detail was done after the highest order of craftsmanship. Gold fluting decorated every section of the marble, but it was not ostentatious. There were no torches or fires, for there was no place in the city where it was dark.

"Come with me then," Neodesha invited, linking arms with her. "You might want to appear in the other gown, however. Vineyard garb wouldn't be appropriate to wander in within the city."

Together they left the bathing chamber through the archway. There were no doors anywhere, nothing closed off. They passed near a surging waterfall, which filled the air with a delicate mist as they passed. The smell of flowers lingered. The city was full of others, talking as they walked, discussing topics that previously would have baffled Phae. The rushing of the waterfall passed behind them and they descended a grand staircase together to a broad plaza, fringed with benches made of polished stone. Spirit animals could be seen as well, some interacting with the many races that were represented below.

The mix of plant life with the stonework of the city garden amazed Phae. She had always imagined Kenatos being a grand place to visit someday, a city built on a desolate island. Mirrowen was beyond imagining and she longed to explore the various hills that were interconnected, to search and discover exotic fragrances or budding fruit trees. She felt alive and free, but still unable to imagine that time had halted, that Shion and her father were somewhere nearby, yet not near. She fingered the Tay al-Ard, wondering if she could use it to leave Mirrowen if she needed to.

"There is the tree," Neodesha said, gesturing across a bridge at the far side of the plaza.

It was the strangest thing she had ever seen. The tree was large and crowned with heavy limbs, but it was not of any variety she had beheld before. The bark was silver-gray and from its roots gushed a fountain of silver water that tumbled down three different channels going in three different directions, as if it were the source of three pure rivers. What tree birthed a water fountain, she wondered? As if that were not strange enough, there were a variety of different fruits growing on the different branches. Some were small and round. Others were thicker and shaped like pears. Some like apples. Some were fruits she had never seen before, with strange and colorful peels.

"Tell me about the tree," Phae asked, staring at it as they began to cross the bridge to it. On the other side of the bridge, two massive, catlike creatures were settled and resting. Both were like Nizeera, except much bigger and with enormous white manes. Their pelts were also white and looked so soft that Phae wanted to dig her hands into them, but she dared not since their eyes were fierce.

"The tree has always been in Mirrowen," Neodesha said. "One must be given permission to take from its fruit. The Seneschal is the Gardener. There are many powers here. Even the moss that grows on the stone can heal any wound. The leaves of the tree cure poison or disease."

"Even the Plague?" Phae asked.

"Especially that. The waters are restorative as well. This is ancient magic, Phae. I don't understand it."

"If the leaves cure the Plague, why hasn't the Seneschal stopped it from ravaging the world?"

As if in response to his title being spoken, Phae saw the Seneschal appear from behind a stone column, near the tree. He spoke to another man, his head bent low and giving instructions. The man bowed, nodded, and then greeted them as they passed over the bridge. He was a handsome man, full of youth, and he wore a Druidecht talisman around his neck.

After crossing the bridge, Neodesha escorted Phae to the Seneschal and did a small reverence to him. "I have done as you asked, Seneschal. I took Phae to the bathing pools and presented her with a Dryad robe. She has been instructed in its magic and now I have brought her to the tree as you bid me to."

"Thank you, Neodesha," the Seneschal said warmly. "That is all."

Neodesha hugged Phae one last time and then retreated back across the bridge again.

"There are many fruits growing on this tree, Arsinowe," the Seneschal said. "But above all others, there is one that mortals desire. All of the fruit on the tree are sweet, save one. There is one that is bitter, yet it holds the most power." He reached up to the branch and plucked a white fruit. It looked like a pear, except the skin was soft like a peach. Phae saw that the underside was white, but the top half was golden. It was small, easily fitting inside her palm as the Seneschal bestowed it.

"Why is it bitter?" Phae asked, gazing up at him.

He smiled wanly. "Many fruits surprise us with tartness or sweetness. I am certain you will come to understand the answer after you have been among us a while longer."

She stared at it. "So if I eat this, I will never die?"

He shook his head. "No, Arsinowe. If you eat it, your body will change. You will no longer age. You cannot be injured or harmed by magic. You will not experience physical pain, but you can suffer grief and sorrow. There is a poison, however, which can slay even an Unwearying One. There is also another kind of fruit, from another tree, which will make you mortal again if you eat it."

Phae experienced a tremor . . . a premonition. "The blade Iddawc?"

The Seneschal nodded. "Iddawc is not a blade. It is a spirit creature. Its true shape is that of a serpent. It's quite small." He motioned to the tree, where she saw several serpents—tiny ones—slinking in the branches. She had not noticed them until he gestured. "Some serpents live in trees, Arsinowe. Iddawc was once a guardian of this one. It was disobedient, and so it was sent to the mortal world."

Phae swallowed, staring at the fruit cupped in her hand. "Will you tell me why?"

"I will answer your questions. But first you must fulfill your Dryad oath. You have been bound to the tree you entered Mirrowen from. When you have tasted of the fruit, you will be allowed to experience the memories you came here for. Only a true Dryad can access her tree's memories."

She stared at the fruit, feeling its weight. She realized she was at a moment that would alter her forever. There was a twinge of fear inside her stomach. What if the Seneschal was deceiving her? What if the fruit in her hand was poisonous?

"Guard your thoughts," the Seneschal said firmly. "Have you let your fears plague you thus far? Conquer them. You must decide and then act—come what may."

Phae took a deep breath and then sank her teeth into the flesh of the small golden fruit.

It was sugary sweet at first, surprising her. The flavor was unlike anything she had experienced, but it was gentle on her tongue and quite interesting. As she chewed, she began to taste a hint of bitterness in the peel. Her nose crinkled at the taste, but it was not disgusting. She bit into the fruit again, finding the same sensations repeated. As she swallowed, she felt the bitterness in her mouth grow, and she felt a slight queasiness begin to swell. Then it was gone.

Her arms and legs began to tingle. She examined herself, seeing no marks on her skin. She felt flushed, alive, full of energy.

Every memory of fatigue or weariness vanished from her thoughts. She believed she could run, even across a mountain, and never tire.

So this is what it feels like to be Shion, she thought with wonder. There was no longer any memory of hunger or thirst either. The fruit was inside of her, feeding her with energy. It was limitless. She recognized that she could eat or drink, that those actions were still possible. But she knew that she would not need to any longer.

"Shion ate this fruit," Phae said, turning in amazement to the Seneschal. "How did he lose his memories? You promised you would tell me these things. Can I truly know them? Must I go back to the tree and harvest his memories there?" She swallowed, feeling confusion and uncertainty collide inside her. "What is the right thing to do? Will I still be allowed to help my father? You know his purpose. Can I aid him?"

"I will let you decide," the Seneschal said patiently. He extended his hand. "Let me see your Tay al-Ard."

Phae removed it from her girdle and gave it to him.

He turned it over in his hands, studying the design of it. "Your father crafted this," he said, nodding in approval. "He did well. You cannot trap Tay al-Ard spirits. They cannot be bound into service. They are important to maintaining the flow of time in your world. With this device, you can go anywhere you have ever been, correct?"

Phae nodded.

"Since I bear the Voided Keys, it authorizes me to go anywhere in time, to places I have been or not. The knowledge you seek will be communicated best if you are shown it. Remember, with your robe and the word of power you can look like you belong anywhere. You can also disappear from the sight of mortals. You can hear any language spoken and understand it, or you can speak any language. We will travel together and see how the curse of the Plague began. There is no book you need to read, though all things are written by me. Instead, I will show it to you. Throughout the lives of mortals, there are always pivotal moments. Most often, those moments are so subtle we barely appreciate how momentous they are. A wayward rebuke by a thoughtless father can doom his children to a misunderstanding of their gifts or abilities. Those small moments, those key moments, are often never seen by the rest of the world. They alter the course of someone's life. It is possible to go watch those moments. To be in attendance, unseen, when they happen. Sometimes, all that is needed is a little push, a little nudge to make the fate complete. It takes wisdom to know when those moments arrive. Come with me, child."

The Seneschal extended his hand. Phae grasped it, and it was warm and strong and firm. He held the Tay al-Ard, looking into her eyes, giving her a feeling of warmth and protection.

He blinked and everything changed.

The next instant, Phae found herself in the great hall of an enormous castle. There were huge trestle tables laden with the remnants of a feast. It was a tidy affair, not a boisterous event, and what few scraps had fallen to the floor rushes were instantly snatched by greyhounds and gobbled up. Torches hung in brackets on the wall, causing a smoky light to fill the hall, revealing a crowd of men and women dressed in fine tunics and gowns. The style was different from what she was used to, but she noticed that her robe had assumed the design and style of the time and that she was walking arm in arm with the Seneschal, who was now much shorter and looking more Aeduan than any other race. He still had his piercing blue eyes and she would have recognized him from across the crowded hall by the majesty of his presence alone. The Voided Keys were fastened to his belt innocuously.

Servants brought in fresh drinks, wine, by the smell of it, and the guests of the feast were quick to fill their goblets, but no one drank to excess. There were beautiful tapestries adorning the walls, hanging from high iron piles fixed to rings. The ceiling was vaulted and filled with wooden timbers supporting the weight of stone above.

"Where are we?" Phae asked the Seneschal, keeping her voice guarded.

"Stonehollow," he replied. "Long ago, according to your reckoning. There is no Kenatos yet. The strongest empire is Boeotia, but she is a peaceful nation. What race are these, do you suppose?"

"They seem Aeduan," Phae replied, but wrinkled her brow. "But different. More stern and serious, though. I can see a difference."

"Yes, you do. Come this way. You will have a good view from over here."

"Are these the nobles of Stonehollow?" Phae asked.

"Yes, but not only the nobles. Their king values the artisans, those with excellence in craft and skill. He rewards those with talent and so many come to perform and display their abilities. He commissions the best, regardless of how humble their origins. Do you see his throne? It's made of stone to be uncomfortable. So that he will remind himself of the weight of his responsibility. That he must counsel with prudence and judgment."

"Where is the king?" Phae asked, searching around and seeing only the empty throne.

"Over there," the Seneschal said. "He is approaching."

Phae saw him. He was probably thirty years old, full of vigor and health. He was a handsome man and spoke to several as he ascended the steps of the dais to the throne. His hair was not the gray she had seen in the grove, but was auburn, like her own, with fringes of gray on the edges near his ears. When he turned and seated himself, a hush fell over the room.

Phae's heart constricted with a spasm of terror. The face was young, but the features were clear. "The Arch-Rike," she whispered in shock.

The Seneschal smiled, patting her hand. "Not yet. He's also known to you by the name Shirikant. But that is not his true name. Quiet . . . watch."

Shirikant sat on the throne, leaning forward as if it were uncomfortable and pained him. He gestured to someone in the crowd. His voice was rich and powerful and he had an easy smile and a natural charm. "My friends, thank you for gathering for the feast tonight. It gives me pleasure that you come to honor my brother, who has returned from his long travels. As you know, he is a Druidecht, and they tend to roam abroad when the fancy suits them. My brother is a wanderer. He does not have the affairs of state to pinion him as they do me, but I don't begrudge him his freedom. Under much pressure and even a little compulsion, I've convinced him to sing for you tonight. Welcome home, Brother Isic. Welcome home. Sing for us."

Phae's heart nearly burst when she saw Shion stand and approach the dais.

"I have written what the Empress has revealed to me about the existence of Shirikant. I find it difficult to believe that there is a being among us who is immortal, who cannot be killed, but I have heard enough such rumors to give it credence. I believe he is part of the nameless race, the race that is persecuted in Stonehollow. Knowledge of that race has been lost forever and it seems systematically so. If there were only a way to recover something that time has so meticulously erased."

- Possidius Adeodat, Archivist of Kenatos

XXXVIII

"They are brothers," Phae whispered, clutching the Seneschal's arm tightly. The impact of the realization struck her with tremendous force. Shion and Shirikant were brothers, born of the same kingdom.

"Watch."

As Shion walked toward the dais, he was admired by many in the crowd, many of them women who seemed to vie to meet his gaze. From her vantage point, Phae watched him cross right in front of her, his expression a mixture of melancholy and resignation. He did not look pleased to be asked to perform in front of everyone.

He had some small stubble on his lower jaw, but there was no evidence of scars on his smooth cheeks. He was smaller, probably sixteen or seventeen—her own age. Her heart thrilled when she saw him unharmed, saw the stormy countenance but not the look of danger and threat. He carried a lute in one hand and then seated himself on the edge of the dais, before his brother's throne. A hush settled across the great hall. Even the murmur of the torch flames seemed to still.

Shion nestled against the lip of the dais, positioning himself, sinking his shoulders as he relaxed, his fingers positioned against the lute strings. Phae stared at him, her heart hammering inside her.

Then there was music.

The sound he coaxed out of the lute strings was nothing like the festive dance tunes she had grown up to in Stonehollow. The chords were plaintive and mournful and penetrated her emotions, wrapping her in a veil of sadness. Then his voice joined the sounds, strong and rich, and it brought the mood from her ears into her bones. It was not the tune from the locket, but she knew instinctively that he was the one who had created that song. The Seneschal looked at her, smiling in approval, and nodded, patting her hand delicately.

The singer and his melody cast a spell across everyone assembled in the great hall. She could almost see the music as streamers of magic, coiling around the minds of those assembled, making them forget the moment, forget even time itself—all there was in the world was the sound of Shion's voice, accentuated by the stirring strains of the lute, mixing together in such a way as to coax tears from Phae's eyes. She saw she was not alone, that others wept. The spell endured, washing over every person until the final note hung in the air, tormented with grief, fading into an echo—then gone.

Shion bowed his head, wiping his own eyes on his sleeve. He slowly stood as the spell unraveled, and suddenly he was mobbed with well-wishers and people who longed to see him. He met them with shy reserve and silence, not deigning to answer questions, looking uncomfortable being the focus of attention.

There were several young ladies, fancily dressed, and they persisted, trying to draw him out. He ignored them, looking around the crowd for a way to escape.

His eyes, desperate for a way to extract himself, suddenly found hers.

"He can see us," Phae whispered in shock.

She saw the slight crinkle in his expression as his look shifted from discomfort to curiosity. He started through the crowd toward them, moving around the bodies that harangued and tried to get his attention.

Phae stiffened, feeling a sense of panic welling inside her.

Watch.

The Seneschal's thoughts were forceful, but calming.

Before he had cleared the ranks separating them, a hand reached Shion's shoulder and his brother hooked him into a brotherly embrace, clapping his back hard. He gestured for Shion to accompany him and the two departed back toward the dais. With the king claiming his brother, the rest melted away. There was a wooden screen behind the throne and Shirikant steered his sibling toward it, the two escaping out the back of the hall.

Phae looked at the Seneschal's face. "Could he really see us?"

"Yes. He did notice us, though his imagination will taint the memory. He will come back and look for us again. He'll spend a good part of the night searching the crowd. He won't tell anyone, because he's not certain what he saw. But we came here for a clue to the riddle you seek. As we follow them behind the screen, they will not be able to see us. Observe. Listen. This is an important night. A crucial one for what it sets in motion. Follow me."

He escorted her to the decorated screen and it felt as if they were walking the aether. No one got in their way or even seemed to notice them. Behind the screen was a dark, heavy curtain, blocking the room beyond. They crossed it without rustling the fabric at all, which Phae did not understand. It felt as if they became smoke for a moment and just wafted past, reminiscent of Kiranrao's powerful sword.

There was a council chamber behind the screen and curtain, with a long waxed table surrounded by twelve chairs, six on each side. Each chair was meticulously carved, sanded, decorated, stained, and polished. Along the wall were a window seat and a mountain of books that filled bookshelves almost as high as the ceiling. Books crowded the room, of various sizes and thickness. She saw Shirikant at the window seat, a heavy book in his lap, flipping through some pages while Shion paced near the table loaded with fruit, cheese, and wine. There were seven others in the room, many with the same regal-looking faces, and there was a Vaettir among them as well as a Preachán. A hulking Cruithne guarded the door on the other side of the room.

Shirikant set the book down on the window seat next to him and faced his brother. "You picked a brooding song tonight, Brother. This was supposed to be a celebration."

"Paideia is dead," Shion said darkly, not turning to meet his brother's eyes.

"What? I noticed that I hadn't seen her tonight, but I assumed she was in the crowd." He stood, his expression turning to shock and sadness as well. "What happened?"

Shion fingered a goblet, but he did not raise it to his lips. He let out a bitter sigh and then rubbed his eyes. "Marq and Tenblec are also dead. The rest survived the woods."

Phae's blood went cold. Was he talking about the Scourgelands? His voice was full of sadness and weariness. He looked weather-beaten and exhausted.

"I am so sorry, Isic. Paideia was your mentor. She trained you in the Druidecht lore. When I sent her on this quest, it was to continue your training as well. I trusted her and I respected her. She was a gracious soul. What happened?" He stood and went to his brother, gripping his shoulder to comfort him.

Shion's expression seemed to soften a bit. Phae could see the brothers were close. Even more, they were friends.

"We searched deep into the woods," Shion said. "Trails and clues existed, but they were mixed and difficult to spot. It seemed we kept getting turned around. But I persisted, knowing that we'd face difficulty before success . . . just as you've always taught me. It took a little while before I noticed the butterflies. They were so blue, a startling blue."

"Go on," Shirikant said, his eyes suddenly eager. His mouth twitched with interest.

"It felt like they . . . were summoning me? I can't describe it." He steepled his fingers over his mouth, looking vacantly at the floor. "The butterflies led us to a gulch. It was dark and muddy, roots clawing at our hair. But at the end of the gulch, we found a tree."

Shirikant's eyes were guarded. He kept his hand on his brother's shoulder. "And?"

"It was not the tree you're looking for," Shion said flatly. "It was beautiful and pale, with thousands of blue butterflies instead of leaves. There was spirit magic guarding it, Brother. There was a pond . . . a brackish pond. The tree was in the middle of the pond and the gully water seemed to fill the pond, which was stagnating. I recall you telling me that the tree we seek has a river coming forth. This tree seemed to be drawing certain elements of the forest to it. There was nothing but the fouled waters, the gully, and the myriad butterflies. Paideia went into the waters and approached the tree, saying she had found our goal. She'd found the tree of Mirrowen. The tree with the fruit that grants immortal life. I warned her to stay back, but she wouldn't heed me. She approached the tree, telling me she could see the fruit." He shrugged helplessly. "I could see no fruit on that tree at all. But she went closer, sloshing and splashing. I had a terrible feeling. I was excited, of course—we all were. But something felt *wrong*. I warned her again, but again she would not heed me and she went to the tree. I saw her reach up and pluck something from a lower branch. I could not see what it was, but I saw the blue wings of a butterfly on it. She took a bite. Then she died."

Shion exhaled slowly, shaking his head. The experience had happened in the past but Phae could still see the lingering effects of grief on his countenance.

"What happened to Marq?"

"He went *mad*," Shion said, grunting. "When Paideia crumpled into the water, he thought she was drowning. He went after her but Tenblec grabbed his arm and struggled to keep him near the gully with the rest of us. Marq isn't a big man, but he was suddenly enraged that Tenblec stopped him. They were struggling and before anyone could break them up, Marq struck him on the head with the pommel of his dagger. Then Marq was splashing in the waters and struggling to reach the tree. By the time he reached it, he'd forgotten about Paideia and he also grabbed for the fruit and died. The rest of us managed to drag Tenblec's body through the gulch. As soon as we tried to leave, the insects all went berserk and fluttered around us, going inside our garments."

Phae trembled at the memory, her eyes riveted on Shion's face. Her flesh crawled.

"Tenblec was dead when we reached the safety of the woods again, his skull caved in where the dagger pommel had struck. I didn't realize how fragile life is, Brother. Three were dead so quickly. The trail was false. It led to a tree with special fruit, but it was not the portal to Mirrowen."

Shirikant breathed deeply, shaking his head in dismay. He hugged his brother and held him a moment, his own expression mimicking the desolation of Shion. "I'm sorry, Isic. That's a blow. That's a hard blow. I'm grateful you didn't succumb to the lure."

Shirikant turned to the Preachán. "What do you think, Odea? What struck you about this tale?"

The Preachán was older than Shirikant, his hair receding. He was fit and trim, not a tall man, and his head seemed full of ideas. He had a pensive, thoughtful look. "I think we're lucky Prince Isic is wise. Wisdom is worth pursuing, lad. You found some in this latest foray. This is not the tree to Mirrowen. This is a setback that would crush the determination of ordinary men. It means we are very close to discovering Mirrowen."

Shirikant smiled at the statement, nodding indulgently. "There is always a setback. An obstacle to overcome."

"I know," Shion said. "You told me before we started this effort that we'd face challenges. I wasn't expecting them to hurt this deeply. But I thought the same thing. Looking back, we should have retreated from the gully and left it alone. The clues warned us away, but I didn't heed them soon enough. Those three paid with their lives."

"I grieve for all their families," Shirikant said. "They will want for nothing. We all accepted the risks. What do you say, Kishion?" He nodded toward the Cruithne guarding the door.

"Best to send me along on the next trip," he said, his voice deep and rumbling. "Can't trust a group of Druidecht with fighting or squeamish business. Let me go."

"You will," Shirikant said, rubbing his smooth lower lip. "Isic—you should stay here for a fortnight or more. You need the rest and the chance to grieve. We'll scour the records yet again to see what clues we find."

Shirikant started to pace the chamber, his shoulder hunched with deep thought. His expression was full of energy, his eyes gleaming with hope. "We are so close!" he said vehemently. "I cannot believe that all the tales are false. Every people, whether they are Vaettir, Cruithne, Preachán, Boeotian, or even Moussion like me—like us—we all have traditions of how the world started. Land coming from the waters. Plants and trees coming next. Then fish and fowl. The Book of Breathings left by the Copts probably has the most detailed descriptions and flourishes to the tales. They speak about a Garden. They speak about a tree with a river gushing from it." He pointed to the Cruithne. "One of the rivers in your homeland is named after it! They speak of the Gardener who allows mortals to come to Mirrowen, to learn the ways of the Unwearying Ones. The tree grants immortality." His voice was thick with emotion, with passion and energy. "How can all of these sundry civilizations all share a common core, a common myth, a common origin story? There must be a pea of truth inside this shell. Master Archivist, say again what happened to this Garden?"

The Preachán folded his arms smugly, his expression revealing delight over being called out again. "It was first on this world with us. But the mortals were driven away. A bridge separates us, guarded by a terrible plague. Only those who know the name of the bridge can cross it. The name handed down through the ages is Poisonwell, though that is only an interpretation of a translation from Hidemic texts. Find Poisonwell, learn its password, and you can cross into Mirrowen, where the Plague will not kill you. The leaves from the tree cure any poison or disease. It would take courage to cross such a bridge, knowing that crossing it will kill you. The only question, my lord, is if the bridge is literal or metaphorical. Is it symbol or is it structure?"

Shirikant smiled broadly. "We've searched every forest in every kingdom. I myself sailed to the Vaettir homeland in my youth and searched there. But the tales all say that this land is the home of Poisonwell. Unfortunately, my kingdom is vast. Where haven't we tried, Master Cartographer? What say you, Gault?"

Gault had a trimmed mustache over his blocky face, his hair well salted with silver. He sat back in his stuffed chair, frowning with deep thoughts. "My lord, we've crisscrossed the lands methodically, starting in the mountains in the east, the plains in the south. We've explored all the reaches of our own borders, went to the seashore beyond the mountains, and finally looked into the woods west. You've personally been emissary to the Vaettir across the sea as well as met the Empress of Boeotia. That leaves one final stretch of woods to explore. It's uninhabited as far as we know. The woods to the north, beyond the lake and the mountains. It's a vast land. By my estimation," he tapped his lips thoughtfully, "it will take four years to fully explore that region. Every Finder who has been there comes back with news that it's a peaceful, forgotten place so far away that no one would ever want to dwell there. It's on the edge of the known world, far from all the trade routes, except for the occasional Romani wagon. But if we want to be methodical about this, Prince Isic should look there next. Now, if you want to know my view, I think it's a waste of time and energy because the roads are . . ."

"No, Gault," Shirikant said, waving him silent. "I've told you before to express your facts, not your doubts. Do not poison our minds with such thoughts." He went back to the window seat and sat down next to the book he had been looking at earlier. He patted it reverently. "Every scrap of lore about Mirrowen has been written in here. Every clue we have pursued. Every scrap. My father started this quest before I was born and his father before him. It is said that my line comes from Mirrowen itself, that we descend from the kings of old. We are the Moussion. We are scholars and learners and artists and sculptors. We are patient. We are patient, and we are determined." He turned to Shion, fixing him with his blazing eyes. "Rest yourself, Brother. Get what sleep and rest you can. But I send you next up north. Take as many Druidecht as you desire. Take Kishion with you. He can train and teach you to fight along the way. I have a feeling . . . no, I have a premonition that makes my blood hot that this is where we will find success. We will find the gate to Mirrowen. You will find it, Isic. I know you will. You have all of my resources at your disposal. But it is not gold or jewels that will make you successful. It is believing that you can succeed and moving forward despite obstacles. We few are a mastermind. We few. As my ancestors have taught, there is great good that can be done in this world if a group of wise men and women assembles toward a common purpose. That is a mastermind."

"What about the Gardener?" Odea said. "What would you give that you might claim one of the fruit?"

Shirikant's eyes blazed with determination. "I would give up my kingdom."

"Memory is the mother of all wisdom."

- Possidius Adeodat, Archivist of Kenatos

XXXIX

The world lurched, spinning rapidly, and then it was still again, the magic of the Tay al-Ard bringing them to another place, another time. Phae gripped the Seneschal's arm, finding herself in a lush forest of oak trees. Light came slanting in from many angles, causing a radiant flash on the bark and glossy leaves. Specks of gnats flitted in the air and the drone of bumblebees wafted nearby. The forest was majestic and beautiful, but it was also poignant, rich with spirit life and full of promise as well as warning.

"Where are we?" Phae asked, looking around. It was unfamiliar to her.

"The Scourgelands," he replied with a knowing smile. "Before the cursing."

She watched a robin flutter down from a tree and hop on a boulder, its head shifting back and forth, studying them. Then it flew away.

"I'm beginning to understand a little," Phae said. "They are brothers then. Born from the same mother?"

"Indeed. There were sisters in between who married nobles from other lands. They were a proud race, but not in the sense of haughtiness. They come from a line of master stonemasons, men who are patient and very hard and formidable. They are persistent yet calculating, not using more force than is necessary to shiver loose a piece of rock. They study the stone they hammer, looking for imperfections. Timing the blow to meet the purpose. They are the Moussion. The lost race."

"Why are they lost?"

"You will see, Phae. You will see it all. Several years have passed since you last saw the young prince, Isic Moussion. He is a Druidecht, but it is a primitive version of what you are familiar with. He studied the spirit creatures from all the lands, taking copious notes of his observations. He began to name the spirits, to understand their powers and properties. To enlist their aid. He roamed the woods with a band of friends from the mastermind. The Cruithne . . . his name was Kishion. He was one of the first teachers of that order, back when they were protectors of kings and not killers. When Isic and his companions came here, to these hallowed woods, they met the protections left to guard here. You can imagine how frustrating it was when they returned to Stonehollow with no memory of why they had even come. Shirikant was wise and realized that spirit magic was robbing their memories. They did not understand the nature of the Dryads. Not yet. But after several years, they began to understand that the bridge to Mirrowen—Poisonwell—was here all along. They set up small outposts to help funnel supplies and men to help narrow the search."

Phae looked up at his face, saw the curious expression. "Why not let them come, Seneschal? Why all the obstacles?"

"There is a price to pay for knowledge, child. Some mysteries must be earned. I test the persistence of mortals. Only those who persist discover the way. Isic was not easily discouraged."

Phae smiled at that, remembering how he came across to her so many times. *Relentless.*

"Indeed," the Seneschal said, responding to her thoughts. "Soon you will see the next turning point. The next crucial pivot. During his wanderings in the woods, Isic began to rely on his insights. He understood a little about my nature. He understood that there was a Gardener in Mirrowen. He reasoned it out that I could hear his thoughts. He began to speak to me from his mind as he scoured the woods for clues. I began to teach him through the whispers. I warned him not to share the knowledge, not to write it down, but to print it in his heart. He began to journey alone, searching the woods for hidden trails. Eventually, he began to trust me. He could not find Mirrowen by searching for it. Not with his eyes. I suggested to his mind, through a whisper, that he would find me if he *closed* his eyes."

Phae's mind expanded with the thought. "Yes," she said, growing excited. "By keeping his eyes closed, he could pass the Dryad protectors without losing his memories. He would not be able to see the direction, but you would lead him on the right path!"

"Yes. After sufficient time, he trusted me enough. He blindfolded himself and took leave of his friends, warning them not to follow him. Through the whispers, he made it to your tree, the one you are bound to now. From that tree one learns the word to cross the bridge. You remember it."

"*Pontfadog*," Phae repeated. "So the Dryad I met was protecting the tree even then?"

The Seneschal stopped, his face turning troubled, if slightly, as if a heaviness passed over him—a cloud momentarily veiling the brilliance of the sun. "No. He met my daughter."

Phae turned to look at him, her expression showing concern. "Your daughter?"

"She was still growing. Fourteen years old . . . just a little thing.

She was being raised to replace her mother as the guardian of that tree. When Isic approached it, she was the one who received him. Do you see them? Over there." A delighted smile broadened his face.

As they continued to walk and passed another row of trees, Phae could see the looming mound of rock and stone just beyond the grove, tall and imposing. There was the forked oak tree, its branch split in two with the gap in between. Shion sat near the tree, a blindfold covering his eyes. He was bigger, sturdier, more weather-beaten than the youth she had seen before. In his hands, he strummed a lute, bringing a lovely melody from the strings that reached in and pulled her heart. He sang softly, coaxingly, his voice and the instrument weaving a spell that struck her forcibly. There was magic in his hands and silk in his voice.

From around the tree, she saw the Dryad-born staring at him. She was beauty itself, so young and innocent. She crouched behind the tree, watching him, her eyes filling with wonder at the sounds coming from Shion's instrument. She had auburn hair, Phae noticed. Her gown was a deep brown with gold threads. She looked wary, nervous.

The Seneschal and Phae approached, observing from the ring of trees. She could sense his magic concealing them.

The music died.

"Play again, Druidecht," the Dryad girl pleaded.

"Tell me your name first," he answered, keeping his head bowed.

"I cannot tell you my name," she answered. "It would give you power over me. Tell me yours, Druidecht."

"Do names hold such power? Then I give you power over me," he answered. "My name is Isic Moussion. I am from Stonehollow. Are you from Mirrowen?"

"Yes."

"What kind of spirit are you? You have a lovely voice. A sparrow perhaps?"

Phae thought about his name—the name of his race. Moussion. So very near to Shion. How strange. She felt a prick of jealousy listening to their conversation. It was an uncomfortable squirming feeling inside her breast.

The girl laughed. "I'm not a bird. I'm Dryad-born. I am mortal, like you."

"Tell me of your race," he pleaded. "You are the guardians of the woods?"

"We are the guardians of the portals to Mirrowen." She stayed half-hidden behind the tree, well beyond his reach in case he tried to grab her.

"I won't harm you," he said softly. "Tell me of your people. Why do you steal our memories?"

"Why do you cut down our trees? Why do you spoil the forests? Why do you kill and spoil for sport?"

"I do not do those things," Shion said, affronted. "I am Druidecht. I protect the woods."

"I know. But you asked why the Dryads steal memories. To protect ourselves from mortals who would harm or steal our secrets. We guard the mysteries of Mirrowen, Isic. Do you seek them?"

"I do. It is why I came."

"Take off your blindfold."

Shion stiffened. "I would rather not."

"Don't you want to see me?"

"Yes, but I know if I look at you, I will forget. I don't want to forget you, Dryad. You have the most lovely voice. It tortures me that I cannot see you."

She laughed softly. "You are doing well, Isic. You are enduring the effects of my magic. A little longer and it will get easier."

"Talking helps distract my mind," Shion said. "Tell me of the Gardener?"

"He is called the Seneschal. He is the oldest servant. He is the master of Mirrowen because he is the servant of this world. He is . . . he is my father."

Shion started, turning to look back at her, even though he was blindfolded. "I would meet him, Dryad. Can you bring me to him?"

"No," she answered. "I cannot bring a mortal there through this tree. There is a bridge to Mirrowen nearby. Beyond this grove, there is a large mound of stone, with broken fissures and caves. If you follow the whispers from my father, you will reach the bridge in the center of the rocks. You must know the name in order to cross, but you cannot write it down. Do you agree, Isic? Will you safeguard the name?"

He sat up, his face growing quite excited. "I do swear it on the soul of my father—"

"No need to swear on anything," she interrupted. "I just need your oath."

He looked confused, but nodded in agreement. "Yes, I swear it."

"The portal's name is *Pontfadog.* I must warn you, Isic. There is a spirit guarding the portal, a powerful spirit. That is its name. By knowing it, you will gain mastery over it, and it will permit you to cross. It has the power to unleash great plagues, Isic. It will infect you with one while crossing it. But in Mirrowen, there is a tree that can heal any plague. That spirit is the final protection of Mirrowen. This guardian is powerful enough to defeat entire armies. Even if an entire kingdom tried to force their way into its lair, it could unleash a plague that would destroy them all. Only with the name can you pass it. My tree is the guardian of the name."

Shion swallowed. Phae could see the sweat streaming down his face, making the blindfold damp. "Why are you telling me this? Why reveal it to me?"

"You could only have come here if you followed the whispers of my father. He brought you to my tree. My duty is to tell you the name of the spirit. Go on to Mirrowen, Isic. My father is a just and righteous being. He is one of the Unwearying Ones who guard and protect this world. Ask a boon of him. Farewell, Isic. You may look at me if you wish. I will not steal your memories now."

"Do you promise?"

"I am the Seneschal's daughter, Isic. I cannot lie."

He hurriedly untied the blindfold and crumpled it in his hands. Turning slowly, he gazed around, looking at the forest floor, the scrub and nest of dead oak leaves and twigs. He saw the hem of her robe and her bare feet poking from the hem. She still clutched the tree, clinging to it as a protection.

Shion gazed at her, his expression softening as he met her gaze.

"Will you not tell me your name?" he pleaded.

She shook her head no, but her expression was pained.

A robin flew into the glade, landing on the branch near the Dryad's hand. A trilling song came from it, a beautiful music.

"Alas," she said sorrowfully.

"What is it?" Shion asked, concerned.

"Your friends are tracking you in the woods. They've breached the lair of the Fear Liath."

"I don't understand," Shion said. "The what?"

"The Fear Liath. Remember that dark feeling you had when you passed by its lair? You had to master your fear in order to come farther. It almost made you turn back, but you were persistent. You were blindfolded and so you did not breach the magic of the lair. You were frightened, but you could not imprint the memory on your mind because you could not see its lair with your eyes. They defend the boundaries set by my father."

"They don't know about the boundaries," Shion said, his voice growing panicked. "What will happen to them?"

"When it is dark, the Fear Liath will hunt and kill them. Unless they make it out of the woods before nightfall." She looked up at the sky. "The day is waning already."

"I must warn them," Shion said, stuffing the blindfold into his belt.

You did warn them the Seneschal thought, his voice whispering through the aether. Shion stiffened, his eyes widening, hearing it.

"The beast cannot hunt you in Mirrowen," the Dryad said. "The gate is open to you now. Go."

The look on Shion's face tortured Phae. He was racked with indecision. She realized that his failure at the tree years before, losing his mentor, was clouding his thinking. She understood herself how dangerous a Fear Liath was, how vicious they could attack and how impossible they were to defeat.

"This isn't fair," Shion protested. "You are saying they will die because of their ignorance? When I have a chance to warn them and stop them, but I should not? A Druidecht protects life. Does the Fear Liath have a weakness?"

The Dryad's expression turned to misery. "I cannot speak it. I am forbidden to."

"Why can't you tell me? What is the purpose of these whispers if they bid us come to our death?"

"No, Isic! It's not like that. You followed the whispers. They brought you here. Those friends are intruders. They did not pass the test, which you did. It is justice that they perish. Mortals suffer when laws are broken. If you slip from a stone while climbing a mountain, you will surely fall."

"I cannot go on and let them be destroyed," Shion said, wringing his hands. "I must warn them. Will my Druidecht magic protect me from the Fear Liath?"

"I cannot tell you."

"Please, Dryad! I beg you to tell me!"

"I cannot. Knowledge must be earned. It is your choice, Isic, but please . . ."

He looked at her, frowning with unhappiness. "I will come back. I will go through the portal to Mirrowen. The Seneschal rewards determination. I will see this through. We will meet again. I promise you."

He turned and stalked from the woods, marching hard.

Phae stared after him in horror, her stomach twisting with dread and despair. Understanding flooded her, followed by emotional agony. "No," she whimpered, feeling tears sting her eyes savagely. "Is this where . . . is this when he gets his scars?"

The Seneschal put his arm around her comfortingly. He rested his chin on the top of her head, stroking her hair softly. "Pain is a teacher."

"When we walk in the forest we see only a fraction of what sees us."

- Possidius Adeodat, Archivist of Kenatos

XL

Phae rubbed her hands together, bitterly anxious, watching as Shion dragged himself from the woods of the Scourgelands and then followed the edge until it intersected with a dusty trail that skirted the forest. Weeds and grass grew thickly, but there were ruts from wagon wheels that carved a path through the green. Reaching the road, Shion finally collapsed, having lost so much blood he could no longer master his strength. His face had been slashed by claws and was blackened by the dust mixed with blood. The claw wounds had shredded his front as well. Somehow, through iron determination, he had managed to force himself onward, despite the pain and suffering. But he was leagues away from the nearest settlement.

And he was dying.

"He's too far," Phae whimpered, seeing his body crumpled on the road. "Is there anyone who can help him?"

"Watch and wait," the Seneschal said. They were hidden within the rim of the woods. Flies began buzzing around Shion's body, drawn to the sickly sweet aroma of death. She cringed, wanting to rush to him, to tend his wounds herself.

"Can we help him?" she begged.

"I've already called for help," he answered.

Soon some birds began to circle above—vultures. She grew ill, thinking about them coming down and goring him with their beaks. Her insides were sick and haunted.

"Look up," the Seneschal said, nodding to the tree line.

Then she saw him. It was a Bhikhu, gliding along the tips of the trees, floating above. Relief surged inside her. The Vaettir noticed the birds and altered direction, seeing the crumpled man far below. With a rush of breath, the Bhikhu dropped from the sky and ran up to Shion's body. He was middle-aged, with just a frosting of silver in the stubble on his head. He approached Shion cautiously, his expression twisting with disgust at the grotesque wounds.

Phae clenched the Seneschal's arm, watching with growing horror. The Bhikhu stared at him, gazing at the half-dead man. Then he knelt and offered a prayer in the Vaettir tongue, which Phae didn't understand. He looked with pity at Shion and then departed, floating away.

Phae stared at him, wanting to shriek with frustration. "Where is he going? To get help? He didn't even touch him to see if he was alive!"

The Seneschal shook his head. "The injuries made him squeamish. He realized how much blood he would get on himself attempting to help. Watch and wait."

The day passed to afternoon. Somehow, it went by more quickly than what she was used to. She could see the arc of the sun in the sky, feeling the world sigh and breathe around her. The shadows stretched and changed. The vultures descended and began poking at the body with their hooked beaks. Shion let out a groan of pain and anger and the birds scattered in fear. They returned again a short while later, bobbing and hopping to get near him again. They started to pick at him again.

The Seneschal waved his fingers at them and the vultures all turned to look at him. One by one, they bowed their necks and then flapped their wings and left.

"They saw you!" Phae said, surprised. "You were here all along? When he suffered?"

"I have been here before and I will come here again," he said softly. "Many from Mirrowen visit this moment in time. Each one who comes scatters the vultures. That is something he could not do for himself."

"But surely you can heal him," Phae said, feeling desperate to do something to help.

"Of course," the Seneschal replied. "What you must understand, child, is that when I intervene in the world, it is not just to benefit the life of a specific individual. I intervene to stop the chaos from swallowing the world. Suffering is important. It teaches so much in a little bit of time. In much wisdom there is much grief. And those who increase knowledge also increase sorrow. He was given a great gift of knowledge when he visited the Dryad tree. With knowledge comes suffering. They are connected."

"But what good will it do?"

The Seneschal smiled, a tear in his eye. "What good indeed. Wait and see, child. Wait and see. When your father fled the Scourgelands, he was going to die. Shirikant had unleashed his many hosts seeking to destroy him, to prevent him from success. Merinda Druidecht gave her life to help preserve his, but it was not enough. The hunters would have caught and killed them both. There was a storm that came and drenched their scent, making them invisible." He put his hand on her shoulder. "I commanded a spirit to summon the storm, Phae. Your father always believed it was random luck that had preserved him. He could not hear the whispers then. He was not like Isic." The Seneschal nodded to the crumpled body.

As Phae turned back, she saw that twilight was upon them. Shion had not stirred or moved at all. He was unconscious, sprawled amidst the grasses like a black stain. She saw a man approaching on the road holding a walking staff. She sighed with relief, seeing the Druidecht approach.

From the belly of the woods, a huge roar sounded. With night drawing near, the Fear Liath had begun to hunt again. One of its victims had escaped. She could feel its anger permeating the aether. Its senses were sharp and the trail of blood was only too easy to follow.

The Druidecht stiffened at the sound. He saw Shion's body in the path. Instead of walking toward him, he darted around, casting a nervous look into the dark forest. He hugged his cloak tighter, looking back once at the fallen man, but he didn't stop.

"No," Phae said in horror. "He's a Druidecht! He can summon a spirit to heal. No! Why isn't he stopping?"

"Fear is a powerful motivator," the Seneschal replied. "He heard my whisper and responded to it, coming down the road as I bid him to. But the cry of the Fear Liath overwhelmed him. He'll feel guilty about it later, and then spend the rest of his life wondering whatever happened to the dead man in the road he had walked past. He'll stop listening to the whispers and eventually forsake his life as a Druidecht. Guilt is a Finder. It hunts and tracks us down, no matter how far we run. His is a sad tale, but you will learn it later. Watch and see."

Phae felt the night descend like a blanket. Trailers of mist began to creep along the ground from the woods, probing and seeking the fallen man. The moon rose, high and silver, wreathed in frost. The temperature began to plummet, but Phae did not experience the chill. The Fear Liath was getting closer, snuffling along the edge of the woods, tracing Shion's ragged steps as he had attempted to flee. Phae clenched her fists, experiencing the terror of the beast, even though the Seneschal was near.

Then she heard the creak of wagon wheels. A lone cart rumbled down the road. A man hummed a tune and a swaying lantern hung from a post fastened to the edge of the seat, lighting the path through the hedge maze. The wagon wheels groaned, the axles needing to be oiled. The cart approached the desperate situation and then the driver stopped his tune, giving a sound like *chup, chup!* The horse stopped, stamping its hooves impatiently. As the wagon master peered around the horse at the dark shape on the ground, he smoothed back some hair and she saw a glittering gold ring fastened there. She stared at him in shock—a Romani!

The Romani leapt from the box seat and unhooked the lantern, bringing it over to gaze at Shion's body.

"Well, good night!" the man said with a wry voice. He knelt by the body, first examining the injuries at a distance. He sighed heavily. "He's more to be pitied than laughed at. Do you see this one, Roke, you old beast? Half-dead. Well, it's as hard to see a bleeding man as it is to see a barefoot duck, but it's no use boiling your cabbage twice, is it? I wonder what you did wrong, fellow, to be left like this? The silent are often guilty."

The Fear Liath roared, sending the horse into a tremor of panic.

The Romani stood and calmed the beast, beginning to whistle a tune again. It was a gentle and soothing tune and the whistle became a low song. The horse quieted immediately and the man stroked his nose. The Romani fetched a bag from beneath the seat and went back to Shion and knelt next to him. He set the lantern down nearby and went to work.

Phae stared in amazement as the Romani began treating the wounds with expert hands. He lifted Shion up and turned him over, exposing the most hideous of the wounds. Then unstoppering a vial of pungent olive oil, he began dabbing it across his wounds and then mopping up the blood and oil with rags that he produced from his bag. He hummed a Romani tune all the while, even as the tendrils of mist began to descend.

Phae tightened her grip on the Seneschal's arm. "Will the Fear Liath harm him?"

The Seneschal shook his head slowly. "He is very wise. He knows how to master himself. He knows how to master fear. The creature cannot threaten him."

Phae's eyes widened. "What is the secret then?"

"Do you hear his tune? It's a love ballad. He sings it to remember his wife while he travels. His love for her is very deep. He bought her and buys her again each time she is ready to earn another ring. He pays handsomely for her, often more than a full year's worth of his trading pay. She works hard while he is gone and helps him earn the price. Remember the secret, child."

Perfect love casts out fear

She felt his thought burn inside her heart, searing her with its power and the gift of recollection. The Romani stopped, cocking his head, hand poised on the stopper.

"Aye, master," the Romani said with a chuckle. "Marriages are all truly happy. It's having breakfast together that causes all the trouble." He laughed to himself and began working again on Shion's wounds. "You're an awful mess, lad. But it looks like I've stopped the bleeding a bit. You'll need some stitches ere we are done, but this isn't the place now, is it? A windy day is the wrong one for thatching. Best get you to the village yonder. Are you ready Roke, you old beast? You never plow a field by turning it over in your mind. Best to get back there, even if the casks of salmon spoil. Not worth a man's life, anyway. I know, Roke, you old beast, everyone lays a burden on the willing horse. That's your duty tonight. Let me lift him up . . . ugh, he's a heavy one even without all his blood."

Shion moaned and the man clucked his tongue. “It’s all right, lad. Worst is over. It’ll be dawn before you know it. Up with you, lad. Let’s set you on the driver’s box. I can walk alongside. Up you go!”

Phae watched him hoist Shion up on the wagon seat. He wrapped him in blankets, gave him small sips of wine and bits of cheese. He used ropes to hold him in place and immobilize him and then turned the cart around and headed back the way he had come, ignoring the mist that hung thickly in the trees, mist that had never descended low enough to dim the man’s lantern.

The Seneschal took Phae next to Stonehollow, back to the castle where she had first laid eyes on Shion. He was wrapped in heavy blankets, sitting on the window seat. Daylight illuminated his face and streaks of water came down outside as the rain lashed against the panes. His face was nearly healed, but she could see the puckered scars still livid and young with tender flesh.

In his lap, he had a book and she could see him sketching on the pages. One was the profile of a girl, a picture he had been working on for some time. As Phae looked at the page, she saw the face, the nose, the calm eyes of the Dryad from the tree. Next to the image, he had fashioned a circle with the Druidecht symbol represented. There was a thick circle in the middle followed by six designs, each with three points that budded from the center circle like a wreath of flowers. Another circle enclosed them all. He stared at the symbol, running his finger on it.

“Why did he draw the Druidecht symbol?” Phae asked the Seneschal.

“He’s inventing it,” came the reply. “Notice that he’s not wearing a talisman. Nor did the Druidecht you saw coming up the road. It’s an idea that came from him. He's going to work with a blacksmith and forge one before returning to the woods. He wants to be able to focus his thoughts, and having the symbol will help him."

"So he invented the talisman then?" Phae asked, startled.

"Oh yes. Here is the conversation you must hear. His brother comes."

There was a gust of wind as the door opened and Shirikant entered the room. He was wearing an elegant tunic with intricate stitch work. It contrasted to Shion's more humble garb. Even though he was a nobleman himself, Shion looked the part of the Druidecht and seemed uncomfortable being ostentatious. Quite the opposite for his brother. He approached Shion and stood behind him, watching him sketch with the nub of charcoal. The king waited patiently.

Shion blew on the page, staring at the symbol he had drawn. His fingers were smudged black.

"Are you certain you want to go back?" Shirikant said softly, his voice concerned. "I won't make you, Brother. I will face the dangers alone, if I must. You've suffered so much already."

Shion smoothed the paper. "I must return. I owe that Romani trader a king's ransom for saving my life, yet he will not accept it. I promised to sing for him and his wife. That was the only compensation he would accept. He has a great voice, Brother."

"Better than yours?" Shirikant said with a smile. "I don't believe it."

"He can tame beasts with his voice. But it's not his voice that does it." He leaned his head against the glass. "He loves his wife. Her name is Morganne. What they have between them . . . what they have is stronger than death. It's stronger than fear. I told you that I heard a voice in a mind while I was nearly dead on the road. Perfect love is more powerful than fear." He swallowed, staring at the drips of rain. "I love her, Brother."

Shirikant was silent a moment. "The girl at the tree. The girl who told you about the bridge to Mirrowen."

"She warned me not to try to save Kishion and the rest. If I had listened to her . . ." He scrunched up his face. "I cannot undo the past. What she told me of the Seneschal. The Gardener. I want to go to Mirrowen, Brother. I want to be welcomed there." He sighed again and set the book down on the seat. "You shared with me the histories. Of mighty men who wanted to father a new race. You have that desire, Brother. I do not. I want to be welcome in Mirrowen. I want to be able to travel between both worlds. I want to serve the Gardener. He's a Druidecht, I think. He's the founder of the Druidecht. I wish to serve him. And if he will let me, I wish to marry his daughter." He looked down at his hands. "Am I a fool?"

Shirikant rested his hand on Shion's shoulder, making Phae's skin crawl. The look in his eyes was genuine, though. She had expected to see a man brooding with evil, but the two were obviously very close and connected. The older brother had different ambitions. But they balanced each other. The respect was mutual.

"I'm not sure what to say, Isic. You could have any girl in Stonehollow, despite the ragged scars." Shion flinched at the words, but the grip on his shoulder increased. "I don't jest, Brother. Your survival will be sung about for a thousand years. What you endured seeking the portal to Mirrowen. I am routinely pressured to *force* you to marry one of your many admirers. Your injuries did not impact your singing. If anything, it made your music even more potent and haunting."

"I can't take credit for that," Shion said. "The Romani are the best musicians, I've learned."

"And that story!" Shirikant said, his eyes delighted. "You were bleeding your last on the edge of the woods when a Romani trader, of all people, rescued you, letting his fish spoil and losing a trade. Not only that, but he stayed with you for several weeks while you convalesced and then paid the innkeeper to care for you until word could reach us here in Stonehollow and I could send healers and horses aplenty. He refused to accept my rewards, which still offends me, for I suspect he is biding his time to ask for even more!"

"He won't," Shion said. "What he did for me, he would have done for any man. I can see why he hears the whispers from Mirrowen so keenly. His heart is right. His thoughts are determined. That is the kind of man I wish to become."

"You already are, Isic." He tousled the younger man's hair. "You're a better man than I will ever be. So you crave the daughter of the Seneschal of Mirrowen. I cannot say you lack ambition, boy."

"I learned about ambition from you, Brother. I have heeded all of your lessons. We are a mastermind, you and I. There are others too, but together, we are our own. I want to help you accomplish your aim. I only ask that you help me accomplish mine, in my own way."

Shirikant smiled deeply. "Lad, if she makes you happy, I will bless her for it. She sounds young."

"She will be immortal, Brother." He stared out the window again. "Isn't that what we both desire? We'll be the first, I think. The first two brothers who entered Mirrowen together. We must bring no weapons. No tricks. The Seneschal can read our thoughts like you can read a book from the Archives. There is no deception. He will know our true motives. While I grieve for the deaths I couldn't prevent, I hope that the good I can do in this world will far outweigh it."

The Seneschal put his hand on Phae's shoulder. "Come, Phae. It is time to meet the brothers in Mirrowen. It is time for you to understand how Shirikant earned that name."

"We captured a Rike today sneaking through the lower city. He was white with fear, saying the Arch-Rike has gone mad, that not only is the city doomed to fall to the Plague but that every race and kingdom will also fall. He described a series of magic portals in the Arch-Rike's palace, connecting Kenatos to the furthest way posts. The Rike insists that Band-Imas intends to poison the lands and destroy everyone. The Empress says we must attack the Temple immediately, regardless of the casualties. There is a council gathering to prepare the assault. What fools we have been. What trusting fools."

- Possidius Adeodat, Archivist of Kenatos

XLI

The magic of the Tay al-Ard sped them away from the gusting rain and when Phae blinked, she found herself back in Mirrowen. Huge thunderheads roiled in the sky and heavy surf pounded against the beach, which was clear of individuals. There were no children playing in sandcastles and nothing remained of their game. There was energy in the air, a frightening raw power that made Phae gape in amazement as the fury of the storm beat down on the hull of Mirrowen's defenses.

"Peace," the Seneschal said, waving his hand absently at the storm. "Enough. All is well. Be still."

Phae watched as the brooding storm slumped in defeat, the waves receding back to the boundaries of the rocks. The clouds scattered, revealing ample blue sky, and a calm breeze flittered past them, replacing the stiff gale that had preceded it.

The Seneschal offered her his arm as they walked along the beach toward the magnificent dwellings built into the sculpted hill. Many from the city began to appear, coming out now that the ferocity of the storm had passed.

"Do the storms rage more fiercely when you are gone?" she asked him.

He nodded. "The waters of the Deep are always trying to destroy the world. They will never stop trying so long as time reigns in your world. Eventually they will all be tamed. I am patient."

"You are," Phae agreed. "What will you tell me about Shirikant?"

"His name is Aristaios. It is from the ancient tongue and it means 'the best.' He was the firstborn son of the King of the Mousion. His parents were loving and wise but both were killed on a storm-tossed sea returning from a treaty journey to the Vaettir homeland. He was seventeen when they died and inherited the kingdom after a brief interregnum from a steward. Some children drastically alter the affairs of a kingdom if they inherit too young, but Aristaios wanted to live up to the name he was given. He took the role seriously, as he did when he assumed the responsibility of being a brother and a father to Prince Isic and his sisters. The death of their parents impacted them deeply. Prince Isic turned inward, nursing a secret grief. He became acquainted with the Druidecht order, which was in its infancy, and sought the whispers from Mirrowen. Aristaios was handsome and charming and had the best advisors, and he hearkened to their counsel, winning himself esteem and respect. He was always ambitious and harnessed that ambition to be a great king. He did not marry for he was seeking a bride who was perfect. While he met many eligible maidens, none had the perfection he sought in a wife."

The Seneschal advanced to the outer bulwarks of the garden city and inhaled, his breath making them rise up to the rampway above. Several spirit beasts bowed in homage to him and he acknowledged them with a gentle stroking of their ruffs.

"Aristaios knew of the Druidecht ways. You noticed the book that Isic wrote his secrets in, his sketches, his explanation of the ways of Spirit magic. The two brothers were close. Despite being reserved, Isic was popular. He did not seek attention but he always got it. That rankled Aristaios, though he buried those emotions. The two brothers came to Mirrowen together, crossing the bridge of Poisonwell and seeking me out. We will wait for them by the tree, of course. When someone exercises sufficient self-mastery to enter this land, I allow him an opportunity to partake of a single fruit of the tree. They can choose it themselves or allow me to pick one suitable for their purpose. As you observe, I will shroud you in my magic so that they will not see you. But through our connection, you will hear my thoughts. Watch and observe. This moment is critical. This moment shifted the course of the future. One decision, one regret, can alter one's entire future. Evil does not bloom all at once. It is nurtured like a seed. It always begins with a thought."

He patted her arm and led her over the ramp to the beautiful tree with its variety of fruit. The silver lions still guarded the area, resting on their haunches but alert and watchful. He motioned for Phae to take a small seat on a bench on the side of the veranda. The waters gushing from the tree passed under the stone beneath her, turning into rivers and rivulets farther down, silvery and clear.

Phae sat on the bench and felt as if a blanket had come across her shoulders. They had not waited for long when a Vaettir approached, the two princes coming behind.

"Kind master," the Vaettir said in formal greeting and a low bow. "Two travelers from the mortal world. They are brothers and seek audience with the Seneschal of Mirrowen."

"Bid them welcome, Taliesian."

As Phae looked up, he saw the Dryad girl she had seen before on the Seneschal's arm—his daughter. Phae recognized her from the previous vision and saw that she was older now. She had a look of calm wisdom, an untroubled face. She wore a simple but beautiful gown and a thin silver tiara—it looked as delicate as spiderwebs. She was a beautiful young woman, and Phae could sense her Dryad magic. The girl looked toward her at the bench, but her eyes did not focus, as if she could sense Phae but not see her. A small wrinkle appeared in her forehead, but it smoothed as the two princes arrived.

Phae's heart churned when she saw Shion. He gazed at the enormous city, his eyes wide with wonder, his face full of fascination and delight at the myriad forms of spirit magic. There were creatures Phae had never seen before, more beautiful than butterflies, with bright gossamer wings and legs of various sizes and shapes. The plethora of beings surrounding Shion was breathtaking. Each seemed to be drawn to him, seeking to commune with his thoughts. He gripped his brother's shoulder, whispering the word, "Amazing!"

Aristaios looked determined, his expression more guarded, but he also seemed overwhelmed by the sights he was watching. However, his gaze was riveted on the tree behind the Seneschal. A look of desperate hunger was clearly in his eyes.

"Greetings, Princes of Moussion," the Seneschal said in a cordial voice. "You are welcome here so long as you abide by our laws. You were both infected with a plague when you crossed the Pontfadog, but my servants have already cured it from you. This is my daughter. Be at peace. Why are you here? What do you seek?"

Shion nodded to his brother to go first. He stared at the Seneschal, his expression turning grave with respect. Both brothers dropped to one knee.

"I am Aristaios Moussion," the older brother said. "I seek a piece of fruit from your tree. You are known to us as the Gardener of Mirrowen. Long have I studied the myths and legends pertaining to you. Their words do not give even a moment of justice to the grandeur I see before me here. I am grateful you have granted audience. In return for a piece of fruit from the tree, I commit all the resources of my kingdom. I had intended . . ." he swallowed, his voice catching. "I had intended to build a temple in your honor, but I see that even with the skilled craftsmen at my command, I could not offer you anything you do not already possess, and by much more skilled hands." He bowed his head. "However, I beseech you to grant my boon. I will erect a place, in the very heart of the forest we just traveled, a place where knowledge of you and of Mirrowen may be preserved so long as there are people left in the mortal world. I seek to build it so that others may learn the ways of Mirrowen, may learn to master their thoughts to be able to hear the whispers. I desire that this shrine, this temple, this sanctorum shall stand when my kingdom has crumbled into dust. I would call it Canton Vaud. Give me this charge, I pray you. And give me the strength of heart to see it fulfilled."

His head remained bowed. Phae saw sweat trickling down his cheek. His jaw muscles were clenched.

"Rise, Prince Aristaios. I grant your boon. I charge you to build of stone this monument to Mirrowen as you described. I will carve a path through the woods that your workers may pass unhindered. I give you the mountains to the south to quarry and polish the stone. They will be your domain, a seat of your power for generations to come. Inasmuch as you seek to preserve the knowledge of Mirrowen, the structure will never fall. May it stand as a tower in the midst of the woods and draw mortals to learn of our ways. You may take one fruit from the tree. You may choose it freely or you may allow me to choose it for you. I must warn you, Prince Aristaios, that the tree contains serpents. If you seek to pluck a fruit and are not worthy of it, a serpent will strike your hand and you will die. These serpents have power over death. Make your choice."

Prince Aristaios' eyes widened with surprise and concern. "I . . . I thank you," he stammered. He crossed the paving stones to the base of the tree, where waters gushed from the roots. He stared at the variety of fruit, casting his eyes across them all, looking for similarities. Phae knew which fruit granted immortality. She could see Shirikant's eyes pass over it several times, pausing particularly at it, but still he searched.

Shion remained kneeling before the Seneschal, but he glanced up at his brother, watching him with a hopeful look.

Aristaios's expression hardened with frustration. This was what he wanted. All his years of studying the legends had prepared him for this moment. But in none of the legends had they described what the fruit looked like. There were twelve choices. How could he know which was the one he desired?

Phae saw the look of determination on his face. He studied each one, but he did not raise his hand.

The Seneschal looked at him gravely, his face impassive. His daughter did not look at Prince Aristaios—her eyes were fixed on Shion's face. Though she clung to her father's arm, her eyes bored into Shion's. She looked . . . tormented.

Prince Aristaios began to reach for one of the fruit. It was the fruit of immortality. Phae recognized it. As his hand came near, she saw a little white serpent raise its head. It was so slender and small, it looked as if it were part of the branch. Small black eyes opened. The forked tongue flicked out once as if to hiss, *I will not bite you, mortal. Trust me.*

The Prince's hand froze midair. He stared at the serpent, his eyes widening with suppressed fear. His mouth twitched with panic. His hand began to tremble. Beads of sweat trickled down his cheeks. He withdrew his hand and backed away from the tree, his eyes never leaving the fruit.

"I will trust your judgment," he said in a hoarse voice. "You pick for me." His whole body trembled.

The Seneschal looked at him with a slight nod. "So be it." He motioned for his daughter and she went and plucked a different fruit, one that was small and blue—the size of a cherry. The Seneschal's daughter brought it to the Prince and extended it to him.

He stared at her, his eyes fixated on the fruit in her hand, then on her face. He seemed to know intrinsically that it wasn't the one he desired.

"What is your name?" Aristaios asked her.

"I will not tell you my name," she replied simply. "It would give you power over me." She offered him the small fruit from her hand.

Prince Aristaios took it, his fingers grazing her palm. He stared at her, lost for a moment, his expression growing pale. Then he blinked quickly and put the fruit to his mouth and bit into the juicy skin. In a moment, he had devoured it.

He stared at the juice stains on his fingers, watching as the blue drops began to dance and then ignite.

The Seneschal bowed his head reverently. "You and your posterity will inherit this gift," he said, his voice firm. "It is called the Fireblood. You will sire a race that bears this gift, Prince Aristaios. It is a fruit of ambition. But it must be controlled. You must control your anger, or the flames of ambition will consume you. Remember these words and teach them to your posterity. *Pyricanthas. Sericanthas. Thas.* If you think these words—in your mind—then you will control the power of the fireblood and accomplish any task that you set your mind to. With it, your achievements will impact generations. I warn you, Prince Aristaios. If you fail to control the fireblood, it will control you. I charge you and your posterity to fulfill your oath." He nodded with finality.

Phae stared at Prince Aristaios—at Shirikant. The horror began to churn inside of her at the realization. She contained the fireblood herself. Was she a descendent of this man?

YES

The force of the Seneschal's thought-whisper nearly made her black out. She blinked in amazement, feeling the realization turn into jagged pieces inside her stomach. This man . . . this *creature's* blood was part of her own existence! Pain and disbelief battled inside.

"What would you seek of me, Prince Isic?" the Seneschal said in a softer tone. Shion was still on his knee. He had been staring at the Seneschal's daughter, the Dryad-born, his face full of intense emotions. He started.

"I seek to serve you," he said, his voice half-choked. He fished inside his tunic front and withdrew a bronze Druidecht talisman, shaped into the design that Phae had seen in his book. He pulled it off and cradled it in his hands. "I made this. With my own hands. These designs represent eighteen different facets I have observed about spirit magic and Mirrowen. I've memorized eighteen precepts about them and how not to harm or injure the spirit beings. There are also eighteen virtues, I believe, which you honor and respect. They are your characteristics, my lord. The circle in the center represents you. A circle has no beginning and no end. I built this . . . this . . . talisman to help me remember what I have learned about Mirrowen. It helps me focus my thoughts when the world distracts me. What I ask of you, my lord, is that you touch this talisman. Bless it in some way that when I wear it, I will be able to hear the whispers more clearly. If I can hear your will, then I will do it. I seek to be your emissary in the mortal world. To serve you as long as you will have me. When any Druidecht has earned your trust, has demonstrated constancy in seeking to protect and defend the knowledge of Mirrowen, then you would give him a talisman to mark your favor." He held out the medallion.

"I grant your desire," the Seneschal said, his voice warm and pleased. He motioned to his daughter and she approached Shion, taking the talisman from his hand. The look on her face was eager and excited. She smiled at him, blinking with tenderness. Phae felt a prick of envy seeing her.

"I also grant you," he continued, "a chance to choose one of the fruit from the tree."

Shion shook his head. "Let your daughter choose for me, my lord. I trust she is wiser than I."

The daughter's face brightened with a touching smile. She looked at her father, nodding vigorously.

"If you choose it, Daughter," he said. There was something in his voice—a hint of regret. "So be it."

The Seneschal's daughter rushed to the tree and plucked one of the immortal fruit from the branch. The serpent did not rear its head that time. Phae watched as she presented it to Shion, offering it to him with obvious delight.

Aristaios's face was hardening by the moment, but he mastered himself. He stared at his brother, still on his knees. A curl of contempt flickered across his mouth and then was gone.

Shion took the fruit from her hands and sank his teeth into it. A surprised look came next, and she remembered the strange bitter taste of it when she had eaten it herself. He devoured the fruit, bit by bit, then slowly stood, his body full of strength and vigor.

The Seneschal stepped forward and placed his hand on Shion's shoulder. "You are one of the Unwearying Ones now. You may pass through Pontfadog without death. You are welcome here. My daughter has chosen you, Prince Isic. She has chosen you to be her husband. I have chosen you to be my heir. One day you will inherit the Voided Keys that were entrusted to me, if you honor your oath to serve the mortal world. My daughter has an obligation to fulfill. But before she is bound to her tree, she would like to visit the mortal world, to visit the kingdom of the Moussion. She wishes to meet and know your people, your kindred. Marry her according to your laws and customs. Then return her here and I will bind you according to ours." He smiled at Shion then, a fatherly look. "This was your secret desire, Prince Isic. I cannot forbid it. May you find joy in your decision. May you endure the pain of it as well."

Phae stared at the Seneschal's daughter and Shion, her stomach clenching with dread and an awful premonition. When she looked next at Aristaios, his face was cold and smooth, betraying nothing of what he felt. His hands were clasped behind his back, clenched tightly. His fingers were glowing blue with flames.

"The Vaettir have a saying that I find of utmost relevance in our dilemma now: Prayer is a groan."

- Possidius Adeodat, Archivist of Kenatos

XLII

Phae's mind whirled with the implications of what she had seen. Sitting on the stone bench, she gripped the edges tightly, squeezing hard. Along with the thoughts came a storm front of emotions as well. The swirl of memories, the places she had been, it all thundered inside of her, trying to sort itself out, to fit together.

When she lifted her eyes, the two brothers were gone. A faint wind rustled the leaves of the majestic tree. A honeyed smell drifted on the air and far away, someone was singing a rich, melodious aria. The smell and sound contrasted to her stormy emotions.

"Good is not good until it is tested," the Seneschal said, his voice thoughtful and reflective. "Aristaios became Shirikant when he failed the test of self. All his life, he had prided himself on his discipline, his wisdom, his good fortune. He came to believe that everything in the world worked together for his good. He was unused to disappointment. He couldn't bear the thought of failure."

Phae stared at him, her face scrunching with concern. "He wanted immortality. I could see it in his eyes."

The Seneschal shook his head. "He wanted that when he came here. But when he saw Mirrowen—when he beheld its splendor for himself, he realized his kingdom was only an imitation of perfection. He began to lust for things that he had not earned. The station I hold. The tree I protect. The daughter I sired. He was used to Isic giving way to his ambition. He could not bear the thought that his younger brother would become all that he desired."

"You knew this?" Phae asked, looking at him deeply. "You knew what he would become when he came here?"

"I did."

"And you allowed it to happen? So many have been destroyed because of that man. Why do you permit him to poison the mortal world?"

The Seneschal reached down and caressed her hair. "Does an ox gain strength if it has no burden to pull? As I've taught you, child, the Decay seeks to rip apart all that has been created. Only the firmness of the Unwearying Ones holds it at bay. It takes strength to resist its inexorable pull. Evil must exist, just as fire is needed to purify ore. Shirikant plays a purpose, though he does so unwittingly. Yes, I allow it. I must. When Aristaios left Mirrowen, he struggled with his feelings. He began immediately to construct the fortress of Canton Vaud. The best stonemasons and builders in his kingdom were summoned. It was a mighty charge and a colossal task. Stone was quarried from the mountains, and they discovered caves beneath the range. It became a secret lair, which he named Basilides. He visited Mirrowen often, gaining ideas for the construction by the designs he saw here. He wanted it to be a piece of Mirrowen in the mortal world, a gatehouse to protect the bridge to this world."

Phae's eyebrows crinkled. "I must ask this, though I fear the answer. The fruit that you chose for him yielded the fireblood. Are we all descendants of Shirikant?"

The Seneschal smiled and nodded. "There are not many of your family left. Not many of the original Moussion, the forgotten race."

"Then how did Shirikant become immortal?" Phae asked. "He must have partaken of the fruit of the tree. How did that happen?"

"His rebellion began on his way out of Mirrowen. He felt he had been robbed of the opportunity to become Seneschal by his brother. Jealousy blackened his heart. He saw the happiness that his brother and my daughter shared. He promised them an elaborate wedding, a royal occasion that would rival any kingdom's. He set in motion a plan to murder his brother and claim my daughter for himself."

Phae's eyes bulged with shock.

The Seneschal approached the tree, staring at one of the gentle fruits dangling from a stem. Crackles of thunder popped in the sky above and Phae noticed the clouds roiling with storm. Vivid forks of lightning streaked through the billows. The Seneschal was peaceful, his hand grazing the edge of one of the fruit.

"He visited several times, as I told you, seeking to mirror the wonders he found here. But all the while, he tested to see if I truly knew his thoughts. He kept coming closer and closer to the tree, seeing if the defenses of Mirrowen would be summoned against him. There are laws irrevocably decreed, child. When one is persistent, when the determination is absolute, one achieves . . . even if it is to his or her harm. He did not believe that I could discern his thoughts. He convinced himself that he would succeed. He was fascinated by the Paracelsus order developed by the Cruithne. He had met, years previously, a caravan of Cruithne with a menagerie of captive animals that were forced into bondage to perform tricks for the amusement of nobles. One of the chief animal tamers wore a torc around his neck, fashioned by a Paracelsus. The torc made wild animals fear him, which allowed the Cruithne to perform feats of astonishing bravery—or so it seemed. Shirikant paid dearly for such a magic charm and he used it to enter Mirrowen and pass the sentinels guarding the tree. Even the serpent Iddawc feared to bite him. He claimed a fruit of immortality. He also took a serpent, concealing it in a pouch to be used to kill his brother. Then he took a bite of the fruit."

Phae sighed, hearing sadness in the Seneschal's voice.

"You see, child, he deceived himself most of all. Having eaten of the fruit without permission, he quailed when I appeared and charged him for his crime. He was banished from Mirrowen forever. I cursed his fireblood with madness that any soul with it who would not control his or her thoughts or emotions should succumb to insanity. Ambition must always be tempered. He was angry at his punishment and threatened in his heart to destroy Mirrowen. Because he had favored the principles of bondage to that of freedom, I commanded the spirits of Mirrowen to never obey him. I allowed Shirikant to take the serpent with him."

The Seneschal turned and faced Phae. "My daughter never returned to Mirrowen. Come with me, child. You must see what happened next for yourself." He extended his hand.

The magic of the Tay al-Ard swept them back to Stonehollow. They were outdoors and the air smelled familiar. They were in one of the lush gardens of the palace, full of trimmed hedges, vibrant flower beds, and gurgling fountains. There were many guests about, savoring goblets of wine, enjoying the singing and instruments of musicians. Decorations abounded, with pennants hanging from tall staves and butlers appearing with silver dishes full of wonderful meats and cheeses.

"This way," the Seneschal said, holding out his arm and escorting Phae. They were both dressed as the nobility around them, blending in perfectly with the costumes of the occasion. Giddy laughter filled the air as the people rejoiced.

"They were married in the Druidecht rites," the Seneschal said. "Scarcely an hour ago. Prince Isic did not wish for all this pomp and circumstance but his brother insisted, managing to delay the wedding for many months as they entertained guests from various kingdoms coming to greet and pay respects to the Seneschal's Dryad-born daughter. By this time my daughter was feeling the pains of the seed traveling through her. She knew her time had come and she longed to return to the grove and claim her birthright. She relented to the persuasions of the king, despite her pain and the longing to return. She hid her discomforts from everyone but Prince Isic. They were inseparable, the closest of confidants and friends. Shirikant's jealousy grew more envenomed. And so he made a pact with the serpent Iddawc to kill his brother on their wedding day. He was deposited in a hedge maze and the guests were warned to stay away, that it was a special reward for the bride and groom. There . . . do you see them?"

Phae looked up and saw Aristaios escorting the Seneschal's daughter by the arm toward the mouth of the hedges. He was speaking to her gallantly, explaining the nature of the maze and that the couple had to seek each other by calling out to each other and finding the way. She would be in the center and Prince Isic would need to find her. It was a charming custom among their people.

Phae could see the worried looks on the daughter's face, and she could recognize the strain caused by pain in her brow. Phae knew how she felt, how the pain of the Dryad seed could be torturous.

Phae clutched the Seneschal's arm. "Does it pain you to see this?" she asked him, feeling the terrible sense of impending doom.

"Yes," he replied, smiling sadly. He patted her arm. "Some memories are painful. But I am proud of her too. Proud of what she did. Let's follow them. They will not see us."

Phae went alongside the Seneschal as he directed them toward the hedge maze. Shirikant was just ahead, causing her to look at the sculpted hedges and statuary decorating it. They passed through the maze quickly, for Shirikant knew the way.

"The Scourgelands is a hedge maze," the Seneschal whispered to her, smiling. "The themes of his treachery always repeat. He can't help himself."

When they reached the center of the maze, there was a hue and cry.

"Ah, the revelers have come," Shirikant said, letting the girl wander freely in the center of the maze. A small fountain splashed in the center with a low bench encircling it. He seated himself. "He'll find you soon, I think."

"Does he know the way?" the Seneschal's daughter asked.

"No. The ways have been changed since he was a boy. But he is clever, do not worry. Have you enjoyed your stay among the Moussion, my lady?"

"Very much, thank you. But I long to return to my home."

"I know you do. Well, my dear, there is one more tradition of the Moussion that I failed to mention." He stood and approached her. "The king of the country must kiss the bride before her wedding night. It's an ancient tradition and awkward considering I am now your brother. A kiss on the cheek will suffice."

The Seneschal stared coldly at the two. "He tries to deceive her," he whispered to Phae. "He knows about the Dryad kiss. He's secretly read all of Prince Isic's notes about Druidecht lore."

Phae clenched her fists, staring at the two.

The Seneschal's daughter looked at Shirikant skeptically. "I would rather not."

A bulge of muscle clenched in Shirikant's cheek. "Come, my dear. It's just a formality." He stepped closer to her, his shadow falling over her face.

She retreated from him, her brow furrowing.

The sound of the revelers was loud, trying to drown out the sound of Prince Isic's calls to his beloved. Phae's stomach twisted with sickness. She wanted to scream and warn her to flee.

"Are you afraid?" Shirikant said, his voice dropping low. "There's no need to fear me."

"Your words belie the feelings in my heart," she answered. "I will go to my husband now." She turned on her heel to escape.

"No!" he snarled, grabbing her by the elbow. His face was frantic.

She looked at his hand gripping her arm. A crinkle of doubt and worry spread across her features. "Release me," she ordered.

"You must wait for him here," he said, placatingly, but his voice trembled with emotion. "Don't ruin the tradition, Sister."

"Let go," she ordered, pulling against his grip, but it was iron.

Phae's stomach clenched with dread. She felt specks of dizziness surround her. Her heart thumped wildly in her chest.

Shirikant looked desperate to maintain control of the situation. "Come sit by the fountain," he offered. "It's a silly tradition. We can ignore it if you wish. I don't want you to be afraid of me. Come . . . sit."

She pulled on her arm again, her look growing more determined. "You hold me against my will. Why?"

He licked his lips, his eyes blazing with emotion. "I'm sorry. I'm ruining everything. Come sit by the fountain. I'll fetch your husband myself." He gently, but firmly, pulled her toward the bench.

"Aristaios," she said, looking him full in the eyes.

He gazed at her, his brows crinkling.

Then she blinked.

He stood dumbfounded, his eyes blinking rapidly. His hands fell to his sides.

She fled the hedge maze, calling out Prince Isic's name in a panic. Phae squeezed her eyes shut, hearing the gasp of outrage and fear coming from Shirikant. A gurgled noise passed his lips as he pursued her. Phae buried her face into the Seneschal's arm, fraught with tension, waiting for the moment.

There was a scream of fright, a startled cry of pain.

"She is dead," the Seneschal whispered, pressing a kiss against Phae's hair.

The group of revelers found Prince Isic, who had been forced to trade his Druidecht clothes for the garb of royalty. The talisman was still dangling around his neck as he knelt weeping by the corpse of his young bride, the daughter of Melchisedeq, Seneschal of Mirrowen.

Phae saw him clutching the body to his chest, heard the wracking sobs as they came like thunder. He begged and pleaded for her to live. Several Shain spirits hovered near him.

She was bitten by the serpent Iddawc, kind master. She cannot be revived.

Only the Seneschal can revive her. Only he with the Voided Keys has that power.

Tears streamed down Shion's face and Phae felt her own following suit. The look of suffering on his face—he had expressed it before in the Scourgelands, when he thought that *she* had died. She shared his misery, shared the suffering he endured. His bride's body was turning pale with each passing moment. On her ankle, two crimson flecks of blood protruded from where the fangs had pierced.

Phae's eyes widened with realization.

When a Dryad chose a mortal husband, she wore a gold bracelet around her ankle in the image of a twisting serpent. Now she knew why the tradition had started, even though time had dimmed the memory to extinction.

"My poor Shion," she whispered, her throat catching and choking. Her heart yearned to comfort him. His sadness was terrible. She watched him weep, watched him press kisses against her temple, as if somehow they would overpower the magic of the serpent's venom.

Shirikant approached them, his face gaunt and haunted by the death. He stared at the girl's corpse, his eyes ravaged by guilt and despair. Seeing the grieving revelers who had gathered in the hedge maze, he waved them off and barked an order for them to disperse and make way.

Shirikant knelt in the thick grass, clasping his brother's shoulder with a firm grip.

"How could this have happened?" he said in pretend amazement.

"I must go to Mirrowen," Shion murmured in desolation. "I must seek help from her father."

"No," Shirikant said, shaking his head. "He'll be furious. He'll likely curse you. Brother, I've been hesitant to say this, but I don't trust him." He rubbed his bleary eyes. "If he truly knew the future, why did he allow this to happen? What father would willingly send his child to die? He must not have known. He's not this wise and all-powerful, benevolent being. He appears the way we want him to be. We've formed him in our minds. Isic—you must not go! If he does not punish you for killing his daughter, he may punish the world! Think of the power in his hands. What he might do to us!"

"Stop!" Isic snarled, shaking his head violently. "You speak nonsense, Brother. I knew the Seneschal before I stepped one foot in Mirrowen. This is the only way I can save her. I must cross the bridge again and bring her spirit back. It is said by the spirits that someone can revive in three days. A horse. I must ride now. I cannot waste a moment." He hefted the body in his arms and handed it to his brother. "I leave her to you. Bring the body to Canton Vaud quickly. I'll ride ahead."

The two brothers stared at each other, their emotions conflicted. Shirikant cradled the girl's body in his arms. "Very well, Brother. I'll await you there."

Isic rushed from the hedge maze, sprinting like a madman.

Shirikant sank to the ground, staring at the dead girl in his arms. He stroked a tuft of hair from her forehead, grimacing in pain. He stared for a long while, tears gathering in his eyes. Then dipping his head, he kissed her dead lips.

Phae quivered with revulsion.

"The greatest injury is betrayal."

- Possidius Adeodat, Archivist of Kenatos

XLIII

They were back in Mirrowen, back to the tree—the origin of the suffering she had witnessed through her visits in time. Her heart panged with sorrow for Prince Isic, unable to see his brother's treachery, unable to discern the twisting of his soul into savagery. So many pieces were coming together, so many cruelties that wrung compassion from her heart and made her long to return to the Dryad tree she was bound to, in order to share what she had learned with him.

She paced the area around the tree, trying to subdue the battering emotions, to quell the burgeoning feelings of loathing and hate.

The tree was the origin of it all. She stared at the silvery bark, the tempting fruit that seemed to whisper to her to snatch another one.

"You feel its compulsion," the Seneschal announced softly. "For all ages and in every civilization scattered amidst the myriad worlds—of which this one is but a type—there is a relentless hunger for immortality. They all search for this tree." He put his hand on her shoulder, a tender gesture. "What they never understand is that there is bitterness amidst the sweetness. There is suffering betwixt the joy. I was given the Voided Keys as a steward, to protect this tree from those like Shirikant who rule with terror and destruction because of their benighted pride. Unwearying Ones from other worlds will visit this one and learn for themselves the fruits of consequence caused by men like Shirikant and the despair that follows. Some worlds are wiser than this one. And there are some that are even worse."

She turned and looked up at him, seeing the look of wisdom in his deep-set eyes. "Are you from this world, then?"

He shook his head. "No, child. I am a custodian. My intention has been to deliver the Voided Keys to someone who will take my place. I will pass to another realm eventually. And so will you."

"You desired that Prince Isic would take your place. Has he forfeited that chance?"

A small smile lit his face. Thunder rumbled overhead, followed by thick, billowing clouds. As Phae stared up into the sky, she saw an enormous gathering storm, with huge anvil-shaped clouds that loomed higher than the heavens. Lightning flashed and struck. A bulge appeared in the clouds, and she watched with fascination as the bulge began to swirl.

"He comes," the Seneschal said, motioning toward an archway.

Shion appeared through the gap, as if he had stepped from another existence into this one. He staggered with heaviness, his countenance matching the storm clouds. He had the look of restless determination in his eyes, the focus that had always made her shudder.

"His brother attempted to stop him," the Seneschal whispered to Phae. "Shirikant sent hawks and doves ahead, warning his servants to forestall him. The safe road was guarded, but the Prince would not be halted. He is a powerful Druidecht and summoned creatures from the woods for assistance. Shirikant's minions tried to subdue him but failed. Now Isic comes again, burning with determination yet clinging to the seed of failure—the doubt his brother planted in his mind. Watch it fester. Watch him fail."

Shion tramped up to the bridge, his face flushed with emotion. He stood there, nodding in respect to the Seneschal, but he could not meet his eyes. His hand trembled on the railing of the bridge. He cast a quick, furtive glance at Phae and she realized she was visible to him.

Shion's voice was hoarse. "I come with grievous news," he said, sinking to his knees in front of the Seneschal. "Your daughter is dead."

"I know."

Anguish of the deepest kind was etched into Shion's brow. He struggled to breathe, to inhale past his tears. "I failed to protect her." He wiped his mouth, his cheek muscles twitching. "I beg you to give her soul back to me. I know her spirit magic persists for three days in the mortal world. Let me revive her, my master. I have already given my oath to serve you. I only ask for this one boon." He wrung his hands together, still unable to meet the Seneschal's gaze. "I beg you."

The Seneschal was quiet, considering. "Your heart is grieved, my son. My daughter accepted her fate when she chose to leave Mirrowen. Would you undo that choice?"

Shion winced at the words. "I did not know . . . I could not see the future. I was careless, but do not let my error allow her life to be purged."

"Was I careless to let her go?" the Seneschal said, his voice deep with meaning. "I—who can see the future? Do you trust my judgment, Prince Isic?"

A spasm of pain seemed to burst open in Shion's face. "If you *knew* it, how could you allow it?"

"How could I *not* allow it?" came the reply. "I cannot force a person to choose."

"You once told me that the Unwearying Ones who created us without our help will not save us without our consent. I ask you . . . I plead with you! Save her. You were her father. Surely it grieves you as well? I ask for this one boon. I will ask nothing else from you. I will give my whole heart to you, even if you reject my plea. There are no conditions. I submit to your judgment. But please . . . if it is possible . . . give me my wife." Choking sobs erupted from Shion's throat.

Phae felt tears trickle down her own cheeks.

"Persistence is powerful magic," the Seneschal said in a near whisper. "You know I can do as you request. You know I have that *keramat*. You know it is possible. Bid me again, and I will grant it. Compel me with your magic, and she is yours."

It will only add to your pain

Phae heard the whisper and watched Shion closely, her heart leaping into her throat. He was being given a choice. She could feel the wrongness of the choice, could sense that the outcome would be terrible. Yet Shion's desire to be with his wife blinded him and deafened him to the subtle pulse of the whisper. His grief was too new, too raw.

Shion bowed his head in grief, trying to control his breathing. His quavering muscles began to calm. The intensity of his feelings was seen in his stormy eyes. In the skies above, a swirling vortex had opened up, painting the clouds in hues of green. The storm could not be felt inside the city gardens, but Phae knew the surf was hammering again.

Lifting his chin, Shion faced the Seneschal. He slowly rose to his feet and outstretched an arm. Opening his mouth, he started to sing.

Phae's eyes widened, recognizing the tune from the gold locket. A tune that generations of those from the Paracelsus Order had captured and bound in trinkets. Shion's song wove through the air, full of pathos and sorrow, building in power as his voice became stronger. Phae's knees trembled with the weight of it, recognizing again how many ties had bound them together. She had first heard the tune huddled and frightened in an abandoned homestead. It was Shion's song—a song he had lost.

Tears poured from her eyes as she listened to the notes fade into stillness. All of Mirrowen was hushed with his mourning anthem. All the Unwearying Ones paid homage to his suffering.

Phae saw tears in the Seneschal's eyes. "Leave Mirrowen. I will send her spirit walking behind you to the Mother Tree. There is a gap in the trunk, a portal to Mirrowen. If you look back, even once, to see if she follows, then she will vanish. Do not gaze back or you will lose her forever. This was your choice. Depart."

Shion bowed his head, nodding in gratitude with a broken, "Thank you," passing from his lips. He started away, walking back across the bridge.

The Seneschal gestured and a gossamer spirit appeared, a lovely young maiden—his daughter, the Dryad-born. Phae could see the wisps of spirit magic trailing from her. She looked at her father, bowing her head in respect and love, and then flitted off after Shion.

"What happens now?" Phae whispered, wiping her eyes.

He put his arm around her shoulders and brought out the Tay al-Ard again.

With a whorl of magic, they appeared inside a dense cave, thick with shadows and streaming with green light. The air smelled strongly of earth and spoiled vegetation and it was unusually warm. There was a strange green moss lighting the walls of the cave, forming a brilliant glow with crystalline stalactites and stalagmites. It was an unearthly place, lit, yet void of light from the sun.

She looked and saw a pool of molten silver in the cave's center. The surface rippled as gusts of heat disturbed it. There were several inset stone pillars surrounding the pool, and each glowed with a round sphere. It was spirit magic.

The Seneschal gestured to the pool of quicksilver.

Pontfadog/Poisonwell

Standing at the edge of the pool was Shirikant, his face haggard and lined with hard edges. He whispered harsh words in another language, his fingers weaving together as he summoned the fireblood. Blue flames danced from his fingertips and then he unleashed it into the pool of quicksilver. As he did so, a greenish mist rose from the moss surrounding the walls, sending dark vapors to fill the cavern. The flames burned hotter, summoned by Shirikant. The mist began to creep from the walls and swell, coiling into Shirikant's skin and clothes. Still the fireblood coursed into the pool, making the silver liquid bubble like a cauldron.

He binds the magic of Poisonwell to serve him—he unleashes a Plague on himself that will strike the workers building Canton Vaud—this is the birth of the first Plague

Shirikant's face twisted with pain as the green mist surrounded him. She could see the effects of the disease blistering his skin, but it did not kill him. He poured the fireblood into the pool of quicksilver until steam began to wreathe his hands and arms, mixing with the mist from the lichen.

He has bound Poisonwell to himself for a thousand years—it will serve only him until another claims its obedience—he will unleash Plague after Plague, destroying every civilization one by one until the binding ends

She turned to look at him. *What can end it?*

The pool must be cleansed by an Unwearying One—it is a bitter cup that must be drunk—the gateway to Mirrowen will remain closed until then

Am I an Unwearying One? Phae thought to him.

You are Dryad-born—you are not yet an Unwearying One—your oath is not fulfilled

In her mind, the pieces began to fit together. She could see the pattern now; she could see what she needed to do to stop the Plagues.

"I understand now," she said, looking up into his eyes. "There is one more stop we must make now, isn't there?"

He smiled tenderly. "You are wise, child. Do what must be done." He extended the Tay al-Ard to her again.

She gripped it and they vanished from the polluted chamber of roiling fumes beneath the scaffolding of Canton Vaud.

In a moment, they stood near the Dryad Mother Tree at the edge of the woods deep in the Scourgelands. Phae could hear the screaming as the Plague attacked and killed the workers from Stonehollow who were gathered there building the first arches of Canton Vaud. Thick green mist hung like a poisoned fog in the air, seeping into the woods, seeking victims.

This was the birthplace of the Plague. Her mind began to trace and see connections, realizing the fear that would spread as word of the devastation spread. The woods would earn a reputation for deadliness. The caretaker of the woods, Shirikant, would make sure the notoriety spread, preventing Druidecht from seeking the bridge to Mirrowen. After centuries the woods would be named the Scourgelands. She could see it all unfolding in her mind.

The Dryad tree was beautiful and healthy, the trunk split in the middle, showing a gap between. From her vantage in the woods, she saw Shion emerge from the tear in the wood, his hands touching the rough bark. He craned his head, listening to the shouts of fear and pain as hundreds perished. He looked alarmed, panicked even, not understanding the devastation happening in the stone hill nearby. She saw the tension in his neck, saw the indecision of what to do.

He had emerged from the portal to Mirrowen at the Dryad tree, not from Pontfadog. No doubt his brother was sealing off the chamber, hoping to trap Isic inside to prevent him from venturing back into the world. It all made sense to Phae, and she saw the look of confusion and determination wilt. Behind him floated a shade of a Spirit, her face the same as the Seneschal's daughter.

Shion turned to look back at her and in doing so, saw past her into the breach, into Mirrowen. His eyes widened with shock and terror, realization flooding him at what he had done.

"No!!" he screamed, reaching to grab the Spirit wife. Her hand reached for his and then she dissolved into tufts of pollen, scattering in the wind.

Stunned, devastated, Shion sank to the ground, clawing the bark with his iron-hard fingers until the bark shredded and came off in chunks. He howled in dismay, screaming with frustration and despair. He struck the tree with his fists, pounding on its immovable trunk. He could not bleed. He could not die. He let out a wail of anguish that pierced Phae's heart. Sobs shook him violently, great racking sobs that added to the chorus of the dying.

Shion sprawled down at the base of the tree, gasping, breaking apart, unable to die of sorrow.

The Seneschal stroked her hair. The day seemed to pass more swiftly, the arch of the sun across the sky fading to twilight, and then night. Near midnight, the last of the screams ended. Those who had fled the construction of Canton Vaud, those who survived, would carry remnants of the Plague back to their communities. Stonehollow would be devastated by it, the first kingdom to fall.

Night began to fade as a pink sky started to light in the east.

Phae nodded to the Seneschal and then quietly stepped forward, approaching Shion's crumpled body. She knelt nearby him, watching the rise and fall of his shoulders. He had not moved for hours. As she knelt, little twigs snapped.

Shion's head stirred slightly. "Who is there?" he whispered in a ravaged, hoarse voice.

She sat silently, hands folded in her lap, waiting for him to rouse.

He was still a moment longer, then his head swiveled and he looked up at her. His face was bereft of life and joy. He was shrunken, defeated, tormented. He stared at her, his eyebrows furrowing.

"I've seen you before," he said in his quiet voice. "I've seen your face."

Phae nodded. "In your brother's palace. I was with the Seneschal."

He slowly pushed himself up on one arm, his expression so hurt and aching that she reached out and touched his cheek. He flinched.

"Who are you?" he asked.

"We will meet again in the future," Phae said. "This is my tree now." She stroked the bark that he had ravaged with his bare fingers. "You must protect me. You must bring me here safely. I charge you, Prince Isic, to reopen the gate to Mirrowen."

"It's closed to me," he said, his mouth turning to a frown.

"Only you and I can open it," she said, giving him a timid smile. "I see that now." She breathed deeply. "You won't remember this. You won't remember any of it. I'm sorry, but I see that this must be." She reached out and touched the side of his face, looking deeply into his eyes, deeply into his very soul. "Until we meet again, Shion."

She blinked, taking away all of his memories. Not a portion—not a slice. She took them all away. They came as a rush, suffusing into her heart, into her mind, all of his memories and emotions, his knowledge of Druidecht lore, even his knowledge of music. She absorbed it into herself, feeling it well up like a tidal wave. She loved him. She understood the boy he was as a child, the man he was at that moment. All of his life experiences rushed past her in a surge.

Phae gathered the memories, hugging them to her soul, and then she filled the tree with them, preserving and safeguarding them.

Shion slumped to the ground, unconscious. His face was reposed, deep with sleep.

She reached around his neck and lifted the talisman away. Then Phae stood and walked back to the Seneschal.

"I am ready," she said firmly.

"These next choices will be up to you," the Seneschal said. "Be wise how you make them. Return to your own era in the mortal world. Save your father. Save your friends. Redeem Poisonwell."

"Be at peace with your own soul, then the heavens and the earth will be at peace with you. The Druidecht are truly wise."

- Possidius Adeodat, Archivist of Kenatos

XLIV

Paedrin stood side by side with the Quiet Kishion, their blades slashing at every angle, defending the Dryad tree in the center of the Scourgelands. Arrows hissed and stuck into the trunk. Somehow, Paedrin avoided every one. His blind sense seemed to move him, and each time the trunk was split and scarred by the heavy weight of impact. Kiranrao flashed again, trying to stab at him, but the Bhikhu was all rage and quickness and his sword had the better reach than the cursed dagger.

Sweat streaked down Paedrin's cheeks, coming down his back in a river of moisture. His muscles hummed with energy, his situation too desperate for fatigue. One wrong move and the blade Iddawc would graze his skin, snuffing out his life. Every stroke counted. Every miss mattered.

"Should I lie still?" Paedrin taunted the Romani. "Maybe you're only used to striking people asleep. I thought you were quick, Kiranrao. Old Master Shivu could run circles around you."

A grotesque look of rage crumpled Kiranrao's face as he feinted and then lunged again. Paedrin deflected the thrust and whipped his elbow around to smash into the Romani's face, but again he vanished in a plume of smoke.

"Smoke and shadows, that's all you are!" Paedrin shouted, dodging another arrow. It thunked into the tree with the others. "A cawing raven. You have no power. You can only steal."

"You will die, Bhikhu," Kiranrao threatened. "That I swear!"

"You could not hit me with an avalanche," Paedrin quipped. "You couldn't hit me with a rainstorm. You've gotten lazy, thief."

There he was again, materializing out of smoke, his face contorted in rage. Paedrin prepared for the attack. Kiranrao's eyes widened with shock. A look of confusion rippled across his face. He shook his head, startled and panicked, and then vanished into smoke again.

Fire exploded from the tree behind him.

Paedrin whirled in shock. There was Phae, perfect and whole. Her clothes were different, clean and unstained. Her red hair billowed from the heat as blue flames bloomed from her hands, streaking into the woods and striking one of the sentinels, turning him into ash. Paedrin saw another one lift his bow and he tried to warn her. He would have rushed in front of her to protect her, but he would have stood in the flood of flames and died himself.

The arrow went straight toward her, striking her full in the heart with a stony clunk before dropping harmlessly to the ground at her feet. She smiled savagely and turned her flames against that sentinel, scattering it into ash as well. Shion whirled with surprise, his face lighting with joy when he saw her. Phae took a step forward and sent a final gust of flames and destroyed the third and final sentinel.

"Away from my tree," she said triumphantly.

"Phae!" Paedrin gasped.

From the gap in the split trunk, twin blurs of silver-white fur came charging out. Paedrin gaped in shock. These were lions, taller than horses, and they bounded into the burning grove and with twin ferocious howls, they scattered the Weir who had gathered around the ancient oak. Their roars sent a spasm of dread into Paedrin's bowels and he watched with awe as their huge muscled limbs shredded through the Weir. Their roars could be heard over the cinders and crackling flames and seemed to mix with the thunder booming from the clouds overhead. The two lions struck down Weir one by one, and the massive cats became the hunted ones and fled in panic.

Phae grabbed Shion in a fierce hug, whispered something to him, and then she rushed to where Annon had fallen. Paedrin and Shion joined her, watching sharply for a sign of Kiranrao, but the thief had not materialized since his stricken look.

The Dryad knelt by the Druidecht and produced a small, damp pouch. Digging her hand into it, she withdrew a clump of vibrant green moss with little flowers—the same kind Paedrin had found in Khiara's belt that he had used to heal Baylen. Paedrin stared with wonder, realizing the Dryad had gotten it from Mirrowen somehow, and then watched as she pressed the moss into the savage claw wounds on Annon's bloodied back. The magic swept over the Druidecht, bringing color back to his pallid cheeks. Annon lifted his head, then pulled himself up on his elbows.

"Phae?" he questioned, his voice raw but his strength returning.

"We must reclaim the Scourgelands," she said, gripping Annon's shoulder. Then she pointed into the woods toward the stark hillside where the ruins were. "It's time to rebuild Canton Vaud. The ruins there . . . built by our ancestors . . . I know all of it now. I know the history. The gate to Mirrowen was closed by cruelty. We go to open it again, to open the bridge. To cross it, you must know its name. I give it to you. *Pontfadog*. Gather the others and fight your way in. Shion and I will go into the depths to counter the Plague. I know how. Meet us there. Go!"

Paedrin's heart nearly burst with joy. He wanted to rush to Hettie, to save her before it was too late. Phae had changed completely, but she was still vulnerable to the blade Iddawc.

"Kiranrao is still loose," he warned her.

She shook her head. "He doesn't remember anything right now. I took all his memories. When our task is done, he will be hunted down and that blade taken and hidden until its binding has ended. I understand what Iddawc is now. Trust no man to wield it."

Paedrin nodded. He didn't need any more reason. Invoking the power of the Sword of Winds again, he flew up into the branches and crashed through the thicket and pierced the sky. He soared up to the clouds that lowered over the crumbled ruins.

"I can't walk," Hettie said to her captors, sitting on the ground near a pile of rubble and massaged her leg. There were three of them, wearing tunics bearing the symbols of Kenatos. They were soldiers, not Rikes, and she could see the fear emanating from their eyes. None of them dared look at her, for she still wore the illusion of Phae's countenance and they had assumed she was Tyrus's daughter.

"Grab her beneath her arms," one of the soldiers ordered, beckoning to another. He sheathed his sword and came up behind her.

Suddenly Hettie swiveled on her ankle and extended her injured leg, a simple Bhikhu leg sweep, and two of them tumbled to the ground. Hettie did a quick forward roll and leapt up at the third, striking his chin with her palm, snapping his head back. She watched his eyes roll back as he staggered backward and fell. Gratified by the easy victory, Hettie spun around and stomped on one of the soldier's arms as he reached for his fallen sword and she felt the bone crack. The other scampered away from her and she kicked him hard in the ribs, knocking him over.

Gazing down at the crumpled men, she nodded with satisfaction and slipped into the ruins, moving stealthily as she could, hiding behind slabs of lichen-speckled stone. The ruins were ancient, the stone pitted and ravaged by time and the elements. Only the barest suggestion of design and purpose could be observed. It was a lofty structure, with some tall buttresses still intact. She grazed her fingers on the rough stone, trying to imagine past the dimness of time to what the structure had originally been. The past was a secret here, a secret she yearned to know.

Voices ghosted through the mist and she stopped, hiding behind a broken column.

"I don't know where Band-Imas is!" the man said in desperation. "His orders went silent."

"What should we do, Lukias? Tyrus made it up the rampway in the fog. What do we do?"

"I don't know, man! I'm trying to contact the Arch-Rike, but the aether is empty. Like nothing is there. Did he abandon us? I don't know."

Hettie maneuvered closer, trying to get a look at the two who were approaching quickly. Two sets of black Rike cassocks appeared, two men hunched over in conversation.

"Do you think he abandoned us?" one whispered dreadfully.

Hettie saw the one—Lukias. She recognized him and scowled.

Another shape appeared out of the mist, one of the hulking Cruithne bodyguards.

"Over here," Lukias called, gesturing. "I want you with us when Tyrus arrives. He's a Paracelsus with the fireblood. The man is deadly and aggravated. He may already be mad."

"I know," the Cruithne said and Hettie beamed, recognizing his voice. It was Baylen.

"Who are—?" The Cruithne swung a meaty fist around and struck the side of Lukias's face, dropping him with the sound of a crunch. The other Rike tried to summon a shout of warning, but Baylen was fast and gripped his tunic at the throat and hammered into his stomach so hard, the man could only gurgle in pain and collapse.

"Baylen?" Hettie sighed with relief, emerging from the shadows and the stone and revealing her true self to him.

The Cruithne looked at her, not registering surprise or delight. "There you are." He brushed his heavy hands together, his jowls quivering as a smile finally crept over his mouth. "I've been lurking up here for a while watching for Paedrin. Been taking advantage of the confusion to thin the herd."

"I thought you were dead," Hettie exclaimed. "Paedrin's here too?"

The Cruithne put his hands on his hips. "A story I'll tell you over a mug of ale. Paedrin said he was coming but it's been a little while. With all the mist, we won't be easy to find."

"He'll find us," Hettie said. "Do you know a way off this rock?"

"Follow me. There's no one leading them right now. I know the way back down. But I also know where they are all coming from. I don't think we came all this way to leave early."

Hettie unsheathed a dagger and nodded.

The smoke from the fires would have normally stung Phae's eyes, but it did not. She thought about taming the flames with her fireblood, but she decided not to. The woods needed a chance to heal and be reborn. Fire would be the womb. She watched Annon disappear into the shroud of smoke as he bent his way toward the ruins of Canton Vaud.

Phae took Shion's hands and marched him back to the tree. There were no longer any Weir, no longer any threats. Rumbles of thunder sounded overhead and she felt a few drops of rain on her wrists and hands. She climbed back up the nest of roots, pulling Shion after her until they came to the portal entrance.

"How long have you been gone?" he asked her, his voice quiet and thoughtful. "To us, it seemed but a moment. You are changed." He reached out hesitantly, brushing aside some of her hair. A shiver went down her back at his touch.

"A lifetime. I've learned so much. I know your name. I know who you are." She squeezed his hands, feeling her throat thicken. She reached to her belt where she had woven the chain of his talisman and quickly unfastened it. It was battered and dull, but she could feel the talisman's power. He stared at it, his face crinkling with confusion.

"This is yours," she told him. She licked her lips. Reaching out, she put the talisman around his neck. He looked confused, worried, anxious.

"I'm frightened," he whispered hoarsely.

She shook her head and cupped his cheek. "There is no reason to fear. I know the truth. I know all of it." With her other hand, she stroked the ragged bark. "Your memories are all here. I've already seen them. Even the recent ones. I've watched your life." She tried to breathe, found it difficult even looking into his eyes. She blushed, feeling the weight of the moment. "Let me help you remember."

A quivering sigh escaped his chest. He nodded mutely, worriedly. With her full Dryad senses, she could tell that they were truly alone. She could sense where Annon walked as if she saw him in her mind. She saw Kiranrao, staggering and falling, running madly through the woods to escape, but there was no escape for him. The defenses of the forest would wall him inside and he did not know the secret of the Dryads any longer. The roots of the oaks ran for leagues and she was tied into them all, connected to the information they shared with her.

Phae leaned forward and whispered to him. "You guarded my tree, so you have earned a boon. I give you my Dryad name. I give it to you freely because I trust the man that you were, even the man you've become. My name is Arsinowe."

As she breathed out the name, she felt magic in the word, magic that began forging a bond to him. She felt it well up inside her, a powerful surge that made her lips begin to tingle and power burn on her tongue. It was a pleasant feeling, a surging tidal feeling. Phae lifted his chin and brought her mouth to his, bestowing a Dryad's kiss.

There was a rush of power and emotion. She felt herself become a conduit for memories as they poured from the tree, through her, and into him. His mind was unlocked, the hidden recesses filled to overflowing. She pressed the kiss harder, connecting to him, feeling his breath begin to quicken, and then he gasped. Not only did his memories return, but her memories joined with his, her experiences with the Seneschal, her following of his life's story.

The rush was intense, deeply personal, and they both floated in the magic, clinging to each other as it sped them fast, weaving through sharp turns and rugged eddies. He tasted wonderful, his scent a mixture of sweat and earth, and full of the forest and trees.

It was finished.

Phae pulled back, gazing into his scarred cheeks.

"I love you, Isic," she whispered, her heart breaking with the words. She smiled at him, a sad smile full of empathy and compassion. "I know your story. I know it better than you knew yourself, for I see the truth that you were blinded to. Your brother's treachery. Your wife's sacrifice. She died protecting you." She swallowed, wondering what she should say. "You were never meant to be together. I think she always knew. But I cannot blame her for loving you. I would have done the same to save you."

Shion's eyes were wet with tears. "You were there," he said in amazement. "You are the one who took my memories. I've always felt . . . that I knew you."

She nodded, wiping a tear from his cheek, as her own flowed unheeded. "We must undo what your brother . . . what Aristaios did. We can end the Plague, you and I. We must end it before it destroys everyone."

Shion stared at her, his face becoming grave. "The pool of quicksilver is tainted. How can it be cured?"

Kneeling in front of him, she put her hand on his wrist. "Only an Unwearying One can cleanse it. I am immortal, but I am not like you. I am bound for a season and I am bound to a specific tree. I can help draw the fire out of Poisonwell. But only you can cure it. You must drink it, Isic. You must drink all of the Plagues. They won't kill you, but you will suffer." She winced, gazing into his eyes. "You must separate the Plague from the well. That is how your brother unleashes it. He drinks from the well and carries it to another land, expelling the disease on the population. Drinking quicksilver would kill a mortal man. But you cannot die."

He stared at her, his eyes full of wisdom and understanding. "I will do this."

Phae retrieved the Tay al-Ard from her belt. She kissed his cheek and then offered the device to him.

They gripped the warm cylinder. Their thoughts were as one, picturing the greenish hue of the subterranean lair beneath the mountain.

Shirikant was waiting for them.

"I do not know how it happened. Someone threw open the gates of the Arch-Rike's palace. Confusion is everywhere. They say the Arch-Rike is hiding in the dungeons. What is true and what is false? No man knows. There is no end to the deceptions."

- Possidius Adeodat, Archivist of Kenatos

XLV

The subterranean cavern swirled with greenish mist and pungent odors. Cracks of light appeared in fissures on the walls, spirits trapped in glass orbs fixed into sconces. The air was sulfurous and heavy, and thick shadows cut in jagged angles and slits along the floor. An oppressive feeling clung to the air, a menace full of dark loathing and cruelty. It made Phae's heart tremble with fear, even though she was immortal. The blackness pressed against her mind, hammering against her thoughts and conjuring malevolent images in the secret places inside her.

Standing across from them at a pool of bubbling quicksilver, she saw Shirikant holding a stone chalice. It looked heavy and deep, half the size of a melon, with intricate carvings set on the outside of the bowl. The lip was ridged and crumbling, and the whole thing looked ancient and defaced. Shirikant gripped it in one hand, the other clutching his Tay al-Ard. His face was creased with savage emotions, his eyes burning with pure hatred as they appeared. He seemed on the verge of lifting the chalice to his lips, but he lowered his arm, staring at them with a look that would have killed them both if it could.

"I knew you would come," he said in a low, even tone. "Do you remember me now, *Brother*?"

Shion put a cautioning hand on Phae's arm and took a step forward.

Immediately, shards of lightning flashed from the walls, hammering into Shion from three sides. The light blinded Phae, and she could feel the energy and heat swell past her, filling her with current.

The energy went into the Druidecht talisman worn around Shion's neck, absorbing the charges before the light winked out.

"*Exacerist*," Shion whispered. There was a chink of glass and spirits emerged from the cracked spheres, swirling in the air, leaving streamers of magic. "*Antonium farsay. Benne.*"

The light remained, the spirits not leaving after being freed. Phae realized Shion was speaking to them in another language, the pure language of Mirrowen.

"You free them but transform one form of slavery into another," Shirikant sneered. "We are no different."

"We are quite different," Shion said flatly, walking forward deliberately. Phae did not hold back. She went with him, coming closer, wanting to connect with Shirikant's eyes, but he would not look at her. He ignored her, turning the full force of his menacing eyes on his brother.

"So different," Shirikant repeated. "How so, Brother? We are born of the same womb. We share the same immortality. You've served me for so long—your entire life! Why quit now? I'm close to undoing everything, to remake this world. So very close. I've set it all in motion. You cannot stop it."

"I can, and I will," Shion said coldly. "You are a usurper. Your throne is stolen. You cannot create, you can only destroy. You are of the Void, Brother. I will stop you."

The feeling of tension in the smoky chamber intensified the dread. Phae felt as if dark shapes appeared at the corner of her vision, flickers of shadows. They weren't alone. She felt as if someone stood beside her and the hairs on her arms pricked. As if someone were reaching to touch her and that touch would destroy her.

"How?" Shirikant said, chuckling darkly. "The Seneschal will stop me? He has done nothing these last ages. He can do nothing with the gate closed. He does *nothing*, but stride elegantly and spew platitudes, and shackle everyone into his own form of bondage. Mine at least is fixed for a season. There are terms and agreements. There is an *end* to the servitude. I would not wish to be an Unwearying One now. You are a slave, Isic."

"I was *your* slave," Shion replied coldly. "How could you do that to your own brother? What did I ever do to you to earn such contempt? I was loyal to you. We were the first mastermind. You and I. Look what you've become."

"Look what I've become?" Shirikant said with a nasty twist in his expression, his cheeks quivering with rage. "I've remade this world. I built Kenatos. It's no different than Mirrowen. I have chiseled and scraped every single reference, every mention of Mirrowen and its decrepit Seneschal from every book throughout the world. There is no mention of him anywhere. Not even the sad Druidecht order—*your* order!—remember him any longer. He's nothing more than a myth and only the Dryads know of him. No mortal has trod this bridge since we did. And no one ever will again."

Shion shook his head, standing across the bubbling cauldron of quicksilver from his brother, the greenish light playing across both their faces.

"You cannot erase the Seneschal," Shion said simply. "In the winter, every tree appears to be dead. He's allowed you to reign during this particular winter, Brother. But the spring comes and thaws the snow. The buds form on the trees again. Except the truly dead ones. Except for yours. You are known in Boeotia as a traitor and a deceiver. Your legend will spread throughout every land and kingdom until your title becomes a curse on men's lips. It is over, Brother. I bring you to justice. I am taking you with me to Mirrowen."

The look in Shirikant's eyes went silver with hatred. "Never!" he screamed, spittle flying from his lips.

"You betrayed your own blood. You betrayed your own heart. Because of what? Jealousy? Because the Seneschal chose to honor me above you because he discerned the variance in our motives? Because he saw what you would become?"

"He sees nothing!" Shirikant shrieked. His fingers gripped the Tay al-Ard so tightly it seemed the metal would rend in his hand. "I hate him! I hate you! Would I could drown you in this boiling pool! I would choke your last breath with my hands."

"You've tried," Shion said, his own cheek twitching. "How many ways and how many times have you tried to murder me, Brother? You've buried me in stone. You've chained me to the bottom of the lake. I remember it all now. To hide your guilt and shame? It festers inside you like a wound that will not heal. It cannot heal now, Brother. There is no spell, no balm that can save you now. You are like the Void, constantly hammering against the defenses. And that is where you will be chained. It is your punishment, Brother. I could not prevent it even if I desired mercy. And I do not. I don't hate you—"

"Do not spit your pity at me!" Shirikant screamed.

"I have no pity for you. You knew what you did when you spoke to that serpent. You deceived yourself before you deceived us all. You never knew what it was to fail. You knew pride, never meekness. You were jealous in the end. What a petty emotion, Brother. It's a filthy broth that will not nourish. You will accept no one to rule over you. So you will inherit a kingdom of chaos."

The silence that followed sent shivers of dread through Phae's heart. The blackness seemed to gather around them, drawn into a vortex of hatred and loathing.

Shirikant's voice was cruel and placid. "I will destroy every living soul in this world. You cannot catch me. You cannot take me against my will. I too have trained with the Kishion. I am not afraid of you, Brother. And I know more about Druidecht lore than you ever will. Dryad—I call you by your true name, Phae Grove, and I bind you to serve me."

Phae felt a whorl of magic rush against her, searing into her skull. It was as if a great hand clutched her mind, gripping it with iron fingers. She felt it, but it had no power over her. She knew that, but she also knew that Shirikant did not. If she could trick him into looking into her eyes . . .

"No!" Shion shouted, his mind connected to hers.

Take his memories she heard Shirikant whisper greedily in her mind.

Shirikant raised the stone cup to his mouth and swallowed several gulps from it. Trickles of silver liquid spilled down his chin. He grimaced in pain.

"No, I forbid it!" Shion said, turning to look at her, to look deliberately into her eyes. His expression hardened into fierce determination. He did not want Shirikant's memories harvested inside her, his evil chained inside her tree.

Now! Shirikant's thoughts murmured to her.

Phae turned to Shirikant, shrugging off the heavy oppressive feeling against her mind. "*That* is not my Dryad name," she announced, looking into his eyes. And she blinked.

The wave of memories struck her like a flood, coursing through her mind, her body, her soul in a hailstorm of evil and gibbering terror. She crumpled to her knees, feeling the weight of the burden suffocating her, soiling her, bringing her in contact with the worst demons of imagination possible. She shrank from the onslaught, uttering a groan of despair as the thoughts and images flooded her mind. The countless murders and savagery he had caused through his many faces. It was worse than she could have ever imagined, seeing the suffering and devastation and ruin that one being had caused throughout the world.

She felt arms around her, holding her, hugging her, and realized that Shion was kneeling next to her, sharing the memories as they passed through her, their minds connected by Dryad magic. It was a never-ending scream, a ceaseless howling that rippled into eternity.

She trembled under the weight of the horror, her own mind faltering to know what to do, and then by instinct, it happened. She began to unload the memories into her Dryad tree, and as she did, the burden began to lighten, the stretching strain against her soul began to ease. Memories shuffled into place, like books on a shelf, sinews of leather and glue and parchment.

There was a retching sound.

It felt as if a million pricking needles had stabbed inside Phae's eyes. She had crumpled against Isic, feeling his strong arms around her, keeping her up. Shirikant knelt by the pool of quicksilver, vomiting silver bile back into the bubbling pool.

He looked sick and confused, his body shuddering as he looked up blankly, staring at the two of them without a shred of recognition. He wiped a trickle of silver from his mouth. "Where am I?" he whispered hoarsely. He looked around the battered cave.

Phae stared down at her hands and then at the stone cup toppled next to Shion's brother. She made it to her feet somehow and hefted the stone chalice. She didn't bother taking his Tay al-Ard. It would be useless to him, for he bore no memories and thus had nowhere to go. She stared at the chalice, at the designs carved into the side. It was a strange engraving of a tree with many vine-like limbs and blooming fruit. There was a man with a strange halo carved into it sitting on a throne. Images of serpents clung to the vines. There were other beings carved into it as well, one kneeling and raising a single hand. Another grabbed a fruit from the vine. It was the story of Shirikant and Shion. The entire legend had been painstakingly engraved into the stone chalice.

"What must we do?" Shion asked her, trembling from the memories they had endured. He stared at her worriedly, his expression tightening with the impending sense of more pain to come.

She stared at the bubbling cauldron, seeing the sheen of it. She understood how Shirikant had cursed it. His memories were now hers too. It would take one with the fireblood to tame the fire unleashed inside Pontfadog. And she knew the Seneschal had foreseen she would have it.

Phae reached out a calming hand. "*Pericanthas. Sericanthas. Thas.*"

She felt heat from the pool gathering together. Blue flames began to dance atop the frenzied churn of bubbles. The flames grew brighter and coalesced into a sphere that floated to her hand and then absorbed into her skin. She felt a rush of magic as her fireblood responded to it, meshing the magics together, taming them. A haze of steam lingered over the pool, the heat dissipating quickly. Soon the pool was a glassy sheen, still as a mirror.

Both she and Shion crouched near the edge of it.

"I must drink it, mustn't I?" Shion whispered, looking at her.

Her heart ached. "Yes. The Plague is a protection to this place, a way of defending it against intruders and to prevent those who haven't earned the right to enter."

"Yes, I know," Shion said. "He joined the magics together, somehow."

"He used fire to bind them," Phae explained. "I've taken that away. If you drink from the pool, your body will separate the

Plague from the quicksilver." She closed her eyes, sorting through the memories. "You must suffer the effects of the Plague in order to rid it from the pool. It will be painful."

He looked her in the eye. "It must be done." He gripped the stone chalice and dipped it into the calm mirror surface. The liquid rippled and filled the cup.

Shion raised it to his lips and drank it down, wincing with each swallow. Phae watched a series of hives appear on his face and skin, boils that swelled and turned livid. He groaned with pain, staring at his arms, his hands, watching the pustules ripple and quiver. He shuddered, his entire body trembling like a tree shaken in a windstorm. Before the first effects of the Plague had run their course, he dipped the cup a second time into the pool and drank it down. Phae watched in mute horror as another Plague was unleashed on him. Then another.

She clung to him and wept.

"This is the last one," Phae whispered, tearstains on her cheeks. The pool was almost empty.

"Help . . . me. Please. To drink . . . it." He lay trembling, exhausted—blistered and pocked.

She dipped the chalice into the dwindled, shallow pool, a volcanic pockmark in the dim green haze of phosphorescent light. Small beads of quicksilver seemed to draw themselves into the stone cup when she tipped it down at the bottom to gather the last. The final Plague sat quivering in the dregs of silver. She stared at it, wondering if she should drink it herself.

"No," Shion said, choking, his face puffy and ravaged. His bloodshot eyes were full of suffering and also with the knowledge that she was tempted to drink it herself. She wiped her eyes on her sleeve and gently raised the cup to his mouth, tilting it so that he drank the final bit, the dregs of the Plague.

He winced, sputtering and choking, his body trembling under the multiple and varied symptoms of the Plagues of mortality. His breath was in shallow gasps, his forehead wrinkled with unbearable agony. He looked at her pleadingly, his expression begging it to be over. Vomit stained his shirt and purple bruises covered his lumpy skin in patches. Every breath brought a pained shudder.

"It is done," she said.

Shirikant sat across from them, staring at the empty pool. He sat in brooding silence, watching but not understanding. He had asked a few questions, but nothing they said made sense to him. He watched, uncomprehending that his entire plan for destroying the world was being purged, sip by sip.

Shion struggled to sit, then leaned against Phae as he trembled with fever and chills. He was as weak as a kitten, spent and broken.

"Help me . . ." he begged.

Phae pulled him up gently, helping him face the pool. He planted his hands on the liquid's edge, his arm muscles quivering as if the effort were more than he could bear. His whole body bucked and heaved, and Phae watched in shocked silence as tiny beads of silver began to gather from the pores of his skin. Little specks trickled down his arms and began filling the pool. He shuddered violently and groaned, experiencing wave after wave of nausea and anguish, and she watched the pool begin to fill with quicksilver. His skin bubbled and popped, thick pustules of silver emerging. It looked agonizing as she watched, her stomach churning with disgust. The stream came faster, and with it, the distant sound of rushing waters began to echo inside the chamber. It was a sound she recognized, the rushing of the waters coming from the tree in the garden in Mirrowen.

A halo of light filled the gruesome chamber, driving away all the shadows. The smell of salt and the sea filled the air, and a breeze tousled Phae's hair. With the light came a feeling of immense peace and relief. Joy exploded inside her heart.

"Isic, I think it is over!" she said, beaming through her tears. "It is finished!"

A window to another world opened up from inside the pool. It was so bright that Phae shielded her eyes for a moment. Shirikant shrank from it, fleeing to one of the edges of the chamber, staring at the light with shock and dread. He cowered in fear.

The Seneschal, Melchisedeq, stepped through the portal and entered her world.

"Well done," he said with a broad smile. "Well done!"

He set his hand on Shion's head and said, *Calvariae!*

The word seemed to gush out from him in a whisper that could be heard anywhere throughout the world. Strength filled Shion's arms and legs and the boils and rashes on his skin were healed. As she stared at him, she saw that the scars from the Fear Liath were still there . . . small and hardly noticeable unless she really looked hard to see them.

"It is time to set things in order," the Seneschal said. "To usher in a new season. Isic Moussion, I bestow upon you one of the Voided Keys."

Isic knelt before the Seneschal, shaking his head. "I am unworthy of such a gift," he said softly.

"With much suffering comes much wisdom, Isic. This is the day I saw when you pledged to serve me. This is the hour I knew would come. You will earn more Voided Keys as you assume more responsibility for governing this world. The keys are mine to bestow upon whom I will. I give this one to you."

He produced one of the ancient, gnarled iron keys with a leather strap running through the empty part. He gestured for

Shion to rise and fashioned it around his waist, so that the key dangled there. Phae stared at him with pride, smiling with pleasure at seeing him finally fulfilling his destiny.

"What shall we do with your brother?" the Seneschal asked. "You must name his punishment."

Shion looked at the Seneschal in surprise. He stared at the cowering form, shrinking from the gaze of the Unwearying Ones. Phae looked at him as well, seeing no trace of power left in him, no threat to anyone.

"He will be imprisoned," Shion said firmly, coldly, but not vengefully. "He has a book of the Paracelsus order. A book where he has written all of his means to bind spirits and the will of men and women. All of his cunning. All of his sources of power are contained in this book. Evil cannot be destroyed. But it can be bound." He turned to face the Seneschal again. "I do not want his memories tainting Phae's tree. Can you bind his memories to the book, bind his spirit to the book? He is too dangerous to be allowed to walk the earth. He is unwilling to obey any power other than himself. Let him be caged like the spirits he caged. The Druidecht order will forbid anyone from reading that book and we will protect it as our sworn duty."

The Seneschal paused, staring at Shion. Phae could tell that he was looking into the future, into a decision made and its impacts down to the ends of time. A slow smile crept over the Seneschal's mouth.

"Phae, you still have the stone your father gave you. The stone that traps a mortal's spirit. Give it to me and I will use it to bind him to the book you spoke of. It is time to heal the Scourgelands, to restore them to their proper use. To fulfill the oath to build Canton Vaud, the Druidecht stronghold. By the Voided Keys, I revoke the curse tainting the fireblood."

He raised his right hand, holding his palm toward the cleft

of rock overhead. An earthquake rocked the cavern, splitting the dome of the ceiling, shattering the rocks and bringing in the natural light of day at last.

Phae felt something change inside her blood, filling her with peace. She grabbed Shion's hand, staring into his eyes, beaming at him.

He smiled lovingly at Phae, his eyes crinkling with tenderness and warmth, and then dipped his head and kissed her.

"Maybe the Vaettir are the wisest of all, not the Preachán. They put it best: Love is not to be purchased, and affection has no price."

- Possidius Adeodat, Archivist of Kenatos

XLVI

Paedrin's heart raced with dread and a welling sense of hopelessness. Gusts of wind whipped him off course as he searched from the sky at the ruins of the fortress for a sign of Hettie, Tyrus, or Baylen. Every moment increased the sense of panic. He was too late. The soldiers were scattering like a hive of ants whose hill had been kicked over by an angry boot. Flashes of lightning from the turbulent skies warned him of the danger of staying aloft much longer. A brilliant bloom of blue fire exploded through the haze of mist below and he altered his course, shooting down to it. Flashes of red light came in response and Paedrin saw four shapes, wearing black, advancing on a man trapped in the middle. As he drew closer, he saw the streak of white light connecting the four men, boxing a fifth man in between.

"Closer! Closer! He's wavering!" came a shout.

A gurgling scream of agony wailed from the midst of the light streamers. Another detonation of blue flame came, toppling one of the arches, and one of the men was crushed beneath the weight.

"Quickly! Don't let him escape!"

Paedrin saw that the men were Paracelsus and he recognized the magic they used, for he had been entrapped by it as well. The more force used against it, the more force was repelled back. Tyrus was hunched over in agony, trying to get back on his feet. The three continued to lean forward, struggling with each step to draw the net of magic tighter, to immobilize him.

A shriek of curses came from Tyrus next, and he spit at them, screaming again as he tried to counter their magic with his own.

"Almost!" one of the Paracelsus shouted in triumph. "Bring him down! Shoot him! Shoot him!"

Paedrin swept into range from above and plunged the Sword of Winds into the lower back of one of the dark-clad Paracelsus. The man crumpled, his legs suddenly useless, and the spray of light went wide.

"No!" another wailed in terror, the net of magic scattering.

Tyrus's head lifted, his eyes glazed with savage fury. He held up his hand, exposing a ring on his finger, and one of the Paracelsus went flying backward, arcing into the sky to smash into one of the stone columns still standing. Paedrin dove forward, coming up into a high leap and smashed his heel into the last Paracelsus's face, dropping him to unconsciousness.

Paedrin whipped the blade around and turned to Tyrus. "Where is Hettie?" he shouted.

Blue flames irrupted from Tyrus's outstretched arms, flooding toward Paedrin. Only his Bhikhu reflexes saved him and he leapt high into the air, summoning the blade's magic to carry him up and over Tyrus's head.

"It's me, Paedrin!" he screamed and realized with anguish that Tyrus's mind was no longer his own. Flames rippled from the man's fingers, which were hooked like talons. There was no euphoria on his face, only malice and madness. Another burst of flames raced at him, and Paedrin swept it away quickly, barely dodging it.

"Stop!" Paedrin pleaded, trying to meet the gaze. It reminded him of the Boeotian Tasvir Virk and his heart crumpled with pain. Not Tyrus—not him. It was too much to lose him.

"You won't . . . trick me!" Tyrus snarled, his body contorting into an unnatural position. He hunched over, as if experiencing horrible pain. His legs seemed rooted to the spot and one arm was tucked tight against his body, as if guarding a deep wound.

"It is not a trick," Paedrin said, changing angles, using the Uddhava to be unpredictable. "Tyrus, please! You are sick. Let me help you. Where's Hettie?"

"She's dead. They're all dead. I couldn't stand alone against the entire world. I bore it all, but I'm dying." He coughed and sagged to one knee, bending over and vomiting black bile. He struggled to breathe, choking.

Paedrin's heart wrung with emotions. It was like watching Shivu die. "No, Tyrus! They're alive. Phae is alive! We must wait for them here. They will come."

"No . . . one . . . is . . . coming," Tyrus gurgled.

"Trust me!" Paedrin pleaded. He needed to get close. If he could strike fast and hard, he could stun Tyrus and knock him unconscious. He came around from behind.

"Too late," Tyrus moaned, shaking his head. Dribbles of spittle came from his mouth.

Paedrin saw his neck turn, saw the cunning in Tyrus's eyes. The hands shot out like serpents, the illusion of weakness shattered by the surge of madness. Blue flames exploded around Paedrin, smothering him, searing his skin. He had seen what happened to a person struck by them before. Ash.

Yet the flames did not burn him.

"Tyrus!" Hettie yelled. Paedrin heard her voice, saw her appear behind Tyrus on the other side, her body crouched, her fingers burning blue as she tamed the fire and prevented it from engulfing Paedrin. It was everything she could do to absorb the fatal blast herself, drawing Tyrus's fireblood with her own. Her face twisted with anguish.

"Now, Baylen!" she snapped.

Then the Cruithne was there, behind Tyrus and wrapping him in his huge arms, pinning his arms to his sides and jerking him away from Paedrin. The flames guttered out momentarily and Tyrus bucked and twisted. Even the Cruithne could barely contain him and Paedrin watched Baylen's hold slipping.

Hettie ran up, her face wrinkled with anguish. "Uncle, stop! I have the cure for monkshood. Baylen, hold him still!"

"No!" Tyrus shrieked. "You'll poison me!" He was desperate, frantic, his eyes blazing with terror.

"He's stronger than he looks," Baylen grunted, dodging his head aside as Tyrus's whipped back to crush his nose. Baylen shifted his hold to a Bhikhu grip, wrapping his forearm around Tyrus's neck, blocking off his air. The Paracelsus slammed into Baylen's ribs, clawed at his face with his nails. Blood streamed from a cut on Baylen's cheek, but he leaned forward, overpowering Tyrus with his pure weight. Both men wrestled viciously.

Paedrin saw several soldiers watching them from behind the shelter of stones, their faces frozen with terror. None of them tried to interrupt the scene. They were frightened out of their wits, leaderless—shattered.

Tyrus was choking, but he was still fighting. Baylen's face scrunched with determination, his broad shoulders flexing as he forced Tyrus's face into the shattered cobbles.

"Now," Baylen grunted, blood dribbling off his chin.

Tyrus's head was forced back, his throat exposed.

He looked at Hettie in wild terror. "Kill me," he croaked. "Please! Just kill me!"

Hettie knelt by him, her eyes wet with tears. She shook her head fiercely. "You didn't kill my mother. You saved her life. You did everything you could." She cupped his sweating face with her hand. "You gave everything, Uncle. I won't let you die."

She took her water flask and pressed it to his mouth. He spat it back at her, swearing violently, choking with rage and helplessness. Baylen torqued Tyrus's arm viciously and his head arched back, mouth wide in a soundless scream. Hettie poured more of the liquid from the flask into his mouth and then Baylen released the chokehold and clamped his hand on Tyrus's mouth. Paedrin crouched nearby, his heart breaking with pity.

The three knelt by Tyrus as he lay panting, chest heaving. He started to weep, great choking sobs that split the air like thunder. He lay crumpled and defeated, unable to move, unable to fight, unable to rage. He sobbed, the sound a hymn of mourning and desolation so fitting for the Scourgelands.

Paedrin squatted nearby, wiping tears from his own eyes, watching the mighty Paracelsus with overpowering pity.

Hettie raised Tyrus's head, resting it on her lap, and she stroked his hair, whistling softly. Baylen sat nearby, struggling to regain his own strength from the contest. He wiped a smear of blood from his chin, shaking his head sadly.

Hettie cooed softly, bending low. "I won't leave you," she whispered to him. "I won't abandon you."

"To your father," the Seneschal said. His magic enveloped her and Shion and they rose with his inhaled breath up the chasm of broken rock to the top of the plateau. As they emerged from the crags of shattered stone, Phae watched the whorl of stormy clouds dispersing, exposing streaks of stabbing sunlight. She blinked, covering her eyes with her hand for a moment. As she looked, she saw her father sprawled on the ground, with Hettie, Paedrin, and Baylen crouching near him. He lifted his head as she approached him, her heart shuddering with relief at seeing them all alive.

"Phae?" Tyrus said hoarsely, his eyes clear and focused.

"He's mad," Hettie said forlornly, her eyes streaked with tears.

Tyrus pulled himself up slowly, his muscles trembling with extreme exhaustion. "No, my thoughts are clearing." He shuddered, trying to stand, but he was too weak to manage it. He shook his head, blinking rapidly.

"Yes, you are, Uncle," Hettie said. "You used the fireblood too much. You were raging a moment ago."

"I was," Tyrus said, nodding emphatically. His eyes were reflective, calm. "My thoughts are clearing like those storm clouds. Phae? Is that you? Shion?"

Phae rushed forward and sank down on her knees, drawing Tyrus into her arms. "The madness is banished," she announced to everyone, her heart throbbing with joy. "The curse of the fireblood is no more. The Plague has ended. Father, it is over. You triumphed!" She cupped his cheek tenderly. "You were right. You did not know all of what happened in the past, but you figured out so much on your own. You've been hearing the whispers from Mirrowen all along. They brought you here. They brought you here to heal the land."

She felt wetness on his back and when she pulled her hand back saw the drops of blood sticking to her fingers. His face was pale, his strength fading with each breath. His body was full of gashes and wounds. She withdrew the strange, moss-like plant from Mirrowen from a pouch at her side and pressed it against

Tyrus's back. She felt her father tense with surprise as the magic coursed through him, closing his savage cuts and healing his wounds and his weariness. Color came back to his cheeks.

She stared at him, stroking his face, smiling through her tears. "Father, we defeated Shirikant! Shion was the one who destroyed the Plague. His memories are restored. I know him now, I know about our race . . . about the history of our family." She bowed her head, unable to speak all that was in her heart, realizing that her time with him was not ending, only beginning—that their time together would be lasting. "You were right in what you chose, Father. All that you sacrificed, all that you surrendered to succeed. It was worth all the hardships! The Plagues have ended. We were immune because of who we are. We're descendants of Shirikant, Father. And we now have a destiny to prevent this evil from returning."

I will speak with him

Phae felt the whisper as it rushed through her heart. She rose, drawing her father up with her. She held him close, burying her face in his chest, feeling his strength but trying to suffuse part of hers into him again. She gripped his hands and then turned, facing Shion and the Seneschal.

"Father, this is the Seneschal of Mirrowen. There is a task he will give you. I know him, Father. Our family must reverse the evils caused by our ancestor."

Tyrus stared at Shion, seeing the change that had overcome his countenance, the steadiness and confidence. The compassion. She could see Tyrus's eyes noticing the talisman around Shion's neck. Then he faced the Seneschal. Slowly, Tyrus eased down on one knee.

"What would you have me do?" he whispered.

The ground beneath Annon rumbled. A sudden jolt from below knocked him flat. A crack—as if the earth had split in half—sounded, deafening them. The remaining columns toppled, causing shrieks of fright to come from the quivering soldiers of Kenatos. Annon rose to his feet quickly, rushing up the final length of the ramp to the upper heights. He had passed the field unchallenged, seeing dead Weir all around. In the mist, he thought he had seen larger beasts ghosting in the shroud of vapor, their bulk twice the size of the Weir. He had hurried across the field, passing the carcasses, until he reached the ramp.

As he stepped onto the top of the hill, he saw the shattered ruins up close. Some ancient fortress seemed to have once stood proudly, but it was toppled. As he stepped over a fallen buttress, he saw a shock of pale hair and recognized it. The dead eyes of Lukias stared absently, a trickle of blood coming from his ear. Annon stared at the corpse, feeling a twist of anguish mixed with relief. He realized in the image that the Order of the Rikes would fade into memory now. Would any remain to carry on their false traditions? What would be said of them in the future? That they were a mad religion that enslaved the races in a prison island known as Kenatos?

Annon stared at the face, shook his head, and then pressed toward the center of the destruction. He felt a strange exhilaration in his blood, a sense of giddiness instead of fear. As he walked, the lightness in his chest grew to euphoria. All around him was devastation and destruction, but he felt peaceful and calm. He heard a whisper coming from the center of the ruins. The whisper sizzled in his heart, making his eyes sting with tears. His pace broadened, his mouth burning with thirst. Was that the sound of water? Up at the heights? He could not understand it. Where was it coming from?

Spirits began to flit through the air. He saw them, dazzled by the streaks of color and intensity. A Shain spirit came up to him with enthusiasm.

Come, Druidecht. Come! The Seneschal is here. The Seneschal of Mirrowen! Come!

Annon felt a surge of relief and gratitude. He wiped his mouth, unable to contain the burst of enjoyment and thrill that surged inside his heart. Had they done it? Had they accomplished the task? As he stepped over the clutter of rubble, he came to a rift in the ground, the center of the hilltop. There were Hettie and Paedrin. To the side, he saw Baylen smirking as he arrived, the giant Cruithne nodding in welcome as they joined. Tyrus! Annon saw Tyrus talking to Phae and Shion, clutching a heavy black book to his chest and nodding. As Annon approached, he saw Tyrus turn and discovered a talisman around his neck.

Annon was dumbfounded.

Annon

He felt the whisper in his mind and saw that there was another standing among them whom he had not seen before. He was a lithe and towering figure, with long dark hair and an expression of humility and respect on his face. The feelings surging inside Annon's heart stunned him. He recognized the man. Somehow, it felt like it did when he saw Reeder after a journey. Annon knelt before the Seneschal of Mirrowen, feeling the enormity of the moment, the thought that most Druidecht lived their entire lives without ever glimpsing Mirrowen.

Rise, Annon of Wayland—one of the Thirteen

His heart swelled even larger and he felt tears trickle down his cheeks. He rose, seeing the greeting on their faces, seeing the joy in their eyes. There were so many questions he wanted to ask, but he felt it would be wrong to speak. That to do so would intrude on a sacred moment.

The Seneschal faced Annon, who rose because he felt compelled to do so.

"Welcome," the Seneschal said, smiling. "Welcome to Canton Vaud. Do you accept your position as one of the Thirteen? You join others, like Tyrus and your friend Drosta. You must restore the Druidecht order under the guidance of its original founder, Prince Isic Moussion of Stonehollow. There is much you will learn about your blood and who you are. Do you accept the responsibility?"

"I will," Annon replied without a moment's hesitation.

"Good," the Seneschal said. He then withdrew a sheathed dagger, which Annon recognized as the blade Iddawc. "The binding on this weapon will last for a thousand years. It must be safeguarded. Return it to Drosta's Lair, where it may continue to remain hidden. The Druidecht must be summoned to this place. The safe road leads from Basilides to cross the Scourgelands. Poisonwell has been opened at long last."

"The way to Mirrowen?" Annon asked, his eyes gleaming with hope.

"When you have all completed your tasks, you will be allowed to enter. If you desire it with all your hearts."

Annon saw the looks on their faces, saw the triumph in their eyes. The world would change forever. He dared not ask it, because he knew he did not need to. If he did what he was required, he would be allowed to enter Mirrowen. And there, he hoped, he would find Neodesha waiting for him.

"The more I understand the lore and mythology surrounding the Seneschal of Mirrowen, the more humbled I am at all that has transpired, how the events of these days will reap a future we can only imagine. I asked Tyrus to try to explain why the Seneschal, powerful as he is, did not come to deliver us personally. Tyrus's answer was fraught with wisdom, his words were simple: He who created us without our help would not save us without our consent.

Tyrus returned to Kenatos with the rightful Arch-Rike, Band-Imas, whose body was discovered in the Rike vaults known as Basilides. He was still alive after many years, his body preserved through arcane spirit magic. He immediately relinquished his claim and status, choosing to become a Druidecht instead and to commence the rebuilding of the mighty fortress of Canton Vaud. He was joined by other Druidecht, who banded together to form a new mastermind, bent on restoring the lost Druidecht knowledge. Tyrus did not stay in Kenatos long—long enough though to set free the spirits entrapped in the city. He collected the volumes of the Paracelsus order, to be archived in Canton Vaud but no longer used. He has already collected most of the records from the Archives of Kenatos. All the records from the Archives will ultimately be transferred there. I am grateful that the one who sought to destroy all knowledge is no longer able to prosper.

Kenatos and Boeotia have a truce. Relations with Silvandom also have begun between the two erstwhile hostile neighbors. The Empress Larei believes it will take several generations to unravel the hatred of her people. I do believe she may be right.

The Cruithne are reconstructing Havenrook, beautifying the city with gardens and waterworks, harnessing the power of the rivers to invent great gristmills and other intriguing contraptions. The Preachán are restless, of course. They resent being thrust out of their ancient homeland. I predict we will see a series of skirmishes between their peoples before they learn to coexist. The King of Wayland is exerting his power more forcefully now. He controls the shipping between kingdoms and seeks to replicate the power the Romani once held. The king of Wayland is a distrustful man. He does not believe the reports from the Scourgelands. He believes it's all a trick of some kind. There are rumors that the Romani have finally infiltrated Stonehollow. I don't give these rumors much credence myself.

For a more detailed history of what transpired surrounding the fall of the Scourgelands and the revoking of the Plague, I suggest the writings of Annon of Wayland, one of the Thirteen of Canton Vaud, when he has finished it. The Druidecht have excellent memories and I know the account will be archived in their histories when the libraries and vaults are finished. What an undertaking, millennia in the making.

For all of my life, I have quested for the answer regarding the secret race of Stonehollow. I can now state with authority that they do have a name. They were called the Moussion, after the house of Aristaios Moussion, the being known as Shirikant. It was his partaking of the fruit that gave his descendants the fireblood. Because he was the originator of the Plagues, his descendants inherited a natural immunity to it. It turns out that their blood was helpful in preventing the disease from spreading. There are no records of the genealogy of this race, but if I could trace Tyrus's line, I am certain to find that he is a direct descendent of the man. I asked him how he felt about that possibility. As with everything regarding Tyrus Grove of Kenatos, he only smiled enigmatically and said, 'We cannot choose our parents.'

I am grateful to have Tyrus as my ally. I consider him a personal friend and the man who rescued these forsaken lands from extinction."

- Possidius Adeodat, Arch-Rike of Kenatos

XLVII

He could not remember his name.

Hunkering against a craggy oak tree, the man shivered with cold and weariness, trembling uncontrollably. Every snap of sound, every cracking twig, caused him to start. He was being hunted by a creature, a creature that came with the mist every night. It roared in menace, snuffling through the woods, seeking his blood. He could not remember why it hunted him. He could only flee until exhaustion caused him to collapse in the shattered remains of the woods. There was no north or south, no east or west—only a never-ending maze of oak trees and desiccated leaves. He had no weapons anymore. Part of his mind nagged that he should have two. Yet he had nothing, not even a water flask. He'd been forced to drink brackish water and eat disgusting mushrooms to stay alive. There was no game and no way to hunt it. There was no ending to the maze.

His throat was scratchy and parched. The only pond he had found was full of strange, puffy fish, which he found too loathsome to try to snare. The water was hideous and made him retch and gag. He touched his face, feeling the sores again. His face and arms were full of sores. His breathing quickened again, hearing the distant cry of some winged creature. Ticking sounds came from his left, startling him. He rose, brushing off the decaying leaves, and started walking once more.

The man's cloak was in tatters and he clutched it close to his neck, trying in vain to remember anything about his past. How long had he been lost in the woods? He tried to walk in a straight line but kept getting turned around. A menacing breeze caressed his neck, making him shiver even more. The air was getting colder. He could see the mist coming out of his mouth.

No, it was happening again! Darkness was falling. Darkness brought the creature out hunting. It could smell him. Somehow, it knew his scent. He wandered through the groves, aimlessly, terrified.

He tripped over a fallen tree branch, sprawling flat on his face. The sticks and burs stabbed him, making him groan with pain as they poked his sores. He scrambled back to his feet, looking at the fallen branch. It was large, fallen from a huge oak nearby. Something about the tree branch was familiar. He cast his eyes around the area, trying to take in as much as he could despite the shadows. The scene was vaguely familiar. Perhaps he had crossed this path before along his journey of never-ending circles. A fallen tree branch. He turned around in a circle and saw the mist swelling from the mouth of a stone cave.

His eyes widened with terror. The cave was the beast's lair. The beast that was hunting him. He heard a gurgling growl come from the blackness and froze in terror. His legs could not move. He stared at the darkness, heard a snuffling breath. His mind collapsed into gibbering fear.

"I knew we would succeed," Paedrin said confidently, walking across the abandoned training yard of the Bhikhu temple. The sun was hot against his neck, but he enjoyed the feel of its burn. Memories, both joyful and bitter, played in his mind.

"Will you never stop bragging?" Hettie said from the shadows, cocking an eyebrow.

Paedrin gripped a long staff in his hands and began whirling it around in dizzying circles. He had always favored the staff in his training. He loved the feel of it, the heft of it, the way it would be made to do intricate maneuvers. He planted the butt of the staff into the cobblestones and spun around its length, coiling to the top like a serpent, one arm outstretched and held in a perfect pose.

"It's difficult not to," he said from that position, eyeing her in the shadows. "Every man must have at least one fault."

Hettie walked into the training yard, arms folded, her frown concealing the beginnings of a wry smile. "When is Baylen going to get back from the bakery with food for our journey?" she asked.

"I think he'll be gone a little while . . . why?"

She lunged forward, dropping low, and swung her leg around in a wide arc, slamming the staff hard enough to topple his stance.

He remained floating in the air, the staff spinning away. He let it clatter. "I knew you were going to do that. I knew you wouldn't be able to resist."

The two engaged in a full-stroke series of punches, kicks, and grappling techniques. Her reflexes had improved immeasurably since the Scourgelands. She did not hold back, and he had to admit that before too much longer, she might be ready to start sanding the calluses off his heels.

Their forearms jarred together in an intricate series of blocks and strikes. She shoved him hard against the chest and did a reverse kick that clipped his cheek. It even hurt a little.

She landed, grinning triumphantly, and he let her enjoy the moment before coming at her like an avalanche. Their arms and legs locked, fingers groping, feet positioning, and switching from one stance to another as they tried to achieve the right leverage. She caught his wrist and chopped at his neck. He blocked with his elbow and caught around her neck, spinning her around his exposed leg and tripping her backward. Hettie tucked her shoulder and pulled him off his feet. He felt his balance lurching.

Hettie grabbed a fistful of his tunic front and then kissed him passionately on the mouth, breaking his concentration completely. He forgot about the fighting, forgot everything except the taste of her, and then realized she was tricking him.

He backed away just as she was about to land her knee in his stomach. He caught the knee, hooked it with his arm and then hoisted her up higher, making her lose her balance. He reversed his hold, swept her final leg, and then watched with satisfaction as she toppled—at last!

Paedrin normally would have tackled her and pinned her, but he was winded from the duel and instead reached and helped her rise.

"I almost had you," she teased, panting.

"You came close," he agreed. He cast his gaze around the training yard, seeing glimpses of the memories it contained. "I'll miss the Bhikhu temple," he said solemnly. "It is colder in Shatalin. Do you fancy climbing the side of the mountain again?"

"Only if you are there to catch me," she answered slyly. "You realize I saved your life in the Scourgelands, Paedrin. When Tyrus was going to burn you to death. He would have, you know."

He gave her an arch look. "You want me to admit it?"

She nodded vigorously.

Paedrin grabbed her around her waist, his mouth crinkling with joy and a wistful smile. He stared hard into her eyes, soaking her in. "You did save my life, Hettie. And I'd like to thank you. The Romani way."

She smiled, nuzzling up against him. "I'd like that."

Annon cleared the branch away, exposing the small hut. It surprised him to see that much had changed since he had last visited Dame Nestra and her husband. He recognized the stump near the fire pit, the whetstone sitting outside the hut. But a barn had been constructed and some of the woods had been cleared. It looked peculiar, jarring with the memories he had of the place. A little prick of disappointment flashed inside his heart, but he stifled it. He had changed much himself since he had last wandered the forests of Wayland.

"Annon?"

It was Dame Nestra. She came from the doorway of the hut, her expression brightening when she recognized him. "Darling, Annon is back! Look at you!" She swept from the hut and approached him, eyeing him with mouth agape. "You're a grown man now, no longer a boy. Bless my heart, but you've changed. It's been so long, Annon. Where have you been hiding all this while?"

He took her hand and then gripped her husband's when he emerged from the hut, stroking crumbs from his mustache. "Bless me, lad. Look at you!"

Annon smiled in spite of himself, feeling grateful for the warm greeting. "I've been away too long. You have a barn now. It's impressive."

The woodcutter chuckled. "We get too many visitors, you see," he said with a shrug. "Word of my wife's cooking has spread in these parts, and folks come out of their way to pass by. Many are Druidecht, but occasionally Romani too or stonemasons from the west. It's safer in these woods, boy. The things you taught us—how to watch for the spirits and not disturb them."

Dame Nestra patted her husband's arm. "He listened to you. We both did. Some of the other woodcutters have accidents. The spirits don't bother us. In fact, they help us. We're always generous to travelers who come through. Now, since you look like a grown man, I'm sure you have a man's appetite as well. I was just going to start on some soup, and the bread will be done ere long. I keep telling him we should build an inn or something with all the visitors we get. You can still sleep outside if you prefer, Annon. You're always welcome here."

Annon smiled at the hospitality and nodded his acceptance. He didn't dare tell them that they were entertaining one of the Thirteen of Canton Vaud and that he could have stayed at the palace of the King of Wayland if he'd chosen. He was glad he had decided to stop to see them on his way to the king's city. He patted the Tay al-Ard fastened to his belt.

Tyrus lowered the cowl of his cloak in reverence. The mighty oak tree looked as if it had seen a thousand winters and summers. The forked trunk was twisted and furrowed. New growth had started from the trunk and the existing branches were crowned with healthy leaves. In the distance, the sound of chisels and stone beating to rhythms faded. The fortress was starting to rise from the rubble, the grounds full of scaffolding, men and pack animals hauling stone from the mountains near Basilides.

He paused before the oak, head slightly bowed, listening for the whispers from the talisman around his neck.

Phae stepped from around the tree, smiling broadly. She came forward and embraced him, kissing his bearded cheek. "Hello, Father. The work is progressing. It will be beautiful when it is finished."

He reached out and clasped her hand, feeling its warmth and strength. "You've seen it already, I imagine."

Phae nodded. "It's a marvelous structure. Canton Vaud will be the center of learning throughout all the kingdoms. You are its first Archivist, you know. The custodian of many secrets. You will even have your own tower again."

He was satisfied by that and squeezed her hand. "Thank you for seeing me, Phae. I don't mean to trouble you."

"It's no trouble, Father," she replied. "I will always be here, even when you are old and gray. Your whiskers are starting to turn, but there is still much you will accomplish in your lifetime. Time passes differently for me. It won't be long before you join us."

Tyrus sighed deeply, longing for that reunion, but knowing there was still a purpose he needed to accomplish first. "I have a question for you."

"Of course." She linked her arm with his and they started to stroll through the glen. She was not wearing the robes he had seen other Dryads with—her attire was better situated to a girl from Stonehollow, the girl she had grown up as. A homestead girl. She was beautiful and radiant, and he flushed with pride at seeing her inner strength, her wisdom, her compassion.

"I'm proud of you, Phae," he said, surprising himself. "I'm so very proud of you."

She caressed his hand. "It wasn't really either of us who deserves the credit. We both know that. Every person did their part, just as you knew they would. You will honor the memories of Khiara and Prince Aransetis?"

"Yes," Tyrus said. "The manor house in Silvandom is a shrine to their memory. The Vaettir pay their respects and give them honor in their way. And Erasmus will be remembered in Havenrook. We must remember those who gave their lives."

"I'm pleased. Why did you come? What do you wish to know?"

"The Seneschal made me the custodian of Shirikant's book. It is a heavy burden, Phae. I don't trust anyone else to even look at it. But I know, child, that someday, long after I'm gone, someone else will seek out its secrets. Someone with the fireblood, most likely. Ambition has uses, for certain, but my mind is heavy with the possibility. I would seek counsel from you. Should I hide it where no one can find it? It will always be a temptation if I leave it with the rest of the Archives. Some knowledge should be hidden permanently."

Phae listened to his words thoughtfully. They continued the pleasant stroll, wandering the grounds around the tree. The roots of her tree were vast, giving her a wide room to walk and be free.

"You cannot prevent evil from occurring," she said, looking at him pointedly. "Nor should you. The Seneschal described its cycle like that of the seasons. We are in the season of spring, when good has triumphed and evil is forced to slumber. The cycle will come again, long after you have relinquished your duty to others. It will be their turn, Father. It will be their duty to stand up to that evil. As you did."

He sighed deeply, disturbed by her answer, yet it felt true. "You will outlive me," he said, feeling the absurdity that she would live for another thousand years. She would see the next cycles come and go. Perhaps she already had. It defied his understanding how she existed in a different manner of time than he did. "If there was a way to prevent the book from being used, could you tell me?"

Phae smiled. "No, Father. The events that occur in the mortal world are caused by the decisions of mortals. You cannot see all things from the beginning, as the Seneschal can. You must make your choices as you deem wise. It is never improper to seek counsel from those wiser than yourself. But you must accept the counsel given, knowing that suffering often accompanies choices. And sometimes that suffering is what we need the most to make us stronger. Try not to predict the future." She paused, stopping, her head cocking. "Let's go back to my tree."

They continued to walk arm in arm until they reached the ancient oak once again. Standing at the base was Shion. He stood tall and at ease, his clothes no longer the garb of the Kishion. A single tarnished key was fastened to a hoop on his belt.

"Hello," Tyrus bid him, bowing his head deferentially.

"Greetings, Tyrus," Shion said, his voice rich and full. Tyrus had heard him sing and had wept with the power of his ability. Then he noticed the woman in his shadow and his heart leapt with amazement. It was Tyrus's wife, the Dryad from the Paracelsus Towers. It was she!

Phae smiled cheerfully. "Hello, Mother. Are you ready?" She leaned her head against her father's shoulder. "She's going to care for my tree for a little while. Shion and I have a journey to make together with the Tay al-Ard. Would you keep her company while we are gone?"

Tyrus stared at his wife, felt tears sting his eyes. She smiled at him with unspoken love, her eyes burning. Phae broke away and hugged her mother, kissing her on the cheek. Then she looked at Shion adoringly, their faces still expressive of their tenderness with each other. Their hands snaked together.

"I will," Tyrus said and then watched as the magic of the Tay al-Ard made them vanish.

The magic unsettled Phae only a little. She did not know where Shion was taking her, only that he had said he wanted her to accompany him on a journey. As soon as the magic ended, she blinked with surprise and then felt her heart throb with warmth. She saw trellises and green vines thick with purple fruit, the slope of a roof that covered a high attic where little children slept. A barn stood to the side in the dusky light. It was the Winemiller vineyard!

Her grip on his hand increased. "What is this?" she demanded, tugging on his arm and forcing him to face her. He had a pleased smile seeing her reaction.

"Do you mean *when* is this?" he asked, his eyes twinkling.

The air was rich with smells and memories, memories that they both shared and savored. She wanted to squeal with delight, but she dared not, knowing that sometimes they visited places unobserved, blending into a crowd with his magic.

"Yes, I'd like to know when this is, please." Her heart was giddy with excitement.

"The grapes are nearly harvested," he answered. "It's autumn, a year after you disappeared. They're going to crush the grapes tonight. I thought you'd want to join them."

She turned and stared at his face, awash with kindness and gratitude. "Shion," she whispered tenderly.

"It will do them much good, knowing you are safe. Knowing you still care about them. Trasen is still here. Will that . . . be painful for you?"

Phae shook her head no. "I cared for him. I still do. I cannot give him back his memories, they are gone forever. But I do not resent the feelings I had for him. Not when I have you." She squeezed his hand, stroking his arm. "So . . . we can see them? It will not harm the future?"

He put his arm around her shoulder. "I am a Seneschal now, Phae. I don't do anything that will not bless the mortal world. I wanted to share this memory with you. Come. Introduce me to your adoptive family. There's a little girl here who has a twin in Mirrowen. You need to tell her not to be afraid."

"You remembered little Brielle? Of course you would. You remember everything I've ever said or done."

Shion smiled and nodded.

"Who do I tell them *you* are?" Phae asked as they walked up the road. Her stomach bubbled with excitement. Just to see them all again, to hug and hold and kiss each of them. Master Winemiller with his stern looks and work ethic. Dame Winemiller with her stories and chatter. She wondered how many more children they had adopted since she'd been gone.

"Tell them the truth," Shion replied enigmatically. He gazed down at her, his eyes deep with meaning, full of wisdom, sorrow, and depthless compassion. "Tell them I'm your husband."

AUTHOR'S NOTE

I hope you enjoyed the final book of the Whispers from Mirrowen Trilogy. When I was a child, I had a favorite book on Greek mythology. This was long before Percy Jackson. One of the stories that haunted me was the story of Orpheus, who lost his wife on the day of his wedding after she was chased by a satyr and bitten by a snake. Orpheus then charmed his way into Tartarus through his music and the power of his voice, and he begged Hades to release his wife's spirit. His music was so powerful that the god relented and told him to return to the mortal world and that her spirit would follow him. But if he looked back, she would be lost to him forever. I learned later, doing research for the Whispers from Mirrowen Trilogy, that Orpheus's wife was actually a Dryad named Eurydice. This theme of love and losing it prematurely is also in one of my all-time favorite movies, *Somewhere in Time.* I love the music from that film.

While I was writing this book, I was given a wonderful gift from a reader who is part of the Mormon Tabernacle Choir staff. She sent me a CD from the Bryn Terfel album, *Homeward Bound.* As I was enjoying the CD during my commute one day, it came to the last song on the album, a duet between Bryn Terfel and Sissel called "Give Me My Song." As the music began and the melody swept through my car, I was stunned by the lyrics as well as the voices singing the duet. Everything about the song reminded me of Shion and Phae, including the words. It was one of the most haunting melodies I'd ever heard. So, if you want to know what the song in Tyrus's locket sounds like, I suggest a visit to iTunes.

I dedicated *Poisonwell* to Terry Brooks, the fantasy author who inspired me to become a writer. In October 2004, we had lunch together in Corte Madera, California, during a writing seminar that he taught. That experience was a major turning point in my life and in my writing. I appreciate the encouragement, wisdom, and motivation he gave me on that occasion to finish my first million words. With this book done, I'm well on my way to the second million. I have many more books still to write—brand-new worlds bubbling in my mind as well as revisiting familiar ones.

Thank you all for joining me on this journey. And thanks for lunch, Mr. Brooks.

GLOSSARY

Aeduan: a race from the southern kingdoms of Wayland and Stonehollow. They are primarily fair-skinned with dominant and recessive traits for hair color, eye color, and complexion. Many consider the Aeduan as mongrels because of the variety of their physical characteristics (hair color, eye color, skin tone). However, they have proven to be very adaptable and most resilient to the Plague. The Aeduan were the principal founders of Kenatos.

Boeotian: a race of tribes from the northern territories known as Boeotia. They have no central government, though purportedly revere an individual known as the Empress. They are nomads with no permanent cities and live off the land. They are strong and typically have brown or black hair and are prone to fight amongst themselves, pitting tribe against tribe. Their skin is heavily veined and tattooed, giving them an almost purple cast. They have sworn to destroy the city of Kenatos and occasionally unify for the purpose of attacking the island kingdom. Silvandom is the primary defense against Boeotia, for they have conflicting ideologies.

Bhikhu: a class primarily found in Silvandom and Kenatos. These are highly trained warriors that specialize in all forms of armed and unarmed combat and are trusted to preserve the peace and dispense justice. They cannot own treasure or items of value and treat life with the greatest respect. They are often mistaken for being cruel for they will punish and deliberately injure as a way of teaching their morality of painful consequences. The Bhikhu are typically orphans and nobility who have abandoned worldly wealth.

Canton Vaud: the seat of the Druidecht hierarchy, known as the Thirteen. These are the wisest of the Druidecht and they travel throughout the kingdoms to solve social and political problems and to represent nature in disputes over land. When one of the Thirteen dies, the remaining twelve vote to replace that person from a promising Druidecht who will join Canton Vaud and travel to kingdoms solving problems.

Carnotha: a small marked coin denoting the rank of thief. Showing it to another ensures cooperation in an activity as well as access to information and illegal items. There are purportedly only five hundred such coins in existence and, in order to acquire a carnotha, one must steal it from another thief. They are carefully safeguarded and hidden from authorities. There is one carnotha that identifies the location of all the others and can determine whether one is a fake. The bearer of this one is known as the master thief.

Chin-Na: a lesser-known class found in Silvandom and only taught amongst the Vaettir and usually only to nobility. In addition to the martial aspects of the Bhikhu, the Chin-Na train their bodies to exist on very little air and have learned to harden their bodies and focus their internal energy to the point where even weapons cannot pierce their skin. As such, they do not float but their attacks are so focused and powerful that they can strike down an enemy with a single blow that damages internal organs. Only the most trusted and dedicated to Vaettir ideals are allowed to learn the secrets of the Chin-Na.

Cruithne: a race from the eastern mountains of Alkire. They have grayish-black skin, ranging in tone, with hair varying from pale blond to coarse gray. They are easily the largest of men, in terms of weight, not size, but not slow or ponderous. The Cruithne are known for their inquisitiveness and deep understanding of natural laws and spirit laws. They founded the Paracelsus order in their ancient homeland and transferred its knowledge to Kenatos.

Druidecht: a class found in every kingdom except Kenatos. Those in Kenatos consider them superstitious pagans, though harmless. The knowledge of the Druidecht is only transmitted verbally from mentor to disciple. It teaches that the world coexists with a spirit realm known as Mirrowen and that the spirits of that realm can be communed with and enlisted for help. A Druidecht cannot heal innately, but it can enlist a spirit creature that can. When a disciple has memorized the unwritten lore and demonstrated sufficient harmony with nature and Mirrowen, he or she will be presented with a talisman that will enable him or her to hear the thoughts of spirit creatures and be able to communicate back. The variety of spirit creatures is diverse and so Druidecht often only stay in one place for a few years and then move to another place to learn about the denizens there. The Druidecht are the only outsiders trusted by the Boeotians to enter their lands unharmed.

Fear Liath: a spirit creature of great power known to inhabit high mountain country. Their presence causes fog and fear to disorient and terrify their prey. There are no recorded descriptions of a Fear Liath. They cannot tolerate sunlight.

Finder: a class found in nearly every kingdom, trained to search for lost items or people. They can track prints, discern clues, and are often hired as bounty hunters or guides. Finders trained in the city usually do not associate with those trained in the wild.

Fireblood: an innate magical ability possessed by a lost race. The race purportedly are the predecessors of the inhabitants of Stonehollow and are much persecuted. They appear to be a mix of Aeduan with some physical resemblance to Preachán for most have red or copper-colored hair. Their race is impervious to the Plague and for this reason they are distrusted and hunted during outbreaks and their blood dabbed on door lintels, which is commonly believed to ward off infection to the household. The real name of the race is unknown, but it is said they can conjure fire with their hands and that overuse of such innate ability renders them permanently insane.

Keramat: a Vaettir word for the innate ability to produce miracles, such as healing, raising the dead, traveling vast distances in moments, and calming storms. The secrets of the *Keramat* are zealously guarded by the Vaettir and have not been disclosed to the Archivists of Kenatos.

Kishion: a class originating in the island kingdom of Kenatos. These are the Arch-Rike's personal bodyguards and administer the city's justice on those convicted of heinous crimes, such as murder, rape, and treason. Only Bhikhu and Finders are chosen to be Kishion and are given extensive training in survival, diplomacy, and poison. They are unswervingly loyal to the Arch-Rike and to the ideals of Kenatos.

Mirrowen: a concept and possibly a location. The Druidecht teach that the world coexists with a spirit realm called Mirrowen and that the inhabitants of each can communicate with one another. The realm of Mirrowen is said to be inhabited by immortal spirits with vast powers. There is little belief in this dogma in the larger cities, where they consider the belief trite and superstitious, a way of coping with the regular horrors of the Plague by imagining a state of existence where there is no death. The Druidecht suggest there is ample evidence of Mirrowen's existence and roam the lands teaching people to be harmonious with nature.

Paracelsus: a class from Kenatos and Alkire. Enigmatic and reclusive, these practitioners of arcane arts study the records of the past to tame vast sources of power. Some Paracelses excel at forging weapons of power to sell for profit in Havenrook. Others experiment with new sources of energy, which they harness into powerful gems to be used by the ruling class. Most Paracelses specialize in specific forces and phenomena and document their findings in great tomes that they contribute to the Archive of Kenatos. The Paracelsus Towers in Kenatos is the hub of their order, though many travel to distant kingdoms to continue unraveling clues from the past.

Plague: a terrible disease that strikes the kingdoms at least once every generation, destroying entire cities and dwindling the population. There is no documented record of the origins of the Plague and over the millennia the kingdoms have drawn closer and closer together for the preservation of their races. Documents discovered in abandoned towns and fortresses reveal that there are complete civilizations that have been wiped out by the Plague and races that used to exist but no longer do. The island kingdom of Kenatos was founded to be a last bastion for civilization and to preserve all knowledge and a remnant of each surviving race.

Preachán: a race from the trading city of Havenrook. They tend to be short, brown- or red-haired, and have an amazing capacity for deductive reasoning and complex arithmetic. They also have a deep-rooted desire for wealth and the thrill of gambling. They employ the Romani to execute their trading system and are generally devoid of morals. The Preachán take pride that there are no laws or rules in Havenrook. Those who rule are the ones who have accumulated the most wealth and prestige.

Rike: a class who lead the island kingdom of Kenatos. They are often mistaken for a priesthood of Scithrall, but in reality they are more like academics, physicians, and lawyers. While many believe them to possess magical powers, their power comes from the artifacts created by the Paracelsus order. With such, they can heal injuries and cure Plague victims. They are frequently dressed in a black cassock, but the most telltale sign is the ring that they wear. It is a black stone that purportedly gives them the ability to detect a lie spoken in their presence as well as to compel a weak-willed person to speak the truth.

Romani: a class that has no country or kingdom. Romani can be of any race. They control the caravan routes and deliver goods between kingdoms with the strongest allegiance to the Preachán city of Havenrook. They are forbidden to enter or to operate within Silvandom. Romani are known for kidnapping and organized crime. Starting at age eight, they are sold into service at ten-year increments. Their value increases in age and training and usually diminishes with age and disability. Each decade of servitude corresponds with an earring, which they cannot remove under pain of death. Their freedom may be purchased for a single, usually large, lump sum.

Seithrall: a quasi-religion existing in the island kingdom of Kenatos. The term is a transliteration of the Vaettir words for "fate" or "faith," as one being under the thrall of one or the other. While the Rikes of Kenatos do not suggest that the term connotes a specific religion, the populace of the city has given it a mystical quality as it is not possible to lie to a Rike who wears the black ring.

Shaliah: a class of Silvandom known for the *keramat* of healing. This ability is innate and comes from their closeness to nature and the ability to share their life force with others.

Sylph: a spirit creature of Mirrowen that is tiny and can travel great distances and provide warnings of danger and healing.

Talisman: a Druidecht charm, fixed to a necklace, which is presented to the Druidecht by the spirits of Mirrowen upon achieving a sufficient level of respect, usually achieved by adulthood. The emblem is a woven-knot pattern, intricately done, and it purportedly allows a Druidecht to commune with unseen spirits.

Tay al-Ard: spirit beings of great power that possess the gift of moving people and objects great distances in mere moments. It is considered a *keramat* to be able to induce such spirits to perform this feat.

Uddhava: a Bhikhu philosophy and way of life that centers on the observation and discernment of the motives of others, and then acting in a way that validates or rejects the observation. Life is a series of intricate moves and countermoves between people, and a Bhikhu who can make the observations and reactions faster than an opponent will win a confrontation.

Vaettir: a race from Silvandom that values life above all. They are generally tall and slender, dark-skinned, with black hair. They do not eat meat and seek to preserve life in all its various forms. Their magic is innate and the wise use and practice of it is known as *keramat*. When they inhale deeply, their bodies become buoyant and can float. When they exhale deeply, their bodies become more dense and solid and they sink.

ACKNOWLEDGMENTS

Many thanks to all the staff at 47North for their hard work and expert advice. A special thank-you to David Pomerico who liked the synopsis of *Mirrowen* enough to sign me up. I was the first author he signed when he joined 47North, and he was my first real editor. Also thanks to my early readers (again) for their feedback and encouragement: Gina, Karen, Robin, and Emily. I also would like to thank the fabulous Chris Cerasi and Clarence Haynes, whose input and guidance improved the trilogy and helped me tug at your heartstrings. And finally, to all my wonderful readers who have waited patiently (and not so patiently) for this series to finish.

ABOUT THE AUTHOR

Photo © 2012 Kim Bills

Author of the Legends of Muirwood trilogy, *Landmoor*, *Silverkin*, and numerous stories and articles for the fantasy e-zine *Deep Magic*, Jeff Wheeler has long been fascinated with medieval history and lore. His inspiration for the Whispers from Mirrowen trilogy stemmed from reading about the Black Death and its devastation in Europe and from his research into ancient Roman and Greek civilizations. Jeff took an early retirement from his career at Intel in 2014 to become a full-time author. He is, most importantly, a husband and father, a devout member of his church, and is occasionally spotted roaming hills with oak trees and granite boulders in California or in any number of the state's majestic redwood groves.

Visit the author's website:

www.jeff-wheeler.com